Summer Island

Also by Shelley Noble

Imagine Summer
Lucky's Beach
A Beach Wish
Lighthouse Beach
Christmas at Whisper Beach (novella)
The Beach at Painter's Cove
Forever Beach
Whisper Beach
A Newport Christmas Wedding (novella)
Newport Dreams (novella)
Breakwater Bay
Stargazey Nights (novella)
Stargazey Point
Holidays at Crescent Cove (novella)
Beach Colors

Summer Island

A NOVEL

Shelley Noble

AVON

An Imprint of HarperCollinsPublishers

SUMMER ISLAND. Copyright © 2022 by Shelley Freydont. All rights reserved. Printed in the United States of America. No part of this book may be used or reproduced in any manner whatsoever without written permission except in the case of brief quotations embodied in critical articles and reviews. For information, address HarperCollins Publishers, 195 Broadway, New York, NY 10007.

FIRST EDITION

Designed by Diahann Sturge
Title page and chapter opener illustration © Mascha Tace / Shutterstock

Library of Congress Cataloging-in-Publication Data has been applied for.

ISBN 978-0-06-311842-3

22 23 24 25 26   LSC   10 9 8 7 6 5 4 3 2 1

To all who are doing their part, large or small,
to make our world a better place

Summer Island

Chapter 1

"It was amazing." Phoebe Adams sat cross-legged on the king-size bed and flourished one hand in the air. "I just went over to the food bank to get a basic who-what-where-when article about their move to larger quarters. Then I met Anita Peters and I knew we had to print her story."

It didn't matter that Phoebe was talking to the back of the editor of the *Weekly Sentinel*. She was psyched.

Gavin Cross turned in the doorway of the walk-in closet and held up two ties. "The blue striped or the yellow paisley with my gray suit?"

"Blue striped," said Phoebe. "She was sent in to streamline and modernize their data base and their distribution system. But get this . . ."

Gavin tossed the blue tie on the bed next to her and went back into the closet.

"Anita was raised just a couple of towns from here and had been homeless as a child. She was forced to drop out of high school and earned her GED sitting in the back of her mother's food truck. Which just goes to show you—"

A pair of dress shoes sailed past her and landed on the duvet next to the ties.

"Anyway, one of the lunch regulars noticed her and was so impressed he pulled some strings to get her a scholarship to college. And from that one man's help, she was able to earn an MA in supply-chain and distribution management and now she travels throughout New England helping local food banks make policy and streamline day-to-day operational changes that could completely overhaul the ability to feed the hungry throughout the region, perhaps the nation. How's that for a story?"

"Fine." Gavin rolled his suitcase out of the closet and opened it on the bed.

"I'm going to make sure it gets column space in next week's edition. It will be an inspiration for the whole community. Right here under our noses. Who knew?"

Phoebe flopped back on the mattress. This was the kind of article she was born to write. Unsung locals doing good for the community. The kind of article that inspired readers to think, to volunteer, to make a difference.

"I'm sure once everyone learns Anita's story, the donations for the new building will pour in and the whole community will be the better for it."

Gavin carried out two pairs of khakis and several shirts on hangers.

Phoebe rolled to her side and braced on one elbow. "As always, I admire your sartorial elegance, but this is the New England Association of Independent Newspapers. The other guys will be sitting around all weekend in T-shirts with coffee stains."

He looked down at her and smiled. He was tall and blond with a patrician nose that reminded her of his father, Simeon Cross, who had published the paper until the day he died and who had been Phoebe's mentor and inspiration. Just looking at Gavin gave her a little rush of satisfaction. Soon she would be Mrs. Gavin Cross and together they would—

"I'm going to take a couple of days after the symposium to check out the operations of some of the other weeklies."

"Oh?"

"Since I have to go anyway, I might as well pick their brains on site. You can handle things while I'm gone?" He glanced at his watch.

"Of course." She'd been handling "things" since Simeon had fallen ill. "Oh, I almost forgot, Alan in design called today; the photo processor is acting up again. I told him to call the guy who usually fixes it, but we're going to have to bite the bullet and get new equipment soon."

"Call him back and tell him not to do anything until I get back."

Phoebe sighed. "You sure you don't want me to go with you? We could work the whole group, see who's got equipment they want to unload, and I could introduce you to the editors you haven't met." Editors he should already know but didn't, since he'd only been to one other symposium since taking over the paper three years ago.

Gavin pulled out a drawer of the built-in dresser and frowned at the contents. "No reason for us both to go. Besides, I need you to touch base with Ed Begland at Cross County Insurance. Strong-arm him if you have to. We need a big repeat advertiser.

Not all this space wasted with two-by-ones congratulating some favorite high school grad."

"Hey, those ads help pay the rent."

"The *Sentinel* owns the building."

"Pay our taxes, then."

Gavin sighed. "Phoebe, could you please focus on bringing some money to the paper?"

"You're just cranky because you have to drive three hours at rush hour to get to the hotel."

"I couldn't get away earlier, as you well know." Gavin went into the bathroom, came back with his shaving kit and toiletry bag. He'd be the most well-groomed editor at the Manchester Airport Hampton Inn.

He'd been on his office phone all afternoon. He hadn't said who it was, but Phoebe guessed it had to do with finances. These days, he was obsessed with overhead and income. Sure, they were always floating right above red alert, but they had been for years, long before Simeon died and Gavin had inherited his father's legacy. Simeon had worked indefatigably to keep the paper up and running. They'd won awards. He'd published a quality newspaper the whole county could be proud of.

Simeon was a true journalist. He'd given her a start when she was even too young to drive, had nurtured her and taught her more than most reporters learned in a lifetime. He'd depended on her to help Gavin get acclimated and to keep the paper running.

That was *her* legacy. And one she was immensely proud of.

Gavin zipped his suitcase and slid it to the floor. "You going to stay here tonight?"

"No, I'd better get home. I still have a lot of packing up if I'm moving in here on Friday."

He kissed her, too quickly it seemed to her, but he hated running late.

"I'll lock up before I go."

"Great," he called, already on his way out the door. "And get those ads sold while I'm gone." The door clicked shut and she was alone on the spacious bed.

Ads. Sometimes it seemed as if she spent more time canvassing for ads, drumming up new subscribers, and keeping ancient equipment running smoothly, while making sure that everyone was paid, than actually reporting.

Seemed? There was no "seemed" about it. Her writing *had* taken a back seat to all her other duties as managing editor of the paper.

She pulled the elastic band from her ponytail and shook her hair free. Then she lay back, rested her forearm across her forehead, and thought about a young Anita Peters, tucked away in a back corner of the food truck, her history book open, while the sting of chopped onions blurred her vision. And now that young girl was responsible for so many.

Phoebe couldn't help but make a comparison to herself. She'd never been homeless, thank heaven, and she may not feed the hungry, but she was a conduit for the people who did. She had found her place in the world, where she could do what she was called to do—make a difference.

That's what local news was all about. Not broadcasting breaking headlines between commercials, not sending a podcast into the ether sphere. Those were good for others. But not for Phoebe. For her, it was go deep, stay local. Local news touched the people closest to it, could make them aware, change their lives, keep them grounded, and get things done at a grass-roots level.

And Phoebe facilitated that. She took a long, satisfied breath and sat up.

She'd start writing the article tomorrow morning . . . right after she met with Ed Begland about a recurring ad . . . and checked with Marty Cohen about the last order of newsprint that came in short . . . and dropped by town hall to see if they had pulled the files on a hit-and-run case from last month that needed a follow-up article. And she would call Alan and tell him to definitely call the repair technician; they needed working machinery.

And then . . . she would write her article about Anita Peters.

Thursday morning, Phoebe was hunched over her computer keyboard in the newsroom, fingers flying over the keys. It had been days since she'd interviewed Anita Peters and she was just now writing the article. No worries. It just had to be in good enough shape to present to the editorial meeting at noon. She glanced at the corner of the screen. Eleven forty.

She'd missed breakfast and was about to miss lunch, and between her growling stomach and the general din of the newsroom, she was having a hard time concentrating. It was amazing, the amount of noise the four full-time and just as many part-time staffers of the *Weekly Sentinel* could make while working with laptop keyboards, cell phones, and the occasional blue pencil.

When Phoebe was a kid and dreaming of becoming a journalist, she'd watched in awe those old-time newspaper rooms portrayed in the movies: Cary Grant shouting into the black candlestick phone as reporters rushed in and out of the room, slamming doors in their pursuit of a "scoop," while old Royal typewriters clacked in the background. It was funny, but thrilling.

Later, as she sat alert through *All the President's Men*, she dreamed of one day being Bob Woodward. Not as portrayed by Robert Redford, but as portrayed by Phoebe Adams, investigative reporter.

But lately she hadn't felt much like a reporter, and today she just felt overworked from all the non-writing duties she'd accumulated since Simeon's demise. The only time she was really fired up was when she was out in the field gathering stories or sitting in the newsroom with Mitch and Nancy, the two other "old-timers," composing at their desks or rushing out to check a fact. Everyone rushing toward deadline.

Willa Davis stopped at her desk and glanced over Phoebe's shoulder at the computer screen. Willa was the feature writer and circulation manager and Phoebe's best friend.

"You hear from Gavin yet?"

Phoebe nodded, without looking up. "Last night. He's on his way back this morning. He said if he's late, start the meeting without him."

"Uh-huh."

That made Phoebe look up. "What do you mean, 'uh-huh'?"

Willa just fisted her hands on her hips and gave Phoebe what they all called the "Willa wither" look.

"I know, I know, but he's been really busy networking. It must have been a productive weekend."

"I'll say. Considering it's Thursday."

"He'll be here. He's probably having trouble getting away. You know how these newspaper people love to talk shop."

"For six days?"

"He's been checking other papers' operating systems and looking for used equipment. Maybe he's come up with a brilliant idea for making us all rich." Phoebe glanced at the corner of her screen. *Eleven forty-seven.* He was cutting it close.

And so was she. She typed faster.

Willa was still standing there when the newsroom door squeaked open. Phoebe had been meaning to get it fixed. Though it didn't seem to bother anyone but Phoebe.

Gavin Cross stood just inside the newsroom, his hand still on the doorknob, about as far as he ever got these days.

She was surprised by how relieved she felt. Of course he would be back in time for the meeting; he was the editor in chief. She flashed him a smile.

He didn't smile back, so Phoebe went back to typing.

"Could I have everyone's attention."

A statement, not a question. And at the most inconvenient time possible. What was so important it couldn't wait the ten minutes for the regularly scheduled editorial meeting?

Conversation quieted but everyone in the *Sentinel*'s newsroom continued to work. Multitasking was a necessary skill for survival in the newspaper business.

Gavin raised his voice. "I have some bad news."

Phoebe's fingers slowed as her mind ricocheted from a hurricane barreling toward the New England coast to the death of someone they all knew and loved.

"I'm closing the *Sentinel*."

Phoebe's fingers froze on the keyboard. Around the room all motion stopped, six *Sentinel* employees captured mid-movement—perched on the edge of a desk, gesturing to a colleague, reaching for a file drawer. All caught in time—death-of-a-newspaper time.

Then slowly their heads turned until all eyes zeroed in on Gavin.

He should have staggered back from the force of their disbelief. But Gavin merely lifted his chin and looked past them to the window.

He's shutting down the paper. For a nanosecond Phoebe thought he must have lost his mind. Or she had. He couldn't do that.

"No." The denial escaped her lips almost as if the word had been there all along, waiting for the inevitable. "No." It couldn't be true. Why would he do such a thing after all their hard work? And after he'd just come back from the symposium. Something must have happened there.

"You all know that the *Sentinel* has been struggling for years," Gavin continued. "We've tried, but times are changing and local newspapers are no longer relevant."

Not relevant? Of course it was relevant. Phoebe tried to catch his eye. To warn him to stop. To meet her outside and explain. Like why he hadn't consulted her before springing this on everyone. But he was focused on the mid-distance, something she realized he did when he wasn't going to budge on an issue—or because he couldn't face her?

"We've run out of money. Today is the *Sentinel*'s last day."

She sprang from her chair, as if she could bodily stop him from continuing.

"You'll be paid for this week. You have until tonight to clean out your desks. After that the offices will be closed and everything will be sold. This hasn't been an easy decision."

Not an easy decision? Phoebe hadn't even known he was considering it.

"I want to thank you for your commitment to the *Sentinel*." Gavin backed out of the room and firmly shut the door.

"You son of a—!" Mitch Rueben, who had been at the paper for forty years, turned his anger on Phoebe. "Did you know about this?"

"No," Phoebe said. "No." She dropped into her desk chair, her eyes settling on Anita Peters's typed name.

She gradually became aware of Willa, her face mere feet away, her eyes questioning.

Phoebe shook her head. Shook it again. Shook it until she thought it might fall off. "I didn't know. I can't believe it. Something must have happened this weekend."

"Something that he didn't tell you about?"

"He didn't say anything." She searched her brain to try to find some clue, some hint, of what he'd been thinking. But her brain was blank.

"You're telling me you had no idea he was planning this?" Willa asked. "What do the two of you talk about?"

"I don't know. Stuff. Actually, between the paper and the wedding, we don't have all that much time to talk. At night we're tired and it's pretty much dinner, sex, and Netflix."

Willa shook her head.

Phoebe pulled Willa closer, lowered her voice. "The *Sentinel* isn't out of money. We've been running on a shoestring for years. I've personally been out selling ads. The bills are mostly paid on time. The readership is up . . . a little. Things can't be that bad. Why would he do this? How could I not know what he was thinking?"

Willa eased herself down on the armrest of Phoebe's chair, slipped her arm around Phoebe's shoulders. "Maybe you were too busy trying to save this paper and our jobs to notice." Willa squeezed Phoebe's shoulder. "Gavin was just not as committed to the *Sentinel* as you were."

"It's just that he was still feeling his way."

"After three years? Face it, Phoebe, you've been running this paper since the day he arrived to take over. Even before that."

"But he—"

"It's not your fault. We know you did your best."

"My best? If I'd done my best, we would still have a newspaper."

Well, she would do something now. She pushed to her feet, dislodging Willa from the arm as her desk chair shot out from under her.

"What are you going to do?" Willa asked anxiously.

"Make him change his mind."

Chapter 2

*G*avin's office was down a dimly lit hallway, behind a heavy oak door with a frosted glass half-window and a brass nameplate that screamed *traditional journalism*.

Phoebe didn't go in immediately; she'd stormed out of the newsroom and down the hall without thinking. She didn't have a plan. She just knew she had to stop him.

She could see his shadow moving through the frosted glass.

She tapped on the glass. It sounded like gunfire, and she choked on a searing breath.

She knocked again. Her hand was shaking. "Gavin. It's Phoebe."

At last she heard a distracted voice say, "Come in."

She licked dry lips and stepped inside just as he slipped his cell phone into his jacket pocket. He was standing at his desk, his back to the window, a mere silhouette against the midday sun.

She moved off to one side, where she could see his features in the overhead light.

He didn't say anything, no explanations, no excuses, just reached for his briefcase and clicked it open.

She plunged in. "What's going on? Did something happen at the symposium? Whatever it is, we can make it work. We always do."

"Nothing happened at the symposium."

"Then what? If the printing is costing too much, we can take it totally online."

"We're closing down. Face it, Phoebe, the *Sentinel* is a dinosaur."

"You're wrong."

"Obviously not, because I've been actively trying to unload it for the last two years. I never wanted the damn thing to begin with."

"You've been trying to sell it?"

"What do you think I was doing for the last six days? Talking about cutting-edge local journalism? It was pathetic, but it was my last chance to unload this albatross. I spent two days trying to convince Bob Evers of the *Island News* to take it off my hands. But he couldn't swing it financially. He was my last hope. There is just not enough interest."

"The last two years? You're lying." She could hardly hear her own words past the hammering in her heart. He was closing the *Sentinel*. Had intended to for two years and she had been clueless. What *had* they talked about? Until Willa asked her earlier that day, she hadn't thought about it. But how could she not have seen what he'd been planning?

"Why didn't you tell me?"

"Because I knew you would get all sentimental and hysterical."

She didn't hear the rest; the buzzing in her ears drowned out his words.

"Sentimental? I worked my butt off for this paper."

He sighed. "All the more reason to unload it. All we do is work—for this." He snatched a folded copy of the latest edition off his desk. "Good God. Look at this front page. 'Mayor Breaks Ground for New Community Pool.' Who gives a shit?"

"All the people in this town, the county. And beyond. A lot of people worked hard to make it happen. The community college will use it for classes. There will be special programs for therapy and special needs. It will have open hours for the public to swim. It will create jobs. People should know."

"They can get the pool hours off the website when it opens."

"But we're the only place they can get in-depth news about what affects them directly. Town council decisions," she carried on desperately. "Water safety and traffic problems, milestones achieved, funerals—we have news that you can't find anywhere else."

"Phoebe, you're living in the past."

"Investigative reporting—" She plowed on, refusing to give up. "Local innovation. The revitalization of the old mill. Willa's idea of Furrever Family Fridays. More pets have been adopted or fostered on Fridays since we began featuring the current occupants of the shelter than ever before."

"Really, Phoebe? You went to Columbia to write about dog adoptions?"

"Well . . . yeah, I did. I want to write about people making a difference. Help them connect to other people."

"God. Don't you have any ambition at all?"

Phoebe reeled back. If he'd slapped her, he couldn't have hurt her more. Everything that made sense, that she cared about, meant nothing to him.

She was too stunned to even move as everything in her world blew apart and shattered at her feet like so many shards of glass. She gasped for breath that refused to come, while heat climbed from her stomach straight to her face where it flared into searing humiliation. There was nothing to say to that, even if she could find her voice, which at the moment didn't seem possible.

"I want to be where the action is, Phoebe. Not whining about some building that got condemned. Or whose freaking cat was rescued from a storm drain. I'm sick to death of it. Sick of this dingy little office, the antiquated machinery, the day-to-day drudgery, the bad coffee, all of it.

"We could go anywhere, Phoebe. I've got contacts. I can land at a big organization. You can write your little human-interest articles for the neighborhood rag. We could have a great lifestyle."

Her little articles? The room went out of focus. Tiny spots floated before her eyes. Everything they had worked so hard for, all their plans . . . had been *her* plans. She saw it now. She'd been busting her butt, neglecting her own writing to keep the *Sentinel* afloat. And the whole time he'd been trying to sell it.

"Why—?" She didn't even have to finish the question. She suddenly knew the answer. Her success in keeping it running would be a perk to any potential buyer.

The realization came in one big lightning bolt of understanding. He'd been using her. Willa was right. He hadn't consulted her, hadn't discussed any of his feelings or his plans, because he didn't think of her as a colleague.

He probably wasn't even sure about her as his wife. And suddenly she wasn't so sure about him.

"You can't do this. If you don't care about the paper, think of your family. They started this paper a hundred years ago. You can't just walk away from it."

"I can and I am. You care more about the damn *Sentinel* than you do about us."

And so should he. "I did my first internship when I was fourteen with your grandfather. I went to work for your father right out of college. He spent his life keeping this paper going."

"And died at seventy-four for his trouble. Phoebe, it's a done deal." He turned away from her to look out the window.

And Phoebe lost it. "You may have turned your back on this paper, but don't you dare turn your back on me." She could hear her voice, shrill and hysterical. This was not the way to approach Gavin. It was not the way she approached anyone. But she couldn't control herself. Her whole world was imploding, and something had snapped inside her.

He turned, slowly, and she knew in that moment that nothing she said, no argument she could produce, would change his mind.

She was facing a stranger.

"Just through the summer," she pleaded. "So many people are dependent on this paper. They work hard. Mitch and Nancy have been here since your grandfather was the publisher. Willa has two kids she has to support. At least give them two weeks' notice."

He didn't even answer, just shook his head.

"Simeon would never—"

"I'm not my father."

No, you're not, Phoebe thought. *You're not even the man I thought you were.* She'd been a fool. She'd thought her enthusiasm was enough for both of them, that in time he would be as determined as she was to save the *Sentinel*.

She'd said she had no idea of what he was planning, but there had been signs. Signs she'd misread, which wasn't like her. His distraction when he should have been listening. His brushing off her plans to grow the paper with an interactive online section. The editorial meetings he missed. She'd hardly missed his input; she knew how to run a newspaper. She just didn't want to.

She wanted to be in the field discovering stories, in the newsroom capturing them on the page, surrounded by other reporters all doing the same. She would never have been so sloppy in her study of an interview subject as she had been with Gavin.

She reached mechanically for the ring on her finger, grasped it with fingers she ordered not to tremble. Very carefully, calmly, she began to pull it off. It stuck on her knuckle and it took several extra seconds to continue the journey.

For a moment she thought he might try to stop her, but he didn't, and she found herself strangely . . . relieved.

The ring finally slid off, the diamond flashing once in a ray of sunlight, the supernova of a dying star. It must have cost Gavin plenty. She could almost hear Willa saying, *Keep it. Sell it or pawn it, but don't get left with nothing.* Of course she would never, but she did wonder just for a second how many salaries it would have paid.

She placed the ring on the desk. Proud of herself for not throwing it out the open window.

Open, because the air-conditioning had broken two weeks ago. She'd wondered why he hadn't called a repairman in. Now she knew. It didn't matter to him. He had already moved on.

He looked down at the ring, but didn't try to change her mind.

"I assume you've made arrangements for the sale of the equipment," she said in as much of a businesslike tone that someone whose world had just disintegrated could muster.

"No. Just leave anything that belongs to the paper in situ. The Brennan Agency has a listing for the whole operation. I'm sorry, Phoebe. It just wasn't for me."

"I'm sorry, too," she said, and slipped quietly out the door.

She was several feet down the hall, walking zombielike back to the newsroom, before she realized she wasn't sorry at all.

She turned back, forcing her feet to move, and opened the office door without knocking. He was on his cell again. He glanced up, looking slightly alarmed.

She didn't blame him. "On second thought, I'm not sorry. I've learned more about you in the last half hour, hell, in the last couple of minutes, than I have in the last three years. But you're right about one thing, Gavin—you're nothing like your father. He was an honorable, serious journalist and you're just a hack."

She backed out and slammed the door.

As an exit, it was right up there with a thirties movie. Phoebe wondered if those actresses' knees shook as much as hers did as she walked back to the newsroom.

Today the hall was deserted, silent except for the squeak of her sneakers on the old linoleum. Silent enough for all the old sounds and memories to rush in to fill the air. The steady clacking and whir of the printing presses before they began sending out their printwork. The arguments spilling out of the editorial meeting room when they fought over column space. Conversations shouted from one door to the other, staff members talking on their phones as they walked, or heads bent over texts.

Then, as suddenly as the memories came, they faded again into a sad, hollow, empty silence, and Phoebe was standing at the door of the newsroom.

She lifted her chin and opened the door just enough to slip inside, hoping to leave that sadness behind.

It followed her in.

There were fewer people waiting than when she'd left a few minutes before. There seemed to have been an exodus while she was in Gavin's office.

Only the long-term staffers remained. Mitch and Nancy were at their desks, heads down, appearing to work on material that would not be discussed at the usual Thursday editorial meeting. Willa still stood at Phoebe's desk as if standing guard. *Over what?* Phoebe wondered.

Mitch stood when she entered, but one look at her face must have told him the worst.

He slumped back into his desk chair. "I guess that's that, then." He suddenly looked a lot older than he had when he'd come in that morning. He tossed his pen on his desk. "At least you'll be all right, Phoebe. Gavin is bound to still have enough money to support you in the style you deserve. He couldn't have blown through his inheritance already. Though God knows he didn't spend it on the *Sentinel*."

Phoebe didn't bother to correct him. Just held up her left hand, displaying her empty ring finger.

Nancy gasped. "Oh, my dear. Not you, too."

"He dumped you?" Willa took Phoebe's wrist in her hand to see for herself.

Phoebe blew out air. "I kind of beat him to it."

Nancy grabbed a tissue and hurried over. She handed the tissue to Phoebe—who was not crying—and burst into tears herself. "And you've already chosen the cake."

Phoebe's breath caught on an intake.

Red velvet with champagne cream cheese icing. And reality hit Phoebe with the full force of the hurricane she had briefly imagined. Not only was the paper gone, but so was her wedding. The venue was booked, the dress was out for alterations, the flowers were picked out, the singer was hired. Her parents had forked out hefty deposits on it all. Maybe it wasn't too late to get some of it back.

"I can't bear it," Nancy said as tears flowed freely down her cheeks. "All our years together. I just can't bear it."

She rushed back to her desk and began clearing it off, placing years of accumulation into a large plastic trash bag that she kept in her bottom drawer. It didn't take as long as it should have to remove decades of hard work and loyal service. And within an hour, Nancy grabbed the bag and her purse and practically fled out the door. Mitch stuffed everything he could into his pockets. Tucked the rest under his arm and strode after her.

When they were both gone, Willa came to stand by Phoebe's side. "Well, girl, new adventures ahead."

"I guess."

"Basically it sucks."

Phoebe nodded. "What will you do?"

"Get a job. You?"

"Call my parents, give them the bad news, and see if they can get some of their deposits back."

"You have a place to stay? I'm taking it you won't be moving in with Gavin as planned."

"Oh shit. I forgot." Phoebe slapped a palm to her forehead. "The movers are coming to put things in storage first thing tomorrow."

"You could cancel them."

"I can't. They've already leased the apartment." Phoebe scrubbed her hair until it stood out from her face.

"I'll have to ask Mom and Dad if I can move in with them at the condo until I decide what to do next."

"Well, I better get going," Willa said. "Gotta start that new job search. You coming?"

"Not quite yet."

Willa nodded. "If you need to talk, call me."

"Thanks, you too."

"Remember, it doesn't matter where we land, we're still besties."

Phoebe nodded. They gave each other a quick thumbs-up like they did just about every day. Only today would be their last.

Then Phoebe was alone. Just a few hours ago the room had

been alive with work, and news, and conversation. Now the desks were empty, the file cabinets left filled but unneeded. The printers and fax machines idle.

It was over, just like Gavin said. There would be no more cutting, proofing, or sending articles to layout. The part-timers wouldn't come and go, usually late, rarely early, but always enthusiastic. Neither Mitch nor Nancy would sit at their desks tomorrow or the next day. They had dedicated their whole working lives to this paper, to the Cross family, only to have their loyalty and hard work thrown in their faces.

Now there was only Phoebe, like the captain of a slowly sinking ship.

She ran her fingers over the worn wood of her desk. This had been her desk since Simeon Cross had hired her as a real reporter six years ago. Fresh out of journalism school, riding high in April . . . actually it was September, after a summer of interning, her sixth.

How naive that seemed to her today.

She'd banked everything on the *Sentinel*. She'd let them all down. No, Gavin had let them all down.

The tears she'd managed not to cry all afternoon trickled down her cheeks. She dashed them away and snapped open the tote bag she kept in her bottom drawer for emergencies. She guessed today qualified. She picked through her office supplies, decided to keep it all; Gavin wouldn't be needing them. The paper, the note cards, the blue pencils. Things left over from pre-computer days, even from before her day, but that she still used. Just for the feel of them.

A dinosaur at twenty-eight, like the *Sentinel* at one hundred.

All she'd ever wanted was to tell the stories of people. She was good at talking to individuals, listening to what they had to say and sharing it with others; sometimes it was the only way their stories would get told, because they were embarrassed, or reclusive, or protective, or just didn't see themselves as special. It came naturally to her. And the popularity of her articles proved that.

And where had that all gone? Into the madness of strongarming people into taking an ad or a subscription, making finances work out so that everyone could get paid. She'd lost her reason for being here long before she'd lost being here at all.

She shut the drawer, grabbed the tote bag, and headed for the door. With a final, quick look around, she walked out of the place that had been her everything for as long as she could remember.

The door squeaked as she shut it. For once, it didn't bother her. It would be someone else's job to fix it now.

Chapter 3

*P*hoebe knew what she was coming home to. Still, she was surprised to open the door to half-packed boxes, open suitcases, and piles of donations.

She slipped quietly inside as if she didn't want to disturb them.

She left her laptop on top of the kitchenware box and walked to her bedroom, where more half-filled boxes awaited. At least she hadn't stripped the bed; she'd have a place to sleep tonight without having to open boxes looking for sheets.

She sank down on the edge of the bed. She didn't even feel like crying. She must be in shock. It was a lot to take in.

First business—call her parents and give them the bad news. They'd be unhappy for her, but supportive. They'd already shelled out a small fortune in deposits for the wedding-not-to-be. Her dad might rant a little, but he would come around. Phoebe knew that no matter how bad things were, she could always count on them.

She fished her phone out of her backpack and made the call. It was still early and her dad might not be home yet. But Phoebe couldn't wait; she needed to get it off her chest, even if she left her mother to break the news to him later. Her mother wouldn't mind; she'd done it for all her daughters more times than they could count. Ron Adams was a serious, hardworking man, who didn't like things upsetting his well-ordered life. So the girls often sent their mother to cajole him into a good humor.

"The truth with sugar," she'd always told them.

Something Phoebe had yet to learn.

She let it ring six times and was preparing what to say in her voicemail message when her mother finally picked up.

"Hey, it's me, Phoebe."

"Hi, sweetheart."

"Mom, just listen, don't say anything until I finish, okay?"

"Okay?"

"Gavin is closing down the *Sentinel*. I called off the wedding. I gave him back the ring. It's over between us."

Complete silence at the other end.

"Don't be upset."

"Oh, Phoebe—"

"Just let me get it all out, okay?"

When her mother didn't answer, Phoebe plunged in.

"He came into the newsroom today and announced it out of the blue, didn't even give the staff two weeks' notice or anything. He didn't tell me about what he was planning, didn't consult me, didn't even ask my opinion.

"He didn't care about how I felt. He told me I had no ambition. No ambition. Maybe he was right, maybe I don't have what it takes, but I loved the paper. And I worked hard to keep it running.

"He said he'd been trying to unload it since he inherited it. Unload. The *Sentinel*. His family's legacy. He doesn't care. He never cared. It's always been about him, not the paper, or us—or me.

"I saw it all standing there in his office. There had always been something off. I thought it was because we were both working so hard to save the paper. But it wasn't. And something just snapped and I knew that I couldn't love a man like that. I've been such an idiot. An idiot and selfish."

"Oh, Phoebe . . ."

"Don't worry about me. I feel terrible, but not as terrible as we both would have felt if we went through with the wedding. I could practically hear him sigh with relief when I told him it was off."

A muffled sob from her mother.

"Mom, please don't cry. I'm sorry. I thought it was perfect, but it wasn't. He wasn't honest with me. We just weren't right together. I hope you and Dad will understand. I'll start calling first thing tomorrow and see if we can get back any of our deposits."

"Oh, Phoebe. I just want you to be happy. But are you sure? Shouldn't you try to talk things over?"

"Mom, he's shutting down the *Sentinel*. He didn't love the news; he's not interested in the town. He didn't care about his employees enough to give them a heads-up. I thought I was really helping him to grow the paper and all the time he just wanted me to fail."

Her mother said nothing.

"Mom, are you still there?"

"Yes, sweetheart. I'm here. I just don't want you to do something that you'll regret later."

"I won't. He's done. I'm not going to fall for that again."

"Oh, don't sound so bitter. I hate to see you bitter."

Phoebe's guilt squeezed the breath out of her. "I'm not bitter." Actually she was relieved. "Just really tired. I think I could sleep for a week. I've been working so hard and trying to get everything in order for the wedding that—"

Her mother's sob erupted in her ear.

"Mom, don't cry. I'll be okay. Really. It's just that my lease is up tomorrow. I was supposed to move into Gavin's, but obviously that's not happening. The movers are coming to put my stuff in storage in the morning and I need a place to stay. Is it okay if I come stay with you and Dad until I can figure out what to do? I know the condo is a little on the small side, but it'll just be for a short time, until I find a new job. Or a new apartment, whichever comes first."

"Tomorrow?" her mother asked.

"Yes." Phoebe frowned. "Is that a problem? I can make other arrangements if it is. I'll be fine."

"I know you will be, sweetheart. You always do whatever you set out to do. We'll see you through this, but I don't know about staying here. Your father—" Her voice broke.

"Is he there?" Phoebe asked. "Let me talk to him. I know he'll be upset, but he'll understand once I explain things to him. Just put him on."

"I can't."

"Why? I'll explain what happened. He'll understand."

Silence at the other end.

"Mom, I'm sorry, but it turned out all wrong. I'm not going to change my mind and Gavin isn't, either. Let me talk to Dad."

"I can't."

"Isn't he home yet?"

"No." Her mother hiccupped the word. She seemed more upset about Phoebe's broken engagement than Phoebe was.

"Well, when he comes back, tell him—"

"Phoebe, your father isn't coming back."

"I don't understand."

"Your father has left me."

"Left you? Like . . . ?"

"Like I-don't-love-you-anymore-and-I've-found-somebody-else . . . left."

There was a long silence while Phoebe's brain crashed. Tried to reboot. Failed.

Finally she managed to say, "When did this happen?"

"Last week."

"Last week? Why didn't you call me?"

"I didn't want to worry you. With the wedding and everything. And . . . I thought he might change his mind . . . After all, it's been thirty-eight years. You'd think he could wait three more months to walk you down the aisle before he had an attack of wanderlust. Only now there won't even be a wedding. I'm so sorry."

"Don't apologize to me," Phoebe said, as the truth began to sink in. Her father had walked out on her mother. And all the rage she'd been struggling not to hurl at Gavin wrapped itself into a tight hot ball aimed at her father.

"It'll be okay, Mom." It was a stupid thing to say. It wouldn't be okay. None of this was okay. "Do you want me to come over?"

"No, absolutely not. I'm fine. Unless you . . ."

"No, I'm fine." It was a lie; neither one of them was fine.

"About tomorrow night . . . He's coming Saturday morning to get his things. God forbid he should miss a golf game. He texted to tell me. Didn't even have the guts to talk to me on the phone. If I'd known what a wuss he was, I would have divorced him a long time ago." A tight breath from her mother. "Oh, Phoebe, I didn't mean to say that. It's just that I don't want to be here when he comes. Frankly, I don't trust myself not to break his golf clubs over his head."

"Okay, Mom, I get it. I can probably get the management to let me stay here one extra night. You can come stay with me tomorrow night and then we can go back to the condo on Saturday when we're sure he's gone. Oh, you can't—my bed and couch will be gone. We could get a hotel room."

"I'm not coming back here. Ever. I texted him and told him to put it on the market. He's the one who insisted we sell the house and buy in an over-fifty-five community . . . Less upkeep, he said. I never wanted to move here anyway. And if he thinks I'm going to stay here alone with a bunch of old people . . ."

"Where will you go?"

Her mother made a strangled sound. "I was thinking about crashing at your place until I could decide."

"You could stay with Daphne and Paul for a couple of nights. It's only a few hours away."

"Good God, no. I haven't told either of your sisters. Especially not Daphne. You know how fragile she is."

More like needy and self-indulgent.

"And Celia would . . ."

Micromanage everything and make them both crazy.

". . . be so upset."

Phoebe loved her sisters. They were caring, well-meaning people, but they sometimes drove Phoebe nuts. Of course, they probably felt the same way about her. *Bullheaded* was the word that came to mind.

"Well . . . I know. Why don't you drive to the island and stay with Granna? I'm sure she'll welcome the company. Since Mr. and Mrs. Wilkins moved away and Mrs. Harken died, she's probably been lonely."

"How could I face her?"

"Granna will understand." Granna always understood. Eventually. Alice Keyes-Sutton was the grande dame of the family, ruling her spreading brood without ever leaving the island she called home. It had become a family joke that Granna Alice had no reason to visit because she could read your mind from miles away. It kept them all toeing the line, just in case it was no joke.

But Phoebe understood what her mother meant. Granna Alice had enjoyed a long, happy marriage, never seemed to get ruffled, was nonjudgmental. Which made her a difficult paragon to live up to. But in spite of her lofty position, she was as down-to-earth as the next person.

There was still silence from her mother's end of the phone.

"There's no place like home in a crisis," Phoebe encouraged.

"Home," her mother echoed. "We did have some good times there, didn't we?"

"Every summer," Phoebe said. Until life got in the way. And suddenly it sounded like the answer to both their situations. A weekend at Granna's. "I know," she said, suddenly feeling brighter. "Why don't we both go?"

"But what if you and Gavin—"

"We won't. I made a big mistake. And so did he. Though I do have to start looking for a job, but I can do that from Granna's house. She has Wi-Fi."

"I don't know. Both our cars are in Ron's name; he'll probably want the Lexus back."

"Mom. Stop it. He's not going to take your car. Anyway, we can take mine. I'll pick you up at the condo." A worse thought occurred to her. "Do you have a good lawyer?"

"Denny Welsh."

Denny was a family friend, a shark, but an ethical shark. He wouldn't let her get short shrift. Leave it to her mother to not lose her head in even the direst situations.

"But don't tell your sisters."

"About Denny?"

"About the divorce. Promise you won't tell them."

"They'll understand." They would never understand. How could any of them understand? How could a man walk out after thirty-eight years of marriage? Three children and . . .

"Promise me."

"I promise," Phoebe said. "So what do you say? Shall we take a little vacation? Just us girls?"

"I don't know . . ."

"I thought you didn't want to be at the condo when Dad came. We can go for the weekend and we'll come back on Monday."

"You're right. Okay, but just for the weekend."

And suddenly Phoebe was the one with cold feet. The movers were coming in the morning. She had to finish packing. Cancel the caterer, cancel the hall, and see if she could get the deposit back on the dress. Put her résumé together and start looking for a new job. And since there was only one paper in town, she'd have to relocate. But all that could be done from a phone or a laptop.

And she could take back the pearls Granna had given her to wear at her wedding.

Phoebe waffled between the thought of a safe haven at the beach and sleeping on Willa's lumpy couch with two preschoolers watching Saturday-morning cartoons at the crack of dawn.

The beach won out in spite of the pearl situation.

"Phoebe?"

"I have some stuff I have to take care of tomorrow, but I can pick you up around five. It's only a two-hour drive."

"It will be rush hour by then," Ruth said.

"We'll take the back way."

"And weekend beach traffic," Ruth added.

"The back, back way. Just pack a few things and we can grab a burger on the road and be there before bedtime."

Phoebe was having second thoughts herself, but she couldn't very well leave her mother to face the divorce by herself. And there was bound to be lemonade and snickerdoodles, Granna's universal cure-all.

Which left her with only one excuse not to go. The one real thing she was afraid of and that she was loathe to admit. Once she left, there would be no going back. As if there was anything left to go back to.

She took a breath. "No more excuses. I'll pick you up around five."

Ruth Adams ended the call, and closed the new memory book she'd bought earlier that month. She'd made one for both her older girls for their weddings. Each was divided into three sections: The first for a little trip down memory lane with photos from the bride's childhood and an empty page for the groom to add his. A second section that portrayed their courtship, though with Daphne she'd had to be a super spy to get any candid shots. And a third for their wedding, and their life together yet to come.

She rested her hand lightly on the new, soft bound scrapbook. Traced the embossed lettering of *Memories to Cherish, Adventures to Come*.

Luckily, she hadn't begun filling out Phoebe and Gavin's book. She'd have to give it to the thrift store. Even if things changed and they got back together, or especially if she married someone else, Ruth wouldn't use the same book.

It just seemed unlucky.

She'd been thinking that a stage of her own life would be ending with the beginning of Phoebe's marriage. She'd raised three strong independent women. She'd done her job. All of them had embarked on their own lives. And now it was time for her.

Or so she had thought.

Of course there would be grandchildren. Their old house had been large, with plenty of bedrooms and a wonderful yard for them to play in. A tree swing and a stream to splash in. Plenty of space for a second generation for children. It *had* become a bit much to manage, and Ron insisted that a condo would give them more time to do the things they wanted.

She hadn't been thrilled about the condo. It was too small for the young families to visit; still, she was determined to make the best of it. Maybe start some new traditions . . . But of all the possibilities, she had never come close to imagining this.

But this feeling of defeat hadn't just begun with moving to the condo, or even with Ron's leaving her for another woman. She didn't know quite when, actually. Just that over the years, she'd gradually defaulted to taking care of the girls and the house, then her committees and her job as a librarian. And finally just keeping the peace.

She let Phoebe's album slip from her hand and saw another white album pushed to the back of the shelf, this one yellowed by age. Her own. She hadn't looked at it in years. She reached toward it, tentatively at first, then anxiously, as if she might find the answer of what had happened to her marriage inside.

Our Wedding. She and Ron standing in that age-old pose of newlyweds, slightly angled and smiling at the camera. Her hair looked nearly the same color as it was today. He'd had a lot more hair and no paunch.

She touched her own nearly flat stomach. She'd worked at it. Just like she did everything in her life.

She turned the page: more wedding photos, her mom and dad, smiling above their names printed in script, *Alice and Henry Sutton*.

Our Years to Come. A photo of Celia as a baby on Ruth's lap with Ron standing proudly behind them. Then Daphne with Celia standing by the arm of Ruth's chair and Ron smiling behind them. Then Phoebe with her sisters flanking the chair, and Ron looking vaguely into the camera. Ruth had never noticed that before. As if with each picture he'd grown more distant, a little out of focus. Resigned.

More photos followed, one from each year. At first all five of them smiled at the camera, then gradually it became photos of the girls and Ron as Ruth took over the duties of photographer.

God, she'd been disappearing since the beginning. She started to slam the book shut, but the words on the next page, *Our Life Before Each Other*, held her hand.

She knew it would be the obligatory childhood photos. But she couldn't resist. As if there might be a clue as to what had happened within those long-ago shots. She turned the page. Ruth as a Girl Scout, her sash filled with badges. On the porch of the house holding a live lobster and squealing in delight for the camera. In her graduation cap and gown from high school when there was still a high school on the island.

And on the last page, two grinning girls, standing in front of Sabatini's Bakery and holding a giant sheet cake, decorated with roses and sunbursts and big blue letters in a florid script. *Best*

Friends Forever. Ruth and Inez Sabatini. Ruth's first summer job at the bakery. They'd had dreams, those two girls. One day they would run a bakery where they only made cakes. Just cakes—Inez would bake and Ruth would decorate. Cakes that would make them famous. Cakes to make people happy.

How hopeful and assured they had been.

A shiver of unease ran over her. How could she go home to the island now? How could she face her paragon of a mother? A failure, rejected by her husband, with any dreams she still had dashed and her future looking suddenly bleak.

How could she have been so oblivious? And so mundane. Dumped in an over-fifty-five community, like a pair of old shoes ready for the vets bin, while Ron ran off to make a new and exciting life for himself.

How would she ever come out whole on the other side?

Well, she didn't have a choice, did she? She'd always managed so far. Through the good times and the not so good, she'd persisted. Now for the first time ever, she hadn't succeeded. Because, slowly but surely, she'd let it slip from her hands.

She'd been slowly becoming irrelevant, until she seemed no more than a fading place marker on the road of life. And if she didn't stop it now, she would finally cease to exist altogether.

She closed the memory book, resisted the impulse to throw it in the garbage. She'd keep it as a reminder of how tenuous dreams could be. How easily a lifetime could be crushed.

And how long it would take to find her grounding again.

Chapter 4

Her parents were divorcing. Phoebe eased down on her bed among all the half-packed boxes. Her cell was warm in her hand. Like a live poisonous thing.

How could her parents be divorcing? It was like she was living in a nightmare from which she'd awaken only to realize she was still dreaming. Her father walking out, her engagement ended, her *Sentinel* killed.

None of it made sense. Just this morning everything was perfect-ish.

She looked around. She had so much to do, no place to go. Except the beach house, where Granna would be surprised and a little disappointed. In the situation? Or in her daughter and granddaughter? Granna never made judgments. She didn't have to. She'd instilled in them a sense of justice and competence and sometimes that was a slippery slope.

Phoebe forced herself to get up. Stay busy. That would help. Actually, she had no choice. She had to be out by tomorrow.

A sound escaped from deep inside her, a sound she didn't even recognize, but she thought it might be despair.

Pull yourself together, she commanded. She had it so much better than most people. So why did her heart feel like it might burst, and not in a good way?

Right now, her first order of business was to finish packing.

She pulled her hair back with an elastic band and looked around her bedroom. Her winter clothes were hanging in two wardrobe boxes. Her summer clothes were packed in suitcases she'd meant to take to Gavin's. She wouldn't take the time to re-pack for the weekend. There was plenty of storage at the beach house.

She began opening and closing drawers. There was hardly anything left to pack.

Into the bathroom. Only Phoebe's toothbrush and some makeup were left on the bathroom vanity. A change of clothes for tomorrow hung over the towel rack next to one old bath towel she planned to toss before leaving.

My parents are divorcing.

A laundry bag was hanging on the doorknob, left out for pack-ing away the sheets and pillows in the morning.

My engagement has ended.

Phoebe moved to the living room.

Boxes, boxes everywhere. Some taped shut and labeled; just as many half-packed and waiting for the last load. There were so many. And one bookshelf still filled with her favorites that she'd left for last.

She sat down on the couch. Pulled her knees up and hugged them tight.

The Sentinel *is no more.*

She rested her cheek on her knees, closed her eyes, felt her cheeks grow wet, but she didn't try to dry them. It seemed like too much trouble.

She would have to be strong for her mother. For herself. That's what Sutton-Adams women did.

When the doorbell rang, it took her a whole minute to understand what it was; she was still scrunched up on the couch, not knowing how long she'd been there.

The bell rang again and her legs jerked out straight.

God, what if it was Gavin? It couldn't be . . . he wouldn't . . . A shiver, a combination of wariness, anticipation, and something that might be denial, skittered up her spine. She just wouldn't answer it.

It rang again.

Phoebe pushed herself off the couch and nearly fell onto the coffee table. Her foot was asleep; she hobbled over to the front door where she stood indecisive for a moment, then opened the door just enough to peer out.

"Pizza delivery," Willa announced.

Phoebe nearly collapsed in relief.

Willa was dressed in jean shorts and a T-shirt, and held a large box from Antonio's balanced on her palm. She clutched a bottle of champagne in her other hand.

She took a quick look into the room over Phoebe's shoulder. "I'm not interrupting anything, am I?"

Phoebe stepped aside and motioned her in.

"No last-minute reconciliation?"

"Nope."

"Thank God, 'cause you look like shit."

"I feel like shit."

"When was the last time you ate?"

Phoebe shrugged.

"Hydrated?"

Phoebe shrugged again.

"We'll fix that in a jiff." Willa maneuvered herself and the box and bottle past Phoebe to deposit them on the coffee table among the rolls of tape and markers.

Phoebe followed behind her, trying to locate the energy to be appreciative.

"Not even a broken heart can resist Tony's house special."

Phoebe's eyes stung. She told herself it was from the heat rising off the loaded crust. "I'm such a fool."

"No, you're not, and I'm fresh out of platitudes, but we've all been there, some of us more than once. It may seem like the end of the world, but—"

"My parents are getting a divorce."

Willa stopped, holding a slice of pizza while the cheese slid slowly off the tip.

"Not . . . not because of you and Gavin?"

"No. Of course not. I think it's because of that damn condo. He made her move, then he left. I don't know. Nothing makes sense."

"Well, sit down. I'll get some paper towels."

Phoebe sat. It seemed easier than trying to help. She didn't know how Willa could be so cheery. She'd lost her job, too, and she had kids to support.

Willa returned with a roll of paper towels, a bottle of water, and two chipped mugs that Phoebe was donating to the vets.

She put the mugs and paper towels down and thrust the water at Phoebe. "Drink some of this, or the champagne will go right to your head."

"Are we celebrating?" Phoebe's mouth twisted.

"We might as well. The alternatives don't sound like too much fun."

Phoebe drank some water. God, she was parched.

Willa tore off two pieces of paper towel and placed slices on them. "Eat up. It doesn't look like you've done much packing today so we'll need our strength."

"Where are the girls tonight?"

"Mindy from across the hall is watching them," Willa said, picking open the bottle's foil cover. "She said you and I both needed a girls' night."

"Some girls' night," Phoebe said, looking around at the cardboard containers that were her future. "You know, the hardest thing to take is that I didn't even see any of it coming."

"If it's any consolation, I can't say that I did, either. Certainly not closing the *Sentinel*. Not you ending the engagement, although . . ."

Phoebe sighed. "You never really thought he was right for me."

"Hey. I was willing to like him for your sake; now I don't have to. But man, Ruth and Ron, that's just so disappointing."

"Yeah, Mom's being brave, but she has to be devastated."

Willa nodded and popped the cork of the champagne. Poured out two mugs and handed one to Phoebe. "But eat something or you'll get sloshed."

Phoebe picked up her slice and took a bite. She hadn't eaten all day, but it was only after the first bite that she realized how hungry she was.

"So do you have a plan?"

Phoebe finished chewing. "We're going to stay out at the beach house with Granna for the weekend. Maybe Granna can help Mom."

"And what about you?"

"I don't think she can help me. I'm a fool and I let everyone down."

"Oh, stop it. Give yourself time to grieve. Time to get angry. Time to regroup."

"Is that what you do?"

"Nah, I just stay pissed off all the time. But I married the jack-ass. That was totally on me."

"But losing the *Sentinel* was on me."

"No, it was entirely on Gavin. I knew there was something I didn't like about him."

"There was something wrong, wasn't there? With Gavin and me."

"Something wrong with him and the world, if you ask me. Well, don't feel bad. A false start or two isn't the worst that could happen. Hell, if he hadn't kneecapped us with closing the paper, you might have actually married him."

Phoebe shivered just thinking what she'd almost done.

"The man for you was his father. But he was married, too old, and now he's dead. We all expected Gavin to be like him. Maybe he couldn't live up to the expectation. Who knows."

"I know I did. I didn't mean to. I wasn't even aware of it really until this afternoon. Oh God. I told him he was nothing like his dad and he was a hack."

"You did go crazy."

"He'll probably have to go to therapy."

"I'll drink to that," Willa said, and held up the champagne. "Shit happens. To everybody."

"The really hard part is that I'm more upset about the paper than I am about Gavin."

"Well, good for you, girl. You're well rid of him. One thing I've learned about men in my thirty-four years is they can be fun but you can't ever rely on them. I learned it the hard way. So just consider this a narrow escape and convince yourself the best is yet to come."

"How can the best be yet to come if they're all unreliable?"

"I'm an inveterate optimist. Now let's get this mess into boxes and get on with our lives."

It was almost midnight before the last box was packed. Her suitcases were bulging; everything that didn't fit had been stuffed into reusable grocery bags. Except for the two slices of pizza left over for breakfast, she was done.

She walked Willa to the door. "Thanks."

"Anytime," Willa said. "And if you need a place to crash, I've got a couch."

"You and the girls have always got a place on *my* couch. Whenever it comes out of storage."

Willa surprised her with a spontaneous Willa hug.

After a moment, Phoebe pulled away. "Listen, when I was

interviewing Anita Peters for the food bank article, she mentioned that with the expansion they'd be looking for a new coordinator."

"Is she leaving?"

"Once it's set up, she'll move to the next place. You might want to talk to her. Tell her I told you about her. I don't know what the salary will be, but I'll give you a great recommendation."

"Thanks, I will."

They stood in the doorway. It was really hard to say the words that were inevitable. Phoebe didn't say them.

"See ya, then. Thanks for the pizza and champagne."

"Any time. See ya . . . soon," Willa added and walked down the steps to the street.

Phoebe lingered until the last minute, then closed the door.

It was the first thing that caught her eye, sitting upright on the bookcase. Placed where it was bound to catch her eye the minute she turned around. She could have sworn she'd packed it along with the first set of books last week.

Willa. She must have seen it in one of the boxes and taken it out as a reminder.

Phoebe lifted the brass plaque from the shelf: TO PHOEBE ADAMS FOR HER FIRST NATIONAL NEWS ARTICLE. It was inscribed by Simeon Cross.

Simeon had called the whole staff into a meeting and presented it to her when her first article had been picked up by the AP. She'd been so proud. The whole staff had been. Her career suddenly blossomed full blown before her.

She'd been eighteen and had written a feature on a man who

had secretly bequeathed his entire life savings to the local historical society. Because of that, they had been able to endow a scholarship program and begin renovations, which in turn led to the discovery of a cache of war correspondence between two generals of the Continental Army.

Just one man's generosity, a little incident in the scheme of things, but it spoke to Phoebe, and had spoken to enough readers that it had been reprinted in numerous newspapers throughout the country.

But even then, she knew it wasn't her great journalistic skills that made the article so appealing. It was the subject. She'd still been learning how to write compelling articles in those days, but she knew instinctually how to recognize compelling characters.

She'd powerhoused through Columbia's school of journalism. Had interned at the *Times* and the *Globe*. Constantly racing to catch the latest breaking news had been ruthless but exciting, adrenaline-rushing, and dog-tired fatiguing. But worth it.

The right story, the right placement, could make your career. Being the first, the most in-depth, the most insightful—it was a constant competition. Success was always just a step away from the smallest desk in the corner to a byline on the front page.

Phoebe had received several offers by the time she graduated. But when she returned home with her shiny diploma, she saw at once where her future lay. Simeon was fighting to keep the *Sentinel* meaningful in a changing world. And what she'd imagined would be her last summer internship segued into her choice for her future.

He asked her to stay on as an editor.

She agreed readily.

Breaking news was exciting, but it quickly cycled out, often before it had ripened. It might take years before she could work into in-depth, human-interest stories. Her hometown needed those stories now. The town needed the *Sentinel*. And the *Sentinel* needed her. She could really contribute to saving something she knew was just as important as all that national and international hubris . . . Local news.

She held the plaque against her chest, as if holding it alone could reactivate her heart, her belief, her fortitude.

Surely that article written a decade before wasn't the pinnacle of her career. It should have taken her to the next level. There had been others that were picked up and disseminated. But the last few years, she'd let her drive to tell the story take a back seat to her need to save the *Sentinel*.

Don't you have any ambition?

Yeah, she did. But not one Gavin would understand. And she'd let him hijack hers.

Well, no more. From now on, Phoebe would play this game differently. Stories first. *Her* career first. She could freelance until she found a permanent place that would give her the opportunity to search out stories that needed to be told, and then write them.

She carried the plaque into the bathroom, placed it on the counter while she brushed her teeth and peeled off her dirty clothes.

She carried it into her bedroom and wrapped it in Bubble

Wrap, but this time, instead of putting it in a box going to the storage unit, she placed it on the top of her suitcase. To remind her. In case she started to forget.

Phoebe awoke with a sense of panic that she'd forgotten to set her alarm. She *had* forgotten. She threw off the sheet and sat up. And that was as far as she got. Her eyes were swollen, and she ached everywhere. Maybe she was getting the flu. But gradually the fog of sleep cleared and she remembered.

The aches must have been from the packing, the swollen eyes from the rest of her life.

But movers waited for no extenuating circumstances. She dragged herself into the bathroom and took a quick shower. Nixed the thought of making coffee for herself and jogged down to the corner deli instead. She was back sitting on the stoop when the movers pulled up to the curb.

It only took a couple of hours to load the truck, another two to drive to the storage place and unload it all.

She waited until the movers drove away before she pulled the padlock out of her purse and secured the lock, securing all her worldly possessions, except what she would be taking to the beach house. And a few things that she'd left at Gavin's. Those she could do without. Forever.

She climbed back into her car, her laptop on the front seat. All she really needed.

By the time Phoebe had returned to her apartment, swept it out to satisfy her lease requirements, and loaded up her Honda with everything that hadn't gone to the storage unit, it was almost five o'clock. She called her mom to let her know she was on her way.

She didn't really need to make the next stop, but she couldn't not make it. She drove downtown and parked on the street across from the *Sentinel* building.

Averting her eyes, she got out of the car, trying not to let her gaze linger on the dull gold lettering across the window.

She would let herself in. Just one last quick look, something to remember indelibly printed on her brain.

But when she found her key and started to put it in the lock she found a lockbox instead. For a moment she could only stare.

A lockbox. He'd locked her out of the building. How dare he? *He'd said yesterday was their last day*, her both-sides-of-the-story journalist's mind reminded her. But this was ridiculous. Mitch and Nancy had been with the paper for forty years and he'd given them a few measly hours to get out.

Phoebe sucked in a long breath, let it out, took another one. No use getting angry now. It was over. Over. If that fact hadn't soaked into her brain and heart before, it did now.

She felt the betrayal as if she were Simeon Cross himself. She'd been his proxy for the last three years, but she'd been his friend and colleague for many, many more.

She backed away from the door, crossed the street to her car, and only briefly looked back at the building that had been her home.

If she ever visited again, she knew the lettering would be scraped off the window. A bright striped awning, all very chic, very upscale, would shelter the big plate glass of a new bistro or trendy dress shop and the *Sentinel* would vanish like the summer. Or maybe it would linger, staying vacant as the building grew derelict, finally to be razed. A heartrending end to generations of news.

Either way, she didn't want to witness its demise. Her eyes filled with tears but she willed them away.

She could cry at the beach, while she was getting a tan. Multitasking as always. This time when she drove away she knew it was for good.

The condo was half an hour in the opposite direction of the beach, and with rush-hour traffic, it was almost seven by the time she actually stopped in front of her parents' over-fifty-five-community condo.

At this rate they would miss regular rush hour, but beach traffic would be worse. It didn't matter.

There were no deadlines tonight.

The condos were arranged in trios of attached houses, each entrance flanked by faux Doric columns. The only way Phoebe could ever find her parents' condo among the others was the garden gnome under the mailbox that her mother, in a moment of guerilla warfare, had placed by the front steps.

When Phoebe pulled up to the curb, the front door opened immediately, revealing Ruth, haloed in the porch light. A perfect photo shoot for an article called "Best Places to Live After Retirement." The complex had everything: easy-to-maintain living quarters, pool, club house, and golf course—though her mother abhorred golf.

Phoebe waved and started up the sidewalk, but her mother was already coming out to meet her, rolling two huge suitcases. A lot of packing for a weekend visit just to avoid her husband.

Phoebe tried to take one of the cases from her, but her mother shook her head. "There's more inside."

Phoebe went inside.

Two smaller cases, several tote bags, and a serious briefcase that looked new were lined up military style in the foyer. Her mother had been a librarian when she wasn't having children and being a stay-at-home mom. But she'd never, ever carried a brief-case.

Phoebe was still standing in the foyer when Ruth returned.

"Oh, honey, I'm so sorry." She wrapped her arms around Phoebe. And Phoebe was tempted to just succumb to the war of emotions she was barely keeping at bay, but she squeezed back and then moved away. This was no time for falling apart.

Her mother seemed right on the brink herself. She was not quite as tall as Phoebe, kept fit, but was looking a little under-weight. Her hair was always meticulously colored and styled into what her mother called "the PTA face frame," but tonight it was beginning to show roots and hung in lank waves about her face.

Not good.

Ruth grabbed two of the totes. Phoebe took the last of the suit-cases and the briefcase. She didn't ask what was in it.

While her mother locked up, Phoebe found places for the last load and stood back, looking at the pile of luggage in the back of her Honda and remembering the day her parents had loaded up their station wagon and driven her to her first semester at college.

It had been Phoebe's first step into the adult world. A glorious day of exuberant expectations and new beginnings.

"Well," said Ruth, coming to stand beside her. "We look just like the Joads on the road to California."

"Not the image I was going for," Phoebe said as *The Grapes of Wrath* burst her happy memory like a bubble in the night.

"Never mind, sweetheart. Never mind," Ruth said, and Phoebe wondered if she was encouraging Phoebe or herself.

Chapter 5

As expected, traffic was heavy, and a trip that usually took two hours in winter was taking twice as long. When they reached the halfway point, they decided to pull into a drive-through burger place. Not Phoebe's first choice of dining experiences, but it was late, and it had been a long day since the slice of pizza early that morning. She had no intention of getting lightheaded and driving off the bridge to Summer Island just because she'd forgotten to eat. And there would be plenty of good food at Granna's house.

"I'll just call and tell her we're going to be late," Ruth said, and pulled out her cell phone while Phoebe ordered. "That's odd. She's not answering."

"It's a little early for bed even for Granna," Phoebe said. "You told her we were coming?"

"I told her we were thinking about coming for the weekend. I wasn't sure if you'd make it to my place by five, so I just left our arrival open. You know how she worries." Ruth held up a finger. "Hi, Mother. Phoebe and I are on our way. Heavy traffic, so we may be really late. Don't worry about us. And don't wait up. Just leave the key under the mat and we'll fend for ourselves."

Ruth ended the call and sighed.

"What?"

"Nothing, sweetheart. How are you holding up? Want me to drive?"

"No, I'm good."

"Just so you know," Ruth said when they were on the road again, "I didn't tell her about you and Gavin."

Phoebe's stomach performed a brief but spectacular acrobatics act and she dropped her burger back into the bag. She'd been hoping that her mother would have eased the way for her to explain things to Granna.

"Actually, I didn't tell her about your father, either."

"Mo-o-om."

"She sounded so happy that we were coming. And I didn't want to worry her. It will be better to tell her in the morning. After a good night's sleep."

"Fine by me," Phoebe said. She had no desire to confess her fall from grace to her grandmother who had lived for "fifty years of wedded bliss to the best man on earth."

And she'd have to return the pearls that would go unworn. They were on the top of her small suitcase, in the black velvet case, worn by several generations of Keyes-Sutton women, and thus far two Adamses. It was a rite of passage. Phoebe was—should have been—the last of the line until the next generation. It was as if she'd broken the chain.

For once, Phoebe actually felt kindly toward the snail's pace of beach traffic. Granna might be asleep when they arrived and they could put off the inevitable until tomorrow. Because if she was awake, they would be outed.

Not much got past Alice Keyes-Sutton, no matter how hard you tried; adult or child, she seemed to see right through you. Though she acted surprised at every "surprise" party, showed no consternation when you confessed that you were the one who'd bounced the ball in the parlor and broken her favorite vase. Even when she caught you sneaking in late at night, smelling of beer and cigarettes, she never let emotions get the better of her. Her judgment was always meted out calmly. No yelling required. Just one quiet "Don't let your grandfather know—he would be so disappointed" made any indiscretion all the more squirm-worthy. Even after Henry Sutton died, the memory of his imagined disappointment was enough to make any of them blush hot with shame.

It made Alice Sutton the consummate matriarch. And the best grandmother anyone could want. It was also hard to live up to such a paragon.

Phoebe glanced across to her mother, who seemed to be dozing—or avoiding conversation. The few times Phoebe had even tangentially suggested they talk about things, Ruth had deflected and changed the subject, and most of the trip had been taken in silence. Which was fine by Phoebe. She hadn't begun to process what had just happened to her own life.

Almost an hour later, they inched across the first bridge from the mainland to the series of islands that ran along the coastline and were connected by a series of old bridges and earthen causeways.

Each island was unique in size, topography, and personality. The first and largest island was the most popular, with a yacht club, several high-end hotels, and many upscale tourist venues. But after they passed the first causeway, and the lights and traffic of civilization receded, they were enveloped by almost complete darkness, lit only by her car's headlights and the stars above, until clouds scudded across the stars and there were only her headlights to lead the way.

They passed through smaller islands where the old fishing villages had not yet been overtaken and disguised by gentrification, passed uninhabited rocky protuberances that dipped out of the night sea and were accessible only by boat.

The Suttons lived on the last island. It was large enough for two small towns, inhabited by a handful of year-round residents and nearly doubling in size between June and September.

The largest town, Kedding's Wharf, was the closest thing they had to upscale shops and tourist attractions. A handful of B-and-Bs and an even fewer number of stately beach houses and summer rentals. It even had its own carousel.

The Suttons lived in a smaller cluster of shops and beach cottages that masqueraded as a town but was merely called the Corners, since it consisted of four of them where Seaside Lane crossed Beach Road.

The Suttons had lived here for generations, and after Alice Keyes married Henry, it became home to the Keyes and then to the Adamses as well.

Phoebe's family had spent every summer here. And as far as she was concerned, Granna's house was home, and always would be to Phoebe as much as the house she'd grown up in. As she and her sisters grew older and Daphne and Celia complained about having to leave their school friends for the summer, Phoebe would always be packed and ready a week before school was out.

So it wasn't strange, perhaps, that as she maneuvered off the last bridge and onto terra firma, she began to relax. Even with her life in turmoil. Even with the prospect of having to explain what had happened to Granna, there would be the house, and the beach, and the waves, calming her doubts and hushing her to sleep.

Phoebe slowed down as she drove through "their" town, all two blocks of it, mostly dark now. But it would be bustling in the morning as the bakery fired up its ovens and the luncheonette opened for early-morning coffee seekers.

The luncheonette always had free newspapers to read and leave, Phoebe remembered. The *Sentinel* sent them two copies for free every week—Phoebe had made sure of that even after Gavin took over and their hard-copy readership began to dwindle. She wondered if the last issue would be there tomorrow.

Phoebe gulped back a sob. No time for looking back now.

Elridge's Ice Cream had one light on in the back. The shop next to it looked abandoned. Phoebe tried to remember what had been there. The shoe-repair shop? In the next block, the bakery had a new neon sign hanging in the window, spelling out in green script *Sabatini's*.

Phoebe turned right and drove slowly down Seaside. There

was a television flickering in the Jamiesons' house; farther along, the McMurphys' was dark. A big dumpster sat in the front yard. The McMurphys were adding on. The new frame rose around the original foundation like a cage, jarring Phoebe's sense of welcome.

"It's so peaceful," Ruth said out of the darkness. "Just like . . ."

"Home," Phoebe agreed. A safe haven from her troubles, time to reboot. And for her mother? Ruth had grown up here; for her, it really was home.

The lane forked almost immediately, the left leading to the Wilkinses' "fish camp," a glorified shack on the Wilkins property where local residents could launch their two-seaters from the bayside or fish from shore. Phoebe took the right hook that looped down to where three houses sat in a semicircle around the secluded sandy beach.

The first was the Sutton house, a gem of New England architecture, all turrets and verandas and oddly shaped rooms, painted a light yellow and finished in white trim.

Next to it, the Harkens' smaller, newer house by half a century was three stories of no-nonsense beach house, strong enough to withstand the weather and three rambunctious growing boys.

Their two houses were separated enough to have a modicum of privacy, but still close enough that you could toss a ball from window to window; hence the broken vase episode. The two families had grown up together, treating each other's houses like their own.

Farther along, and separated from the other two by a full lot of pines and scrub oak, the Wilkinses' sprawling cottage had once been the scene of a near-sacred up-island tradition. Every Saturday, the local men would congregate under a massive oak tree to work on cars and drink beer. It didn't matter whose car or how long it took to fix it as long as the beer was cold and the company was friendly.

Phoebe turned into the first driveway.

"Look," Ruth said. "There's a light on in the Harkens' living room. The rest of the house looks deserted." She sighed. "Poor Lars. I should have made more of an effort to stay in touch, but he didn't tell any of us how ill Delores was. I don't think I've seen him or the boys since the funeral. I'll make sure to let him know how much we all care."

Phoebe nodded. She could hear music coming from somewhere. She opened the car window and the ocean breeze rushed in—along with loud Caribbean dance music.

Ruth reached out and grabbed Phoebe's shoulder. "Remember, not a word, until tomorrow."

"Chill, Mom, she's probably been asleep for hours." Then Phoebe saw the bright red Range Rover parked next to her grandmother's Lexus.

"Whose car is that?" Ruth exclaimed.

Phoebe maneuvered the Honda beside the two cars, turned off the ignition, and stared. Instead of being quietly dark and sleeping, the house was lit up like Christmas and the Fourth of July together. Music blared through the open windows.

For several seconds, neither of them moved. Just sat looking at the spectacle that was meant to be their haven.

Someone was having a rip-roaring good time inside.

Ty Harken turned from the window.

"Well?" his father demanded. "What's going on over there?"

"Looks like they're having a party. You should go over. I'm sure Alice would be glad to have you."

"It's Mrs. Sutton to you," his father said.

"She told me to call her Alice when I turned thirty; that was seven years ago." Why did he even bother? His father was just trying to pick an argument.

Ty had been here almost two weeks, and the only time his father showed the least bit of life was when he tried to pick a fight with his middle son.

"What were those lights?"

"More guests, I suspect. Why don't you get up and see for yourself?"

"Don't care. Music's too loud." His father fumbled with the remote and turned up the volume of the television that neither of them was watching.

And so another day passed, Ty desperately trying to do what couldn't be done. He'd known that before he'd come, but he'd let his brothers persuade him. In their eyes he didn't have an excuse not to spend the summer trying to get his father to return to the land of the living. They had families and jobs they went to every day. Ty didn't have either.

To them, that meant he didn't have responsibilities. And the fact that he was sometimes "between projects" just reinforced their belief that he couldn't keep a real job. It had always been that way. "He marches to a different drummer," his mother always said. "Making excuses for him," his father always countered.

His mother had been his rock. She'd understood when he turned out to be so different from his business-oriented brothers and father. She supported him when his "absentmindedness" led him away from what they considered "important jobs with a future."

Ty had a job. Plenty of work. He even had an office that he kept for a small staff to run so he wouldn't have to, but it was work they didn't understand.

They weren't bad people, just unimaginative.

So here he was trying to break through to a man who had tried and failed to understand his middle son, and had finally given up.

But his mother had. And now she was gone.

"What are you standing there for? You're young, why don't you go over and have some fun? Maybe you'll find a wife. Don't know why you came here in the first place."

"Because the house needs fixing up, Dad. I'm good with my hands."

"Nothing's wrong with the house. Don't know why I bother keeping it."

His brothers had tried to convince their father to move to a condominium nearer their own homes. He'd thrown a fit and declared he would never leave the island.

"You want some ice cream? There are fresh strawberries."

"I'm not supposed to eat ice cream," Lars said, not bothering to look away from the neon colors of the Red Sox game.

Except Ty had caught him eating it right out of the container the night before. There was no reason he couldn't enjoy a dessert now and then. The doctor had said that he'd suffered several panic attacks, not heart attacks.

"Ya bum!" Lars yelled at the TV. Like he actually cared what had just happened on the field. Even that would be a blessing. Because Lars Harken didn't care about anything these days.

And that was the real reason Ty was here.

You couldn't push away grief, wrestle it out of your heart, trample it underfoot, ignore it until it went silently away. You could only live through it.

Ty knew about how hard it was to grieve. Unfortunately he didn't seem to be able to share that grief with his father.

And he was afraid his being here was only making things worse, instead of better.

I don't understand, Ruth said, staring ahead and not making a move to get out of the car.

"I think she's having a party," Phoebe ventured.

"Never. Not like this. The neighbors would complain."

The neighbors would be too shocked to do any such thing, Phoebe thought. It wasn't that Alice Sutton didn't know how to have fun, but her idea of a good time was homemade ice cream on the beach with all the neighbors invited, a Sunday family dinner at the yacht club on the big island, or a neighborhood clambake and home before dark.

This was—

"She didn't mention renting it out?"

"Of course not. She would never."

"And she knew we were coming?"

"Yes."

"Well, maybe we should go in and find out what's going on."

"We certainly will." Ruth opened the car door and marched across the packed sand toward the house.

Phoebe had to rush to catch up.

Ruth knocked on the door.

Before Phoebe could suggest that they might not hear her over the music, she knocked again. Tried the doorknob. The knocking turned to banging. The banging to calling. Phoebe was about to walk around to the beach side when the door opened.

Her grandmother stood in the entryway. She was wearing capris and a nubby silk tee that would be perfectly normal except she was barefooted and had a Hawaiian-print scarf wrapped around her head like a latter-day Carmen Miranda.

"Ruth?" she mouthed, or maybe she said it out loud; it was impossible to make out with the music filling the air with ear-splitting exuberance.

She threw out her hands in welcome and staggered back slightly. "This ish a shurprise."

Phoebe's mouth dropped open.

"Mother?" Ruth said. "I told you we were coming." She was practically yelling to be heard over the music.

Alice smiled and nodded. "You didn't tell me you were getting here tonight. But come on in."

"I did. I called you from the road to say we'd be a little late. Didn't you listen to your messages?"

Alice shrugged. "I guess I didn't hear my phone."

"I don't doubt it with this racket."

Alice turned to Phoebe. "And how's my little bride-to-be? Come give Granna a hug." Phoebe did and got a double-dose whiff of alcohol. Her grandmother had been drinking.

"If I'd known you were getting here tonight, I would've cooked dinner, but we got takeout. There's plenty left. I think."

"We?" Ruth asked, pushing past her. "Who's *we*?"

"Didn't I shay? Come this way." Alice turned and wove conga-line style down the hall.

Ruth cast a panicked look at Phoebe, then ran after Alice. "Mother, have you been drinking?"

Alice made a little turn and grinned back at them. "Absh-o-lu-u-u-utely."

"Mother! What exactly is going on here?" Ruth took off again after the whirling Alice.

Phoebe followed.

They were halfway down the hall when the kitchen door opened and someone backed into the hallway, carrying a pitcher of green liquid in one hand and a salt shaker in the other. She was tall and skinny as a post with wild gray hair pulled back and bouncing on the top of her head.

She turned and saw the others. Froze somewhat like the Statue of Liberty would if Liberty had been a cocktail waitress.

"Ruthie! Alice said you might be coming. And is that Phoebe? My, I won't say how you've grown, but how you've grown! And such acclaim. I loved your article on the hidden letters in the wall. And you won that award for it, too. I would have called to congratulate you, but I was in . . . let me see . . ." She waved the salt shaker. "Someplace with no cell reception, no electricity. Marvelous. Had the time of my life. C'mon in. Alice and I are just getting started.

"Ruth, you look slim enough to be a model. Don't know if I like it. For myself I've tried to gain weight my whole life. You should try it. Put some zig to your zag. I'll get more glasses. Hold these." She shoved the pitcher and shaker at Ruth—who took them out of sheer surprise—and disappeared back into the kitchen.

Ruth managed to shut her mouth long enough to form one question. "Vera?"

Phoebe sat on a wicker club chair, sipping her margarita and trying to take in her three companions. Her grandmother—Granna Alice, the matriarch of the whole island, the person the town came to when they needed a hostess for a fundraiser, who held an annual picnic-and-beach day for the local community center, and who had sat on several insurance company boards and even chaired one—sat across from her, legs crossed, tailor style, sipping her second margarita since Phoebe and Ruth had arrived.

Great-aunt Vera Keyes, whom no one had seen for years, was the black sheep—if there was such a thing—in the family. World traveler, self-confessed rolling stone, whose rare visits never lasted more than two days, she stretched out on the floral chaise with the trademark élan of all the Keyes-Sutton women.

Vera was always exuberant, but Phoebe thought that tonight her energy seemed forced. Of course, she hadn't seen her great-aunt since before college, and she was getting older, early seventies, Phoebe guessed. But she held an awe-filled memory of her independence and self-assuredness and mystery. It was a wonder how two sisters could be so different.

Her mother sat on the sofa next to Granna Alice. She, like Granna, was the quintessential rational woman, organizing home, career, children, husband, and a myriad of special interests and organizations. But tonight she clearly was not comfortable with any of what was happening. And though usually a white-wine drinker, she was making good headway through the margaritas. She sat primly upright but was beginning to list slightly toward her mother.

It was like being at a carnival and seeing her family in the distorting mirrors of the fairway sideshow.

Great. Her life was falling apart and the universe had sent her a Fellini movie.

Phoebe stood up. "I think I'll go down to the beach."

The other three women looked up and stared at her from owlish, inebriated eyes.

"Want us to come, too?" Ruth asked.

"No, no. I just . . . well, just want to see the beach. It's been so long since I've been back." Phoebe slid her margarita glass onto the coffee table, and, already feeling light-headed, she carefully made her way to the side porch.

She wished she could blame this feeling on the margarita, but she wasn't drunk. She was painfully sober. And as she slipped out of the house and slowly made her way across the sand, it finally hit her, the magnitude of what she had done.

"Well?" Vera asked, as soon as they heard the screen door slam shut. She turned her overly inquisitive eyes to Ruth. So did Alice. And it was impossible for Ruth to avoid their unspoken question.

Why are you really here?

This had been a terrible idea. What had she been thinking? She was so frantic to get away from the condo, she'd forgotten that Phoebe was moving this weekend.

Now she'd gotten them both in an untenable situation. Damn Ron and his typically clueless male timing. She should have just thrown his golf clubs out on the street and told him to pick them up at the curb.

"Take your time, dear," her mother said.

Ugh, sometimes she hated her mother's ability to know everything. Of course, she didn't know everything. It just seemed to Ruth that even as an adult, she was still the child.

"Is this a celebratory family weekend?" asked Vera. "Or a cry-in-your-margarita weekend? Should I make another pitcher?"

"It's a long story."

Vera reached for the pitcher. She also had her sister's sixth sense. And Ruth had to admit, at least when it came to her children, she had it, too. So why had she missed Ron's change of heart?

"You'd better hold off on the margaritas, Vera," Alice said, eyeing Ruth and transforming from her conga-line persona to the administrator-of-justice mother Ruth remembered. "I wouldn't want to forget any little detail in the morning."

Ruth slumped against the cushions. Straightened up again. What should she say? Should she confess that her husband had left her? Or should she start with Phoebe's broken engagement and keep her own bad news to herself?

That wouldn't be fair to Phoebe. But a broken engagement was not the same as a divorce after thirty-eight years of marriage. And there was still a chance that Phoebe and Gavin would make up. There was no chance that her marriage could be saved. It had been limping along for far too long. She saw that now, saw how she'd enabled it to happen. And she wasn't proud of herself.

Tomorrow would be soon enough. Telling them about both might be a bit too much even for her mother and aunt to take in, especially after all the margaritas they'd imbibed. And then she'd just have to recount it all again.

Or, worse, they might try to change her mind. And she wasn't sure she could hold out against their assuredly rational arguments tonight. But there would be no going back for her and Ron. He'd grown tired of her. If she was honest, she'd grown tired of herself.

Ruth bit her lip. Tried not to look at her mother and aunt waiting patiently for her to come clean. *What to do?* Tell them the whole sordid story of Ron's betrayal? It would upset everyone; it might take hours to explain and her mother certainly needed her sleep, especially with Vera around. On the other hand, maybe it was best to lose a little sleep and get it over with now. That would be the most rational, reasonable thing to do, the way Ruth always dealt with things. She would do it.

She cleared her throat, thought, *Here goes*, and said . . .

"Phoebe has called off the wedding."

Chapter 6

Phoebe walked along the sand, letting the ocean air cool her heated cheeks. She felt better now, but for a moment in that room, with the people she loved, even Great-aunt Vera, whom she hardly knew, she felt like she'd let them all down. Had let herself and Simeon down. Where had she gone wrong?

And what did it matter? It was done now and she'd have to crawl her way back up to a place where she could live with her choices.

A setback. Everyone had them, just not necessarily on the same day, the same hour.

For the briefest second, with the wind blowing her hair, she wondered what life would have been like if she'd taken the *Boston Globe* job right out of school. She could be well on her way to national recognition. Was Gavin right? Had she settled for too little?

She looked out to the sea, deep and unfathomable. Walked back to where the sand was dry and sat down, closed her eyes and just listened. It helped. The constancy of the waves breaking on the shore sent a calm through her that she hadn't felt in a long time.

Phoebe didn't know how long she sat there; she may have dozed for a bit. She only knew that when she looked up again, the moon was overhead and the clouds had broken up to create a flickering play of light and dark across the waves.

She stood, stiff from packing, driving, sitting, and the turmoil of her life, and brushed off the seat of her jeans.

As she turned from the water, she was greeted by the full silhouette of the old Victorian house, its turrets and eaves, balconies and porches glowing almost magically in the moonlight.

Next door, the Harken house was dark, almost foreboding. One lone, dim light managed to flicker from the window of an attic room. It was hard not to imagine who might be imprisoned there.

Phoebe shook her head. That was taking the fairy-tale theme a bit far. The two houses had always been filled with laughter and love and a few broken vases. It was the moonlight and her own mind playing fanciful tricks.

As she watched, the second-floor bedroom lights in her grandmother's house popped on one by one. The others had gone to bed. Good, she would have the house to herself. She could creep to her own bedroom and sleep.

Tonight she was glad she'd come back. Tomorrow would be soon enough to face the world.

She trudged slowly up the sand to the house . . .

She remembered which stairs creaked and instinctively stepped over them. She had successfully tiptoed across the wide landing when her grandmother's door cracked open. Granna's face appeared, then her long beringed fingers motioned for Phoebe to step inside.

Phoebe started, snatched back into the lingering fairy tale she'd conjured. *Come in, come in, you have nothing to fear.*

Recovering herself, Phoebe obeyed. There would be nothing scary on the other side of the door. This was Granna Alice, not a witch out of the Brothers Grimm. Phoebe owed her grandmother an explanation, and it would be better to get it over with and without an audience.

Granna shut the door and motioned for her to sit down on the bed. Phoebe noticed that the mattress had been lowered from its original height, but the bumpy pattern of the chenille spread was the same as ever, and she felt a flicker of optimism.

It didn't last.

Granna pulled over the little slipper chair from her dressing table and sat down facing the bed. Phoebe appreciated that. It would be so much harder to explain with her grandmother towering over her or pacing the room as she sometimes did when she was thinking.

"Your mother told us about you and Gavin."

"I'm sorry," Phoebe said. "It just didn't—"

Granna's upheld hand stopped her. "Even someone my age can guess it didn't work out. Tell me what really happened."

So Phoebe told her the unvarnished truth. One that she hadn't totally appreciated until now. "He sold the paper, he didn't care about it, never cared about it."

"But what about you, Phoebe?"

"Me? I cared. I cared and he didn't ask my opinion or even let me know in advance. So I ended things. He didn't even try to stop me."

"I mean, did he care about you?"

"Yes," she said, but had he? Really? She'd never questioned their relationship. And it turned out that she didn't know him at all. "I guess he did, but not enough to save the *Sentinel*."

"Would you change your mind if he did?"

"I . . . I . . . I hope not." There, she'd said it. She looked at Granna for her reaction.

But Granna was a well of inscrutability. She'd always been like that. Even when Phoebe was a child, she would listen to her just as if she was one of the adults. She would give her opinion, but in her own good time. Her advice, if she had any, would take longer. And sitting here tonight, Phoebe thought she understood.

And suddenly she couldn't stop talking. "He said . . . he said I cared more about the paper than I did him. That I wanted him to be like his father. He was right. Simeon cared about the paper. It was his life. It was mine. Oh, I don't know—I brought your pearls back."

Granna's thin lips curved into a soft smile. "Why don't you just keep them for a while."

"We're not getting back together."

"Perhaps not, but he's not the only man in the world."

"No," Phoebe agreed. "He certainly wasn't the one for me."

"And you had the good sense to recognize it before you rued the day you walked down the aisle."

Phoebe stilled. Had her mother told them about her dad leaving? Was she sorry now that she ever married him?

"I was lucky," Granna said. "Your grandfather and I were a match made in heaven. Not that we didn't have our moments." Her eyes twinkled. "Some real knock-down drag-outs. What I'd give for just one more. Making up was such a pleasure."

Phoebe had to force her mouth to stay shut. She didn't even want to think about what those making-ups might have been like, and Granna normally would never wander into that territory. It had to be the margaritas.

"You'll figure it out. And you're welcome to stay here for as long as it takes."

"Thanks, Granna. I was at the end of my lease and—" Phoebe hiccupped trying to stop an escaping sob. Was this where she finally lost it? Over a broken lease?

Granna reached behind her to the dressing table, pulled several tissues from the ornate container, and handed them to Phoebe.

"Thanks. Sorry. I don't know why I'm acting like this."

"No? Well, you will. Now you just have a nice cry. And then perhaps you'll tell me why your mother is here."

Her words shocked Phoebe into momentary calmness . . . and just a bit of trepidation. "She—"

Granna flashed her hand in the air, the big emerald-and-diamond ring she always wore even at the beach catching the light. "Yes, I know, she wanted to be supportive. She told us that much."

Phoebe nodded and hid her face in the tissue. Her grandmother had always had an uncanny way of making them think she knew everything already, even before they confessed. And they always confessed.

No one in the family would ever downright lie to Alice Sutton. Not because she'd punish you. She never did. But because you didn't want to disappoint her.

She never lost her cool even in the face of tragedy or celebration. It made her the consummate matriarch, ruling over her family with an even hand that held all the compassion and understanding—and justice—you could wish for.

The silence grew, and Phoebe knew she was alone in feeling uncomfortable, but she also didn't think it was fair for her to rat out her mother. She'd been married for decades and had children, and her hurt must be so overwhelming. It made Phoebe sick to even think about it. And here she was being whiney and self-indulgent over a broken engagement and a lost job . . . and no place to live . . .

Not able to chance a little white lie—if she could have even thought of one, which she couldn't—she asked, "Didn't she say anything?"

"Just that she came to be supportive. She didn't elaborate, which said everything." She laughed softly. "After all these years, you'd think she'd know me better. You'd think you all would."

Granna was the kindest, calmest, most forgiving person Phoebe had ever met. And yet they were all a little frightened of her. Which made absolutely no sense at all.

Granna clicked her tongue, the closest she came to disapproval. "What a sack of phooey. She and your father could have both been supportive in their new condo and given you a place to stay while you got back on your feet. But since she never goes anywhere without him—and since she hasn't mentioned him once—I gather she has a very good reason for being here and it involves him."

No question, Granna Alice was a witch. A white witch, perhaps; clairvoyant, indubitably.

Phoebe licked dry lips.

"You don't have to answer. That was more a statement of fact than a question. I expect she'll tell all after breakfast. That's her usual time. She's always had a hard time admitting failure."

Phoebe bristled. "She isn't a failure."

"Of course not, she never has been. I have complete confidence and respect for Ruth. But she does have that tendency to regard whatever she can't fix as a failure."

Suddenly Phoebe wished she hadn't been so absorbed in her own unhappiness that she hadn't shown more concern for how her mother was feeling on the car ride here.

"Now clear your head and go to bed; you look dead on your feet. Whatever it is, it won't be solved tonight. And I confess, I'm rather sleepy myself. It's been a long time since I've drunk like a fish. Vera's fault. She always brings out the wild in me."

"Mom didn't mention she was going to be here," Phoebe said.

"Probably because she didn't know. It was a surprise to me. She showed up two days ago with a blender and enough tequila to sink a battleship. Usually, she would be gone by now."

"Is this a special occasion?"

"Said she was on her bucket list."

"Great-aunt Vera? Oh no."

"Well, if she is, it must be a long list. She's not about to die. The Keyes women are known for their longevity."

"How can you know for sure?"

"I know my sister. No, she's here for some other reason. She didn't say. Though she may be a harder nut to crack than your mother.

"Now off to bed. I have a feeling tomorrow is going to be a full day. We can count on Vera to make sure you don't have a minute to feel sorry for yourselves. Now shoo." She took Phoebe's hands and pulled her off the bed. Gave her a quick kiss on the cheek and ushered her to the door.

Phoebe was standing in the hall, alone, before she knew what had happened. She yawned and padded down the hall to her room. So much for a quiet, contemplative, regrouping weekend. Vera would make that impossible.

Maybe that was a good thing after all.

Tyler Harken shielded his eyes from the early-morning sun as he balanced on the top rung of the extension ladder and studied the closest section of roof. This part of the roof was on the island side of the house and hadn't taken the same harsh battering as the beachside had, but the tiles were pretty worn.

He leaned over to try to see the flashing around the chimney; the aluminum joints creaked under his weight. The ladder should probably be replaced, too.

But the roof definitely. It was probably better to have it completely replaced.

His father would balk over the cost, as he did on just about every decision from roofing to what to have for breakfast. Ty could try to get his brothers to go in on it with him, or he could just pay for it himself.

Any decision he made would make them all pissed off. Sometimes you couldn't win. And Ty was pretty sure this would be one of those times.

But family was family and he was glad to have one. There were so many people who didn't.

He let his eyes rove out to the strip of sand and beach grass between the Harken and Sutton houses. They'd had a wild time of it last night. Granna Alice was usually as quiet as anything, so when he saw her lights on at ten last night, and heard the music crank up, he knew it could only be one thing. Her sister, Vera, was still here.

He'd literally bumped into her the day before as he was unloading several black lawn bags from his SUV. She'd come barreling through the yard between the houses, and reached the backyard where he was parked just as he turned. The inevitable collision followed and two dozen empty gallon milk jugs flew out in all directions.

His father, who had been watching from the window, was not amused, but it did start a conversation with Alice Sutton's globe-trotting sister. It had been so long since someone had shown real interest in his work, he'd kind of gotten carried away. But he managed to wind down before her eyes had completely glazed over. She'd helped him put the jugs back in the bags and then left, starting up again at her pre-collision pace, and trotted up the lane toward town.

He was fairly certain she was responsible for the good times last night. Now they had another visitor. The Honda he'd seen drive up last night was still parked there this morning. They'd carried on late into the night. Which was why he was looking at the roof instead of mending the porch steps.

They would most likely have hammering heads without the addition of his external one. He'd give them another hour, then get to work. Until then he'd check to see if his dad was up and get himself a cup of coffee.

As he started to climb down the ladder, the back door of the Sutton house opened and a woman came out. Not Vera, not Alice, but a young woman, probably in her late twenties. One of the Adams girls. They all had the same honey-gold hair. This one wore hers long, but pulled back into some kind of twist at the top of her head.

He squinted down at her. And then as if he'd actually called out to her, she looked up at him, frowned—probably just the sun in her eyes—and waved.

He waved back, but she had already turned and continued on her way up the lane in the direction of town.

She definitely had the Sutton-Adams look. If her face hadn't convinced him, the way she strode up the pavement did—she had that Sutton walk. One of the granddaughters. But which one was this?

Celia must be midthirties or older. So not her. Daphne was

always larger boned than the others—this one was skinny and petite. It must be the youngest one . . .

It took a few seconds to remember her name: Phoebe. Of course, how could he forget. Tiny little chatterbox, annoying as hell with twenty questions every time she could run him or anybody else to ground. They used to call her Magpie. She thought it was a compliment.

He wondered if she was still as annoying as she was then.

He finished his descent and went into the kitchen, hoping that he would have just a few minutes to drink his coffee in peace before the daily confrontations began.

Mr. Harken must be getting his roof fixed, Phoebe thought as she walked up the lane toward town. The house looked like it could use a coat of paint, too. It wasn't like Mr. Harken to let things go like that. He took pride in the classic shingled beach house.

Phoebe hurried on, suddenly curious to see the rest of the town in daylight. But mainly she needed coffee and she didn't want to wake anyone up by using the grinder. And to be honest, she wasn't ready to face her mother, grandmother, and great-aunt en masse.

And she really didn't want to be there when her mother blurted out that her husband had left her.

Of course she wouldn't blurt it out. Granna was right. Her mother didn't blurt things out. She would inform them matter-of-factly. Their phone call had been an aberration, one that had frightened Phoebe. Her mother only cried at old movies and classical music and the plight of refugees. Phoebe couldn't remember a time—before two nights ago—when Ruth Adams had ever cried for herself.

Phoebe, coward that she was, didn't want to witness her mother's undoing. Besides, it would be better if she told Granna and Great-aunt Vera without Phoebe present. She probably wanted to say things that she wouldn't want to say in front of her daughter.

But surely things weren't as bad as her mom thought. Her father would never do something like this.

But he has. He's walked out on your mother. And Gavin walked out on the Sentinel *and you.* Not a good week for men in Phoebe's book.

She started walking faster. Trying to quell her sudden burst of emotion. The beach was no place for anger.

And she was angry. Angry and surprised. But mostly confused. Her dad had a good life; her mom saw to that, like she saw to everything. Phoebe couldn't recall her mother complaining or nagging him to do something. He always got his way. He had no reason to complain.

And if Phoebe was angry, she could just imagine what her mother felt, no matter how hard she tried not to let it show. Granna was the matriarch of the family, but Ruth was the matriarch-in-waiting. Phoebe knew her mother wouldn't want to appear less than capable of handling her own affairs.

There was a slight incline toward the center of town, and after a few minutes, she was out of breath. That's what happened when you had a one-track mind, spent all your time at a computer instead of going to the gym. The walk was doing her good. Even if her lungs felt like a fish in the last gasps before the frying pan.

She passed the McMurphys' house. There was, as she'd thought last night, work going on. The dumpster was there, plus a large construction shed and some big hoe-like machine that had been only a silhouette last night.

What wasn't there was the house.

Phoebe stopped dead in the middle of the street and stared.

There was a new foundation twice, maybe triple, the size of the old house. Surrounded by a high mesh fence, it took up every square inch across the front and lapped at the edges of the houses on each side.

The McMurphys' house was about to become a McBeach house.

She thought of the handyman at the Harken house and prayed that he wasn't fixing it up to put it on the market. What would happen to the island if this replaced all their houses?

Phoebe quickly looked away, turning in a circle, searching for signs of impending demolition. So far, all the old houses were still standing. But for how long? Wasn't there a zoning law? She'd have to find out.

No she wouldn't. She wasn't here on a story, she was here out of desperation. She wasn't staying; it wasn't her business to get involved. On the other hand, this was Granna's home. Their home.

No one was going to tear down Sutton House. Not if Phoebe had any say.

Businesses were just opening for the day. There were several new green awnings, which from her experience meant new stores, new owners, and the old pushed aside or out altogether. She desperately hoped she wasn't looking at the future of the Corners.

She passed the old luncheonette where they'd spent many a Sunday brunch feasting on blueberry pancakes. She wouldn't go in. She knew there would be no *Sentinel* stacked on the counter waiting to be read and passed around.

Across the street, John Jacobson was opening the hardware and beach supply store. Next to him, the shoe-repair store had gone out of business. A trendy coffee bar had taken its place. She crossed the street, ordered a latte from the walk-up window, and drank it as she continued down the sidewalk.

She passed the pharmacy, where the familiar row of metal newspaper boxes were lined up at the curb. She stopped to look inside though she knew the *Sentinel* wouldn't be there. One held several *Pennysavers*. One for the weekly *Beach Goings-On*. One was empty; the last held a double stack of real estate pamphlets.

Not one newspaper in the lot. Another tradition slowly being erased. The news shared each morning over eggs and pancakes and orange juice. Or read lazily on the porch, each section then dropped by the side of your chair, growing like a hill of words at your feet.

"Excuse me." A man in shorts and a polo shirt reached past her and grabbed two of the real estate brochures, before hurrying off down the street.

Phoebe stepped away and continued on. She arrived at the front of the bakery without thought while she pondered the death of journalism.

Luckily, her feet knew the way. And her dismal mood wasn't

anything that one of Inez Sabatini's sticky buns wouldn't cure. She mentally crossed her fingers that Inez hadn't retired.

There was the usual display of pies and cakes in the showcase window as well as a HELP WANTED sign near the door at eye level. *Part-time counter position. Experienced decorator. Inquire inside.*

Well, there was always that if Phoebe ran short of funds. Not as a decorator; that would be a fifties comedy routine in the making. Her mother was the one who excelled at baking and decorating. She'd even had an after-school job here as a cake decorator.

Phoebe pulled the door open and stepped inside.

The sweet, yeasty aroma wafted across her nose and dispelled the black cloud over her head, replacing it with sweet memories.

Her mother and sisters and her standing before the counter, Inez standing behind, while they decided what they wanted. Jelly donut? Crumb cake? Maybe one of the cupcakes decorated like Oscar the Grouch. Or the little squares of iced cakes with the tiny purple violets in the center of each one that were said to have been her mother's creation.

Phoebe looked up from her reverie to see a woman standing on the other side of the counter; she was older, but Phoebe recognized her immediately.

"Mrs. Sabatini!"

"Good morning." Inez Sabatini leaned forward to peer at Phoebe through the top of her bifocals. "Phoebe? Phoebe Adams? Is that you?"

Phoebe grinned. "It is indeed."

"My goodness. How long has it been? How's your mother?"

"It's good to see you," Phoebe said. "It's been too long. And Mom is . . . fine."

"She come down with you?"

"Yes. She and I decided to visit Granna for the weekend, and Great-aunt Vera had the same idea."

"Everyone together again. How lovely. Are your sisters coming?"

"Not this trip. They're both busy with work and families."

"Well, that's too bad. But I'm sure you can Zoom with them and it will be almost like old times. What can I get for you?"

"I thought I'd pick up something for breakfast and maybe dessert for after dinner tonight. But I'm having trouble deciding. Do not let me order one of those cupcakes," Phoebe said, pointing to the rows of pastel rainbow-colored icings. "I'll have snarfed the whole thing down before I get out the door."

"I'm making more tomorrow; I'll save you one. Strawberry, right?"

"You didn't forget."

"I never forget the likes and dislikes of my special customers. Why don't I make you up a box of your family's breakfast favorites." She folded a white box with slow but efficient precision, frowning a little as she tucked in the flaps.

She filled it with pastries and tied it with red-and-white worsted string; it was the first time Phoebe noticed her slightly gnarled fingers. But if her movements were slower than they once had been, they still showed the loving care that was the Sabatinis' hallmark.

Inez slid the box across the glass counter, glanced over Phoebe's shoulder, and motioned someone in.

"It's Charley Wilkins. I just want to give him some rolls I made this morning."

The bakery door opened and a tall, slightly stooped man stepped inside, dragging an old army cap off his head to reveal ragged patches of white hair and a scarred scalp.

Phoebe smiled in greeting and stepped to the side.

"I just wanted to make sure you didn't forget this, Charley," Inez said, carrying a white bag around the counter to him. "You remember Phoebe? She's one of the Adams girls, visiting her grandma, Alice Sutton."

Charley nodded toward Phoebe, before giving Inez his full attention.

"Thank you, Inez." Charley took the bag, said, "Ladies," by way of goodbye and put the cap back on his head.

Inez and Phoebe both smiled and waved until he was out of sight.

Inez sighed. "I try to help out where I can."

"I remember him from when I was a kid, but he didn't have those scars. What happened?"

"The army. Got them over in Iraq. Came back a broken man. Poor soul hasn't really been the same since."

"Is he back living with his parents?"

"For a while, then this past fall they sold up lock, stock, and barrel, and moved to a retirement village in Florida." Inez crossed herself and looked to heaven. "Florida. They wanted to take Charley with them, but Charley refused to go. So they parceled him out the property on the Point and fixed up the fish camp for him to live in."

"You're kidding," Phoebe said. "He lives in the shack?"

"He does. Where else would he go? And he has every reason to stay."

"Girlfriend?" Phoebe guessed.

"Lord, no, he built himself a big garage where he turns old cars into houses for homeless veterans. Now there's a story somebody should write."

Chapter 7

Ty was pouring himself a cup of coffee when his father shuffled into the kitchen.

"Pick your feet up, Dad, you're going to trip over your uncut toenails and give yourself a shiner."

His sarcasm went right over his dad's head. It had been a year since his mother died. They were all heartbroken; her sons were coping, but his dad made no effort to rouse himself.

He was young, sixty-five. He should be out playing golf, or at least down at the diner complaining about the Red Sox. But he just sat, the television on but unwatched, the newspaper opened but unread, just sitting in his damned chair.

Lars managed to assume a normal walk for several steps until he passed Ty, then relapsed into an even more obvious shuffle.

Just to annoy his son, whom he never really understood, never worked up much interest about, and resented like hell that he was here for the next three months.

Ty had gotten the job by default. His brothers were far too busy and involved in business to cede their time, so they volunteered him for Dad Watch, but Ty was beginning to think it was a futile effort.

But since he wasn't scheduled for another project until September, Ty had been glad to do his part. God knew he hadn't kept in touch with his family as regularly as families should.

And with all the needed repairs on the house, he would keep his physical chops primed, something that you lost sitting behind a drafting table all day. And enough downtime to fine-tune his next project while his father napped in the afternoon.

"Nap," Ty mumbled, resigned. His father didn't need a nap. He needed interest in life.

"You say something?" Lars asked, taking the mug Ty had left on the counter and filling it halfway with coffee. "Damn noise last night kept me awake till all hours."

"All night until eleven o'clock. You should have gone over and joined them."

"Couple of old broads acting like fools."

Ty put his mug down. "Dad. Stop it. You sound like some Neanderthal on reality TV. Show some respect." He bit his tongue. Hard enough to make his eyes water. Started over again.

"I think maybe the Adamses are visiting. I saw one of the girls coming out of the house this morning. Why don't you go over there later? I'm sure they'd be glad to see you."

His father turned from the counter. "Going to read the paper."

"Well, at least sit down. I'll make you some breakfast."

"I'll get cereal later." Lars started to shuffle past him.

It was infuriating; it was like he was doing it on purpose, just to yank Ty's chain.

"I want to discuss something with you."

Lars slowed down, let his shoulders stoop just enough to let Ty know that he was too infirm to do any work.

Ty gritted his teeth. "I was looking over the roof this morning."

"There're some shingles in the shed."

"I'm thinking we should consider putting on a whole new roof."

"Shingles will do."

He shuffled out of the kitchen.

Ty banged his forehead on the oil-cloth tablecloth. He hated to see his dad this way. He'd always been smart, energetic. He worked hard and took care of his family. That had all changed a year ago.

Ty knew he wasn't the best choice for this project; he and his dad had always brought out the worst in each other. He knew his dad loved him, but he had more in common with his other two sons. And that was partially Ty's fault, too. The only time he readily agreed to accompany them on some outing was when they went to the Wilkinses' house where they worked on cars every Saturday.

Cars were the thing that bonded all the guys on the island, like a private club that everyone wanted to join. Except Ty. Ty wasn't interested in cars. He was interested in engines and moving parts. But only so far as they gave him ideas for his own interests.

It might be a little late, but now they had three months to get to know each other, and for Ty to reverse the ravages his mother's death had wrought. And he didn't have a clue as to where to start.

Ty fixed things; he fixed things for people who couldn't fix things for themselves. Usually it was mechanical things, but there was no reason he couldn't apply those methods to his dad. Somehow he would figure out how to push him back into the land of the living.

Cars into houses. Phoebe tried to imagine them as she waited for Inez to go to the back, where she had the "perfect dessert" for Phoebe to take home. It did sound interesting, but Charley didn't seem like someone who enjoyed talking about their work. And Phoebe had more important issues of her own. Like finding a job.

Inez came back carrying a cardboard plate holding a dozen little square cakes, each covered in the palest yellow icing with a delicate purple violet in the center of each.

"I can't believe you still make these," Phoebe exclaimed.

"Your mother will always be the undisputed queen, but we do our best. They sell out every time I make them, which"—Inez unconsciously rubbed her fingers—"isn't so often these days."

She put them in a box, tied it up, and handed both boxes to Phoebe.

"How much do I owe you?"

"Consider it your welcome-back present."

"No, I couldn't."

"I insist. Just tell your mother to drop by for a visit before she leaves, though I know you'll all be busy while you're here."

"I'm sure she'd love to see you," Phoebe said, not knowing if her mother would be willing to face anyone for a while.

She walked back thinking about her mother making intricate icing violets and Charley Wilkins turning scrapped cars into homes. An old veteran giving back to other veterans who didn't have the luxury of living in their own home. Ironic, really—his own family home sold to be reconstructed as a summer mansion, and Charley relegated to the fish shack. Now there was a story begging to be told.

Except that she had no place to publish a story like that . . .

She ruthlessly cut off the rise of excitement she always felt before beginning a new piece. First things first. Be a support to her mother and look for a job, then she would think about writing again.

The day promised to be sunny and warm, and Phoebe tried to remember where she had packed her swimsuit. Or if she even had a swimsuit.

The handyman was still up on the ladder at the Harkens' house. It didn't look like he'd done much work while she'd been gone. It didn't look like he'd even moved.

As she turned into her own drive, a silver Lexus pulled up in front of the Harken house. A woman, daily-spa skinny, wearing white capris, a silky off-the-shoulder shirt, with hair in a platinum French twist, got out, then reached back in for what looked like a casserole dish.

Phoebe reached her own door and went inside.

There was no one in the kitchen, but coffee had been made, so she deposited her boxes on the table and went in search of the others. She found them huddled together at the parlor window, their noses pressed to the pane.

"What are you doing?" Phoebe asked.

Her mother squeaked; Alice turned briefly to frown at her and shush her with a finger to her lips; and Vera motioned her over with a rapid flap of her hand.

Phoebe obeyed.

"A husband hunter," Vera explained.

Phoebe raised an eyebrow at her great-aunt.

"Don't blame me. That's what your grandmother calls them."

Alice frowned at both of them and added another "Shhh" for good measure.

Phoebe squeezed in to peer out the window.

The woman was climbing the Harkens' steps in clunky cork wedges and holding the casserole dish in both hands like one of the kings with his frankincense.

Mere feet away, the handyman had sprung into action, rappelling down the ladder like a seasoned athlete.

"What's *he* doing?"

"Heading her off at the pass," Vera said gleefully. "We saw three yesterday. None of them got past Sir Speedy."

"Who is . . . ?"

"That's Tyler Harken," Alice said. "You remember him."

"That guy on the ladder is Ty? I didn't recognize him. I thought he was the handyman."

"I'm sure he is," Vera piped up as they watched Ty take the casserole from the woman so she could ring the doorbell. "And cute, too. Tall, dark, and handsome."

"What's he doing back here?" Phoebe asked, interrupting Vera's enthusiasm.

"Keeping his father safe from the husband hunters," Vera volunteered. "Oops, too late."

The door opened and Lars Harken stepped out, hair standing on end and looking like he hadn't changed clothes in a week. The woman beamed at him. He scowled and said something that even mimed through the window couldn't be construed as friendly.

He stepped back inside and slammed the door. The woman clomped back to her car. And Tyler was left alone on the porch, holding the casserole.

"That wasn't very nice of Lars," Ruth said as they all moved from the window.

"He hasn't been very nice since Delores died," Alice said. "He's let himself fall apart. That's why Tyler is here. Looking after him."

"Ty? He seems like an odd choice," Phoebe said in surprise. "He was always such an airhead."

"Just marched to a different drummer," Alice said.

More like wandered off to a meandering flute, thought Phoebe. "Well, I brought breakfast *and* dessert from the bakery. Mrs. Sabatini says hi, Mom. And said she'd love to see you before we go."

Ruth flinched. "If we have time."

It was exactly what Phoebe knew she would say. Ruth wouldn't want to see her old friend when her life was in upheaval.

"Well, she really would. It looks like she has arthritis—"

"In her hands," Alice commented, shaking her head.

"—and there were HELP WANTED signs in the window. She sent a box of lemon violet petit fours and didn't charge me for any of it."

"It seems like everyone is falling apart," Ruth said on a sniff. "Excuse me." She hurried away.

Vera and Alice turned to Phoebe.

"There are sticky buns and bear claws, too," Phoebe said, her attempt at rousing her mother obviously failing. "Ugh. I need more coffee."

Phoebe, Alice, and Vera were busy frying bacon and scrambling eggs when Ruth returned, pretending she was fine.

The other three pretended not to notice that her eyes were red-rimmed and swollen and not even semi-successfully camouflaged by concealer.

Ruth automatically began to set the table; Alice turned the egg spatula over to Phoebe and began making more coffee. It was a routine so ingrained over the years that it ran smoothly from one step to the other, even with the addition of Vera, who had slid seamlessly into the operation. Just like she did into their lives, before sliding out again.

Soon they were sitting around the old table, passing eggs and bacon and choosing delicacies from the two platters sitting side by side in the center.

It occurred to Phoebe that none of them looked their best. Though she wasn't sure how much was drama and how much was the number of margaritas they'd imbibed.

Across the table, Ruth passed the eggs to Vera and glanced at her watch. Phoebe glanced at the wall clock. Almost ten. Her father would be arriving at the condo about now. She took the eggs from Vera, suddenly feeling queasy. Her father was leaving her mother. Maybe he'd changed his mind. Maybe he was just having some midlife crisis and it would blow over.

Unlike her relationship with Gavin, which had blown up in her face and was truly finished.

Phoebe added a piece of bacon to her plate and pushed her eggs around while Vera exclaimed over the bear claws with what seemed to Phoebe's ears to be overly bright enthusiasm. They were good, but they were bear claws.

She took a deep breath, reached for a pastry, and saw her mother check her watch again.

Was Granna right? Would Ruth finally tell them the whole story after breakfast? Did Phoebe really want to hear it?

The clock struck ten. A little smile curved her mother's lips.

Ruth's cell phone pinged.

Ruth jumped as if she'd touched a live wire. She didn't pick up the phone, just reached over and swiped right. Read. Let out a breath. And closed the message.

It pinged again. She swiped right.

Any semblance of conversation ceased as they all zeroed in on Ruth's cell phone.

Seconds ticked by, then a minute. Phoebe reached for her sweet roll.

The phone pinged.

She put the roll down.

It had to be her father. What was he saying? Why wasn't Ruth answering him?

This time Ruth was slower to swipe. And after reading the text, she turned her phone off completely. "Is there more bacon?"

Phoebe pushed the plate of bacon across the table to her. Her mother didn't look at her, merely chose another piece and pushed the plate back.

They all ate in silence after that. Even Vera's unrelenting enthusiasm seemed to give up the ghost. Phoebe's nerves were strung so tightly she thought she might throw up, but she kept forking in food and sipping coffee and thought, *What a waste of wonderful pastries.*

After a few long minutes, when it was clear no one was still eating, Vera went for the coffeepot, filled all their cups, and returned to her seat.

Granna put her fork down. "Well?"

Ruth had known it would come to this. She'd never had any doubt that she would tell all before the day got much older. But she hated it. She hated everyone knowing her marriage had failed after almost three decades of what she thought had been happy. Happy enough, anyway.

She still couldn't really make herself believe that it was actually happening.

But it was definitely happening. Ron had texted her just like clockwork.

She wasn't surprised, considering what she had done. It had been so out of character that she was astounded her inner good person had allowed her to do it. "An expensive waste for spite," Ron would say if anyone else's wife had done it.

There had been a time when she would have nodded, then laughed at the wayward husband who deserved what he got.

Now Ron deserved it.

And he'd reacted just as she knew he would. In all caps. *WHAT THE HELL? The police are here.*

She'd quickly turned off the phone before he could have them call her and ask if it was okay to let him in.

Screw his golf game and screw him. She placed both palms resolutely on the table.

"Ron has left me. I assume for a *younger* woman." She could only hope that his new love could match his socks. Lord knew he couldn't. How many important meetings would he have attended in one brown and one black sock if it hadn't been for her.

"That was him. I changed the locks, and he couldn't get in. When he tried the window, the alarm went off and the police came. He's a little miffed. He'll probably call here next. Or Phoebe's phone. Just don't answer, sweetheart. There's no reason he should badger you. He'll be wasting his and your time. I won't be talking to him." *Ever again*, if she had her way.

Who decided to leave their wife after thirty-eight years of marriage and announce it in the same way he would have announced a Rotary Club luncheon? What kind of man would humiliate and hurt the person who had loved him, taken care of him, supported him all those years, slowly letting him take over her life as insidiously as an unseen malaise.

"You changed the locks?" Phoebe asked.

"Well, there *has* been a rash of burglaries lately," Ruth explained. And he hadn't told her *not* to change the locks on him.

Just that he was coming at ten, and he thought it would be better if she wasn't there, since he didn't want a fight.

Ron had always been good at giving instructions, without actually giving them.

When he asked, "Shall we take the children for ice cream at seven?" he really meant, *Have everyone ready and in the car at seven*. When he asked, "What do you say we have steak tonight?" she got out the steak to defrost.

It hadn't always been that way, but over the years it just became easier to acquiesce over the things that didn't really matter. Seven or seven fifteen? Steak or pork chops? She had to cook it anyway. It didn't really matter to her.

Later, the non-demands had gotten larger, and more demanding. And even then they didn't seem to matter that much to her.

But suddenly now it mattered. She'd created a monster in her husband. And she was petrified that she'd created one in herself, too.

"Earth to Ruth," Vera said, breaking into her thoughts. "We're sitting on pins and needles here and you're drifting out in la-la land."

Ruth looked up to see Vera, Alice, and Phoebe sitting up in their chairs as attentive as any group of schoolchildren waiting for library story hour. She'd liked being a librarian. But not as much as she loved the bakery.

"Dear, would you like to elaborate?" Alice asked.

Her mother's voice was calm and unruffled as always. There

was something comforting in her constant evenness, but there was something terrifying as well, never knowing if you would get swallowed down the infinite well of her compassion.

"I—" What had she been saying? Ruth took a breath, pushed her plate away, slid her coffee mug closer so she could hold it in both hands.

"Ron left me."

"We got that part," Vera said.

"Phoebe, I'm so sorry." Her youngest daughter, the only one who hadn't moved miles away, shouldn't have to listen to the implosion of a marriage. Especially not on top of her own broken engagement. Ruth should be putting her energy into helping Phoebe see her way clear, instead of nursing her own broken heart.

That was the most humiliating thing of all. Her heart had broken, not over Ron's announcement the week before, but little by little over the years, and especially after the move to the condo, the sheer complacency of it all. His latest announcement had just scattered the final brittle pieces.

"Why don't you tell us what happened," Alice coaxed.

"Mother, I really think . . ." She glanced at Phoebe. Ruth was a firm believer in not letting your children be held captive to the foibles and shortcomings of their parents. And they should never hear the things Ruth was thinking right now. She would have to watch her tongue.

Alice smiled benignly and waited for her to continue.

So she did. Told them everything, from the night he'd announced his intentions until she and Phoebe arrived at the house the night before.

"I didn't see it coming. Though he must have been planning it for a while. He just marched in and told me he was leaving. He dumped me in that condo like it was some kind of storage unit for worn-out wives and walked out. I'm sorry, Phoebe, but it's true."

Phoebe shook her head, a slight movement that Ruth recognized as discomfort.

Her mother didn't show the least surprise. Of course, Alice Sutton never did. Phoebe already knew a lot of it, just not the details, but even Vera didn't register shock. Just picked at the edge of a sticky bun that had been left on the serving platter.

"That's why we came this weekend. I of course wanted to see you, Mother, but . . ."

Alice waved it away. "I understand completely."

"Then when Phoebe called . . ."

Vera licked her fingers. "One rat bastard at a time, please."

"Ron is not a rat bastard. He's not a rat bastard, Phoebe."

Phoebe didn't say anything.

"What if *he* locks *you* out?" Vera continued. "He'll probably change the locks again."

"Let him. I've had a week to move everything I care about into a storage unit that he knows nothing about."

"That's our girl."

"And I've always had my own bank account. Father insisted."

Vera nodded. "But can he declare desertion if you leave the condo?"

"Let him try. I'm visiting my mother for the weekend. As for the condo, I never wanted to move there. He can sell it for all I care. Or he can buy me out and live there with whomever, if they allow teenagers in an over-fifty-five community."

Phoebe looked stricken and Ruth could have bitten her tongue.

"You shouldn't be listening to this, Phoebe."

"Yes, she should," Vera said. "From what you told us, she just got out in the nick of time."

"Vera!" Ruth admonished.

"You should never let a man rule your—" Vera broke off abruptly, coughed, patted her chest. "Crumbs," she managed.

"Has he served the papers, dear?" Alice asked. The question, as indelicate as it was, came as a welcome respite.

Ruth shook her head. She was feeling like she'd jumped out of a plane without a parachute, but Alice's pragmatic question made her think she might land on her feet, bruised maybe, but still whole. Ruth wished she could have inherited just a bit of her mother's whatever it was.

"Maybe you should serve them first."

"Actually, I had my lawyer—well, a friend, who is a lawyer— draw up papers. I haven't had him file them yet. I just felt like I should wait. That somehow it was all my fault."

This roused a reaction from all three.

Ruth held up both hands. "I know. I know. I'm not a victim. I've had a good life. It's just . . . well, I'd forgotten how much he complained. And how he always made it my fault. Not overtly, but . . . I don't know. It was a habit we slid into over the years—

that I let us slide into. It was easier just to ignore him. I think I wasn't all that surprised when he made his big announcement."

The house phone rang from its place on the kitchen wall. Vera jumped up.

"Vera, no. Don't answer. It's probably him."

"Well, we can't let him call all day. It will drive us crazy. I'll be nice.

"Hello, Sutton residence. Sorry? No, I'm sorry, this is Mrs. Higginbottom." Vera paused to wink at the others. "Yes. We've rented the house for the summer . . . No, she didn't say where she was going . . . No, no, nor when she plans to return. We have a lease agreement through August. I do have an email. And the number of the local handyman." Her shoulders twitched as if stifling a shiver of excitement. "No, no, of course, I'd be glad to. Goodbye now." Vera hung up. "That should give us some peace."

"But what if there's an emergency?" Ruth demanded.

"He can text."

Phoebe's phone rang.

Vera snatched it out of reach. "Now how shall we spend the day?" She looked around the table.

Alice pushed to her feet and began clearing the table.

"I'll help with the dishes," Ruth said. "And then I think I'll take a nap."

"And I have phone calls to make," Phoebe said. "And I have to see about getting the wedding deposits back."

"No you don't," Vera said. "I'm guessing your father paid for them. Let him try to get his own deposits back." She winked at Ruth.

Ruth was so taken aback that it took a second before she thought, *Yes, let him deal with things for a change.*

"Besides, we can't have the two of you moping over your single-source coffee." For a second, Vera seemed to forget what she was saying, then continued with a flourish of her fingers. "Things to do, places to go, family to enjoy. How about the wharf, the grocery? Definitely the liquor store. And then we'll hit the fish market. Have a barbeque. I know . . . we can invite grouch and son from next door and make a party."

Ruth shook her head. Her aunt was always exhausting and Ruth was already exhausted to begin with.

"I think I'll stay here," Ruth said. "I've been so busy the last week, I need a day to relax."

"Nope, we're not leaving you here to mope and worry about Ron or to get cold feet about standing your ground for once."

"For once?" Ruth said.

Vera glanced at Alice. "You know what I mean. You're always so accommodating. At least when I've been around."

"Which you hardly ever are," Alice reminded her.

"I've been seeing the world. I highly recommend it . . . especially to certain people who never go anywhere." She punctuated that with a pointed look at her sister.

Alice rolled her eyes. Something that she never did—except when Vera was around, Ruth realized. "Well, that's fine for some people, but if Ruth needs a day off, then she should take it."

"She doesn't. She'll sit here and work herself into a mope, then a guilt and—"

"I'm right here," Ruth said. "I'm fine. I'll come with you."

"Good."

"If that's what's best for you," Alice added, casting another disapproving look at Vera.

Ruth rolled *her* eyes. "I'll just change into something more presentable."

"And, Phoebe . . ." Vera began.

"I'll be right back," Phoebe said, and fled before they could turn their attention toward her.

Chapter 8

*P*hoebe came downstairs fifteen minutes later to find the other three already outside and standing by the cars. Alice, dressed in crisp summer slacks and a flowered knit shell, and Vera, in a wide sun hat and Bermuda hiking shorts, were arguing over which car to take and which one of them was going to drive. Ruth stood by, looking determinedly enthusiastic about the upcoming activities.

Phoebe sympathized. She really wanted a few hours of quiet time to touch base with her friends and former coworkers and decide what to do with her life, but like her mom, she was determined not to be a drag on the others.

"Why don't I drive?" Phoebe said.

Vera and Alice turned from each other to frown at Phoebe.

"Oh, you don't have to do that," Alice said. "You're a guest. I don't mind driving and I know my way around the island."

"So do we all," Vera pointed out. "Great idea." She shooed Alice toward Phoebe's car. "Come on, then. The day is passing."

Phoebe took Ruth's arm. "Are you up for this?"

"Of course. I'm fine. Really."

"You sit in front," Vera told Alice.

"No, I'll sit in back," Alice said. "You're the one with the day planned out. You can navigate."

"I want to talk to Ruth."

"Don't you dare put your nose into the middle of—"

Phoebe unlocked the doors and practically pushed Ruth into the front seat. The other two could bicker to their heart's content in the back.

"Oh, look, there's Tyler coming out of the house," Alice announced. "Phoebe, why don't you run over and invite him and Lars for dinner tonight?"

"Sure." Phoebe strode over to the porch where Ty was retrieving a rusted bicycle.

"Hi," she said.

"Hi."

"I was appointed to invite you and your dad over for dinner tonight. My great-aunt Vera is here and she wants to have a barbeque."

"Uh," Ty said, and looked back at the closed door.

This was Tyler Harken? The "uh" sounded like the younger Ty. But the rest of him had definitely changed.

"Tell him none of us are looking for a husband!" Vera yelled from where she was still standing by the car door.

Phoebe felt her face heat up. "They saw the woman with the casserole this morning."

"It's getting pretty ridiculous," he said. "We'd . . . I'd love to come. He's, uh, resting right now. So . . ."

"Five o'clock for cocktails," Vera called.

"Just say yes," Phoebe said. "You can always cancel later. No pressure."

He laughed, a quiet expulsion of air that hinted at resignation. "Thanks. In that case, we'd love to come. If I can get him out of the house."

"Great. See you later." Phoebe hurried away before Vera volunteered any more comments.

When she got back to the car, the others were already seated. Her mother was wearing designer sunglasses and faced stoically ahead. Behind her, Vera and Alice were arguing over a pair of sunglasses Vera was trying to foist on Alice.

"Sun is very bad for eyes—especially old eyes."

"Stop calling me old—you're only three years behind me," Alice complained.

Vera held up three fingers and made a show of counting on them. "You're only seventy-five? Maybe it's not too late for you to learn to surf. Hawaii is great this time of the year."

"Oh, give me those." Alice snatched the sunglasses and shoved them over her ears. They were cat-shaped with rhinestones.

Vera smiled victoriously and donned her own pair, big black circles that covered a good portion of her face.

Phoebe looked over her shoulder. "Where to first?"

"Kedding's," Vera ordered. "Full steam ahead."

Phoebe slid on her own sunglasses and backed the car out onto Seaside Lane. When they reached town, she turned toward the old wharf where they'd spent many summer days stuffing themselves on pretzels, ice cream, and fried clams and watching the boats come in. But as Phoebe drove she wasn't thinking about the wharf or any history except her own. She'd been startled to see Ty Harken up close. He wasn't at all like she remembered him. Granted, she had never paid all that much attention.

She'd been so busy trying to keep up with the others and get Scottie, who was closest to her age, to play with her that Ty had become sort of a blur, even as a kid.

Middle-kid syndrome, her mom had explained. Though Daphne was the middle girl and she'd always gotten plenty of attention. Ty was always sort of the odd man out. Tall, skinny, gawky, he was dark haired, unlike his brothers' light brown. They used to tease him about being adopted; he never cried or whined, but one day he went inside and made Mrs. Harken show everyone his birth certificate. He was a Harken, but it didn't stop the teasing.

Sometimes he would join them in a game of Frisbee or volleyball, but even when he deigned to play with them, it always seemed like part of him was somewhere else. Before long he would wander off, sometimes not showing up for hours, and then would reappear dragging all manner of junk by a piece of nylon mooring rope that he always seemed to have hanging out of his shorts pocket.

He'd definitely been weird. Though watching him on the ladder, Phoebe could tell he'd grown out of his gawkiness and into his height. He was muscular without being bulky and could hold his own in a not-too-shabby contest. But he still had a slightly distracted air. Like part of him was somewhere else. He hadn't grown out of that.

And why was a man his age living with his father?

"Why is Ty back home?" she asked over her shoulder.

"Taking care of Lars," Alice said. "So sad. I've never seen a man fall apart like that. It was tragic, Delores's illness. But it's been a year and life goes on. I'm not sure it was the best thing to have Ty taking care of things. Lars doesn't even appreciate it. If you ask me, Lars should be doing for himself. It isn't healthy to just give up like that."

Beside her, Vera snorted. Phoebe didn't know if it was for Lars Harken or for Granna. Henry Sutton had been dead for almost ten years. He'd died without warning in his sleep. Granna had grieved but she hadn't given up. She took over the reins of her family and carried on. It's what the Keyes-Sutton, and now Adams, women did.

Phoebe wondered which was worse, the surprise or the knowing and waiting for the inevitable.

She shivered in the car's air-conditioning. "Is Mr. Harken sick?"

"Sick at heart, though he did have an episode a few months back. It wasn't a heart attack, but it scared his sons into trying to get him to move into assisted living."

"Lars Harken?" said Ruth incredulously. "He can't be more than sixty-five; he was always so vigorous. And fit."

"He's getting plenty of exercise running from the husband hunters, that's for sure," Vera said.

"How long is Ty staying?" Phoebe asked.

"The whole summer supposedly," Alice said. "I think he got voted onto the island since he was between jobs."

"Excellent," said Vera. "See, Phoebe, things are already looking up."

Phoebe coughed out a response somewhere between heartbreak and anger. She couldn't believe that Vera would even suggest that she just forget that her life was in shambles and start up with the first available man. And one who was apparently unemployed to boot. "Thanks, but I'll pass."

"Why? He's charming."

"Between jobs? Sounds ominous . . . If I was interested, which I'm not."

"Can Ty cook?" Ruth asked.

"I think he might be a little young for you," Vera quipped.

"Vera! I merely wondered if they were eating properly. Lars was always like a bull in the kitchen. He could barely manage the grill. Ron had to—" She stopped. "But times change, I guess."

"True," Alice said.

"Irrevocably," echoed Vera, in a voice that made Phoebe glance in the rearview mirror to see what her expression was. All she saw was those big round sunglasses looking straight ahead.

A few minutes later, they reached the wharf and Phoebe slowed down to look for a place to park.

Kedding's had once moored numerous fishing vessels and the occasional sailboat. Over the years the marina had ceased to operate, but Kedding's had flourished by transforming itself from bait-and-tackle shops and a few fish vendors to beach stores, souvenir shops, and ice cream stands. It grew rapidly as the number of summer visitors increased. The shops and vendors poured out onto the street.

Restaurants had cropped up on the side streets, along with several real estate offices and high-end clothing boutiques. Then someone had the idea of adding a carousel.

Now only one landing area for a few small crafts and a bronze tourism plaque gave a nod to the wharf's history.

Today, on a sunny summer weekend at the shore, it was packed. Vera and Alice were craning their necks looking for parking places.

"How about there?" Alice pointed ahead.

"Fire hydrant," Vera said. "What about that?"

"Too small," Phoebe said.

"We should have brought the Jeep. It can fit in anywhere. Even Manhattan."

"Except our teeth would be rattled by the time we got here," Alice retorted.

Phoebe pulled into a parking lot and stopped. "You guys get out here while I look for a place."

They all piled out. They were still bickering when Phoebe met them on the sidewalk a few minutes later.

A cell phone rang. They all turned to look at Ruth, who shook her head.

Vera fished hers out of her oversized bag. Checked caller ID. "I have to take this. You go ahead; I'll catch up in a minute." She didn't wait for answer but turned and hurried away in the opposite direction.

Phoebe, Ruth, and Alice wandered through several boutiques, exclaiming and admiring but not buying anything. Every time a shop door opened and a new customer entered, Alice would turn around, purse her lips, then frown when it wasn't Vera.

Then Ruth would frown at her mother, and Phoebe would frown at both of them. Was something going on that she wasn't privy to? There was definitely an undercurrent of something that she sensed but didn't understand.

So she asked, "Are you worried about Great-aunt Vera? Shall I go look for her?"

"Heavens, no," Alice said. "She's probably discovered something interesting. Once during the International Festival, she disappeared for two hours and came back with three sombreros. Said she won them in a poker game. They may still be in the attic."

Alice picked up a pastel floral scarf from a display table just as Vera swept into the boutique.

"Did I miss anything? What? I don't see any shopping bags. You really haven't bought anything?"

She saw the scarf Alice was still holding. "That's pretty, Alice, you should buy it."

"I don't need it."

"That's beside the point. Phoebe?"

Phoebe slid her sunglasses up and took a quick look. "Nice, but not my style." She pushed the sunglasses back down over her eyes.

"Oh, well. But look at that. Now I could go for that."

They all turned to look at the multicolored caftan displayed on the wall.

Vera lifted it off the hook. "This would look great on you, Ruth. Want to try it on?"

"It's lovely," Ruth agreed. "But I don't have any place to wear it."

"No? Then I think I'll try it. Back in a sec." She headed toward the back and the dressing rooms.

Alice leaned close to Phoebe. "You know you don't really need those sunglasses indoors."

"I might," Phoebe said, feeling her voice wobble.

"Oh, dear. Ruth, will you help Vera with that muumuu thing she's gone to try on? I'm going to sit on one of those nice benches outside to wait. Phoebe is going to accompany me."

"Oh," Ruth said. "Shall I come, too?"

"No, no, I'll depend on you to talk Vera out of buying that thing if it looks too awful. We'll be fine. Take your time."

"If you're sure you'll be all right."

"As rain. Phoebe and I haven't had a chance for a nice visit." Alice took Phoebe's elbow and maneuvered her out of the shop.

Of course, they had just talked last night and Phoebe wasn't certain whether Granna really needed to rest or if she thought Phoebe was about to lose it. Which she was.

As soon as they were outside, Phoebe said, "Sorry. I don't know what has come over me."

"Probably that your whole life has blown up in your face." Alice guided her down the brick sidewalk away from the wharf. "I wondered how long it would take for it to really hit you."

"Sorry." Phoebe dashed away tears that slid out below her glasses.

"Don't be. Everybody is trying so hard to hold in whatever they're feeling around here. It's just exhausting. Do you know that there are cultures in the world where mourning is a group activity? The women get together and cry and wail with the mourner and for themselves, too, I imagine. Vera told me about them. Being a world traveler like she is. Too bad she didn't take a lesson from them."

"What do you mean?"

"I have no idea. I assume she'll tell us before too long."

"Great-aunt Vera, too?" said Phoebe with a sense of impending doom. "But you're okay . . ."

"As fit as a fiddle."

They'd come to the end of the street, where a wrought-iron fence was covered with climbing hydrangeas.

"I think this bench has our name on it," Alice said.

"It has *someone's* name on it. THE ANTWERPS IN MEMORY OF CLAUDIA."

"A nice tradition," said Alice as she sat down.

Phoebe sat beside her.

Alice handed her a tissue.

Phoebe blew her nose and repositioned her sunglasses. "I shouldn't have come out shopping. I have so much to do."

"Like what?"

"I should check on my colleagues, see how they're doing. Some of them had been at the paper a really long time; they'll need jobs, they're all my friends. And I meant to call the caterer, the bridal shop, the venue, to cancel and try to get some of the deposits back. But when I called Mom to tell her— How could he do such a thing?"

"Gavin? You didn't ask him?"

"I meant Dad. Everything is so messed up."

"Oh, my dear, men do stupid stuff. It seems to be part of their makeup. But your parents have rubbed along for a long time, they'll figure it out. Or they'll go their separate ways. It's their choice."

"Mom didn't want to come; she was afraid you would be disappointed in her."

Alice shook her head. "I think they call that transference. She's disappointed in herself, though I don't know why. She'll see her way through. You're the one I'm concerned about."

"I'll be okay. I guess . . . I mean, I don't really have a choice."

"You have lots of choices. And there's no rush. You can stay here for as long as you need to."

"I can't believe he did that."

"Well, maybe he just wasn't the man for you."

Phoebe blinked. "Oh, he wasn't. I think I knew that all along, but it just seemed like . . . I imagined us carrying on the tradition of local news. Stupid, I know. I just— He just—" She gulped back a sob.

"Now, now." Alice patted her shoulder. "We can set up one of the spare bedrooms as an office for you to work in."

"I don't have any work." Now Phoebe broke down. Not over her ended engagement, not over her mother's impending divorce, but over the career, the dream, that had been snatched from her, torn to pieces, and thrown in the garbage.

"You will. I've never known you without a story to tell."

"But nowhere to tell them. Not even for my latest article, an important one. Yesterday was the last edition of the *Sentinel*. I didn't even get a chance to see it in print. There won't be any more. Not one. Gavin let us all down. And betrayed his family's legacy. I'll never forgive him for that." Phoebe blew her nose again. Wiped her eyes. Took a deep breath. "There. I'm fine now."

"Good, because here comes your mother and Vera. Looks like Vera is wearing her new dress."

"Wow," Phoebe said, as Vera stopped in front of them and made a graceful twirl.

"It's gorgeous," Ruth said brightly. "I would have never even thought to try it on."

"And we're going to work on that," Vera said.

"But Vera is dazzling in it," Ruth said, ignoring her. She was being so determinedly chipper that it gave Phoebe the willpower to finally pull herself together.

"Well, in that case," Alice said, easing herself off the bench. "Let's get to the fish market before all the good pieces are picked over. There's a farm stand on our way home. But tomorrow we'll have to brave the supermarket."

They struck off down the street discussing menus and grocery lists and whether they were stocked with enough wine and tequila and piña colada mix for dinner, like none of them had a care in the world.

They ate clam rolls and drank lemonade on the picnic tables outside the fish market. Then bought fresh flounder, clams, and soft-shelled crabs for dinner. A quick stop at the roadside farm stand where they enthusiastically purchased more than they could possibly eat and they were on their way home.

And somehow the day had turned from a mission to keep their minds off their troubles to a day of closeness and fun.

This is what family is for, Phoebe thought as she drove toward home. The final bastion when you need it the most.

Chapter 9

*I*t was after four when Tyler wheeled his bike around the back of the house and into the shed.

He hadn't gotten much of his own work done because he'd helped Charley Wilkins unload some parts and they'd started talking. He'd gotten to know Charley as a kid. Charley was a good ten years older, but he knew his way around an engine and didn't mind explaining things when Ty had asked. He'd joined the army when Ty was just starting high school. And had come back a few years later injured in body and spirit. But he was a good guy, did good things. Ty liked him.

Every afternoon while his father took his habitual two-hour nap, Ty pedaled down to the Point to help out Charley and work on his own project.

He stored his bike in the shed and stopped at the outside spigot to scrub the dirt and oil off his hands, then went inside to see if his dad was awake and getting ready to go to Alice Sutton's house for dinner.

Knowing there would be an argument, Ty had just informed him that they were invited to dinner at five o'clock. His dad didn't say anything, so Ty finished with "Maybe a shower would be in order," and left.

He heard the television before he even got through the kitchen. And found Lars sitting in his chair dressed in the same clothes he'd had on for the last two days.

"Dad," Ty said. "I thought you were going to take a shower before I got back."

"Not going."

"It's a little late to cancel; they went to the fish market and everything."

"How do you know?"

"Because Phoebe said they were having fish. Phoebe Adams," Ty reminded him. "The youngest one. She and her mother are visiting." They had been through this earlier. His father wasn't senile, just being stubborn. Because he was grieving and wouldn't let go.

Still, it was hard to be patient all the time.

"You go on upstairs and take the first shower."

"You go without me."

"Dad, that's rude, and you always liked the Adamses."

Lars snatched up the TV remote and turned back to the news. "Fine. I'll call them and tell them we're not coming."

"You go ahead. I'll just make myself a sandwich."

Baloney and cheese. He had the deli deliver it whenever Ty refused to buy them.

"You loved fresh-cooked fish."

"Can't stand it. Not anymore."

Sometimes he broke Ty's heart; other times he just pissed him off. "Then I'm going. I'll have my cell. Call if you need anything."

"Fine."

Ty didn't try to argue. It would just escalate into increased stubbornness. Maybe he could find a local therapist who made house calls. He certainly wouldn't be able to convince his dad to go to an office.

He was the wrong man for this job, but he hadn't been able to convince his brothers of that. *They* had businesses to run. They had wives and children. He didn't.

They were right.

Out of pure selfishness, he'd agreed. He thought it might give him and his dad a chance to start over. But what he really hoped was that it would bring him closer to his mom. He'd been out of the country when she died. He'd tried to get home but didn't make it in time.

Not that it mattered to her. She'd been so pumped with morphine that she wouldn't have known him if he had made it back. But he knew his father resented him for not being there.

God, Ty missed her. Her death had left a big, empty space inside him. Another reason he'd agreed to Dad duty. She would have been heartbroken to see her husband succumb to his grief.

Ty and Lars had never agreed on much, but his father had once known how to have fun; he loved his family, even Ty, whom he never "got." A lot of people didn't "get" him. His mother did. And that was enough.

Sometimes in his darker moments, Ty wondered if he'd just imagined her belief in him. Her pride in his accomplishments. But then he would remember her face and the questions she'd ask, and the intelligence in her eyes, and the world would tilt right again.

And so he'd come.

There was nothing wrong with Lars, according to his doctor, except depression. And that was exacerbated by a bad diet, lack of exercise, bad lifestyle. Hell, just getting him to take a shower was an all-out fight.

Ty didn't feel like fighting tonight. And he didn't feel like cooking for himself. He would enjoy someone's else's company; his dad could eat his baloney with Ty's blessing.

He came downstairs a while later, clean and refreshed. He stopped by his father's chair. "Last chance. You don't want to slight Alice or Mrs. Adams. Friends are important."

"How would you know?" his father grumbled. "You don't stay in one place long enough to make any."

"I have friends." Ty pushed Lars's cell closer to his elbow. "Call if you need me."

"I'll be fine," Lars said, and increased the volume on the television.

"There's leftover spaghetti in the fridge. Microwave it on medium for a couple of minutes."

When he didn't get a response, he left. He'd made it to the kitchen door when he realized he should have thought to bring something. A bottle of wine. Some flowers. He had nothing. Oh, to hell with it. He'd send them a thank-you note in the morning.

Phoebe had just enough time to text Willa that she'd call her after dinner before Vera called her downstairs for an opinion.

She was pretty sure her mother hadn't called Daphne and

Celia with the news, but she was certain they already knew. She'd had four texts and several voicemails from her father during the day. No doubt he'd been texting them, too. He'd better not be trying to turn them against their mom.

Granna and Vera were standing at the sink discussing the best way to clean the clams, something they had been doing for decades, but still seemed to require much discussion. Her mother was sitting at the table picking through green beans and cutting off the tips.

"Mom, have you talked to Dad?"

Ruth shook her head without looking up.

"My phone is filling up with texts and voicemails from him. I can't keep ignoring them. Have you at least talked to Celia or Daphne?"

Ruth shook her head and kept snapping the beans. "I haven't exactly had time."

True. Vera seemed determined to keep them busy every minute. So they wouldn't have time to wallow in self-pity. Phoebe felt like she deserved a good wallow, but she'd just have to stand in line. Mothers first.

Phoebe's phone pinged again. She clenched her teeth and opened her messages. She held up her cell to show Ruth. It was from Celia. *Call me.*

"You should have told them," Phoebe blurted out, losing her patience. "You're their mother. They should know your side of the story. You know he's whining and bad-mouthing you while you're sitting here trying not to upset anyone. You know Celia and Daphne; they're going to be upset anyway. Especially if they're hearing his side of the story first." Phoebe clapped her hand to her mouth, but it was too late.

"Phoebe!"

"I'm sorry. But it's true."

"Phoebe, hon, will you get the butter out of the fridge?" Alice asked, her voice calm and smooth as butter itself.

Phoebe practically fled to the fridge, yanked it open, and let the cool air waft over her face. She'd never intended to say those things. She'd never even let herself think them about her dad. She retrieved the butter, handed it to her grandmother. Turned back to her mother. "Sorry, it's just I'm sure they're worried."

"You're right. God knows what he's said about me."

"All the more reason to call them. Do you want me to set up a Zoom call, all four of us?"

"No." Ruth shoved the colander of beans away. "I'll do it."

She grabbed her cell and trudged out of the room.

The other three let out their breath. The clams were set to rinse without further opinions. Phoebe cleaned the fresh greens and cucumbers, first of the season. They wouldn't buy a tomato for another month.

Phoebe wondered where she would be in another month.

She gathered plates and flatware and took them out to the screened porch, which was why she saw Ty come out of his house alone and walk toward their back door. He was wearing khakis and a short-sleeved button shirt. He had dressed for the occasion.

She finished setting the table and went out back to greet their guest.

"That old grump," Vera said, as Phoebe came back into the

kitchen with Ty. "Oh well, his loss. We'll send him a plate, and if the clams are rubbery it won't be our fault."

"I'm really sorry," Ty said, sounding like it wasn't his first time saying it.

"No matter," Alice said. "He'll come around when he's ready. Can I get you something to drink? There's beer and white wine in the fridge and red over on the counter."

"I was going to make piña coladas," Vera volunteered, "but it was getting late. I could whip up a batch now."

"Not for me," Ty said, sounding a little panicky. "A beer would be fine."

Alice was handing Ty a bottle when Ruth burst into the kitchen. "He told them both I locked him out of the house, the— Oh, Tyler, so nice to see you. Where is Lars?"

"He couldn't make it. He, uh, meant to, but he was just not up to it. I would have called, but I was hoping . . . I'm sorry."

"Well, don't be, that means more food for us," said Vera with a forced smile. Phoebe could tell it wasn't genuine because Vera always showed a straight line of teeth when she was faking it, as if both ends of her mouth were resisting the lie.

No more was said about Lars's absence or what Phoebe's father had told her other two siblings. Phoebe really wanted to know, but she really didn't want to hear it in front of the others.

Ruth picked up a serving bowl and carried it out to the porch, pausing long enough as she passed Phoebe to say, "They want to do a Zoom call after dinner. I told them I would as long as their father wasn't invited."

Phoebe just nodded.

Dinner went off pleasantly. Ty was a decent conversationalist, a talent he must have honed after leaving home, because Phoebe couldn't remember him finishing a sentence without wandering off somewhere to do something else.

He didn't give out much information about himself. Just that he was between jobs and luckily had the time to spend with his father and make some much-needed repairs on the house. "With my mother's illness and then the funeral, my father didn't have time or energy to deal with the maintenance."

But he was vague when it came to what his jobs were, and why he was between them, and Phoebe, probably her journalist's curiosity, suddenly wanted to know. Was it because they were temporary, or because he lost interest and just wandered away from them like he did when they were all kids? Was he incapable of holding a steady job?

They talked about the weather, and the new businesses in town. Vera regaled them with anecdotes about her latest trip with someone named Jon. Alice mentioned the McMurphys' house being torn down, which led to the pros and cons of gentrification.

During a temporary lull in the conversation, Vera said, "What is it that you do as your vocation, Ty? If you don't mind me asking."

She didn't care whether he minded or not. And for once Phoebe was glad of Vera's direct approach; she was curious, too.

"Well, I have a degree in mechanical engineering."

"Oh?" Vera said, encouraging him to continue.

"I sort of work in water reclamation."

"You do?" Vera said.

"This is where your eyes start to glaze over," Ty said.

"My eyes were glazed over before you even got here. It's the white wine, does it every time. Besides, Phoebe wants to hear more. Did she tell you she's a journalist?"

"Uh, no. Print or televised?"

"Print." Phoebe really didn't want to wade into that one right now. "So what kind of water do you reclaim?"

"Non-potable."

"And you make it potable?"

"My team does . . . if we're lucky."

"Lucky?" Vera said. "I would think that science had more to do with it."

"Well, it does, normally. Well, always. It's just we don't always have access to computer systems or high-tech equipment. Or sometimes even electricity."

"You work in remote areas?" Alice asked.

"Some of the time, but you'd be amazed at how small the nexus of actual working science is. Step across the street and you can move from a modern functioning neighborhood to one where even the rainwater is toxic." He leaned forward on his elbows. "My team goes in and tries to figure out a way to make the water not so toxic, usually by removing large irritants so the water can be filtered and then purified for drinking. A lot of the communities we service have very little access to the standard equipment for removing large amounts of debris.

"So we basically make giant water 'strainers' from things that are readily accessible. Trash, for example." He stopped, blinked a couple of times. The enthusiasm vanished from his face to be replaced by embarrassment. "Sorry. I didn't mean to run on. People don't usually get past the water-reclamation part."

"I think it's fascinating," Vera said. "Don't you, Phoebe?"

"What? Actually, I do." She'd been thinking it sounded like the perfect job for the boy who wandered off and returned with . . . trash. "What kinds of trash?"

"Depends on the stage of the contamination and the availability. But it's hardly a dinner-table topic. What section of the paper do you work on?" he asked Phoebe.

She was so used to being the one asking the questions that it took a moment for her to answer. And how should she answer?

"Well, the truth of the matter is that before yesterday I was managing the paper while neglecting my real job of reporting. Usually I write local news, human interest, community issues."

"There's a dearth of local news these days," Ty said. "It seems the little that manages to make it on the air before the national news are the stories with the biggest, most blaring headlines."

"Which is why it's important to keep local papers alive," Phoebe said enthusiastically.

"Exactly—they're the conduit for news that people need to know. The best way for getting a community to—"

"I'll just go get the dessert," Vera said. "Alice?"

The two of them went into the house.

Ruth started gathering up the plates. Ty stood. "Let me help you."

"No, no, you and Phoebe just sit here. It won't take us but a minute."

Ruth speed-walked into the kitchen. "What are you two up to?"

Vera blinked in surprise. "Whipping cream for these strawberries. I sent Alice in search of the brandy. But since you're here . . . those two are getting along like a house on fire."

"Vera, do not push these unsuspecting children together."

"Hardly children."

"They are to me. So do not start playing games with them. Phoebe is in a very precarious state. I don't think she's fully realized all the implications of calling that wedding off."

Vera grimaced. "Please tell me you're not hoping she and her publisher boyfriend will get back together."

"No I don't. Not if he can't make her happy. But she doesn't need you playing matchmaker."

"I wouldn't dream of it. But Ty's a lovely man."

"It's too early."

"It's never too early and it would be a nice summer diversion for the both of them."

"We only came for the weekend."

"Okay, suit yourself. Oh, there you are, Alice."

Alice came back in the kitchen. "We seem to be out of brandy. I have apricot cordial."

Vera made a face. "Put it on the list for tomorrow." She grabbed a spoon and catapulted the pile of strawberries and angel food cake with spoonfuls of whipped cream. Then she picked up the platter. "Ruth, bring those bowls, will you? Wouldn't want to leave those two alone for long."

"Mother, don't let her interfere."

"I'm sure she won't do anything to embarrass Phoebe," Alice said. "But let's not leave her alone to test the theory." And she hurried after her sister.

Vera served big bowls of fresh strawberries and local cream and all intelligent conversation gave way to *ahh*s and *mmm*s. So they all jumped when a phone rang.

"Not mine," Ruth said. "I muted it."

"Me too," Phoebe said, wondering which one of her family members had decided to move on to Granna. Only Granna hadn't brought her phone to the table. Who could be calling now?

"Sorry," Ty said. "It's mine. I told Dad to call me if he needed me."

He pushed his chair back, looked at the screen. "My brother. I'll just be a minute." Instead of going back into the house, he stepped out into the night. Walked a ways from the porch for privacy.

"Shall we clear the table?" Phoebe said, aware that over the caesura of the waves she could still hear Ty's voice. "Make coffee?"

"Daniel, didn't he tell you that he was invited to come? He opted out at the last minute. Yes . . . yes . . . Dan, I'm ten feet away, for crying out loud. With the door open, he doesn't even have to speed-dial, he can just yell and I'd hear him. Plus I can see the damn television from where I'm standing."

All four women turned to see if indeed he could.

"Nothing is going to happen to him. Would you just listen?"

The four women put down their plates and platter and stopped all pretense of not listening.

Ty lowered his voice, but it sounded urgent and frustrated. "There is nothing wrong with him except bullheadedness. Yes, I talked to his doctors, all three of them. Yes . . . yes . . . I know you are. We all are. There's really no reason to . . . Fine . . . Fine . . . Anytime."

His end of the conversation ceased.

"Somebody say something," Phoebe hissed to the others as Ty pocketed his phone and headed back to the table.

"Oh. That was delicious, Vera," Alice said. "I'm glad you spotted those strawberries. Ty, dear. Sit down and have some more dessert."

"I . . ."

"Ty, would you care for coffee?" Ruth asked.

"Thank you, but I should be going. I'm really sorry. But . . ." He threw up his hands. A simple gesture that managed to convey frustration, acceptance, helplessness, and capitulation without being overly dramatic.

"My father."

"Don't think anything of it," Alice said. "I'll just get his plate from the oven. Ruth, put some of the strawberries in a bowl. I'm sure Lars will enjoy them. They're straight from the field."

Ty shook his head.

"If you don't want to wait," Vera continued, "I'll take them over myself."

That startled a laugh out of Ty. "That won't be necessary. But thank you."

He waited silently while food was packaged up to make the ten-foot walk to the house next door. He left with compliments and thanks, and the four of them watched him until he went inside and shut the door.

"Selfish man," Alice said.

"Ty?" Phoebe said.

"Lars. You heard Ty," Vera said. "There's nothing wrong with the man but wallowing in his grief."

Ruth wiped her eyes. "They're all grieving. Lars should be there for his sons. A father should do that. He should be their support in the good times and the bad. I'll go see him tomorrow. We were good friends once. Maybe I can help."

"Maybe," said Phoebe. "But first we're going to Zoom with Celia and Daphne. They're beside themselves."

"Tomorrow," Ruth said.

Phoebe held up her cell so Ruth could see the screen. They both had called during dinner. "If we don't call, they'll have the police out looking for you—and me."

"You two go ahead," Alice said. "Vera and I will do the dishes."

Ruth reluctantly got out of her chair. Phoebe took her arm and they trudged up the stairs like two prisoners headed for the gallows—or, Phoebe thought, the Joads on their way to California.

Well, that wasn't so bad," Phoebe said as she left Zoom and the screen returned from shocked, horrified, accusing siblings—the explanation, the disbelief, and the mutual tears—to a calm blue background with way too many works-in-progress documents dotting it like little sailboats.

Ruth stood and returned the boudoir chair she'd been sitting in to the corner. "The nerve of him to say I locked him out of his own house."

"You did," Phoebe pointed out. She stretched her back, wishing that she hadn't added to everyone's shock by the announcement that she was no longer engaged to Gavin.

"But that was a reaction to his action, not the other way around."

Phoebe merely nodded. Her father had told her sisters that he'd come home to find Ruth gone and all the locks changed, deflecting the fault from himself to his wife. He'd twisted the story to make it some aberrant behavior of Ruth's, rather than his own.

He'd obviously swayed Celia and Daphne to his side and Ruth had come so close to breaking down and returning home in defeat that Phoebe had had to step in and set the record straight. At least as straight as she saw it. After all, she only had one side of the story. She hadn't talked to her father yet, and at the moment she really didn't need any more excuses from men.

Celia pled with her mother to reconsider.

"You can make him change his mind," Daphne insisted. "You always could."

"No I couldn't, so I just stopped trying. He betrayed me."

This provoked loud denials from the other two.

"No? What do you call a husband who strolls into the kitchen one day, says he doesn't love you anymore and that he's found someone else? Someone who really understands him. He's not that hard to understand." Ruth's hand went automatically to her mouth, but too late to stop the words.

Silence.

The silence grew. Even Phoebe couldn't help with that. It was the first time she'd heard that whole version. Her father was having an affair.

Celia was the first to find her voice. "It's just a midlife crisis. It will blow over."

"Can't you forgive him?" Daphne asked. "Please."

"I could."

"That's great, Mom, call him right away."

"But I'm not going to."

"You're not being fair."

"You don't understand," Ruth said.

"Well, how can we?" Daphne asked. "Everything was fine and suddenly you're locking Dad out of the house."

"Everything wasn't fine. And that's not what happened."

"I know you could work it out if you'd just be reasonable."

"Daphne!" Phoebe and Celia yelled at once. "You're not helping."

"I'm sorry, Daphne, Celia, Phoebe. But I've caved my last for your father. No more. I won't do it anymore."

"Mom, you don't mean it," said Daphne. "You're just upset. And you're hurting Dad. Talk it over. Please. He just made a mistake."

"And I've been living one." Ruth burst into tears and left the room.

"Good move, Daph," Celia said.

Daphne turned her pleading on Phoebe. "She'll listen to you. Do something. Make her go back."

"It's not up to me. I think we should all stay out of it. We're adults and we can cope. It's on him."

"Well, you took Mom's side quick enough," said Daphne. "Did you talk her into it?"

"Daphne, stop being a brat," Phoebe said, beginning to lose her patience. "How could you even ask that?"

"I don't know. I'm just so upset. And you're there with her." A pause. "Where are you?"

"We're fine. You have my cell."

"You're at Granna's, aren't you?" Daphne demanded. "We're coming, too. Tomorrow. And talk some sense into her."

"Don't you dare. Celia's halfway across the country; school isn't out and she can't get off; and your office will fall apart without you."

"I don't care."

"Then come if you must, but she won't be here if you do."

"Why?"

"You have to ask?" Phoebe had suddenly had enough. "They're adults—let them figure it out."

"Daphne, Phoebe's right. These things take time."

"Oh, shut up, Celia. It's so awful."

"Oh my God," Celia exclaimed. "Phoebe, is Dad still going

to walk you down the aisle? Will they sit together? What if they make a scene? That would be terrible."

"Rest easy. Gavin sold the paper and I gave him his ring back."

Silence from Celia, but Daphne erupted into wails. "Everything's so awful."

"Look," Phoebe said. "Let's take a little time to let things work out. I'll keep you posted, but please don't keep calling and don't tell Dad."

Ruth slipped back into the room, but stood out of camera range.

"If only they'd talk things out," Daphne insisted.

Ruth shook her hands in a desperate pantomime.

"They will when she's ready. Look, we're all wrung out. I'll call you sometime tomorrow okay? But don't keep calling and texting."

"Okay."

"Promise?"

"We promise. We love you, Mom," Celia called. "And you, too, Phoebe."

"Love you, too," said Phoebe. "Sweet dreams." She left the conversation. Closed her laptop.

"I can't go back," Ruth said tentatively.

"Whatever you decide," Phoebe said, wishing Granna would come into the room. She always knew what to say. Phoebe didn't.

"I didn't want you girls to know. But they just kept at it. I shouldn't have blurted it out that way. But your father cheated on me, on us, on all the promises he made. He can move on, but he'll do it without me. But he's your father and you girls don't have to be caught in the middle."

"You absolutely should have. You can tell us anything you need to tell. We're not children."

"I know, sweetheart, but you've had your own disillusionment to deal with. I should be there for you. You shouldn't have to carry me. I think I'll go to bed," Ruth said.

Phoebe nodded, kissed her mother. "Good night."

She waited until the door closed, then opened her laptop again. She didn't know if she was wired or exhausted beyond words. Definitely too agitated to sleep. Too tired to start looking for a job—too bleary-eyed to peruse Zillow for an apartment.

But not too late to call Willa. She picked up her cell.

Chapter 10

Phoebe made sure her door was firmly shut, then carried her phone over to the bed, piled up the extra pillows against the headboard, and climbed onto the familiar seashell coverlet.

Willa answered on the second ring.

"It's not too late?" Phoebe asked.

"No, in fact I was about to call you."

"We had dinner with a neighbor and then we had to call my sisters."

"How did that go?"

"Dinner fine, the sisters not so much."

She gave Willa a streamlined version of the call. "Celia was perturbed that we hadn't called. Daphne took Dad's side as usual. They both wanted to come out to the island. I threatened that Mom and I would leave if they did."

"How *is* Ruth?"

"Hanging in . . . barely. I have no idea what to do. I'm hoping that my grandmother will. But what's happening at home? I feel like I'm on a different planet. Did you talk to Anita Peters at the food bank?"

"I did," Willa said. "She was shocked that the paper shut down. And concerned. I told her you would try to get the article on the community website."

"I'm planning to call the communications person on Monday and tell her I'm sending it. Did you discuss any openings for you?"

"I'm meeting with her on Monday but the pay sounds as bad as the *Sentinel*'s."

"Ugh." Phoebe readjusted the pillows. "I hate that this happened. I'm going to call all of the others as soon as I get a second to myself."

"I talked to Nancy; she's decided to finally retire."

"How did she sound?"

"Pretty depressed." Willa's sigh reverberated in Phoebe's ear. "Mitch hasn't returned my calls. Everybody's still pretty much in shock. What a shit way to fire life-long employees."

"Ditto to that," Phoebe said. "How could I not have noticed that things were going south?"

"I'm sure you've already asked yourself that a hundred times."

"At least."

"But there is one other thing that you need to know."

"Bad?"

Willa's silence gave her the clue.

"I wanted to drive out and tell you myself but I can't get away. The girls are starting town camp. I applied for unemployment, but I have to find a job pronto."

"It's okay. Hit me with it."

"Some of the guys from design were down at Smitty's bar last night."

"And?"

"And they heard that Gavin was moving out of his apartment and relocating to Boston."

"Boston?"

"Yep."

"Why?"

"Evidently he's going to be working at the *Globe*."

"The *Globe*," Phoebe repeated as the obvious sledgehammered into her.

"Evidently some higher-up had known Gavin's dad and grandfather. He must have used those connections as well as being publisher of the *Sentinel* to get an in."

"Doing what?" Phoebe demanded.

"They didn't know, only that it was something high up in the food chain. Something corporate maybe, but don't quote me."

"Corporate? He must have been working on the deal for months," Phoebe said. "And using the paper and me to do it."

"Not you, I'm sure he—"

"Don't," Phoebe said. "Don't start defending him now. He used us as a bargaining chip. He didn't care about the paper or journalism or— Just money and prestige. Ugh. I should have guessed."

"Well, you didn't. And once the shock wears off, you'll thank your lucky stars to be rid of him."

"Actually, I already am. I have been since Thursday in his office. He wasn't who I thought he was then. And he really isn't now. I wish he had just sold the paper when he inherited it and let the rest of us get on with our lives. The *Sentinel* might still be in business."

"What a jackass."

"I get why he never discussed things with me, but why let me go on heedlessly planning the wedding? Why did he ask me to marry him in the first place?"

"I'm sure he really—"

"Do not make excuses for him." Phoebe reached for a laugh. "You didn't let him off the hook when we still liked him."

"Well, I never really liked him all that much," Willa admitted.

"I know, and I should have paid more attention. I was just so—"

"So wedded to the paper that you couldn't see what was happening. And neither did anyone else. We just thought he was incompetent."

"Which he is."

"True," Willa agreed. "Which doesn't bode well for his success at the *Globe*."

"Which I couldn't care less about," said Phoebe.

"That's my girl."

"No wonder he'd been pushing me to sell more ads, make more money. A healthy paper made him look good, when he actually hadn't done one damn thing to save the *Sentinel*. And I played right into his hands. Ugh. That's just the icing on the cake—the cream cheese champagne icing on my red-velvet cake."

Willa snorted out a laugh. "Sorry. But we can get another cake."

"If we have to pay for this one, I'll invite everybody and have a party."

"I'm sorry to tell you this way, but I didn't want you to hear it through the grapevine. Now you can forget him and get on with your life."

"I intend to. You know, I could have gotten over a last-minute breakup. I would have been hurt, but I would have gotten over it. I won't get over this."

"Yeah you will."

"Over *him*, yeah. But my career. The *Globe* offered *me* a spot as a regional reporter when Simeon died. I turned them down. For the second time. Because Simeon asked me to help his son with the transition. But there was never going to be a transition. He never intended to make it work. I'll never forgive him for that. Never. What a snake."

And suddenly the last three years welled up inside her, a mushroom cloud of anger that exploded in her head and heart. She'd almost made the biggest mistake of her life.

Gavin was right about one thing. He was nothing like his father.

"What are you going to do?" Willa asked.

"Me? I don't know. I put my career on hold for the last three years. I hope it's not too late to get it back."

"You'll figure it out."

"Stay in touch, okay?"

"Of course I will. You already invited me and the girls out to the island. Speaking of which, I'd better go. The little princesses will be up at the crack of dawn."

"Give them noogies for me. And Willa, thanks for telling me."

"Ciao."

Phoebe ended the call and lay back against the pillows. Sat up. Dropped her feet over the side of the bed; crossed her arms and hugged herself; rocked a bit. Then caught sight of her engraved congratulations plaque where she'd placed it on her dresser. And she saw red.

She crossed the room, opened her door a crack to peek outside. The hallway was dark; no lights showed under the doors of the other bedrooms. She tiptoed across the landing and down the stairs.

As soon as she made it outside, she ran to the beach, holding in the yell of rage until she was standing ankle-deep in the surf.

"You coward!" she screamed. "Coward! Coward! Coward! You ruined everything!"

And she had helped him.

Sleep eluded Ty, as it often did when he was working out a problem. He had several at the moment; water filtration, he could fix with a few adjustments or updates. But he had no idea how to fix his dad. So tonight Ty had waited until his dad was asleep before climbing the stairs to the attic.

He liked it here in the attic, even though most of the time it was hot as hell. This had been "Ty's workroom" since he was twelve. In those days he came up here almost every night to work on ideas without disturbing anyone. His old drafting table was still set up in the corner, sharing the space with the usual attic castoffs.

In the mornings when he didn't show up for breakfast, his mother would climb two flights of stairs to find him slumped over a spread of unintelligible papers.

They weren't unintelligible to Ty.

She'd take him down to breakfast. Smooth things over if his brothers kidded him for being in the same clothes he'd worn the day before, and his dad pretended he didn't hear them.

But that was then . . .

Tonight he'd come as close to losing his temper like he hadn't lost it in a long time. He'd waited on his father, encouraged him, badgered, pleaded, done everything he could think of to reignite the spark of life his dad once had.

Nothing had worked. There would never be any kind of understanding between them. That much had been made pretty clear over the last couple of weeks. It was driven home in spades tonight.

Except for the two hours a day while his father napped, Ty never left except to run errands and grocery shop.

Tonight when he was actually having a nice time within sight of the house, his father had called Dan complaining about Ty's neglect.

There was no reason for him to be like this. No reason for taking his unhappiness out on Ty when he was only trying to help. And Ty didn't resent being here, like his dad had told everyone who would listen. He hadn't resented it until tonight.

But tonight he'd realized that he couldn't help his father. He would never be able to help him. Because his mother stood between them. In life she'd been a channel connecting them; now her memory had become an impenetrable barrier.

He'd come close tonight to telling Dan that he was leaving and to send the old man to whatever facility they chose. Maybe they were all just enabling him to continue to wallow in his unhappiness.

But the thought of his mother stopped him. It was as palpable as if she'd reached out and held his arm. And he knew he couldn't leave. Two months to go. If he didn't lose his mind or his cool before then.

He stretched, pushed his chair back, and went to stand at the window. The night had cooled off and there was a breeze coming off the ocean. He stared out at the dark swells, letting the pull of the tides calm him, thinking how amazing water was, and how its potential power could change people's lives.

Only a couple of months to go. Then he would have "real" employment that couldn't be delayed. If things hadn't improved by then, his brothers could decide what to do.

He had started to turn from the window when movement on the beach caught his eye. A shadow against the moon, sweeping across the sand like a bird racing to the waves. For a full ten seconds he stared, wondering if it would take off and fly out to sea.

Then it stopped at the surf and he saw that it was . . . Phoebe Adams.

What the hell?

He braced his hands on the sill and leaned out to get a better look. Was something wrong? He'd seen women run like that before, when a dam broke or when the rumor of a water truck on its way raced through a village and they were desperate to get in line before the water ran out.

What could Phoebe have to be desperate about?

He looked toward the Sutton house, dark now. Nothing seemed amiss. Still . . .

Instinct took over and Ty bounded down the stairs, not stopping until he was outside and standing in the shadows of the eaves of his house. Now she was pacing up and down in the surf, gesticulating wildly. Not desperate. Pissed off. She was having a royal meltdown.

He was kind of mesmerized by the gyrations she was going through. Like a wild dance, her arms and legs expressive, her body thin and supple and . . .

And she was turning back toward the house next door.

He automatically stepped farther into the shadows. Which was stupid because she would pass right by him on her way to the Suttons' side porch. But he couldn't get back inside his own house without going the same way. And they would be on a collision course.

Of course if he didn't move, she would discover him lurking there like some kind of pervert.

He stepped out to intercept her.

Phoebe jumped about a mile, made an "Eek" sound right out of a cartoon, and stumbled back.

Ty held up both hands. "Sorry, I didn't mean to scare you. I just saw you running . . . and I came down to see if everything was all right."

She seemed to have frozen in place.

"*Are* you all right?"

"Huh? Oh, yeah. I'm . . ." She whooshed out a breath. "I was just out for a . . . a . . . run."

"I do some of my best running at night," he said.

"You jog at night?"

"Not for fun."

She crooked her neck to peer at his face. Frowned. Frowned more than she already was. "Oh . . . I get it . . . I think. Well, thanks for caring . . ."

"Ouch." He wasn't always socially savvy—well, hardly ever— but he knew a brush-off when he heard it.

"Sorry. I didn't mean to— Well, if you must know, I was having a meltdown and I didn't want to wake anyone."

"You're polite even during meltdowns?"

"I don't normally have them."

"Are you better now?" What else could you say to a semi-stranger who was still definitely in the freak-out range?

"I will be."

"Good." He started to walk away, turned back. "Want to talk about it?"

"No," she said, sounding horrified.

He was horrified that he'd even asked. It must be the weeks with only his dad and Charley to talk to. Neither of them was much of a conversationalist. Actually, neither was he, except for tonight at dinner when he was yammering on about toxic water. What had possessed him?

"Well, good night, then."

"Good night," she said, but still stood there as if she didn't want to turn her back on him. He didn't blame her.

So he turned his back on her.

"I'm such an idiot."

Ty spun around to find her now standing in the porch doorway, and for a split second they just stared at each other.

"Can you provide some context?" Ty ventured.

She eased the door shut behind her and stepped back into the yard. "I wasted three years of my life trying to save a paper so Gavin and I could live happily ever after running the *Sentinel*. And the whole time he was working to sell it."

"And you didn't know?"

She shook her head. "How could I not know?"

"Caught up in your own world? Just a guess."

"Yeah, stupid."

"I don't think so," Ty said. "I spend a lot of time there myself."

"In my own world?"

"No, in mine."

She made a kind of snorting sound and for a panicked moment Ty was afraid she was going to cry.

Instead she laughed.

Feeling completely unsure of what reaction to have to that, he waited for her to stop.

But when she stopped, she started pacing in front of him.

"I see it now."

"Maybe we should move away from the house if you don't want everyone else to see it, too."

"You are so weird." But she moved away, closer to the sand.

He followed her.

She started to pace again, though at a slower pace, thanks to the sand. "I gave up the chance of writing for a big paper because I thought local news was important and because it was so important to Simeon Cross. He was my mentor, but he died and his son took over and stuff happened and we got engaged, but while I was trying to save the paper, he was trying to sell it. Sell it! I wasn't writing and bringing the news to people, I was abetting his plan and I didn't even realize it."

Ty opened his mouth while he tried to think of something to say. He didn't get the chance.

"I've wasted years for nothing."

He was on firmer ground here. "I wouldn't call it nothing."

She turned on him. "No? What would you call it? I'm out of a job, homeless, and my parents owe a fortune in nonrefundable wedding deposits . . ."

He laughed.

"You think it's funny?"

"I'm sorry, wrong response. I do that a lot. But you're not homeless, you'll get a job, and from everything you've said about the fiancé, good riddance."

"We'd already chosen the cake," she said between gritted teeth.

He tried not to laugh again. He really did. But it just burst out. He held up a hand. "Sorry, sorry."

She glared at him. Her mouth worked, then she started laughing, too. "It's not funny. I don't know why I'm laughing. Everything's so messed up."

"Sounds like it just got simpler to me."

"Really? *Really?* How do you figure that?"

"I dunno. You've got a clean slate. Seems like now you could do anything you want to do."

That stopped her.

Ty braced himself. "I know, none of my business. But think about it."

"I am. Give me a minute."

"Don't you know?"

"No. I mean, I did."

"That seems like a decent place to start."

"I want to write about people. People who make a difference, who deserve to be known, be respected. Not the famous ones, but ordinary people who are changing the world. Like a pebble in water that ripples outward. And don't say it. I know it sounds corny and naive."

"I don't think it sounds corny and naive. I get 'water.' I think you should do it."

"You do?"

"Yeah." He walked her back to her door, hoping she wouldn't ask for suggestions.

"Then can I ask you a question?"

"Sure, I guess."

"Why don't you stand up for yourself?"

"I do when it counts."

"Not with your brothers—or your dad. We sort of overheard your telephone conversation."

"Oh, that. I figured out years ago that it wasn't worth the

aggravation. One of those ne'er-the-twain-shall-meet things. It's getting late. Maybe you should get some sleep."

"Did I overstep? Sorry, but I am a journalist. Or at least, I was."

"It's fine." Thank God, they'd reached her door. He opened it for her. "You'll probably have it figured out by the morning."

"Probably. Thanks." She went inside and Ty hurried away before she changed her mind again. Heart-to-hearts with women he barely knew were not in his wheelhouse. Actually, heart-to-hearts with women he knew didn't fare much better.

Chapter 11

*P*hoebe was dead to the world when her cell phone rang. She reached over and turned off the sound. It started vibrating. She pulled the sheet over her head, but the sun was telecasting from her open window. She rolled back to her phone. Daphne had left a message.

It was almost ten. Phoebe never slept to ten, but of course she didn't usually stay up to the wee hours running on the beach or blabbing her whole life story to a relative stranger.

How would she ever face Ty Harken again?

Her door opened and her mother peeked into the room.

Phoebe stifled a yawn. "I'm up."

"Good, breakfast is ready."

Phoebe groaned but she got up. She splashed water on her face—puffy but not as puffy as her eyes, which she tried to roll like any self-respecting Keyes-Sutton-Adams woman. It just made them hurt. She wondered briefly if it would be in bad taste to wear sunglasses at the breakfast table, but decided it was useless.

She scrubbed at her hair until it looked messy enough to have come out of an expensive salon, dressed in shorts and a T-shirt, and padded downstairs to the kitchen where Granna was waiting with a cup of coffee.

The look she gave Phoebe told her that she wasn't hiding anything. But they all pretended not to notice. Just like they pretended not to notice how precarious Ruth's attempt to appear all right was the morning before.

"*Frittata alla chevre et pomadore*," announced Vera.

"Goat cheese and dried tomatoes," translated Alice.

"Served with *pain de campagne*," Vera continued, unfazed.

"Eggs and toast," Alice said. "Have a seat."

Phoebe joined the others at the table. No one spoke as they ate and as soon as they were finished, Vera said, "Hurry up now, we're going to church."

If they had been speechless before, they were really speechless now. Ruth stared at her plate, littered with pieces of uneaten frittata. Phoebe focused on the salt shaker.

"Vera, really," Alice began.

"What? It's Sunday. We have a perfectly lovely church here, and I know it's still holding services because I saw the sign when we passed it on our way back from shopping yesterday."

"You want to go to church? You haven't been in the last forty years at least."

"It's never too late to start up again, and at my age . . ."

Alice rolled her eyes. "You're younger than I am, and in better shape."

"That may be so, but I want to get a look at this new preacher. At my age you never know when you might need his services."

"I hope that's a joke," Alice said.

"Oh, come on, you can wear your new Easter hat." Vera turned to Phoebe. "We're actually of the age that we can remember when they still put Easter hats on little girls."

Phoebe and Ruth exchanged looks.

"Oh no, not you, too. Ruth, how could you?"

"The girls were always so cute dressed up."

"It didn't last long," Phoebe reminded her.

"No," Ruth said, and took her plate to the sink.

"If you don't mind," Phoebe said, "I'll stay here. I have a lot of work to do."

"On the Sabbath?" Vera asked in what had to be mock horror.

"I have to get my résumé together and I have to find a place to live." And try to recall what nonsense she'd spouted last night on the beach.

"Tomorrow is another day."

"I can't go, either," Ruth said, turning from the sink.

"Why on earth not? I'd think you'd appreciate a little Christian solace."

"Reverend Lester will want to know where Ron is."

"No, he won't; he wouldn't be able to pick Ron out in a lineup, which is where, if you ask me, he belongs."

"Vera," Alice said. "We'll all go. Meet back here in twenty minutes." Then she yanked Vera out of the room.

The Island All Souls Church was a small white clapboard building topped by a square little steeple. Phoebe, Ruth, and Alice had changed into summer slacks and appropriate tops, and

Vera, much to everyone's relief, wore a long linen sheath, cinched at the waist. She was sporting, the only word for it, a straw hat with an extremely wide brim, which Alice snatched from her head just before they got out of the car.

"You're no fun," Vera complained.

"You don't have to live with these people."

The look Vera gave her said a lot, none of which had to do with quarreling sisters or taste in hats. Though Phoebe, whose life's work was studying people and finding what was special in them, didn't have a clue as to what it did mean.

The church interior was painted white with arched, clear-paned windows that cast rays of sun and dust motes around the well-worn, sparsely filled pews. Several people nodded or waved at Alice as they walked down the aisle and Phoebe concentrated on not thinking about her own recently aborted trip down a future aisle.

They scooted into a pew directly in front of the pulpit, only three rows back and miles from the door. Phoebe didn't usually get weepy in church. But this wasn't a usual time and she wished they were a little closer to the exit.

Pastor Lester climbed to the lectern. He was well past middle-aged, with iron-colored bristled hair and a slight paunch beneath his summer suit. Because he was new, at least since the last time Phoebe had been to church here, she had expected him to be younger. Three days away from the newspaper and already she was losing her edge. *Don't cloud the facts with your own expectations.*

How true was that. In her own life, too.

The pastor had a friendly voice, softly modulating his sentences in a reverential flow of speech and Phoebe relaxed enough to let her mind wander.

Several times during the service she saw Alice glance at Ruth, quietly pat her hand where it clutched her hymnal on her lap. Vera sat on her far side, attentive, standing at the appropriate times and joyously singing every hymn along with the sparse congregation and the even sparser choir.

It seemed to Phoebe she was overdoing it a bit. But not in a mocking way, which Vera was fully capable of doing, but something else. It didn't quite seem like enjoyment, which made Phoebe wonder what her feelings really were.

Fortunately, the sermon was short and uplifting; there was no Communion, being only held on the first Sunday of each month. The pianist took the closing hymn at a spritely clip, Pastor Lester pronounced an enthusiastic "Go with God," and they were back to the sidewalk without any of them breaking down or making any outrageous faux pas.

"That was fun," Vera said as Alice drove them back to the beach house. "We'll all have to do it again next week."

Phoebe saw Alice glance toward Ruth. They were only staying for the weekend, weren't they?

"What a perfect day for lazing in the sun," Vera continued. "A day for lemonade. Do we have lemons? We'll have to pick up some from the store tomorrow."

They pulled into the drive.

"There's Lars talking to Tyler," Ruth said. "I should go over and say hello. It would be rude not to."

"Too late," Vera said. "The competition has arrived. HH alert."

A green Suburban passed by and came to a stop in front of the Harken house. A woman got out of her car, lifted a basket, complete with checked cloth cover, from the seat, and headed for the two men.

Phoebe was sure she could see both of them stiffen.

"You can't help feeling sorry for the man," Alice said, and opened her car door.

Phoebe took her lead and got out of the back.

The woman with the basket was thin and attractive and she didn't seem put off by Lars's slovenly appearance. Phoebe was pretty sure he was wearing the same clothes she'd seem him in the day before when the last husband hunter had dropped in.

The woman had almost reached Lars and Ty when Lars exploded. "Why can't you people leave me alone? I just want some peace." He brushed past her, knocking against her shoulder and jostling the basket.

The woman stared after him, dumfounded—as did the rest of them.

Tyler was the first to recover. "I am so sorry. Are you all right?"

"I just thought the two of you would like some homemade banana bread. I didn't mean to be a nuisance."

"We do and you're not. It's just . . . He's having one of his bad days. He has these spells. He didn't mean anything he said. I'm sure he'll feel terrible when he realizes . . ."

"What a bunch of hooey," said Vera, who had come to stand next to Alice.

"I understand," said the woman. "Poor man." She practically shoved the basket at Ty, hurried back to her car, and drove away.

Tyler stood looking after her, holding the basket à la Little Red Riding Hood on her way to Grandmother's house.

The front door opened. Lars stuck his head out and looked around. Then he came out and marched up to Tyler.

"Why did you take the damn thing? They'll never leave us alone if you keep groveling."

"Banana bread," Ty said, and held out the basket.

"Throw it in the garbage. I don't want it."

"Dad, she was just trying to be a good neighbor. She went to the trouble of baking you something out of kindness."

"What do you know about it?"

"I know when someone is being kind."

"Just go away." Lars swatted the air as if his son was an annoying insect. "I don't need you here."

The four women had stopped halfway to their door, shamelessly listening to the exchange.

"That's enough," Ruth said. "I don't know what's gotten into Lars, but he's not the only man who ever lost a wife. To take it out on his son is unacceptable. Hold this." She shoved her purse to Phoebe and marched across the drive to where the two men were standing.

"Come inside," Alice told Vera and Phoebe.

"Oh no, I wouldn't miss this for the world."

Phoebe had to agree. She didn't often see her mother get angry, but when she did, the world better watch out.

Ty saw her coming and stepped out of her way.

"Lars Harken. What has gotten into you? I can't believe what I just witnessed. I meant to come say hello, but now I'll say something else. There is no reason for you to act like this toward a neighbor or toward Tyler. If Delores was here, she'd give you a good smack for being so rude. Though if she were here you wouldn't be so thoughtless."

"Well, she isn't here, and you didn't even come to say hello."

"I've only been here one day, and we invited you to dinner. You didn't bother to come. What is wrong with you?"

"I don't need you yapping at me, and I don't need Ty hanging around twenty-four seven. The only reason he's here is 'cause he can't keep a decent job and Daniel and Scottie made him come."

Tyler sighed, but said nothing.

Phoebe moved closer to Alice. "Why doesn't Ty stick up for himself?"

"I suspect it would be wasted energy," Alice said.

Phoebe vaguely remembered Tyler saying the same thing last night. "Is it true that he can't keep a job? All that talk about reclaiming water. Was he just daydreaming like he used to?"

"It sounded real to me," Vera said.

"Do you think he got fired?"

"I have no idea," Alice said. "It doesn't matter if he did. He gave up his summer to come take care of his dad. And that's good enough for me."

Lars's raised voice ended their speculation and they all turned back to the confrontation. "You don't know what Delores would do. Because she's dead. Dead. You have no idea. So if you want to harp at me, wait until Ron is dead and you know what you're talking about."

"Dad! Stop it!"

Lars turned and stormed into the house. The door slammed behind him.

"I'm so sorry, Ruth," Tyler began. "He's not getting better, he's getting worse, and mean. I don't think me being here is any help."

"I'm sure you're doing your best. You're always welcome at our house when you need a little respite." Ruth patted his shoulder and came back to the others, visibly upset.

"I don't even recognize him."

"It's okay, Mom. You tried."

"For all the good it did."

They walked slowly to the house.

"I shouldn't have said those things," Ruth said. "It was cruel."

"Sounds like it's about time someone did," Vera said.

"How about some iced coffee and cookies?" Alice said.

"Thanks," Ruth said, "but I think I'll take a little nap."

Phoebe walked her to the stairs. "Are you sure you're okay?"

Ruth smiled and patted her cheek. "Yes, just a little tired." And she climbed wearily up the stairs.

When Ruth didn't come down for lunch, Phoebe excused herself. "I'll just go see . . ."

Alice pushed her back in her seat. "You stay here and eat. I'll take her up something."

She came back downstairs almost immediately. "She apologizes and says she has a headache."

"Who could blame her," Vera said, not even turning around but looking out the window over the sink.

"Vera, that's enough opinion from you. Phoebe and Ruth have both had their lives upended. A little sympathy would not be out of order."

"You're right. I apologize." Vera threw her dish cloth over the spigot and turned an over-the-top smile at them. "Who wants to go to the grocery store?"

"Thanks," Phoebe said, "but if it's okay I'll stay here . . . in case Mom needs anything."

"Right you are," Vera said. "What kind of ice cream do you like?"

"Um, any kind, but . . . but we were only planning to stay for the weekend."

"What? You have some better place you need to be?"

Phoebe bit her lip, shook her head.

"Oh hell, I have no sensibilities." Vera leaned over and smothered Phoebe in an impulsive hug, then stood back, hands on her narrow hips. "This is a good place to be. Just give into it. Go sit on the beach. Take a break. Let life come to you." The "you" warbled into falsetto, truncated by a choke and a cough. "Hairball," Vera said with a shrug.

And Phoebe laughed.

"Come on, Al, time's a-wasting. I don't want to buy picked-over produce."

Granna disappeared long enough to get her purse. "I don't suppose we're making a list?"

"Live dangerously," Vera said. "Anything special you want, Phoebe?"

A job, an apartment . . . "No, thanks." *I have you.*

"Get a move on, Al. And don't try to talk me into buying the biggest cucumber. The seeds are always too . . ." The door closed behind them. A minute later Vera's Jeep backed out and headed for town.

Phoebe sat at the table. Vera was right. This was a good place. And strangely enough, talking to, or rather at, Ty had clarified a few things. It was time to put her money where her mouth was.

She carried her laptop and cell onto the porch and tried to concentrate on her job search. But just ended up wondering where Ty was, and if he and Mr. Harken had carried their argument inside.

Her cell began to vibrate. She hadn't thought to turn the sound back on after church. If she hadn't been a creature of breaking news, she would have left it at the house. She glanced at the screen.

Daphne: three texts. Celia: a text and a call. So much for their promise not to interfere. Even her father had texted. *Call me. ASAP.*

ASAP? Not in a million years.

She wasn't going to plant herself in the middle of that upheaval. Her mother's rash-of-burglaries excuse worked fine for her. But Phoebe found herself hoping that it had really been the one vengeful thing her mother had ever done in her life. Sometimes you had to get down and get angry.

Phoebe certainly had. She still was.

For the umpteenth time, she thanked the powers that be that she'd found out before her wedding what future might have been lurking for her down the line. She was lucky.

So why didn't she feel lucky?

After twenty minutes of the same questions looping in her brain, she gave up and went down to the water, where she rolled up her slacks and waded out into the surf.

She would have liked to take a swim; tonight she'd rummage through her suitcases and see if she could come up with a suit. Right now it seemed like too much trouble.

She splashed along the shoreline, letting the tide pull the sand out from under her feet, leaving her off-balance and fighting for a foothold.

She didn't miss the metaphor.

She just kept walking along staring at the sand ahead of her as if it might lead her to her future. She passed the Wilkinses' house, all boarded up, and tried not to think about what its future might be.

She kept her eyes focused on the point of the island where a bayside inlet carved the land into the shape of a fishhook. Appropriate, since Charley Wilkins's fish camp sat in a clearing, between the bay and the tributaries of an inland lake.

The "camp" itself was just an extended lean-to with a tackle room, cleaning sink, and main area where you could sit and have a beer if the fish weren't biting. It did have running water, as she recalled, because Mr. Wilkins said he didn't want the guys peeing in the woods or the water since it might be offensive to the ladies and the fish.

She wouldn't bother Charley, just skirt the clearing to the path that led back to Seaside Lane and Granna's house.

The fish shack itself had aged to a dark brownish gray. The front porch held two chairs—metal retro kitchen chairs. A new, narrow pier led down to a small bayside boat launch. Beyond the shack, the old picnic pavilion had been replaced with what appeared to be a garage with three wide bay doors.

She didn't see Charley. She stopped to listen but didn't hear any evidence of work going on. She continued on her way, passing between a stripped Chevy minivan resting on a metal frame and an old Volkswagen van with oblong skylights running along the top. The side door was open. She was about to peek inside when a shadow moved into the light and Charley Wilkins stuck his head out of the opening.

He didn't look happy.

"I didn't mean to bother you," Phoebe said.

His frown deepened.

"I'm Phoebe Adams, Ron Adams's daughter? We said hello at the bakery yesterday."

The head bobbed slowly upward until it looked like it might just keep going until it rolled back over his shoulders. But it settled back into place, and he said, "I remember."

"I was just walking on the beach. I hope it's okay. We always used this path to get back home."

"I remember that."

Phoebe smiled. He didn't give her much encouragement to continue talking but Phoebe wasn't a trained journalist for nothing. She accepted the challenge.

"My dad used to come down every Saturday to work on cars with your dad and you and your brother and Lars and his sons. I often thought he wished he didn't have so many daughters. None of us were interested in cars."

"Three of you. I remember that, too. Your dad was pretty handy with a spanner for a city boy."

City boy. Phoebe had never thought about her father being an outsider to the island locals. Of course, there were lots of things she hadn't thought about when it came to her father.

"Your dad still work on cars?"

"No," Phoebe said. "He doesn't get much time off."

"Too bad. Cars are good for keeping things in place."

She'd always thought of cars as going places, not keeping them in place. "How?"

"I've always worked on cars. Could always make them go, sometimes when other folks couldn't. That's a good thing. My dad always said I'd have job security." His brow furrowed and his gaze slid away from Phoebe and wandered around his landscape of auto skeletons until it stopped at a newly painted Suburban.

"That one was nothing but a shell when she came in. Worse than the Chevy."

"And you turned it into that? It's amazing. It looks almost new. Does it run?"

"'Course it runs. What's the use of having a car that don't run?"

"True," Phoebe said, wondering if Inez had gotten it wrong.

"I've been working on car engines my whole life. Went off to the army and I worked on engines in the army, too, only then it was trucks and transport. You know anything about engines?"

"Not much," Phoebe confessed.

"They'll let you down sometimes. But at least you know why

when they do. Good to see you." He turned away as abruptly as his conversation had ended, and disappeared into the van.

"Wait!" Phoebe called.

His head appeared out of the van's open door. "Huh?"

"Inez said you turned these vans into houses, but I don't see any houses." Phoebe turned in a full circle.

"They're all around you."

"You mean these vans?"

"Of course that's what I mean. Transport and bivouac with a roof all rolled into one."

"You refurbish them into campers," Phoebe said, trying to peer over his shoulder into the VW, but he'd braced his hands against the doorframe like a sentry forbidding her entry.

"More than campers. Places to live. A man serves his country. Risks his life. Then he comes home and they let him sleep on the streets. That's wrong."

"It is," Phoebe agreed. "And you give them a place to live."

"I do what I can. Not everybody is as lucky as me."

She couldn't prevent her gaze from sliding toward the old fish shack. "Charley? If I come back one day will you show me around?"

"Why?"

"It's interesting."

"I guess."

"Great, thanks. See you soon." Phoebe headed to the path before he could change his mind.

"But don't come poking around by yourself. There're sharp, rusted things all over."

"I won't. Thanks, Charley. See ya."

But Charley had retreated into the van and didn't respond.

Phoebe hurried ahead, feeling that recognizable tingle of anticipation whenever she discovered something or someone who begged to have their story told. A man who turned useless vehicles into homes for homeless veterans. There was a story there.

Though how could a person live in the back of a van for longer than a weekend or two? What about cooking and running water? Where could they park? Certainly not on a city street. And what about sanitation? And how did he connect the "homes" to the vets?

Suddenly her mind, which had seemed so dull a few minutes before, had a thousand questions. And among those thousand questions was the one Ty had set off last night: *What do you want to do?*

And she knew. She wanted to tell Charley's story.

Ruth powered down her phone. She'd read Ron's texts over and over, then Celia and Daphne's texts; she'd listened to their messages until she thought she would scream.

How had she gotten here? Deserted, rejected by her husband, blamed by her daughters, except Phoebe, who was too busy trying to hold her own world together and needed her family's support.

Was this merely Ron's midlife crisis? But Vera had nailed that one. He was way beyond midlife. It couldn't be his need for sex. She slept less than four feet away from him. Maybe he was no longer attracted to her.

But dammit, she was still attractive.

Maybe he'd just grown tired of her.

Though she had to admit she'd grown a little tired of him, too. Ron had lost some of his appeal along with his hair and his waist-line. But it was more than looks. More than growing older.

It was . . . the settling. They'd been settling. For a long time.

Settling into retirement. Settling into old age. Hell, she was only fifty-six, and a young fifty-six at that. Or at least had been. When had she stopped being young? Not young in age, but young enough to still embrace life.

She hadn't embraced life in a while. But it wasn't until they left the house they had raised the children in—spent birthdays, anni-versaries, and holidays in—that she realized something had died.

Living in the pristine brand-new construction magnified the emptiness of what was left. It was like their history had ceased to exist, and they didn't seem to have anything left in common.

She couldn't pinpoint exactly when it happened or how. She'd blamed it on the condo. But the condo was merely a symbol of everything she had already lost.

She was being erased. A slow disappearing act, so gradual that she hadn't noticed until it was thrown in her face. And she had fled, dragging Phoebe along. That was selfish. Phoebe had had her world pulled out from under her and had come to her mother for aid and understanding. And Ruth couldn't even offer her a place to stay.

She couldn't go back. And she didn't want to think about it anymore. She wanted to sleep and forget. Sleep and forget. Sleep and . . .

Chapter 12

By evening, it was obvious that Ruth had no intention of coming downstairs. Alice had finally taken her a tray filled with her favorites, which she only picked at.

"She'll be fine," Granna said. "She just needs some space."

But when she didn't show up for breakfast the next morning, Phoebe began to worry. It wasn't like her mom to squirrel herself away. Or was it? Her mother had always been there for her daughters, but Phoebe couldn't remember a time they had ever been called on to be there for her. Had they just not been paying enough attention?

Phoebe pushed away from the breakfast table. "I'll go check on her."

"Don't bother," Vera said, pouring fresh-squeezed orange juice into three glasses.

"It's no bother—she's my mom," Phoebe said.

"Well, she may be your mom, but she isn't upstairs."

"Where is she?"

"I haven't the slightest."

"Vera, this is no time to play coy," Alice said, shaking her head at the glass of orange juice Vera held out.

Vera's mouth puckered into a fastidious prune. "I don't know where she is. I heard the shower going around six this morning, then the front door a little later; figured it wasn't you two slug-a-beds, so it had to be Ruth. Unless one of you ladies had a late-night visitor . . ."

"Not amusing," Alice said.

"Did she take my car?" Phoebe hurried past the two women to the door and out into the parking area. Her car was still there. So were the Jeep and the Lexus. She looked up and down the lane but there was no sign of her mother. She ran out to the edge of the lawn, but no one was on the beach.

Ty wasn't even outside doing his chores, so she couldn't ask him if he'd seen her, not that she wanted to see him in the daylight after their unexpected tête-à-tête on the beach Saturday night. What had she been thinking? And worse, what had she actually said?

"I wouldn't worry about her, would you, Alice?" Vera said when Phoebe returned to the kitchen.

"Of course not," Alice said. "She's a grown woman; she can take care of herself."

Phoebe sighed. She should have been more supportive on their Zoom call while Celia pummeled her with questions and Daphne spread blame and needled her to make things right again. Phoebe should have stood up more for her. Why hadn't she? She stood up for perfect strangers in her articles all the time.

But she'd just sat there listening, too absorbed in her own unraveling life to support her mom, while her mother had to stand up for herself alone.

Ruth walked purposefully down the sidewalk, chastising herself for succumbing to self-pity. For being such a coward. For being afraid to see her oldest best friend.

She'd accused Lars of wallowing in grief and now she was coming close to doing the same. Which was why she'd hauled herself out of bed and was slowly making her way toward the bakery.

Halfway down the block, the aroma of fresh baking filled the air around her. Ruth stopped to breathe it in. She would recognize that distinctive aroma anywhere, anytime. Inez's cupcakes.

Across the street, the bakery had a new awning and two round lemonade-style tables and chairs out on the sidewalk that must be new. She hadn't even come downtown during her last few trips home. At first she'd been busy with moving from the house and then so unhappy in the condo she didn't want to do anything but get back to it and try to make it work. She certainly didn't want to see her old friend when she was in such a state.

She and Inez had been best friends since the day they'd met forty years ago. They'd stayed friends but had gradually lost touch once Ruth's girls grew up and they no longer spent summers on the island. These days Ruth made infrequent hit-and-run stops to check on her mother and see if she needed help with anything.

The height of arrogance on Ruth's part. Alice Sutton had been running her family for close to sixty years; she was certainly capable of keeping up the old house or calling a professional for things she couldn't do.

Ruth's stomach rumbled, a betrayal borne part from hunger, part from nerves.

There had been a time when she'd practically run to the bakery each morning, her young world filled with sweetness and excitement, knowing she could do something that she did well that would bring joy to others.

She could hardly remember that girl now. And she halfway hoped that Inez had started closing on Mondays, just so she could avoid facing her old friend.

She swallowed and pushed a strand of lank hair behind her ear. She should have styled her hair before she came.

The bakery door opened and a young women with three small girls walked out carrying a large white box. Just like Ruth and the girls had done years before.

And her reluctance evaporated there on the sidewalk and was replaced by a sudden irrational need to be inside the bakery again. To see Inez, to sit over the old battered worktable, icing cupcakes and drinking ginger ale and telling each other their most secret of secrets.

She crossed the street, but hesitated outside the door. The signs Phoebe had mentioned were still in the window. There had been a similar sign in the window that first summer, too. Ruth had stood outside the door just as she was doing now.

Of course, in those days, there had been plenty of high school and college kids looking for work. And even though she was

Inez's friend, she knew she wouldn't be hired unless she passed Nonna Sabatini's inspection.

But that was then. She opened the door and stepped inside. The same little bell tinkled above her head. There was no one at the counter, but a curtain depicting an artist's renditions of French patisseries wavered as a petite, dark-haired woman stepped through from the kitchen.

She'd aged since Ruth had seen her last. So had Ruth.

Inez saw her and hurried around the glass display case, wiping her hands on a well-worn work apron. "Ruth, I can't believe it's you. It's been years."

There was a brief, semi-awkward pause, before they simultaneously held out their arms for a hug.

"I know. I just don't get back much anymore," Ruth explained. Which was true. And now for the first time, she wondered why.

"Well, come on back. I just put on a pot of coffee. Luckily Monday is a quiet day, while everyone recovers from overeating all weekend, and I'm too pooped to think straight. I've just taken a batch of cupcakes out of the oven. We can talk while they cool."

Ruth followed her back to the kitchen, which was already quite hot even with the air-conditioning running. An upgrade since the days of their youth when they relied on an open screen door and overhead fans.

"I saw the signs in the window. Surely you can get some teenagers to man the counter. It's summer."

"You'd think. But hardly anyone has applied. I have two girls that help out in the afternoon, but they have no baking or decorating skills and don't seem to be interested in learning. Lord, you're a sight for sore eyes," Inez said, going straight to the coffeepot and pouring out two big mugs, one that read, GRANDMA LOVES ME MORE THAN COFFEE, and another one, GRANDMA IS #1.

She handed one to Ruth and Ruth noticed the swollen knuckles of her hands.

"Sit down and tell me what you've been up to. I want to hear everything."

Ruth sat across from Inez at the old worktable and studied the steam rising off her coffee. She suddenly felt tongue-tied. "Oh, nothing much. I've retired from the library. They've had to cut hours, because of funding, and didn't really need all of us. We"—the word stuck in her throat—"sold the house and moved to a condo. No garden. Less work. Celia and Daphne are fine, but they're both busy with families and don't have much time to come visit."

Inez looked up over her mug. "And Phoebe? She's so grown-up and sophisticated. I almost didn't recognize her."

"Oh, Inez. She just broke off her engagement to a lovely man. Three months before the wedding."

"That's terrible. What happened?"

"I'm not sure, but . . ."

The doorbell jangled and Inez pushed herself slowly out of her chair and went to answer it.

Inez was the culmination of generations of bakers. She had always been more nimble-fingered than Ruth, but most of all she was a heavenly baker. "It's in the genes," Inez's mother, Maria, would say, and Nonna Sabatini would answer, "It's not about the genes, it's the love."

Genes or no genes, Nonna had taken one look at Ruth and said, "You. You will ice the cakes." Ruth had iced untold numbers of cakes, cupcakes, petit fours, and other forms of pastries. One day, Nonna said, "And now I will show you how to make a flower."

She'd demonstrated how to make perfect petals and leaves and watched Ruth's attempts. Demonstrated and watched, and demonstrated again. It had taken weeks, but one day Ruth had created a flower that Nonna declared worthy of being put in the display case. Ruth's sense of accomplishment was beyond description. She, like her dozens of almost-flowers, blossomed. And by the end of that first season, she had made her violet-topped cakes one of the best sellers at the bakery.

"You're my little honorary Sabatini," Nonna would say.

When Ruth took her second batch home to show the family and told them what Nonna had said, Granna said, "Sabatini, my foot. That's a Keyes-Sutton violet if there ever was one."

Her father had looked over Alice's shoulder, and grunted. "Definitely a Sutton violet."

Ruth swelled with residual pride just remembering.

Inez returned, then checked the cupcakes on the cooling rack before transferring them to a display tray and bringing it to the table. She took a bowl out of the fridge and placed it on the table, along with several icing spatulas.

"Arthritis," she said, picking up a knife and loading it with chocolate icing. "Slows me down considerably. I need to find somebody, but you can't imagine how hard it is to find experienced people." She looked up at Ruth from beneath her thick eyebrows.

"Don't look at me," Ruth said. "I'm only here for the weekend. Though it seems the weekend is gone already. Just for a few more days . . . until Phoebe is feeling better."

"You were about to tell me about Phoebe." Inez placed the frosted cupcake on a display tray and picked up another.

Ruth told her about Phoebe's phone call. Her broken engagement, and losing her apartment. She didn't tell Inez about Ron's defection or her own humiliation. Instead, she asked about Inez's children and the ever-burgeoning clan of Sabatinis scattered along the Eastern Seaboard.

All the while Ruth watched Inez's slow, deliberate movements, and finally picked up one of the spatulas. "I'll give you a hand. I might not be at the top of my game, but I've made a few cupcakes since I worked here. I can do the basics and you do the finish." She picked up a cupcake and scooped up a spatula of icing.

Soon they were working away and chatting like no time had passed at all.

But it had. They were both older. Inez's hands were beginning to fail her. Ruth's husband was leaving her.

"Tony broke his hip this past winter. I told him not to try to break up the ice without one of the boys, but the stubborn man wouldn't listen. Now he's had to stop all heavy lifting. He thinks he's going to rebound. But . . . it was pretty bad."

"Who's doing the deliveries for him?"

"The boys, the ones who live close enough, are taking turns. I'll have to hire a driver soon, though. How's Ron? Did he come with you this trip?"

"No," Ruth said, nearly dropping the cupcake she'd just finished. "Just Phoebe. A girls' weekend away."

"That sounds nice."

Every few minutes the doorbell would jingle and Inez would get up to wait on a customer. Each time she returned, she would give a rundown on who it had been and what they'd bought along with a tidbit of gossip. Ruth didn't even recognize half of the names. She'd been gone for a long time. Too long.

When the cupcakes were finished, Ruth wiped her hands on a dish towel and stood. "I'd better be going; they'll be wondering where I am."

Inez followed her to the front. "I'm so glad you came."

"Me too," Ruth said, feeling unexpected tears beginning to prickle at her eyes.

It was a sad, bittersweet moment. For a few minutes, time had not passed, and they were young and hopeful and full of dreams.

They hugged, and Inez opened the door.

Another quick hug and Ruth started down the street. Inez waved from the doorway. Ruth lifted her hand, then turned her back on the place and the friend that held so many fond memories.

She walked past the pharmacy, the luncheonette, and the new hair salon where big photos of beautiful young things with stylish cuts and perfect makeup were lined up in the window. And above their heads staring back in the reflection of the plate glass was Ruth Sutton Adams. Mrs. Ron Adams. Mother of three. Member of so many committees she couldn't name them all. Retired librarian.

And she looked it. She'd kept in shape; that's what suburban mothers did these days. She exercised, took online seminars, followed the latest diets to keep her trim figure. Kept up with the almost-newest technologies, Noom and Zoom and chat rooms. Add to that a tasteful, slightly overpriced wardrobe, a semi-expensive face-framing hairstyle, subtle but expensive makeup, and she was a camera-ready suburban mom, a mover and shaker in the neighborhood.

But she wasn't. Not anymore. There would be no more couples nights for her. Did divorcées get invited to cookie exchanges? Widows did. Sally Hicks always made twice as many cookies as most of them. As if extra cookies could make up for what she had lost.

Ruth had never thought about these things before. It had never occurred to her that she might have to.

She didn't want to think about them now. She wanted to be young and pretty and ready to set the world on fire. Not this sad, lost woman wondering where it had all gone wrong.

She turned from the window and the beautiful young models and continued down the sidewalk. She'd go back to the house. Tell Phoebe it was time to go. She and Phoebe could live in the condo until things were decided. She'd been living there for almost a year; a few more months—or however long it took for the divorce to go through—wouldn't kill her.

She'd go back to the condo and serve papers to Ron before he served them to her. But did it really matter who divorced whom? It wasn't exactly something you could brag about. Oh no, *he* didn't divorce *me*, *I* divorced *him*. But it would feel good, she supposed.

She'd be fine. Maybe she'd volunteer for story hour at the library. Maybe she'd . . .

Ruth stopped in the middle of the sidewalk. What was she thinking? She was fifty-six years old. She had a few good years left.

She'd chastised Lars for wallowing in grief. He at least was mourning the woman he'd loved all his life. Ruth had been mourning something more elusive. Something she'd lost sight of along the way. She'd been turning into a fossil for a long time and it was her own damn fault.

Which was a stupid thing to let happen. And if there was one thing she wasn't, it was stupid. She turned around and marched back up the sidewalk.

She didn't stop until she opened the bakery door and the bell tinkled above her head.

Inez looked up from the other side of the display case. "Ruth?"

"There's something I didn't tell you."

Ty hunkered over the wheel of his bike and raced down the lane toward the fish camp. This was about the only exercise he was getting besides minor construction work on the house. Sanding rusted bumpers and hauling plastic jugs through mire and muck was a placeholder. He longed to be out really working. Climbing trees with nothing to aid him but a piece of nylon strap rescued from a spring flood, just to run cable hundreds of feet above a ravine. Standing waist-deep in a spring runoff to clear detritus that was damming the flow, before it flooded a nearby village.

It was early, and his father was still asleep, which made Ty able to make a stealth run to help Charley. If Ty was on a "real" job, he would have already been at it for several hours by now. Some places he went were too hot to work much past ten.

Not like here, where the sun was warming his back in the gentle way of the northeast coast.

He turned down the foot path and came to a stop by the conglomeration of old vehicles. He leaned his bike against the newest acquisition, a panel truck that maybe had been used for dairy deliveries at one time, but had long ago been painted over in psychedelic mandalas, which in their turn had mostly faded away, barely discernible now.

Charlie was squatting down at the back of a 1979 Volkswagen van, tinkering with the engine.

Ty walked over.

"You didn't have to come right away. How's Lars doing?"

"Still asleep," Ty said, leaning over to peer in at the engine. "He's sleeping a lot these days."

"Depression," Charley said. "Hope he's not getting strung out."

"No, he's not taking anything. He won't even go to a therapist."

"It's a hard place to be." Charley pointed to the workings of the engine. "I might have to replace the whole damn thing."

Engines weren't really Ty's thing. He believed that the fewer the parts, the less chance of a breakdown you had. Engines were Charley's expertise. He not only fixed them, but he believed in them. A man Tyler could relate to.

Two different paths, one to war and trauma, the other to college and a chance invention, both leading to the same end.

Recycle something that nobody wants into something someone else needs. In Charley's case, for homeless veterans; in Ty's, for drought-riddled villages.

One man's trash . . . and all that.

"Show me what the hang-up is." Ty squatted next to Charley and they considered the engine.

"Ya know," Charley said after a couple of minutes. "One of those Adams girls was over here yesterday."

Ty straightened up and banged his head on the hood. "Phoebe?"

"Uh, yeah, I think that's what she said her name was. She was at the bakery before that."

"Small town," Ty said, rubbing his head and returning to his study of the engine. "I think we're going to have to take her out."

"Phoebe?" Charley asked.

"The engine."

"Oh. She was pretty in a sprite-like way."

"Sprite-like, huh? She works for a newspaper. What was she doing down here?" And why had he thought intervening in her meltdown was a good idea? She probably hated him for letting her spill her guts to him. Not that he'd had any choice once she got going.

"Don't know," Charley continued. "Said she was taking the path back to her house. Guess she'd been walking on the beach."

"Yeah, she seems to like walking on the beach."

"Probably like it more if she had somebody to walk with."

"You volunteering?"

"Hell no," Charley said. "I'm crazy as a loon and ugly to boot.

A girl her age . . . Hell, she oughta have someone young who can treat her right. Now are we gonna take out this engine or not?"

Ruth and Inez sat in the same places in the back room of the bakery that they had just vacated a few minutes before. Fresh cups of coffee and piping bags of frosting were sitting at their elbows.

This time as they sat drinking and talking, they decorated Mr. Ganhowser's ninetieth birthday cake.

"There was one big thing I didn't tell you, Inez. It was stupid, but I feel so . . . Oh, I don't know."

"We never had secrets in the old days."

"No, we didn't." So Ruth told her the whole story. Beginning with Ron's announcement, Phoebe's phone call, and their decision to come to the island.

"Now he's badgering the girls with texts for me to come back and act like an adult. And Phoebe seems more angry than heartbroken, but she still needs a competent, caring mother, not one who's distracted by her own mess of a life."

Inez frowned across the table at her, her heavy brows straightening and almost meeting in the center. It was an expression Ruth remembered so well, a combination of sympathy and exasperation that all the Sabatinis were masters of.

Then Inez shrugged it away. "So both of you. Whoo. Better you should be together at a time like this. Phoebe's young, she'll get over it, but you and Ron . . . who would have thought."

"I didn't. That's for sure. But I wasn't really paying attention. While the girls were growing up, I was busy. I loved every minute of it—well, almost every minute. But Phoebe's the youngest. She left for college ten years ago, hasn't really lived with us since. I see her more than the others because she lives in the same town, but it isn't the same.

"Since the girls left, I've been gradually . . . I don't know . . . disappearing. I didn't even have a career like Ron did to fill the empty places when they left."

"What about the library?"

"It was okay, but it was really just something to pass the time. I mean, I liked it, but . . . it wasn't a passion. That sounds unappreciative and I'm not. I just don't like what has been happening, but it's on me; I let it happen."

"Remember all the plans we used to make?" Inez said.

"Lately, I've been trying to remember," Ruth said. "We were going to start our own bakery. You'd bake and I'd decorate. No breads or biscotti or cinnamon rolls . . ."

"Just things with icing." Inez sighed. "Now I bake, decorate, sell everything. My kids don't want to work their fingers to the bone, literally, for the meager returns." She paused to glance down at her gnarled fingers. "We barely have enough savings to retire on. Actually if Tony can't get back to work, I can't retire. I can't manage the patisserie by myself, but I can't afford not to." She threw out her hands, a gesture uniquely reminiscent of Nonna Sabatini. "What am I saying? I'm doing what I was destined to do, and it's been mostly good, so I can't complain. What do you think you'll do now?"

Ruth shook her head. "I don't know. I won't go back. I was so humiliated at first, I couldn't even tell anyone. I just hid in that hateful condo. He came to pick up some clothes, and I locked myself in the guest room so I wouldn't have to face him. And then Phoebe called, and I couldn't hold it in another minute. She came to me for support and I dumped my failures on her instead."

"I'm sure that isn't true. Thank God you have each other. And Alice."

"And Vera," Ruth added.

"Lord, Vera's back?"

"Yes, evidently she's been here the good part of a week, and shows no signs of leaving, and none of us has quite figured out why."

They finished decorating the cake, added some candles, and shed a few tears for the past, for growing old, for birthdays.

By the time Inez walked Ruth to the door, everything had changed.

Ruth stopped at the door. "You know, as soon as we started for the island, I felt a huge weight lift off my chest. Though I'm not sure whether it was relief or a sense of freedom. Now I'm kind of optimistic."

"Well, I'm glad for it."

"In that case . . . are you still looking for a decorator?"

Inez's eyes widened. "I don't know what to say."

Ruth laughed. "Well, are you?"

"Yes!"

"Then take that sign off the window. I don't know how long I'll be here but while I am, count me in."

Inez reached past her and snatched the DECORATOR WANTED sign off the window.

"I'll see you tomorrow," Ruth said.

"Six o'clock sharp-ish?"

Ruth stepped outside and they grinned at each other through the glass before Ruth hurried away. She had one more stop to make before she went home to tell the others.

Phoebe spent the morning taking care of business, liaising with the community website to publish the information about the food bank and looking out the window for Ruth to return. She saw Ty leave on his bike and wondered briefly where he went every day. She Googled homeless veterans, learned about students living in parking lots in RVs so they could afford college. She texted her mom's phone. When she didn't receive a text back, she texted her again. And still didn't get a response. What could she be doing that she couldn't answer a text?

She proofed two articles on the food bank and sent them off. She pulled up her incredibly-out-of-date résumé, looked out the window again, and saw Ty cycle into his yard, lean his bike against the house, and go inside. She checked her phone. Nothing.

She tried to start reworking her résumé, using an online template, but it was so old she didn't know where to start or what to highlight. She had several awards and achievements that were impressive enough to garner attention. If there were even any jobs out there.

She pulled up one of the huge job sites. Scrolled through possible journalism jobs. Then made a list of people to call.

By the time Granna called her down for lunch, she was feeling better about the future and wishing she hadn't spilled her life story to Ty Harken.

Phoebe, Granna, and Vera ate lunch at the kitchen table, very much aware of the empty plate for the MIA mother/daughter/ niece.

"What do you think she's doing?" Phoebe asked.

"She's taking a personal day," Vera said. "Isn't there a new spa in town?"

"Mom?" Phoebe said incredulously.

"Well, it's about time she did something nice for herself."

Phoebe wanted to ask, *How do you know?* But Great-aunt Vera was right. Her mom was probably . . . What did her mom do all day? Phoebe didn't even know; she just assumed she had things to do.

"Should I go look for her?"

Granna glanced out the window. Phoebe was pretty sure she was a little worried, too. It wasn't like her mom to just go off. She was always so considerate. "No, she'll come back when she's good and ready."

So they waited.

And waited.

They decided on what to have for dinner. At Vera's insistence, they made suggestions of places to visit because, as Vera pointed out, "We're not just going to sit here all summer worrying about some man that done us wrong."

"Us?" Alice said, eyebrows raised.

"Them," Vera corrected. "I just said *us* to be inclusive."

"You're staying all summer?" Phoebe asked, surprised.

Vera threw her head back in exasperation. It made it impossible to read her face.

"It was just an expression, though I suppose as a journalist you insist on the literal as opposed to the metaphorical or the—"

"Yeah, but I thought maybe—"

"Where the hell is your mother?"

When the hall clock chimed three, they were back in the kitchen for tea. The kitchen had the best view of the lane from town.

Granna had made snickerdoodles during the interim, but today even they couldn't tempt Phoebe. "That's it. I'm going to take a walk into town and see if I can find her."

She grabbed her phone and headed to the kitchen door.

It opened just as she reached it and she took a surprised step backward.

Ruth walked in with a tentative smile on her face.

For a moment Phoebe could only stare, then she blurted out, "Mom, your hair!"

Chapter 13

Ruth hadn't been prepared to be met at the door by three shocked faces. She'd planned to sneak in and take a quick moment to compose herself in the powder room before making her grand entrance.

She'd checked on her new look in every shop window she passed on her way home. Completely studied herself from every angle in the three-way mirror of the boutique where she'd impulse-bought several outfits she would never have considered before their trip to Kedding's Wharf.

But here she was. And here they were. And they were all dumb with surprise.

Ruth turned in a circle, not just to show off her new look, but mainly to keep from having to look them in the face, because she was afraid they hated it.

Maybe she'd gone too far. She had to admit it was a bit extreme. But confronted with the photos of those beautiful models with their perfect hair, she'd had an epiphany—or else she'd lost her mind in one fell swoop.

Then she'd bought the clothes to match her hair.

"Well?" she asked, hoping the tremor she heard in her voice would pass as excitement.

"It's fabulous," said Phoebe. "Turn around again. Slower."

Ruth turned around. Looked at her mother.

"Very stylish," Alice said.

"Lethal," Vera added. "And with highlights."

"Too much?" Ruth may have been too enthusiastic about the blond-on-blond look. "Mother?"

Ruth tried not to fidget while Alice gave her a closer, more scrutinizing look. "I think I'll like it once I get used to it. How did they get it to stand up like that?"

"Is it too much?" Ruth asked, suddenly second-guessing herself. "It's just gelled into those spikes. It washes out."

"No!" Phoebe and Vera cried at once.

"Leave it," Phoebe said. "I love it."

"Me too," Vera said. "I'm trying to think of a word that's trending right now that means 'You done good, kid.'"

"I agree," Alice said thoughtfully. "A new look for a new beginning."

Ruth could have thrown her arms around her mother and wept for joy. Of course, one didn't throw one's arms around Alice. A peck on the cheek and a quick squeeze spoke volumes among the Suttons.

"Okay, that's a unanimous vote," Vera said. "The gel stays. What's in the bags?"

"Clothes. Just a few outfits. And I can thank you, Vera, for that."

"Moi?"

"Yes. I've had the same look for half my life. Tasteful suburban. I decided to go for something a little more . . . something. But don't worry. Nothing outrageous."

"It's never too late for outrageous." Vera flicked her fingers at the shopping bags. "Let's take a look."

Phoebe marveled as her mother brought out several new outfits, not so colorful as the kaftan Vera had bought the other day, but more vibrant than her usual neutral chic.

And Phoebe wondered if this was really what her mother envisaged as her new self or just a knee-jerk reaction to recent events that would fade away with the blonde.

"Did you eat?" Alice said, bringing them all back from their own thoughts.

"Yes, pastries and then lunch. There's a new Italian place in town, quite good."

"You have been busy," Alice said.

"And I'll be busier starting tomorrow."

They all waited for the next shoe to drop.

"I have a job at the bakery. Only mornings. Inez needs help. It's the least I can do for an old friend."

"I guess that means you'll be staying longer than just the weekend," Vera said.

Ruth frowned suddenly and turned to Alice. "If that's okay?"

"Of course it's okay. Better than okay. You and Phoebe will always have a home here."

Phoebe didn't know whether to be relieved or agitated. She

couldn't stay here; she had to get her life together. But where did one get one's life back together when nothing much was left? *With family.*

"Phoebe?" Ruth asked. "Does that work for you? I don't mean to strand you here. You don't have to stay. I'm fine."

"Of course she'll stay," Alice said. "As long or short a time as you want, Phoebe. It will be nice having family around."

"And when Alice Sutton speaks," Vera began. "Which gives me a great idea."

Alice groaned. "Which means you've been hatching it all weekend."

"I think it's time to get down and get dirty," Vera continued, ignoring her sister. "Unless you're worried about your new 'do?" she added to Ruth.

"Depends on your idea of down and dirty."

"I thought we could get out the lawn furniture."

"Lord," Alice said. "I haven't brought out that old furniture in years."

"Well, it's about time you did."

"It's bound to be filthy; the cushions are probably rotten."

"Only one way to find out," Vera said enthusiastically. "So everyone go put on some work clothes and meet me by the shed in ten minutes."

What the hell are they doing now?" Lars asked, staring out the sliding glass doors to the lawn.

Ty leaned over him and watched Phoebe, Ruth, and Vera lug out an ancient chaise longue from around the house and drop it to the grass. Several old familiar chairs were already sitting haphazardly across the yard. "Taking out the lawn furniture from the shed."

"Why?"

"A crazy guess? They're planning to sit on it."

"Stupid. That old stuff has been stored away for years. It's probably all rusted and rotten."

"They don't use it anymore?"

"Why would they? Everybody's gone."

Not everyone. Ty tried to ignore the accusation in his voice. You just couldn't win with his father. If you didn't visit, he complained; if you did, he couldn't wait to get rid of you. Or maybe it was just Ty he couldn't get along with. "Well, there certainly seem to be enough people to enjoy it now."

"Crazy females." Lars turned away from the glass, a scowl settling over his face, carving out deep lines that he'd never had before . . . before his wife died.

He padded back into the living room, where the TV flickering was the only light in the dark room, since his father kept the drapes drawn and the windows shut like some gothic recluse.

"I think I'll go see if they need help," Ty called after him. He didn't wait for a response, but slid the door open and strode across the grass. "Need a hand with the heavy lifting?"

"Perfect timing," Vera said. "The bench is still inside. Don't know why they ever moved it. It weighs a ton."

"Well, let's see."

"Phoebe will help you," Vera said, and gave Phoebe a shove. "Let us know if you need anyone else."

Ty didn't miss the tail of Vera's smug smile as she strolled off to the opposite side of the house. He sure as hell hoped she wasn't going to play matchmaker. Just because he and Phoebe were both here at the same time was no reason to start down that road.

There was nothing wrong with Phoebe. She'd grown up to be pretty attractive. But he couldn't quite forget the annoying kid who asked a million questions and followed him when he just wanted to be left alone to think. Scrambling behind him, peering over his shoulder, curious about everything, but annoying as hell. *Magpie.*

Of course he never called her that out loud, unlike his brothers, who were ruthless in their teasing. She didn't seem to mind. She'd just ask more questions. About everything. Nonstop.

The last summer before he left for college she'd been nine or ten, still energetic and birdlike and determined. At least by then she'd started pursuing Scottie, who was closer to her age.

Amazing what the good part of a decade could do.

"What are you smiling at?" Phoebe asked, breaking into his reverie and reminding him of why *Magpie* might still be applicable.

"Just feeling pleasant," he said, and peered into the shed. The cushions were piled in one corner and looked like they would need a good cleaning, or possibly replacement. *The canvas might be strong enough to reuse for something, but . . .*

"Are you going to move it or just contemplate it all day?"

"Huh?" Ty looked over his shoulder at her. She was stand-ing with her hands on her hips, waiting, and none too patiently. For some strange reason that made him smile even more. He scratched his head. "Just trying to gauge the best way to get the bench out of here."

"How about we pull one end to the door, then we can push the rest from behind."

"Brilliant," he said, not able to suppress the grin that insisted on spreading over his face. She was a breath of fresh air after deal-ing with his father all day. "I was just thinking that myself."

She thumbed him to move over and he did. Together they got one end turned to the door.

"Why is this so heavy?"

"It's made of concrete." She lifted both eyebrows toward him, which he was pretty sure was her rendition of the Sutton eye roll. "And hell to move," she added, grunting as she attempted to get it over the metal threshold.

"A little teamwork might be more efficacious." He nudged her over, took his place next to her, and placed his hands next to hers on the bench arm. "Ready?"

She nodded.

"Then heave."

They pulled and lifted and the front two legs jumped over the metal saddle; then they dragged the back legs to the saddle, where they stuck. They dropped the bench onto the grass and exchanged looks. If they lifted from the back, the front legs would stick in the grass.

"I'll ask Mom and Vera to help."

"And accept defeat? Hold that thought." Ty looked down at the bench structure, then turned and considered the aluminum umbrella clothes dryer that stood a few feet away.

He made a few calculations, then squeezed between the bench and the doorjamb and wriggled back into the shed. He came out a few seconds later with a coil of yellow marine rope, which he tied to the free end of the bench.

He walked backward, uncoiling it until he reached the clothing umbrella that had stood in the yard for as long as he could remember. He knew it was anchored in concrete. Opposite but equal forces. He ran the cord over the cross pole, then wrapped it around his forearm and hands and dropped his weight. The rope pulled taut, then the front end of the bench lifted a few inches from the ground.

He tied it off and went back to Phoebe, who was waiting. "We should be able to lift the back and swing it to the grass without damaging anything."

"Amazing," she said, and took her place beside him.

After several intense moments the bench was sitting on the lawn.

"I don't suppose you have another calculation that will get this bench to carry itself to the other side of the house?"

"Not yet. But I'll work on it."

They each took an end and carried it a few feet before Phoebe called a halt. She shook her arms and grabbed her end again. "Okay, go." With only three stops, they made it to the front of the house. The others ran to help carry it the rest of the way, which turned out to be its original place on a tiny stone patio, sheltered by beach grass and now overgrown with chickweed, but once in position it had a clear view to the sea.

Ruth breathed in a deep breath. "Ah, that's nice."

And Phoebe thought it was a sigh of contentment.

The cushions were salvaged next and laid out on the lawn.

"Maybe they've seen their last summer," Alice said.

"Nonsense," Vera said. She walked over to the outside spigot, detached the hose from its storage hook, and screwed it to the spigot. Then making sure the nozzle was closed, she turned on the water and dragged the hose to where they were all standing by the cushions. "A good spray-down and they'll be just like new."

She tried to open the nozzle, but it was stuck tight; the hose jumped and unrolled across the lawn as it filled with water while Vera struggled to open the nozzle.

"Damned salt," she said, and turned to Ty. "Put some muscle to—" She handed the nozzle to him; it snapped open and water sprayed over the two of them, drenching them both.

Phoebe jumped out of range.

Ruth cried, "My hair!" and skittered away.

Only Alice stayed, laughing so hard she had to hold her side.

A second later the spray had been turned on her. Vera doused her completely, then shoved the hose at Ty and ran in the opposite direction.

"I'll get you, my pretty," Alice said, shaking her fist and laughing.

And Ty turned the spray on Phoebe.

Pretty soon they were all wet, including Ruth, though miraculously her gel spikes were still intact. They arranged the table and chairs in the side yard just where they had always been, and finally turned their attention to cleaning the pillows. Soap and scrub brushes were brought out, and soon the cushions were clean and drying in the sun.

"Nothing like a little fun and laughter and a job well done," Vera said, batting away a clump of soap suds from her shoulder. "Now if old grumpy puss was in range, I'd give him a healthy soaking, too."

They all turned to look back at the Harken house, just in time to see the door slide shut and a shadow walk away.

"I'd better go," Ty said. "Can you manage the rest?"

"You go on," Alice told him.

"No," Ruth said. "I'll go. I owe him an apology."

She walked resolutely toward the house. Knocked on the glass of the sliding doors. Got no answer. Walked around to the side door. Knocked, tried the handle, and when it opened, she stuck her head inside. "Lars?" She waited. "Lars, it's Ruth. Can I come in?"

After a minute she looked back at the others, who had stopped to watch. Shook her head and came back. "I guess you'd better go."

"Don't worry about it," Ty said. "He came out to see what we were doing. That was actually progress." Still he walked away from them a more sober Ty than he'd been just moments before.

Vera rolled up the hose and returned it to its hook by the spigot. Phoebe went to stand by Ruth and Alice, who were looking over the new arrangement of table and chairs. She thought she knew what they were thinking.

It looked just like it had for all her childhood. Now none of them ever came back for a long enough visit to warrant the hassle of taking it out.

Such a big family, so spread out. Was Granna lonely without them? The Wilkins gone, with strangers living in their house. Delores Harken passed away, and Mr. Harken a mean-spirited recluse.

Well, they were here now, some of them anyway. It was a start. A new beginning.

A cell phone rang from the porch. They all looked toward the sound but Vera reached the door in a flash and the ringing stopped. They waited for her to come out again, but she didn't.

Her sudden absence seemed to freeze them into immobility. A kind of unexpected letdown, as if Vera had been buoying them up and without her, they deflated.

Phoebe didn't really know her great-aunt. Every time she'd visited, she'd been a bundle of energy, always on the move, almost as if she *couldn't* stay still.

That energy was even more pronounced these last few days . . . except when those phone calls came in. As if the interruption made Vera falter in her own energy. And then the way she always walked away from the others, like you did when you didn't want anyone to overhear what you were saying. The next moment, she'd be back like nothing had happened, which made Phoebe wonder if anything had.

They might not be serious, just private. A big real estate deal. A secret lover. A surprise party. Did anyone have a birthday coming up? Phoebe didn't think so.

But it was more than that. Phoebe hadn't spent her adult life ferreting out other people's stories to not wonder if there was something Vera wanted to keep from the others.

Certainly her right, but so unlike the Vera that Phoebe remembered.

And what about this surprise visit? And Vera's uncharacteristic length of stay. Was she worried about something? Could it be that her joke about the bucket list wasn't a joke but real?

Surely not. She didn't look sick.

So why was she staying? Then an even worse thought hit her full force. What if it wasn't Vera, but Granna?

What if she wasn't fine, like she'd said? A chill ran up Phoebe's spine.

What if this wasn't a new beginning but a— No. She wouldn't think about it. She was a journalist. She'd gather her facts without jumping to conclusions. Because she didn't want to lose any of them. She felt like she was just finding them again.

Chapter 14

Ruth went to bed early; she wanted to be at her best for her job at the bakery. *Her job at the bakery.* She loved the sound of that. So what if she'd be mainly frosting cupcakes and cutting brownies? She was happy to do whatever Inez needed help with.

It wasn't actually a job. Inez had asked what she would need in a salary, much to both of their embarrassment. Ruth had put her off as long as she could and finally said, "Whatever the going rate is. Remember, I'm a new hire, not an experienced pâtissier."

Inez accepted it. They shook hands on the deal, but ended it with grins. Just a formality. Inez and Ruth working together again.

But now that Ruth actually needed her sleep, she was too excited, and perhaps a bit anxious. When she'd left the bakery for the second time, she'd convinced herself that she was just helping out a friend. But that idea only lasted until she reached the salon.

You didn't need a new hairstyle or new clothes just to help out at a beach town bakery. And yet she had both. Because this was all a part of the new Ruth Adams.

She'd been the dependable wife and mother for as long as she could remember and she wasn't comfortable with this *new* her.

But you will be, she told herself. *You will be.*

Her stomach growled. Anticipation, nerves, and the acknowledgment that she might be irrevocably moving on from her old life had kept her from eating much at dinner. She'd been hoping Ty and Lars would join them, but neither of them showed up.

Maybe she should suggest they start eating dinner together. That way Lars would eat better and Ty would get a break from his father's unrelenting unhappiness. The women would cook and the men could bring one of the many husband-hunter casseroles that must be piling up in their freezer.

She went downstairs to make a cup of herbal tea and cadge a couple of snickerdoodles from the cookie tin, then took her cup and a cookie out to the porch to let the night air calm her restlessness.

Someone else had the same idea. She could see the top of his head over the beach grass. He was sitting on the old concrete bench, looking out to sea.

And she knew who it was.

She stood watching for a few minutes, then put her cup down and slipped out the door. Quickly tying the robe she'd thankfully put on to come downstairs, she crossed the lawn to the dune.

His head was bowed, and he didn't look up when she sat down beside him.

"Lars?"

He didn't seem to hear her, so she sat silently beside him, listened to the shush of the waves on the beach below them.

She was startled out of her own reveries by a raspy voice she hardly recognized.

"We used to sit here every night looking at the stars."

"I remember. I used to envy the two of you."

"I bet you don't envy me now."

How could she answer that? She still envied his and Delores's deep love, something she suspected was still elusive for her. "No."

"I can't— I don't want to go on without her."

Panic skittered up Ruth's back. "You have to. You have to learn to embrace life again. For Delores. She wouldn't want you to give up. She wouldn't want you to give in to your grief."

"Can't help it." He shook his head. His hair was thinner now, and unkempt. His clothes hung on him, limp and dirty. He needed a shower; beyond the perspiration, he smelled like he'd given up.

"Your boys need you, now more than ever."

"No they don't. They foisted Ty on me because they didn't have time, but they felt guilty. Ty resents me for . . . for everything."

"That isn't true. He's doing his best, but he feels your disapproval. Your disdain. Your stubbornness. And you're not being fair. All three of your boys are grieving and they need you to be there for them."

"He was always her favorite."

"Who?"

"Tyler. I didn't get him. Still don't. The other two, Danny and Scottie, I got them. But not Tyler. She got him. Pampered him—it didn't make him strong. He's only here because he didn't have a job."

"You are so wrong. He's between projects, not jobs. Do you even know what he does?"

Lars lifted one shoulder. "He's always running off to places no one ever heard of, doing God knows what. Projects. Huh. He oughta have a steady job, one that can support him and a family. A house. Children. He's thirty-seven, for Christ's sake. He needs to settle down. He has an apartment in Cambridge, like he's some kind of professor. Even that would be okay. He went to a good school, but what has he done with it?"

"You'd be surprised. And proud. If you weren't so stubborn."

"Why doesn't he talk about his work, then?"

"Because no one but Delores ever showed an interest."

Finally he looked up. His face carved in stark recesses by the moon. "I miss her so much." He broke down and sobbed.

Ruth waited. She didn't try to console him, or tell him everything would be okay. She didn't know that it would. And who was she to promise such a thing? On her way to divorcing a man who no longer loved her.

Finally his shoulders relaxed and he straightened up. "I hope you know how lucky you are to have Ron."

Ruth took a breath. "I don't have Ron. He left me for someone else."

Through the fog of sleep, Phoebe heard the shower running and knew her mother must be getting ready to go to the bakery. It seemed so odd. Her mother had worked off and on while she and her sisters were growing up. But she never left the house until the girls were off to school.

A little niggle of guilt embedded itself in Phoebe's gut. She should be the one going off to work. Journalism was a competitive business and while she was at the beach with her family, someone else was probably taking her potential job.

But she didn't get up, just lay there, enjoying the ocean breeze that wafted through the open window.

The shower shut off; minutes later a door opened and closed. The next time a door opened, Phoebe slid out of bed and went to stick her head outside her room. Her mother was just coming down the hallway.

"Good luck on your first day," Phoebe whispered.

Her mother grinned back.

Phoebe was taken aback. Her mom looked happy.

Ruth cupped Phoebe's cheek in her hand as she passed. "See you this afternoon," she whispered and practically floated down the stairs.

Phoebe went back to bed, and when she woke again her first thought was, *People don't really float down the stairs.* Then she reminded herself she was a journalist and not a novelist, and people didn't actually float anywhere except in the water.

Nonetheless, her mother had definitely been floating down the stairs.

Phoebe didn't feel like floating but she definitely was looking forward to the day . . . for a change.

As soon as breakfast was over, she slid her recorder into one pocket, her notebook and pen in the other, and headed off down the beach toward the Point and Charley Wilkins.

She hardly noticed that the day had turned overcast; she was too absorbed in her plans on how to draw Charley into conversation. But she knew what to do: give him a chance to volunteer information.

Most people she interviewed couldn't wait to tell the world about their past, their latest project, their plans for the time ahead, their dreams and sometimes their pipe dreams. It was all important to them, and because of that, it was important to Phoebe.

Sometimes she ran across someone whose story she had to coax from them. She sensed that Charley was going to be one of those.

She walked down the lane to the path that led to the fish camp. It was darker and cooler beneath the pines, definitely a potential storm on the horizon. Hopefully it would hold off until she was home again.

At the end of the path, she slowed down, took a few organizing breaths, and stepped into the clearing. She'd expected to find Charley hard at work, but the place looked deserted. There was a heavy ceramic plate on the old picnic table at the edge of the clearing. Two gulls high-stepped their way across the wood, squabbling over a scrap of bread that she hoped was left over from his breakfast and not his breakfast itself.

"Charley?" she called, not too loudly. She didn't want to startle him or appear too aggressive. She wanted him to be glad to see her.

It was crazy, this thing that came over her. She could tell from the get-go—most of the time anyway—how a story would unfold.

Whether it would fizzle out or be relegated to two inches of column as a PSA. Then there were those that made her blood race with anticipation, the hunger to draw the best from those she was interviewing and from herself.

So what if she didn't cover world-shattering events? Didn't scramble to keep up with the latest news cycle? Some bit of newness that devoured space and time as if it were the only thing happening in the world and everyone's future depended on it. It created excitement, fear, even hatred for a few hours only to be replaced by the next big thing the next day or the day after.

Phoebe had always believed the real news was close to where people lived. The things that made a real difference in their daily lives, could shatter their local world, or save it, while in the distance the news "cycle" endlessly churned and changed and moved on whether the problems were solved or not.

Maybe she was naive. After her disaster with Gavin, she was pretty sure she was.

"Charley?" She peered around an old paneled truck that had materialized since the last time she'd been here. Picked her way past the faded psychedelic hippie caravan and tried to look inside, but the windows were covered. She poked about the vans, looking for Charley and peeking into windows trying to catch a glimpse of his handiwork.

The VW van door was open, so she figured Charley must be inside. She stopped a few feet away. "Charley? Are you in there? It's me, Phoebe."

No answer. She listened and, not hearing any movement within, took a quick look around, and poked her head inside.

Charley wasn't there and the interior was in shadow, but she could make out a counter along the far side, built-in storage below. At the back was a loft, where maybe a mattress would be. It would be a perfect bed as long as the occupant wasn't too tall.

She leaned in to see the side nearest her. It had been completely ripped out except for a tangle of mechanical things that she imagined would become some kind of heating or cooking apparatus. And was that plumbing? A tiny house on wheels.

"You back again?"

Phoebe yelped and jumped back. "Good morning. I called out but you didn't answer."

He looked from her to the interior of the van.

"Several times," she added.

"Could be I didn't hear you. Could be I was hoping if I didn't answer you'd go away."

Well, she hadn't been expecting this. He'd been a lot friendlier the last time she'd come here.

"Is this a bad time?"

He squinted at her. He was wearing baggy camo pants and a faded blue T-shirt with a rip in the sleeve that looked like it had been made by a nail. "For what?"

"I thought you could show me around and what you're working on. Tell me a little about how you got started doing this. Inez said you refurbish these old heaps for housing veterans."

"Yeah."

"How does that work? It looks like this one is going to have gas and water."

Charley walked past her and climbed into the van.

She took that as an invitation and followed him. She'd learn soon enough whether it was or not.

The moment she stepped into the van, he turned to face her. Of course he couldn't stand upright and neither could she, so they hunched over, looking at each other like a couple of disgruntled turtles.

"I guess you get used to it," she said.

"It's cozy, and better than the streets."

"Definitely. When did you start doing this?"

"Working on cars?"

"Making cars into homes."

He reached past her and picked up a large wrench. "A few years now."

Phoebe breathed out a wary sigh. "What made you start?"

"Hold this." He positioned a piece of pipe in her hands and guided it into a metal cylinder. "A buddy and me were gone down to Portland, and we see guys, women too, living on the street after giving their everything to serve their country.

"We decided we oughta do something. His family owns one of those campsites up the coast a ways. Got land and the hookups but can't afford the liability insurance. So he made an arrangement to let vets camp there until they can be placed in a proper home, none of that shelter stuff. People need their own space. Some of the sites even have a water view."

His mouth quirked and Phoebe tried to decide if he'd just made a joke.

"Keep it steady," he said, and plied the wrench to the other end of the pipe.

"But he didn't have the RVs and campers," Phoebe said, nudging him to continue.

"Nope. But I had an old utility van I'd bought for parts. And figured we could gut it, insulate it, put in some basic amenities. He already had the hookups. I just needed to fit 'em out with something to hook to them.

"But first I had to get the engine running to get it up there; it's a couple hours away. And it was only the one. Some guys scored their own transport. But that's no good for the winters. They need to be insulated. So I took those and fitted them out, too."

"But how did you end up with all these different vehicles?" He was amazing. She really wanted to turn on her tape recorder or take notes but she wouldn't take the chance of turning him off.

"You sure are nosey," Charley said.

"I'm interested. Where did all these others come from?"

Charley sighed. "People started to donate, or I found a real good deal and I'd bring them here to gut the innards and build up from there. Another guy was doing the same thing out west somewhere, so I got in contact with him and he gave me some pointers on how to streamline the process."

"How many vans and trucks have you converted?"

"You can let go now."

Phoebe loosened her grip on the pipe. "How many?"

"Not near enough. Can always use more. The three I got there are already spoken for."

"Do you sell them?"

"Nope. Walter, my friend with the site, sends somebody down

to pick them up. He's got a whole system up there. It's not a free ride. Don't you think that."

Phoebe shook her head.

"He gets them hooked up with the VA, with health services and job placements and all that. It's all there, but a lot of paperwork. It's hard to navigate, especially when you don't have even a table to fill out forms on.

"And you have to be able to meet certain criteria to get a spot. Drug free or willing to sign up for a program. Able to take care of yourself physically, or they have to try to find you a spot in a facility. Not everybody's willing to go through the drill. So it isn't perfect, but at least Walter can give them a place to themselves."

The rat-tat of the first raindrops sounded on the roof.

Charley slowly twisted his head from his stooped position to look up at the roof. The rat-tat soon gave way to a flood of drops. He listened for a moment, then said, "It'll pass."

Then he turned back to Phoebe. "Tyler says you write for a newspaper."

"I did," Phoebe said. "It folded just last week. I'm currently out of a job."

"Good."

She jerked up, banged her head on the roof.

"What I mean is, I don't want you writing no articles about me."

"Why? You're a really interesting man, and you're doing good. The world should know."

"I'm just doing what I do. No more, no less. I'm one of the

lucky ones, and it's our duty to take care of those who weren't so lucky."

Phoebe nodded. She looked at this aging man, living alone in an old shack, working on cars for others, no family around him, and wondered how he could think he was lucky. But she knew. You only had to listen to him to know that.

And he was right.

"I won't publish until you say it's okay. I promise not to even show it to anybody until you say it's okay."

"Guess that's okay, then."

The rain was letting up and Phoebe thought she should leave before the next wave came, but she was reluctant to go just now when he was open and communicative.

"But just think, if people knew what you were doing, they might give more vans."

"Got all I can handle."

"People would volunteer to help."

"Don't want help. Well, you can help. Since you're unemployed. It'll give you something to do. Can't pay you."

Taken aback, Phoebe opened her mouth, then realized it might be exactly what she needed.

And she also realized something else. She had just fallen into the same trap as Gavin. *What you're doing isn't important enough. You need to get more—more cars, more financing, more news coverage.* And she was horrified at herself.

"You'll let me help you work on the vans?"

"Yeah. I'm starting on that new panel truck tomorrow. Needs a lot of demo, but you look like a strong girl."

"I am." She eased back. "But I better get back home now. They don't know where I am. I'll come back tomorrow, then."

"Okay with me."

"Then . . . see ya." She jumped down from the VW, but Charley had gone back to work.

She crossed the clearing, past the garage where today all three bay doors were shut.

She was so immersed in thought about Charley and his friend, Walter, and the veterans living in campers in an old campsite that she was surprised to find Ty's SUV coming down the lane toward her. It stopped beside her just as the next barrage of raindrops began.

Ty reached over and opened the passenger door. "Get in, I'll drive you home."

"I won't melt."

"I hope not, since Dad said we have to bring a casserole to dinner tonight."

"What?" She got into the SUV and Ty turned it around to return home.

"Yep, I don't know what your mother said to him, but he announced that we had to take a casserole to your house tonight. As penance, maybe?"

Phoebe looked over at him and smiled. But her attention was arrested by several plastic transparent garbage bags holding empty white plastic milk jugs that filled the back seat.

"Recycling? The center is back the other way."

"Yeah, I know. I just came from there."

"You went to recycling to un-recycle?"

"Why recycle when you can reuse?"

"True. What are you going to use them for?"

"You sure ask a lot of questions."

"Charley said I was nosey."

"That, too."

"I'm a journalist, remember? Though Charley said since I was unemployed, I could help him refurbish the vans."

"As long as that's all it is," Ty said.

"Yikes! What is that supposed to mean?"

He turned into the drive toward their two houses. "Just don't make Charley an object, okay?"

"Of what?"

"Your journalistic enthusiasm."

"I thought I was making him a subject."

Ty stopped the SUV at the back of the Sutton house. "Seriously. His life is a fine balance. He doesn't need to be upset by undue publicity and people coming to gawk."

"And are you Charley's self-appointed therapist, too?"

"No, but I care about my friends."

Phoebe grinned. "Sure you're not out to save the world?"

"No. And please don't say stuff like that about me."

Whoa, she hadn't seen that reaction coming. "I won't ever say anything at all about you," Phoebe assured him. "Since I only report the truth."

"What's *that* supposed to mean?"

"Nothing, just tit for tat. I won't make assumptions about you or Charley. I wouldn't use him for my own career gain, if that's what you're thinking. I wouldn't use anyone."

"I'm not thinking that. I'm just watching out for Charley."

"Well, you don't have to with me. I just thought if people knew more about him they might want to help. And I would never print anything without the interviewee's consent. If I even had a place to sell an article. Which I don't. Thanks for the ride."

She got out but stopped with her hand on the car handle. "I suppose you're not going to tell me what the milk jugs are for."

"Not today. I'm on a tight schedule. I have to get these down to Charley's and back before Dad wakes up from his nap."

"But you're still coming to dinner?"

"If I'm still invited."

She just gave him a look.

"Not quite yet," he said.

"What? What are you talking about?"

"The look you just gave me. Keep working at it. You haven't quite perfected that Sutton eye roll. But I'm sure with practice . . . You're getting wet. Go inside."

She shut the door and he backed out of the drive. Phoebe ran into the house, but she stopped at the kitchen window to watch him drive away through the rain.

The rain had stopped and the sun was shining when Ruth came through the kitchen door. She was carrying two bakery boxes and wearing a smile.

Phoebe thought they all breathed a sigh of relief. They were just finishing up a late lunch and discussing plans for the afternoon.

"I hope Inez is paying you in more than pastries," Vera said, taking the boxes from Ruth. "Or we'll all have to take up exercise. And I might hurt myself when I jiggle when I should be out jogging. Coffee?"

"I just need to take a little nap," Ruth said, stretching.

Vera gave her a look.

"A power nap, fifteen minutes and I'm good."

"First have lunch," Alice said. "There's chicken salad and fresh fruit cocktail in the fridge."

Phoebe jumped up. "I'll fix you a plate."

Ruth gave in and sat down, while Vera perused the contents of the bakery box.

"I hope we're planning on having dinner at home tonight," Ruth said. "Because I invited—well, sort of ordered—Lars and Ty to join us."

"Well, well, well," Vera said. "When did this happen?"

"I came down to get a cup of tea last night. I was so wound up about getting up early that I couldn't get to sleep. And I saw Lars sitting out on the bench. I forgot that he and Delores used to sit there. He really misses her. It's made him blind to the pain his sons are going through."

"You told him that?" Alice asked, shaking her head at the brownie Vera was offering.

"In so many words. I didn't want to push him back into that cloud he's encased himself in. I told him to bring a casserole. I don't know if he'll come. But we should at least try."

"I agree," Alice said. "Steaks on the grill? I remember Lars used to enjoy those."

"Do we still have a grill?" Ruth said.

"It should be in the shed," Alice said. "If it isn't, we can certainly buy a new one. I don't want Lars moving and selling off his house to some HGTV addict. I'd rather have a grouch as a neighbor than what's happened to the McMurphys' house down the road. Such a lovely old home." Alice sighed.

And Phoebe got another germ of an idea. What the race to the biggest and most impressive lifestyles by outsiders did to a local community.

The old ways pushed out by the new—longtime neighbors moving away; memories slowly fading; the depth of understanding and love for the land being buried beneath an onslaught of outside acquisition.

But it seemed that every job opening she'd seen thus far in her search was for media news or big syndicated newspapers with a decent salary, or independently owned local newspapers that could only offer a pittance if they offered a salary at all.

There had to be something in between. Something that connected people, not blasted them with breaking news twenty-four seven. She didn't want to do televised reporting, a sound bite of human interest between makeup and microphones and commercial breaks. She didn't want to do podcast stories of unknown people to unknown listeners whose lives would never intersect.

She was a human-interest writer. And dammit—

"Phoebe!"

Phoebe jumped. "Sorry?"

Her grandmother pointed to the napkin stand at Phoebe's end of the table. "I asked if you could hand your mother a napkin."

Phoebe snatched one of the napkins and passed it down to Ruth. Here they were, three generations of women. Each with her own tie to the house, the beach, the experiences of a lifetime. Charley making a difference at the end of a little island. Even Inez and the bakery.

That's what she should be writing about. That's what she *would* write about. She would just have to figure out a way to make it all work.

After Ruth finished eating, she headed upstairs, and Phoebe, Alice, and Vera went outside to search the shed for the old grill. They found it in the farthest corner in the back, and wheeled it out into the sunlight.

The three of them stood, arms akimbo, studying the old rectangular grill, large enough for a dozen steaks.

"Like the three witches in *Macbeth*," Vera said. "Can either of you conjure a clean grill with a propane tank?"

"There's nothing wrong with this one," Alice said. "It's fed hundreds of people over the years. It'll feed a few more. We'll just have to remember to get charcoal when we go out for the steaks."

"Do they even still make charcoal?" Phoebe asked.

"Of course they do," Alice said. "Island Market always keeps it in stock for us purists."

"It isn't exactly healthy," Phoebe said.

"For God's sake, Phoebe," Vera snapped. "Don't go off on a tangent about carcinogens. We could get hit by a freight train on our way to the store before we ever light the damn thing."

The heat shot to Phoebe's stomach. "I'm sorry, I—"

"Vera!" exclaimed Alice. "What's gotten into you?"

"Sorry, sorry. I was just joking. Accept my apologies please, Phoebe."

Phoebe nodded. But she was shocked at her great-aunt's reaction. That was no joke. It was strident and harsh, not at all like her usual kidding. There was something going on with Great-aunt Vera. She was sure of it.

Phoebe's stomach hit bottom. She didn't even want to consider the possibility that Vera or any of them might be sick. She refused to do it. As if not thinking it could make it go away.

Chapter 15

$\mathcal{V}$era and Alice made it to the store and back without getting hit by a freight train. Phoebe scrubbed the grill until it looked usable, and Ruth woke up from her power nap in time to make the Sutton marinade.

Everything was ready by six o'clock. The grill was fired up, giving them just enough time for a preprandial cocktail before the charcoal was ready for the steaks. The fridge was stocked optimistically with beer, red wine was breathing on the counter, and the margaritas were chilled.

Now all they needed were their "gentlemen callers," as Vera, who had already started on happy hour, dubbed Ty and Lars. "I'll just go light the citronella candles and check on the fire," she said, and carried her glass outside.

Phoebe really hoped Lars would come tonight, though it was bound to be a little uncomfortable at first. But she could tell it meant a lot to her mother, and she knew it would help Ty in his effort to get his father interested in living again.

But six came and went and they didn't arrive. Ruth poured

Alice a glass of wine and a margarita for herself and Phoebe. They all went out to the lawn to wait.

Ruth had just decided to knock on the Harkens' door when Ty appeared, backing out of the kitchen door holding a casserole dish between two oven mitts.

"Sorry, but it took longer than I expected to heat this thing through. Not sure what it is." He put the casserole on a trivet placed on the picnic table for the purpose, and looked back at his house.

They all looked, too, eyes trained on the Harkens' kitchen door as if it were a limo at Oscar night.

"Can I get you a beer, Ty?" Ruth said, releasing them all from the spell.

"I'll help," Vera said, and steered Ruth into the house.

Phoebe and Alice bustled about the table. Only Ty stood watching the kitchen door.

Ruth returned with a beer and the wine bottles just as the door opened and Lars Harken stepped out.

Phoebe heard Ruth's sigh of relief. Phoebe did a double take. Gone was the stooped-over, shabbily dressed invalid of the last week. He'd shaved and his clothes were clean and ironed. His hair was still long but it was parted and combed back from his face.

"Come on over," Ruth called over her shoulder in one of those perfect hostess gestures guaranteed to make an awkward guest feel less aware of the spotlight that was inevitably being cast on him.

The others took the cue and kept moving.

Lars finally made it to the table.

"Thanks for inviting us," he said awkwardly.

"We expect you two every night," Alice said. "Unless you have other plans, of course. But tonight, Lars, we need your expertise with the grill."

"Sure thing," he said, and went automatically to where the grill was. And Phoebe remembered other nights, other dinners, the kids running around, the women chatting and laughing, and her dad and Lars stationed at the grill.

She glanced at Ruth to see if she was remembering, too. But her mother had turned away to toss the salad.

As dinner progressed and everyone exclaimed over the steaks and the desserts, Lars opened up considerably. He even joined in on the conversation, subdued but not morose or angry as he'd been since Phoebe and Ruth had been there.

Phoebe occasionally glanced over at Ty. He was watching his dad with a combination of caution and relief. He was more quiet than usual, as if he were afraid of shattering the delicate balance.

But when Vera announced that they were going to play Parcheesi, Phoebe came to the rescue.

"Too many people. Ty and I will do the dishes, you guys go ahead."

She hadn't gotten the whole sentence out of her mouth before Ty stood and began stacking the dessert plates.

Phoebe gathered whatever was left and followed him inside, passing Vera on her way back from the games cabinet.

"Have fun." She winked at Phoebe.

Phoebe rolled her eyes in response and followed Ty into the

kitchen, where he had deposited his dishes on the counter and was slumped against the sink.

"Parcheesi," he said, looking bemused.

"It's a trip down memory lane," Phoebe said. "We used to always play board games after dinner, remember?"

"Not really."

"Probably because you were always off in the ether. Everybody had to yell to get your attention when it was your turn."

"Huh. Do you want to wash or dry?"

"Wash."

He moved over and pulled a dish towel off the rack.

Phoebe filled half of the sink with hot sudsy water. She slipped her hands into Granna's rubber gloves and caught Ty smiling at her.

"Keep your eyes off these gloves. They're reusable."

He laughed and made a show of preparing to dry. "So how's the job search coming?"

Phoebe bobbled the dessert plate she was holding. She'd actually forgotten to angst for a while during dinner. "I've been sending out virtual applications, beefing up some articles I was working on. Putting the 'best of' my published articles into a portfolio. A virtual portfolio, and . . . Ugh, all the 'virtual' interaction just doesn't really resonate with me, you know?"

"Yeah, but it does cut down on a lot of unnecessary time-consuming chatter. And paper."

"You know what I like about local news?" Phoebe asked.

Ty shook his head and took a dish from her.

"It's working face-to-face. Getting to know the people you're writing about, the community that it affects." She waved the dish brush at him, splashing suds. "The personal aspect, that quiet moment when you connect with someone whose life might touch yours."

"Yeah," he said.

"Yeah," she echoed. "Everyone says local news is dead. That's just wrong. Media these days is too big, the news dire, and the people reported on have to be famous or infamous, with maybe a second or two dedicated to a little someone somewhere doing something special squeezed in before the commercial break. Print is better, but it tends to shove those people into three inches of type between 'more important' news."

"Yeah," he repeated.

"You wouldn't be interested in giving more useful advice than 'Yeah'?"

"I'm just agreeing. Act local, think global. It's the same in anything, the microcosm reflects the macrocosm. I think we've been duped by the trickle-down principle."

Phoebe stopped washing completely and stared at him.

"Not politics," Ty continued. "But like if the local stuff is messed up, it's not going to get better by trying to fix it higher up. You have to go to the source. The— Sorry."

"Don't be, I totally get it."

"You do?"

"Yes, it's people at the grass roots, doing what they do. My town didn't have a physical therapy facility that could do aqua therapy. So this one man helped changed that. He was making a three-hour round trip three times a week to give his daughter aqua therapy. She'd been a competitive swimmer, then was in a car accident.

"I was covering the town hall meeting when he spoke. Afterwards, we talked for a bit—lots of times, actually—and the talks became an article. It got picked up by other local papers. And things started happening. The town in conjunction with the local college raised the money for a joint-use community pool, and the pool was built, and now it serves a college swim team, swimming lessons, therapy, and is open to the community to use in its off hours. They would still be arguing about doing an expensive ten-year study if Mr. Jenkins hadn't pushed because of his daughter. And the *Sentinel* did its part. That's news that counts."

The smile he gave her made her wonder what he was thinking, but before she could ask, an uproar broke out from the Parcheesi players.

"You rat," Granna cried.

"Nah-nah," Vera taunted.

"Those two," said Phoebe.

A burst of laugher followed the exchange. And for a moment time seemed to stop.

Ty glanced toward the door. Back at Phoebe. "Was that my dad?"

Phoebe nodded.

The expression on Ty's face was so open and thankful, she wanted to hug him. Of course, she caught herself just in time. Still, she was happy to have witnessed that moment when the barriers slipped down. She wished Lars could have seen it, too.

The game ended and Phoebe realized that the dishes had been washed, dried, and put away while she and Ty had been talking. She couldn't even remember what all they talked about, just knew that it had been easy, comfortable, natural. And they were standing way too close.

She glanced over to him. Was he feeling the same thing? Or was he off thinking about potable water?

He must have felt her watching him, because he turned, still holding the dish towel. "What?"

Phoebe shook her head. "We're finished."

"Huh." He looked at the counter, into the sink, back at her. "We are."

They both stood for a second, looking at each other and then looking away. Then Ty put down the towel. "Guess we'd better get back out there."

They joined the others, and father and son fell back into their normal contentious relationship.

There was an invisible wall that seemed to keep them distant from each other. More like strangers thrown together at a party where they both knew the host but not each other. And at this rate they never would.

Over the next few days, life settled down into a routine—as routine-like as things ever got with Great-aunt Vera around. It was also very productive, for Phoebe, at least, and she suspected for her mother, who left for work at the bakery each morning before six and returned sometime after lunch, later and later each day, with a spring in her step, a lift to her chin, and a bakery bag in each hand.

Phoebe spent the mornings rewriting and editing articles that she'd never finished or hadn't made the cut, but ones that she deemed still timely. She tested the waters of available journalism positions, even heard from one or two, but they weren't what she was looking for. Though to be perfectly honest, she wasn't sure she knew what she *was* looking for and had to fall back on the old "I'll know it when I see it."

Sometimes she'd take her laptop down to the beach and write her thoughts to the counterpoint of the waves and Ty's hammering. Occasionally she'd look back toward the two houses and see him perched precariously on the roof installing new shingles over old, their deep color broadcasting like open maws against the faded older ones. And she assumed that he had lost the roof-replacement argument.

Around midmorning, she would find herself wandering up the beach, portable notebook and gel pen in her pocket, to talk to Charley.

One morning Phoebe was sitting at the picnic table frowning at her laptop when Ty hurried over.

"Hey, are you busy?"

She shielded her eyes with her hand and looked up at him. "If you call worrying about being unemployed and not finding a thing that looks promising 'busy.'"

"Well, I can take care of the unemployment thing at least for the next hour or so. Charley had to go to the mainland for some appointments and I need an extra set of hands."

Phoebe closed the laptop. "Then I'm your man."

"That bad, huh?"

"Pretty much."

"Well, the pay is shit, but I'll let you in on the mystery of the plastic milk jugs."

Phoebe jumped up. "Let me just put my laptop inside."

"You'd better change into some muck-about clothes and shoes, and meet me back here in a couple of minutes."

"How mucky?"

"Pretty mucky."

"Not a problem. I can do muck." She hurried into the house.

Five minutes later she returned, wearing a pair of old cargo shorts that she sometimes used for hiking and an old T-shirt that she should have thrown out last season. She didn't have any muck-about shoes, so she picked her least favorite pair of running shoes.

She came back downstairs to find Ty talking with Granna and Vera and holding a pair of Granna's Wellingtons.

Phoebe looked suspiciously at the Wellies.

"Last chance to back out," Ty said.

"She wouldn't think of it," Vera said, as Phoebe said, "I wouldn't think of it."

"Thanks," Ty said.

"Don't forget to bring her back," Vera said as they got into Ty's SUV.

"Where are we going?" asked Phoebe when they turned toward town instead of toward Charley's shack on the Point.

"Over to the bay side of the island."

"To the nature park?"

"Yep."

"You're doing something with a carload of plastic milk jugs in the nature park? Isn't that protected land? Are we going to get arrested?"

"Hope not," he said, then took mercy on her and grinned. "I've got a permit. The county has a real problem with trash, both natural and human disregard for nature, especially at the sand beaches around the inlets. The tide rises and picks up not only debris that it had deposited a few hours before but also a few extras, like empty beer bottles, pizza boxes, and that ilk, and carries it out to sea. Which is a bad thing in itself, but it's gotten so bad that it's preventing the natural flow of the water, which in turn floods the surrounding area twice a day. The habitat is not happy."

"And you're adding to the garbage? For some kind of study?" asked Phoebe, wishing she'd brought her notebook; there was bound to be a story here. It was too weird not to be a story.

"Just the opposite. Actually, they jumped at my proposal, even if they thought it sounded a bit far-fetched. They were planning to bring in dredging equipment, but they won't have the budget until July. Until then, they've been relying on posting some DO NOT LITTER signs and sending the park personnel out to pick up the garbage. So they're letting me work on a prototype river sweeper we designed for a project I have in the fall. I'm still adapting it to the particular clime and needed a place bigger than Charley's garage to test it out."

"You asked the county if you could put up stuff and they said yes?"

"Yeah."

"That must have been a nightmare of red tape."

"Usually it is, but I have clout." He thumped his chest in a way that made her laugh.

"Well, good for you. I can hardly wait."

It took nearly twenty minutes to arrive at the protected land entrance. Ty stopped at the ticket booth, where the attendant merely said, "Morning, Ty, your taste in helpers is definitely improving," and waved him on.

"And you know people in high places," Phoebe said.

"That, too."

She had never seen him so carefree—if that was what this mood was.

He pulled to a stop in front of a chained-off maintenance path and jumped out to open the lock. And Phoebe began to think maybe he wasn't kidding about having clout.

He relocked the gate once they were through and they continued down a narrow sand lane flanked by a jungle of head-high underbrush. Phoebe wasn't quite sure where they were going. The park was home to a number of small creeks and streams that flowed into several inlets before emptying into the bay.

A few minutes later the path came to an end. Ty pulled to a stop and cut the engine.

"Do I really need these?" Phoebe asked, holding up the Wellingtons.

"Only if you're squeamish."

"About what?" she asked.

But he had jumped out and was headed toward what looked

like a footpath through the overgrowth. He seemed to have forgotten Phoebe. So she tucked the Wellies under her arm, just in case, and hurried to catch up, thinking the more things changed, the more they stayed the same. Ty still wandering off, lost in his own thoughts, and Phoebe chasing after him.

Only now she understood a little about what he was doing.

She passed small patches of sand that hugged the water and that people had definitely been using as picnic areas and probably more. She had to force herself not to stop and pick up something that looked like a disposable diaper that had caught on a low-lying branch, probably the only thing that kept it from being swept out to sea. Two crushed soda cans were half-buried in the sand.

For a protected area, there was certainly a lot of trash.

She could tell by the smell that they were surrounded by the marshes. Not her favorite smell.

Ty had disappeared up ahead.

She caught up to him about fifty feet before the inlet emptied into the bay. And stopped. Ahead of her, stretched from one bank to the other, was a gigantic tennis net at least six feet high. It was strung across the water and tethered to metal poles on opposite banks.

The net billowed above the waterline, where it was attached at two-feet intervals to the by-now-famous plastic milk jugs. She could see that the net continued below the surface since the milk jugs were being pulled out by the tide.

It looked like an elaborate science fair project.

Ty turned to her with a grin so big that her heart skipped. And then his grin faded as if he'd given too much away. And Phoebe imagined the boy who dreamed different dreams from the other kids. And who was still dreaming those dreams.

"Wow," she said. "That's amazing. But before we go to work, would you explain what exactly it is?"

"It's a prototype for a river sweeper."

"Gotcha. And how does it work?"

"That's the beauty of it: very simply. We of course don't expect it to round up the smaller toxins, but it should be able to filter out the largest pieces as a first defense, so that the water can clear more quickly and be cleaned sufficiently to go through the filtration process."

"And the milk jugs are standing in for . . . ?" She ended with a lift of her voice because she couldn't imagine what they would become. Giant plastic buoys? Drones that could detect debris?

His eyebrows rose. "Milk jugs," he said, as if that answered her question. "Well, milk, juice, water jugs, whatever turns up in the refuse piles."

"Wait," Phoebe said, finally catching on. "This isn't to help the county, but to test your own water-filtration projects."

"Yeah, but it also helps the county, too, while they're waiting to be able to afford their expensive equipment."

"So there's no automation involved at all?"

"Man—and woman and kid—power. In fact, in some of the villages where we've installed similar systems, the women are in charge of the water."

"Makes sense. So people who don't have access to technology would be able to adapt things they use every day to clean the water they depend on."

"Exactly—you send in some high-tech machine, the first time it breaks down, it becomes useless. And since there are usually no trained technicians to maintain it or fix it, and no parts to be had, it becomes a victim to junk collection, or worse. The people in the village we're introducing this one to have to buy drinking water. The rest is trucked in. There's a river close by, but it's downstream from a processing plant. Its runoff is toxic.

"But they have lots of jugs that are being dumped and adding to the problem, since there's no recycling program. They fish; there are always nets. The net is held to the bottom with weights, but anything heavy will do."

"And each one of your projects is adapted to a specific place?"

"Yeah. There is no one-size-fits-all."

"From castoffs to clean water," said Phoebe.

Ty's eyes flashed. "Wow, that would make a good ad."

Phoebe took a little bow and sighed. *All my months of pitching the newspaper to advertisers.*

"Garbage is clogging the rivers of the world," Ty continued. "I mean really clogging. And it's killing the inhabitants. We work with another group that brings in aerating and filtration systems and teaches the locals how to use them. But even then, there's too much garbage that needs to be separated from the source before the machinery is usable. That's where we come in. Send out a recce crew to analyze what usable parts they have access to from everyday castoffs and adapt it to the use."

"Save the planet with a double whammy, recycle and reclaim," said Phoebe.

"Our little bit, anyway."

"And who are the 'we' you keep talking about?"

"I have several crews whose job it is to find sites that can be adapted."

"You personally have crews?"

"It takes every loop to make a chain."

Did he just deflect her question?

"Why does your dad say you're between jobs? Does he know what you do?"

"In a vague way, and actually I am between jobs. I don't need to be on-site again until September. And this gives me a chance to pre-test some ideas in situ instead of in the workshop. Come on, I need to get this cleaned out before the tide changes."

He waded into the water, ankle-deep, knee-deep . . . and when it was up to his thighs, Phoebe tossed her Wellies to the ground and waded in after him. The tide was strong, pulling at her so that it was a struggle not to drift downstream.

She had a million questions to ask him, about the river sweeper, about the places he had helped, but more about why his family didn't seem to appreciate what he did.

Ty was waiting on the far bank and reached down to pull her up to land. They stood for a minute dripping into their shoes while Ty explained what he wanted her to do.

"This is a pretty flimsy structure; the end product will have a better infrastructure with crossbars and stabilizers, but for now, just help me hold the pole upright and pull it across to the other side."

Phoebe nodded.

"Just stand back a little. I have to release the pole and there will be some rebound. As soon as it's free, grab it with both hands and hang on. So will I. Ready?"

Phoebe nodded. *Grab the pole.* Seemed simple enough.

Ty bent down and released whatever was holding it in place. Stood and caught it in both hands as it rebounded, bracing his weight against the pole.

"Now," he called.

Phoebe found a handhold and braced against the pull of water.

Together they began to pull the pole toward the opposite bank. It wasn't easy. Between the tide pulling one way, and the weight of whatever they had collected dragging the net down, they stumbled and fought, bumping shoulders and stepping on each other's feet.

By the time they finally made it back to the other side, Phoebe's arms and legs were shaking, and they both looked like they'd gone for a swim, but they had quite a collection in their net.

Ty hauled the pipe out of the water, where he released the net. Together they dragged the net to higher land.

"We'll have to clean out the net and leave the garbage for the park people to pick up when they make their rounds," he told her. "This is the mucky part. Hold on." He walked away to a large metal box that was anchored to a stone platform and unlocked it. He rummaged inside and came out with two pairs of heavy-duty work gloves. He handed her one pair.

"Have you had your shots?"

"What?" Phoebe looked at the array of things they'd picked up. "This doesn't need Wellies and work gloves, this calls for a full hazmat suit."

"Probably nothing is toxic. You don't have to help with this part."

"I wouldn't miss it for the world," Phoebe retorted and leaned over to wrestle a tree limb from where it had threaded itself through the openings of the net, then tossed it to the side. The limb was followed by clumps of marsh grass and mud, cardboard, cellophane, a pair of work pants, paper, and bottles, all of which they tossed into the pile to be collected.

"And this is all from just twelve hours," Ty said, tossing a muddy backpack onto the pile.

Phoebe followed it with a cracked yellow Frisbee.

When the net was finally free of garbage, they rolled it up and stored it in the box, along with the gloves.

"I only do one tide a day," he explained. "And none on the weekends. Are you okay? Charley carries a little more heft than you."

"Piece of cake," Phoebe said, wondering where she was going to ache the most in the morning.

Ty double-checked everything, then they walked back up the path. Phoebe could tell he was already off thinking whatever he was thinking, but Phoebe was happy just to be walking by his side, enjoying the feeling of accomplishment she hadn't felt in quite a while.

She glanced over to her companion and wondered how anyone could underestimate him.

He wasn't between jobs. He wasn't scatterbrained. He didn't lack ambition.

He was saving the planet one river at a time.

Chapter 16

*P*hoebe and Ruth's weekend visit turned into one week, then two. No one mentioned leaving, and Phoebe began to wonder if her mother planned to ever go back. She knew her father had called her mom, because she'd overheard Ruth tell Granna as much. Phoebe didn't hear if she'd actually spoken to him or not. And she wasn't about to ask. But she thought they must be having some sort of communication because he hadn't tried to call Phoebe again. Unlike her sisters, who had taken to "touching base" each day, which Phoebe had quickly insisted be done by a group text.

Vera, too, seemed to have settled in for the duration. The phone calls she'd been getting were coming more often and at more erratic times. She never mentioned what they were about, but it was taking her longer and longer to get back into her usual frame of mind after each one.

Phoebe asked Alice about it, but Alice said, "Whatever it is, it's none of our business. Either it's not that important or she's waiting until the proper time to tell us."

"That sounds ominous," Phoebe said as her skin crawled with unease.

"Not something you should worry about," Alice said, but while her words were reassuring, the eyes behind them weren't.

Phoebe tried not to worry. She'd just settled into a place of optimism. With her résumés floating around in the Ethernet, she was just happy to have a supportive place to stay while waiting for the next chapter of her life to begin. Sometimes she would feel a surge of panic, or a stab of anger that she'd been so taken in by Gavin. But all in all, things were looking up. But not if Vera or Granna were sick.

Every morning Ruth would go to the bakery, and every afternoon she returned home flushed and slightly disheveled, bearing boxes of fresh bakery goods and looking more satisfied and alive than Phoebe had seen her in a long time.

Which made Phoebe wonder how she had missed the gradual deterioration of her mother and father's marriage. Of course, she'd been so busy trying to save the paper that she hadn't even seen the collision course of her own engagement.

Alice seemed pleased to have her family around and was "using the extra hands" to reorganize the pantry and several closets, occasionally calling on Ty to lend some muscle to the heavier items. He was invariably accompanied by Lars, who told him how to do it.

On cooler days, they would troop up to the attic and spend an hour moving things around since Alice refused to throw anything away.

"I'm not a pack rat," she would say every time Vera pointed to some abandoned piece of the past. "I only keep the important things. They just need dusting twice a year."

So they dusted—old suitcases, a lamp that had belonged to a local suffragette and was at least a hundred years old, a passel of fishing rods that had belonged to her grandfather. And stacks and stacks of plastic bins, color-coded and carefully labeled.

One held Alice's wedding dress wrapped in yellowing tissue, which she let them peek at without taking out of the box. Souvenirs, old toys, and memorabilia were stacked neatly on shelves under the eaves.

Phoebe found a box of old photo albums and insisted on carrying it downstairs. After dinner that night, everyone crowded together on the old chintz couch, drinks in hand, heads together, poring over the old pictures. They had some good laughs over Vera and Alice as teenagers posing for the camera. And some groans over later ones of the Harken and Adams children.

From Ty: "I remember those two ponytails sticking out from the side of your head. You could tell you were coming from a mile away."

"Is that why you were always so hard to find?" Phoebe said.

Ty pretended to fend off a blow. "For my own preservation. I've never known anybody to ask so many questions."

"And she grew up to be a great newswoman because of it," Vera added. "We have the plaques and trophies to prove it."

"An unemployed newswoman," Phoebe mumbled. Vera patted her hand. Phoebe turned the page to a portrait of the two families together, the kids looking impatient and anxious to get back to their games, Alice and Henry standing next to Ruth and Ron. And next to him was Lars with his arm around Delores, who was smiling happily at the camera.

For a moment no one seemed to breathe, then Lars said, "That was the summer the boys decided to build a raft and float down the inlet. The tide was going out and they were almost to the ocean before we caught up with them."

"I remember," Ruth said with a shudder. "We were so worried they'd capsize once they hit the open water."

"One of Ty's cockamamie ideas," Lars said.

"At least it floated," said Ty. He glanced at Phoebe.

She wondered if Lars knew about Ty's latest "cockamamie" use of that inlet.

And while they were bantering, Alice smoothly turned the page.

In the afternoons Vera insisted on taking field trips. And since Lars's need to nap had miraculously disappeared, he would often accompany them. Ty was harder to coax into joining in. Phoebe knew he would rather have the time to himself to work on his own projects or to help Charley with the vans. But he usually caved under their cajoling and came along.

One afternoon, they trod silently through the historic society, which was housed in a stuffy cottage at the edge of the shopping district. They dutifully looked at each artifact and fishing document until they were all sneezing from the dust and mold, and decamped thankfully to the sunny parking area and the local ice cream truck.

The next day they climbed up to the lighthouse and looked for buildings they recognized on the mainland. The lighthouse was small and placed on a point of land about equidistant along the shore of the island. It was surrounded by grass and walking paths dotted by benches, picnic areas, and a telescope that looked over the waves.

Lars was watching Ty, who, true to form, had wandered away from the group.

He sighed. "That boy is still wandering off like he always did."

They all turned to watched Ty, who suddenly bent down and peered into something that looked like a drain pipe. Phoebe had to admit, the guy had a one-track mind; no doubt that piece of piping held the possible kernel of a new idea. But she didn't think Lars Harken would ever understand.

"Running all over the place doing stuff that will never get him ahead. For people who can't even help themselves. He went to MIT, for hell's sake. He oughta be head of some corporation by now, rolling in the cash, settled down and raising a family. But no, he's still tromping around collecting garbage out of the water. They have machines for that. What a waste. I don't know why the boy can't settle down and be happy."

Phoebe wanted to stand up for Ty, but she didn't want to make things more difficult for him if she said the wrong thing, so she just kept her mouth shut.

Vera felt no such compunction. "Maybe he's happy the way he is."

Lars harrumphed. "How could he be; he's alone."

Almost every night the two families got together for dinner, and soon the supply of casseroles began to dwindle. Evidently, once word had gotten out about the new arrangements, the husband hunters had become less enthusiastic about feeding their prey.

They learned the reason why one afternoon when Ruth burst into the kitchen, deposited her bakery boxes on the table, and stood with hands fisted at her hips.

Phoebe, Vera, and Alice looked up from the bushel of farmers market peas they were shelling.

"Can you believe it?" Ruth started without introduction. "Lucy Goode came into the bakery just as I was leaving and asked me straight-out if Ron and I were still married."

She waited for a reaction from the others. Not getting one, she continued. "Implying that the reason for Lars's disinterest in the ladies of the neighborhood coincided with me coming to the island." She paused for breath. "She didn't even buy anything, just practically asked me what my intentions were." Ruth slumped into a chair. "I was mortified."

Vera got up and got her a glass of water. "Next time someone has the impertinence to suggest that," Vera told her, "tell them I'm the one who has my sights on Lars. The difference in our ages should keep their minds off of you." She frowned in thought. "Does that make me a cradle robber or a cougar, I wonder?"

"Makes you a crazy old woman," Alice said.

Vera made a face.

That did earn a little chuckle from Ruth, which she immediately cut off. "But please don't tell Lars. It's too embarrassing. And so wrongheaded."

From behind Ruth's head, Vera raised her eyebrows at Alice,

who immediately frowned her into not saying whatever was on her mind to say.

A couple of nights later, after the Harkens had gone home after dinner and Ruth, Alice, and Vera had gone inside, Phoebe lingered in the yard curled up on the chaise. It was dark now . . . and quiet, and Phoebe just sat there trying to enjoy listening to the waves and the crickets while trying not to think about the perilous state of her life.

She'd almost succeeded when she heard a phone ring from inside the house. She recognized the ring by now. Vera's cell.

The ring was followed by Vera bursting out the side door. She walked right past Phoebe without seeing her.

"Dr. Ivan. Thank you for calling." Vera listened for a while.

Phoebe held perfectly still, caught between trying to slink away and staying there and listening to Vera's conversation.

"Are you sure? Of course you are . . . How much time do I have?"

Phoebe flinched and tried not to breathe.

"No, I appreciate you telling me. No, I don't know whether I'll come or not. I'm at the beach at my family's home. Just an hour or so away. Yes, that's why I'm here. I can't decide whether to come there or stay here and let it all end as we planned."

The end. The end? She'd planned her own demise? Phoebe refused to believe it. She was only hearing Vera's side of the conversation, but it had to be bad news.

"Yes, I'll let you know. Soon. Yes, I understand that I may only have a few days left. Thank you."

Vera ended the call, and Phoebe tried to make herself invisible and pretend she was asleep at the same time.

But instead of going back into the house, Vera stood on the edge of the lawn for a minute, then walked down the slope to the deserted beach.

Phoebe pressed her hands to her abdomen to stop the waves of nausea. What should she do? Did Granna know? Did Ruth? Should she tell?

Phoebe sat in the dark, indecisive. Should she tell the others what she'd overheard? What if she had misconstrued the conversation? Should she keep it to herself until she knew for certain? She tried to think of times when Vera might have said something that would point toward her imminent demise. *The bucket list.* Alice said it was a joke. But it didn't sound like a joke tonight.

Phoebe's feet headed for the beach before she could stop them. She slowed down, though, when she saw Vera sitting on a piece of driftwood in the sand.

Her arms were wrapped around her bent legs; her chin rested on her knees. A mere silhouette in the dark. A shadow of despair.

Phoebe waited, not knowing quite what to do, whether to sit down beside her or tiptoe silently back to the house and pretend she hadn't heard or seen. But she trod slowly over the sand to sit down beside her great-aunt.

Vera didn't seem startled by her sudden appearance. Just turned her head to acknowledge Phoebe's presence, then turned it back to the sea.

They sat there for a long time not speaking, until Phoebe thought she couldn't stand it any longer.

"It's beautiful, isn't it?" Vera said, her voice sounding like a loudspeaker in the night. "Truly one of my favorite beaches in all the world . . . and I've seen a lot."

Phoebe's throat felt thick and tight. For once in her life, she didn't know whether to keep silent or press Vera to talk.

The minutes slipped by.

"One night we were on the coast in Chile, not a soul around. Not a light from earth. That night the stars were so thick they looked like bunches of baby's breath in the sky. It was amazing. I've never seen so many stars. I mean, stars have their place, they're there night after night, year after year, for eternity. You expect them to be there, but not that night. As we watched, one of them flared and died. And you couldn't even tell where it had been."

A chill crept up Phoebe's spine.

"Gone and not missed among all those stars. Scientists have a name for night skies like that. But no one that night cared one whit about what it was called or why it happened. To all of us it was a gift, which we accepted wholeheartedly and with reverence.

"Sometimes it's best not to know the how or the why of things but just to accept them. Accept them gracefully and gratefully." Vera took a long breath. "I always wondered about that star. How it would be to cease to exist while the others lived on."

Phoebe held her breath, willing herself not to burst into tears, but to be strong for Vera. For them all.

"It doesn't seem fair."

Is that why you came back, so you wouldn't have to die alone?

Vera stood abruptly, brushed off the seat of her slacks. "Don't know why I'm even talking about stars. I suddenly feel the need of a summer-night hot chocolate. What about you?"

Phoebe stood. "Okay." It was all she could manage.

She had to practically run to keep up with Vera's long strides back to the house. She didn't know what to think.

"Aunt Vera, is something wrong? Are you okay?"

"I'm hunky-dory, Phoebe."

Then the only person who Vera would be staying for—"Did you come back to take care of Granna? Is she sick?"

Vera burst out laughing. "Me, take care of your grandmother? What for? She'll outlive us all."

The same thing Granna had told her about Vera when Phoebe asked why she had come.

"Where did you get such a notion? Because of that nonsense I was jabbering about just now? Well, don't be alarmed. Sometimes I realize how vast the universe is and for a moment I feel very small. Definitely hot chocolate. With a touch of Kahlúa. I wonder if we have any Kahlúa?"

It was near the end of the second week when Phoebe finished polishing the first installment of her Charley story. She had enough material for a series, but she wanted to run the first one by Charley before she spent a lot of time organizing and writing.

If he agreed, maybe she could send it out as a pitch for the rest. But she still needed to find that one thread that would run through the whole article and make it rise above the rest. It was there, she could feel it, but she was working with a recalcitrant interviewee and she didn't want to push too far, too fast.

She slid her laptop into her computer bag and set off for the fish shack. She chose a time when she knew Ty would be there. She couldn't be sure whether he would be an ally or push Charley in the opposite direction. But she needed to know.

When she reached the clearing at the fish shack, she didn't see Charley, but Ty was pacing in front of the panel truck, talking on his cell.

He saw her, raised a finger to tell her to wait, and said a couple of "Uh-huhs" into the phone before ending the call and sliding the phone into his pocket.

"Charley's in the garage working on a Ford Escort somebody brought in."

"A paying job he takes when he isn't working?" Phoebe asked.

Ty grimaced. "Yep." His cell phone rang. He groaned and strode away to answer it, much like Vera had been doing. Phoebe had been acutely aware of Vera's moods since that late-night talk. She'd even made tentative inquiries to her mom and Granna. And learned nothing.

And now Ty. The last time she'd heard him talking on the phone it had been to his brother, and that had been anything but cordial. She was beginning to really hate phone calls.

She wandered toward the garage. She'd never been invited inside before so she stood at the bay door until Charley's head appeared from under the hood.

She waved.

He nodded, grabbed a wrench from a red cart, and dove back under the hood.

She stood in the doorway until she saw Ty coming toward her, but he didn't make it before the cell rang again. He stopped to answer it.

She strained to listen, but he was still too far away to make out anything. Not that it was any of her business, but since when had that stopped her? It hadn't stopped Woodward and Bernstein.

Of course, she doubted Ty's phone call would be breaking news, but you never knew. At least that's what she told herself. What she was really experiencing was pure nosiness.

At first Phoebe thought it might be Lars. But from Ty's gestures, she dismissed that idea. Much too forceful to be dealing with his father.

This call went on for longer than most of the calls she'd been witness to. Maybe there was a glitch in his next project.

And maybe he'll tell me if I ask. She finally sidled over toward the Escort and peered into the hood and over the top of Charley's ravaged head.

He didn't stop working.

Soon, a third head joined them. "Sorry. My publicist just quit."

Phoebe's ears pricked up. "You have a publicist?"

"Not me personally."

Charley kept working, either not interested or not feeling the need to comment.

Phoebe was, however. "Why do you need a publicist?"

"To do publicity," Ty said, and looked under the hood. "That hose looks shot," he added to Charley.

"I've been thinking," Charley said.

"About what?" Phoebe asked, wondering if he was talking about publicists or car hoses.

"Maybe I do need some publicity. About the vans. Like you said."

"You mean you definitely want me to publish the article about you?"

"I don't know, but maybe I could use a few more donations."

"You might get buried in donations," Ty said, "the way she writes."

Phoebe frowned at him. "Is that a good thing or a bad thing? And how do you know how I write?"

"First thing Alice did when I arrived was show me all your articles. You have a real whatever that thing is."

"Grammar? Sentence structure? Humanity?"

"Yeah, all that. And 'voice.' That's the word I was looking for. Hand me that socket wrench and I'll disconnect this piece of garbage."

Charley reached out and grabbed a tool without even looking. He handed it to Ty.

"That won't do," Charley said. "Somebody already called the county on me."

Phoebe switched gears again. The two of them talking was like listening to non sequiturs in stereo.

"The hell they did," Ty said. "On what grounds?"

"An eyesore 'cause of the cars."

"You can't see them from the road or the beach."

"That's what county told 'em." Charley looked up long enough to grin at him. "The county clerk is a vet."

"Good one," Ty said. "I'm thinking Phoebe may be right. She could write a zinger of a story."

"Thanks?" Phoebe said, hoping that had been a compliment.

"We'd just have to build a firewall between you and the well-meaning public."

"Lost me."

"You can't have people dumping all sorts of shit in your yard," Ty explained. "Or other people showing up at all hours begging for a handout. Or being overrun with interested sightseers."

"Maybe it wasn't such a good idea. Just forget it."

"No," Phoebe said. "It can be done. If you wanted to ask for donations, you just have them made through a third party. So that you aren't a part of the acquisition process. I cover these things all the time," Phoebe assured him. "You can have donations funneled through the county or your friend with the campsite. Somebody who could vet the donations, accept the ones that pass muster, and pass them on to you. You could be as selective as you want."

"I don't know . . . No. I don't know." Charley scratched his head and disappeared back under the hood.

"Too much, too soon," Ty suggested.

Phoebe shrugged. "People want to help other people. It could be as simple as a GoFundMe page."

"Charley needs vans, not money."

"Trust me. Everybody can use money. I spent a good percentage of my time working the business angle for the paper." Something that had wasted a huge amount of time the last few years when she should have been promoting her own career. Something she didn't plan to do ever again.

"Let me think about it," Charley said from under the hood. "But now I gotta finish this."

She knew when not to push an interviewee.

"I'll walk you out," Ty said, putting an end to her visit.

Disappointed, she hoisted her computer case to her shoulder and walked with him out of the garage.

"Let it sit with him for a while. He's content to be the way he is. That's not a bad thing."

Wasn't it? Gavin certainly thought so. He'd accused her of being content with local news. And it had stung, but she *was* content with local news. It was important. And so was what Charley was doing. Could it be done on a massive scale? Sure, but it wouldn't have the same human caring, the connection between people. And that, Phoebe thought, was something that everyone needed, and that Charley had to give.

Each river was different, each van, every person who had a story to tell.

It was like the pebble in the water, or the butterfly wings creating a tornado.

"Just don't try to change things, okay?"

"What?"

"I know you mean well, but good ideas are fragile, easily overwhelmed and destroyed."

"Trust me, I know."

"I don't want that to happen to Charley. He's doing good, but because it's him doing his bit."

"I get that. I want him to keep doing that. Just let me see what I can come up with before you judge me."

"I'm not judging you."

"Yeah you are. And I get that, too. You're not exactly the recipient of understanding yourself."

"Touché."

"But that frees you to do what you want, right?"

"The cost is pretty high."

She nodded. What did you say to that?

"I won't do anything that will cause Charley grief."

She waited.

"No sending it out until he's okay with it."

"Absolutely not. I would never. Not until you're both okay with it."

"Deal."

"But just so you know. I'm a professional. I know what I'm doing."

"I've never questioned that. Write your article. Then we'll see."

"I will." What she didn't tell him was that she'd already written the article about Charley. It was all there, slung over her shoulder in her computer case. Just the bare bones until this afternoon. But now she had the angle she'd been looking for.

It was after two when Ruth stood up from her stool and stretched her back. She was spending longer and longer hours at the bakery. With the weekend coming up and the first of the summer people hitting town, they were already busy with extra orders. Inez had turned most of the decorating over to her.

Inez burst through the curtains to the bakery kitchen. "I have Helen Kirschner on the phone. She's having the annual garden show luncheon tomorrow. She heard you were back and wants to know if we can make four dozen of your lemon violet petit fours by then." Inez grimaced. "I can't do it on my own. My hands just won't work that long or that intricately. It would mean staying late tonight. And if you have plans or it's too much, I totally understand. I'll just tell her no."

The annual garden show luncheon. Every pooh-bah on the island and a few from the mainland would be there. Definitely good for business.

Inez waited. Ruth could tell she was trying not to get too hopeful. How could she let her old friend down? She'd stepped up and given Ruth a job, a safe haven, a place where she didn't have to deal with the demands of an errant husband.

Ruth had been creating roses for the last few birthday cakes, but violets . . . "I don't know if I can still do them. The violets."

"Of course you can," Inez said. "It's like riding a bicycle. What do you say?"

Ruth's mind went blank. Should she try? What if she failed? She would wreck Inez's and the bakery's reputation. But if she succeeded, it would be repaying a long-overdue debt she owed.

She took a shaky breath. "Tell her yes. Then come back and let's make a plan."

"Brava!" Inez hurried off to inform Helen, and Ruth called the beach house. Alice picked up.

"Hey, it's me. We just got a last-minute order at the bakery. I'm going be late tonight. Inez really needs me to help out. It's a very important order. For the annual garden show luncheon. They want my lemon violet cakes."

"We'll save you some dinner. Have fun."

Alice hung up. But Ruth just held the cell to her ear. She didn't know why. Maybe she'd been expecting her mother to tell her not to do it. Or that they needed her at home.

Inez came back into the room. "Is everything okay?"

Ruth swallowed. "All set."

"Great, let's just get the cakes in the oven and we'll order dinner in."

The cakes were a simple but elegant recipe and they were soon in the oven. It would be another hour or so before they could finish them with the lemon glaze they would pour over the cakes to create an even, glassy sheen.

They had a quick dinner and then mixed the icing, a large batch of purple, that Ruth fussed over until she'd achieved just the right shade. Then a green batch for the leaves and two more of white and yellow for the tiny centers.

Ruth got out the icing bags and surprised herself by remembering exactly which tips to select. She carried them all over to the decorating table and carefully filled the first bag with purple icing.

When the cakes were cool and they'd been glazed to an even shine, Inez set a row of the little cakes before her.

With a mostly steady hand, Ruth twisted the bag, slanted the tip at just the right angle, and slowly guided the icing into a perfect petal.

Chapter 17

*I*t was late Sunday afternoon, and they'd been to church again at Vera's insistence. It was so out of character that Alice accused her of having a crush on the pastor. Afterward, they'd stopped by their favorite fish restaurant for lobster rolls and then drove back to the beach house.

Ruth and Vera had challenged the Harkens to an afternoon game of croquet the evening before, and the two men had set up the hoops and cleaned off the mallets and were sitting drinking beer when the women stopped in the driveway.

Since the older ones couldn't remember the exact rules and Phoebe and Ty were oblivious that there *were* rules, it quickly devolved into groans and laughs, taunts from the leading team and whoops when anyone made a good stroke.

They were making so much noise that they didn't hear a car drive up and the engine turn off.

Ruth made a perfect shot and raised her mallet in triumph. Then she stopped, the mallet dropping to her side, her face frozen with a look of sheer horror as she stared toward the drive.

Phoebe turned to look and found her father standing at the

edge of the lawn. He was wearing golf pants and a pale pink polo shirt, but his face was bright red, redder than his usual golf course sunburn.

She automatically started toward him, but Granna held her back. "This is between the two of them. You'll have your time later."

"What are you doing here?" Ruth asked.

"I came to talk to you."

"Go ahead."

He finally realized that everyone was still standing there watching them. "Maybe someplace a little less public? I don't think everybody wants to hear this."

"I wouldn't be so sure about that," Vera said under her breath.

Alice stepped on her toe.

"Let's take a walk."

"I'll walk you back to your car," Ruth said. "Anything you have to say to me, you can say to me there."

"Fine." He walked back the way he had come.

"Mom," Phoebe said.

"It's all right, sweetheart. Go on with your game." Ruth followed him out to the drive.

"He didn't even wait for her," Phoebe said.

As soon as they were both out of sight, Vera and Alice rushed inside the house.

Phoebe knew what they were doing. She deliberated for a second. She really shouldn't encourage them to eavesdrop, but . . . "I'll be right back," she told Ty and Lars. She shoved her mallet at Ty and hurried after them.

By the time she reached the kitchen, Granna and Vera were both standing at the sink, perched forward to the open window.

"We're just making sure she's okay," Alice said.

"In case he tries to kidnap her," Vera added.

"Vera, you're not helping." Granna put her arm around Phoebe's shoulders.

Phoebe bit her lip. "How will they ever work it out?"

Phoebe didn't miss the look that passed between her grandmother and great-aunt. They didn't think things could be worked out.

Unless her mom gave in and went home, and Phoebe had to admit she couldn't remember seeing her so happy as she'd been for the last few weeks.

"Shhh!" Vera commanded and they all turned back to the open window.

Fortunately, they only had a partial view because of the parked cars, which was a good thing since that meant neither Ruth nor Ron would catch them spying on them if they happened to turn around.

"I don't understand you," Ron said. "You running off for a weekend to complain about me to your mother is one thing, but you had to drag Phoebe into it? No one knew where you were. I didn't know if you were alive or dead."

"I'm sure one of the girls must have told you I wasn't dead. And I haven't discussed this business, much less complained to anyone."

"When are you coming back? There's stuff rotting in the fridge. The bills are piling up and I don't know where the checkbook is."

"It's the brown one in the top right-hand drawer of your desk."

"Just come home where you belong. I don't know why you ran off that way."

"Because my home was sold against my wishes. You wanted the condo, you can have it."

"Look, I know you're upset. I know you've been mad at me since I bought the damn thing. But trust me, it's better for us. We'll have more time to do the things we like if we don't have all that upkeep."

"Ron, there is no 'us.' You walked into the kitchen one night and told me you didn't love me and that you were leaving. You have a new 'us.' Or so you said, and you can keep her."

"But I didn't mean it. I was just feeling cramped. I needed a change."

Vera snorted. "Guess the new honey didn't work out."

"Shh," Alice warned.

"Well, now you have a change. Enjoy it."

"Ruth, don't be like that. I made a mistake. You know this isn't right, you leaving and running home to your mother."

"Where else should she—" Alice began.

"Shh!!" from Phoebe and Vera.

"Ruthie. We have a good thing. We're comfortable together. Good for each other. We're meant to grow old together."

"You know I always hated it when you called me Ruthie," Ruth said. "I was *too* comfortable with you; I was slowly dissolving, and dammit, I'm not ready to grow old. With anyone. And certainly not with you. It's time for us *both* to move on."

Vera pumped her fist in the air.

Alice grabbed her wrist and pulled it down, adding a scowl for good measure.

"The new honey definitely didn't work out," Vera said. "Didn't take too long for him to come crawling back."

Alice poked her in the ribs.

"Sorry, Phoebe, but you might as well hear it firsthand."

"I know, it's just so sad." Phoebe bit her lip. "But she's right. Even I saw it. I wonder . . ."

"Does it have to be like that?" Vera finished for her. "No it doesn't."

"What would you know?" Alice said.

Vera didn't answer. The sisters moved back to their post at the window.

"But I don't want to move on." Her father sounded whiny and petulant.

"But I do," Ruth said. "Actually I already have."

The silence this announcement caused drew the three spies even closer to the window.

"Is it Lars? It's Lars, isn't it."

"Lars? What are you talking about?"

"What is he doing over here? Carrying on like that, with Delores hardly passed."

"He's our neighbor and she's been gone for over a year. And those kind of accusations don't become you, Ron. You're the one with the roving eye. Not me."

"I told you it was a mistake. It happens to guys. It wasn't my fault."

All three of the voyeurs groaned, quickly shushed each other, then ducked behind the sink in case their reaction had been over-heard.

"I would be surprised if you did think it was your fault. So whose fault was it? Mine? Or whoever you thought you could trade me in for? No, don't answer that.

"It was both of our faults. It has been for a long time. We just let things go on and on until there was no going back. I'm done with settling into a lifestyle and calling it life. I can thank you for making me finally see what was happening. Goodbye, Ron."

"You can't mean it. It's Vera, isn't it? She was always putting strange ideas into your head."

"No, Ron, it's all me. You and I did this without anyone else's help. You walked away first."

"But I told you it was a mistake."

"Oh God, he's going to cry," Vera groaned.

"Go away, Ron. I'm sorry. I gave you thirty-eight years; now I'm taking the rest of what I have left for myself."

"Ruth, honey. Come back. I just made one little mistake."

Ruth, who had been headed toward the house, turned back. "Ron, you made a mistake. I've been living one."

This time when she turned away, she didn't stop and headed straight to the back door.

Phoebe, Alice, and Vera barely had time to move away from the window before the screen door opened and banged shut.

Ruth found them mindlessly pretending to rearrange dirty dishes.

"I guess you heard all that?"

No one answered.

"I don't know why men get to walk away, try something else on for size, and if they don't like it, expect to be taken back."

Phoebe and Vera shook their heads, but Alice just opened her arms.

Ruth practically fell into them. "I hope . . . just hope my girls don't hate me." And she burst into tears.

"I don't," Phoebe blurted out.

"Thank you, sweetheart." Ruth straightened up, sniffed. "Sometimes these things happen. We'll just have to make the best of it."

Phoebe nodded. She couldn't think of anything to say. Her dad's whining and blaming had made Phoebe's skin crawl. This was not the dad she wanted to remember. She shouldn't have come inside. She should have stayed in the yard with Ty and his dad. But it was too late to pretend she hadn't heard. Sometimes having a nose for news was a curse.

As soon as the Adamses left the yard and the other three women hurried into the house, Ty grabbed his father's arm and trundled him into their own house.

"What the hell are you doing?" Lars groused. "Why are we going home?"

"Because they may want some privacy."

"Ron and Ruth?"

"Yes. Phoebe told me their marriage is having a rocky patch."

"Is that what they're calling it?"

"You know something I don't know?"

"I have most of my life."

Ty let that pass; hopefully it was his dad's new attempt at humor.

"What an ass," Lars said. "The man didn't even bother to say hello before he started demanding things of Ruth. If I were Ron, I would try being a little more humble. But then, humility was never one of his strong points."

They stopped at the kitchen and Ty went to the fridge. "You want a soda or something?"

"No. I wanted to beat the socks off Vera at croquet. But now that the afternoon is wrecked," he grumbled, "I might as well see if there's a game on." He brushed past Ty and retreated into the living room. A minute later, "He was safe, ya idiot!" echoed all the way back to the kitchen.

Ty's heart stuttered. His dad had been doing so well lately; he sure hoped the Adamses' family squabble wasn't going to undo all that progress.

Ty leaned his forehead against the fridge door and said a prayer to whoever might be listening.

He was contemplating whether to take a beer into the living room and join his dad for the game, knowing that watching TV with his father was like watching it by yourself, and he didn't even like baseball that much.

Before he could decide, he heard the sound go off. He braced himself for another complaint against Ron Adams, or against Ty or even the baseball game. But his dad didn't appear. Ty heard the porch door open and close. His dad had gone outside again. Probably down to the spot where he and Ty's mom used to sit in the evenings. Ty had seen him there a few times since he and Phoebe had hauled the bench out of the shed.

He took a beer out of the fridge and sat down at the kitchen table. There was a lot he should be doing. The roof still wasn't finished. By the time he finished patching the damn thing, he'd have a whole new roof. He could paint the back steps. He could look over the timetables for September. See if Brandy, his office manager, had started looking for a new publicist.

But instead he just sat sipping beer and scratching the label off the bottle.

He was so intent on the pile of tiny label pieces growing on the table that he started when a knock sounded on the kitchen door.

Hopefully, it was Phoebe giving the all-clear. The marital strife between the Adamses had upset his dad. The sooner it was over, the better.

Before he could get to the door, a second, more persistent knock disabused him of that idea.

He opened the door to Ron Adams, who looked angry. "Mr. Adams."

"Where's your father?"

"I'm not sure. Can I help you?" Ty didn't like the look of the man. He'd always been nice enough as far as Ty remembered. He was anything but that at the moment.

"You were both outside a minute ago. Is he still there?"

He didn't give Ty a chance to answer, but turned around and strode down the front lawn.

Ty should probably stay out of whatever was going down.

Maybe the guy just wanted to commiserate with an old friend. His dad could take care of himself. But still . . .

Ty grabbed his beer and hurried through the house, then stepped outside. His dad was sitting on the bench as he thought he would be. Ty managed to reach him just as Ron Adams came around the corner of the house.

"Mr. Adams is looking for you," he said. His dad stood and went to meet Adams on the grassy verge of lawn between the houses.

"Ron," Lars said. He stuck out his hand, then dropped it when Adams didn't reciprocate. "How you been?" Lars persisted.

Ty wondered if he had any idea of what Adams had in mind. Ty wasn't sure he did, but the man's anger was now definitely aimed at his father.

"I suppose she told you what happened."

"She did."

Ty looked at his dad. When had his dad and Mrs. Adams had time together to discuss things? She certainly hadn't mentioned any of this in front of Ty.

"Well, there are two sides to every story," Ron said.

"Why are you telling me this? It isn't any of my business."

"It is if you think you're going to take advantage of Ruth at a vulnerable moment—"

"What the hell are you talking about?"

Ty sucked in his breath; neither he nor his dad had seen that coming.

"Keep your hands off my wife."

"Why should I?" Lars answered back. "You walked out on her."

"Dad!" Ty meant to curb the escalation of this conversation, but the word came out in a whisper. Was his dad thinking of having an affair with Mrs. Adams? He'd never even looked at her in anything but a complacent way. At least not when Ty had been around. But of course he left every day while his father was napping. He forced his mind back from that precipice.

"Because I said so."

"Oh, stop trying to be so macho, Ron. You cheated on your wife. You lose. You better run on back to whoever she is before she changes her mind about keeping you."

"I don't want to run back. I made a mistake, okay? I thought I needed a change and, man, Lisa was a real catch, or so I thought. But she can't cook, sends all the laundry out, even my underwear, and she hates golf."

"You should have thought about that before you gave up Ruth."

"I wasn't thinking clearly. And I didn't give her up. Not exactly. She was just . . . I don't know. It's that damn condo. She hasn't been the same since we moved there. I thought it would be less of a hassle. But Ruth wasn't having any of it. I didn't know what to do. I'd sell the damn thing but I can't make money back on it. The market is glutted with empty townhouses. And Lisa was so understanding and listened to how I felt. And one thing led to another; it's not like I meant to cheat. And I'm ready to go back and make everything right. But Ruth is being stubborn."

And Ty thought, *Good for Ruth*; he really didn't like this guy.

What kind of man worried about real estate when you should be doing everything you could to make amends?

"Well, I'm sorry for you, Ron," Lars said, not sounding sympathetic at all. "But you blew it. Way to mess up a marriage."

"It's not my fault. She should have been more understanding. Let me know how she felt. But she just let things go south."

Ty had to bite his lip to keep from saying, *You're blaming your behavior on your wife?*

His dad said it for him. "That's pretty lame, to blame everything on Ruth. Pretty lame."

"Come on, Lars. You and I've been friends for years. Help me out here. She'll listen to you. Tell her she should come home."

"I will do no such thing."

"Why?"

"I told you. It's none of my business. Clean up your own mess. If you can."

Ron Adams's hands clenched into fists. He was probably one of those guys who threw down his clubs when he missed a shot. "Leave my wife alone."

Lars took a very slow controlled breath as his fingers curled and released. Ty cringed. It was well known that Lars Harken could hold his own in a fistfight. On Saturday nights after a day of beer and working on cars, the pub was a hotbed of hot tempers.

But not these days. Actually, Mr. Adams didn't look like he was in such great shape, either. And it was definitely beginning to look like the two old friends might actually try to duke it out between them.

It was times like these when Ty really missed his mother. She could always defuse a fight, make peace between Lars and his sons.

But his dad surprised him.

He stepped back. "You're a fool, Ron. You don't deserve Ruth. Actually, Delores and I never thought you did. As I see it, she's no longer *your* wife. You gave her up. Kicked her to the curb. She's free to make her own choices for a change. God knows, she never got to when you were married."

Adam's fists tightened. "We're still married."

"Not for long," Lars said as if to himself, but loud enough for both Ty and Mr. Adams to hear.

"Why, you—" Adams put up both fists. Before Ty could move, Ron threw a clumsy punch, missed his target, and stumbled forward, right into Ty's father's fist.

Adams staggered back, tripped, and fell onto his butt in the grass. As he sat there rubbing his jaw, Lars stepped toward him.

"Dad, don't!" Ty tried to step between them, but his dad slipped around him.

Lars leaned over and stuck his index finger in Mr. Adams's face. "Put your pea brain to rest, Ron. I'm not making moves on Ruth. I think she's a lovely lady, but I married Delores. If I could have her back even for a moment, I'd be content to live alone till I die. But I can't. And I'll be married to her for the rest of my life.

"You had a good wife, too, Ron, and you didn't appreciate her. And you hurt her. I hope she doesn't take you back. *You* deserve to lose her." He lowered his head and walked back into the house.

For a moment Ty didn't know whether to follow him, or stay behind and make sure Ron didn't go after him.

But finally Adams got to his feet and strode across the grass toward the houses. A minute later, Ty heard a car rev up and drive away. And Ty breathed a huge and wonderful sigh of relief.

Lars stuck his head out the door. "Do you think dinner is still on?"

"He's gone?" Ruth said.

"Yes," Phoebe said, turning from the kitchen window. "I wonder what happened to Ty and Mr. Harken?"

"What do you mean?" Ruth asked.

Phoebe looked at her grandmother, then at Vera.

"We forgot about them. I mean, we were worried that Ron might try to take you by force so we all ran in here to make sure you were okay."

"You thought he might kidnap me? Ron? He would never do something so romantic. Or abusive." Ruth frowned. Laughed. Cried, then grabbed a napkin out of the holder and blew her nose. "What have I done?"

Phoebe covered her face with her hands. Was her mother having a change of heart after her father had just driven away in a temper? Unfortunately, fingers over the face was hardly a way to ignore a problem.

She sat down next to her mom. "Do you want to go back?"

Ruth shook her head. "If I had any second thoughts, I don't after today. But I feel like I've let you girls down."

"You haven't," Phoebe said. Though convincing Daphne and

Celia might take a little time. But they hadn't heard the things their father had said. Yet.

Ruth smiled. It was forced but Phoebe appreciated it. She was feeling pretty confused about her own escape from the altar. Was that how her life with Gavin would have turned out? Was it how all marriages turned out? Well, she'd never know about Gavin, at least.

Thank God for that. The thought of playing out what she had just heard some thirty-odd years down the road with Gavin . . . She shuddered. She couldn't even imagine life with him for that long. He'd been right. She'd expected him to be like his father, and he wasn't. But that wasn't Gavin's fault. They'd both come very close to a bad mistake.

Chapter 18

Ruth breathed a sigh of relief when she saw Lars and Ty, carrying a casserole dish, walk across the lawn to the table she was setting. She'd been afraid that they would be too embarrassed to face her after Ron's visit and the spectacle he'd made of himself, standing there acting pathetic like he was the victim instead of the rat he really was.

She took the casserole from Ty and he immediately went over to Phoebe, who was nose-deep in her laptop, probably checking her email for an answer to her job search. Ruth would breathe easier when Phoebe was settled again.

She was all too aware of her inability to support her daughter when her own life was such a mess. But she put on a good face like she always did and tried to engage Lars in conversation. He shrugged and mumbled something and took the platter of marinated chicken over to the grill, where he stayed until dinner was ready.

Ruth's tenuous hold of her emotions began to slip, but she lifted her chin and willed herself to face whatever their opinions might be with calm.

But she couldn't deny their increasingly comfortable relationship had been upset by Ron's visit. Lars was taciturn during the entire meal. Phoebe and Ty both seemed to be lost in their own thoughts.

No one mentioned Ron's visit, which made things even more awkward. Ruth knew she should say something, but she couldn't bring herself to broach the subject.

So when the first drops of rain fell and Alice suggested they have dessert in the dining room, Ruth sprang to her feet. No one balked, but grabbed whatever they could carry and hurried inside.

Ty and Lars left right after their last bite of cake. Lars was so grumpy that Ruth was glad to see him go. But Ty, who had taken to doing the dishes with Phoebe, left, too, and Ruth hoped she hadn't created a rift between him and Phoebe over the scene that afternoon.

She knew she couldn't keep living in limbo; it was upsetting everyone.

She and Phoebe did the dishes, and Ruth went to bed as soon as the last plate was in the cabinet. She lay awake for a long time while random thoughts bounced around in her brain. One niggling doubt after another.

Maybe she was being selfish. Maybe she should just go back to Ron and the condo, and continue down the road she'd started thirty-eight years ago. But the very thought made her sick to her stomach.

She wouldn't go back, condo or no condo. Ron had broken their trust. It was over. And yet, she didn't want to spend her future as a divorced middle-aged suburban housewife. If she didn't go back to Ron, she wouldn't go back to her old neighborhood. It was either the whole package or nothing. Only one answer bubbled to the surface: nothing.

But where would she go? She couldn't live at home with her mother forever. Though she supposed that wasn't the worst option. Women did it all the time.

It wasn't the prospect of life with Alice, but the knowledge that Ruth had somehow failed as a wife and mother, whereas her mother hadn't. Alice never judged. Never outright. But she had a way of making you judge yourself for her.

This was a problem of her own making, hers and Ron's. She would make the decisions for herself and accept the consequences of those decisions.

As soon as she figured out what was right.

Two of her girls were desperate for her to go back. Ruth didn't understand why, except they were both married and might see their lives reflected in hers. And poor Phoebe, who was at such a crossroads in her own life, needed a capable, strong mother, not one who waffled over her own decisions.

She didn't want to set a bad example. She didn't want her girls to think that they didn't have options. Daphne's husband wasn't the easiest man to get along with. Celia's was a workaholic, but so was Celia. And Phoebe? Would she ever want to take a chance on another relationship after witnessing the breakdown of her own parents' marriage?

Gavin and Phoebe had seemed like the perfect pair. Their love of journalism and each other. How wrong they had all been. At first Ruth had brushed aside the slight out-of-sync-ness of their relationship to how hard they were both working. They didn't have much fun time together. Ruth never heard Phoebe laughing with Gavin the way she did with Ty. She seemed to be blossoming since coming to the island.

Ruth wasn't sure if that was just not having the responsibility of running the paper or the influence of the island, her family—or the boy next door. She shoved that thought aside. Too soon. Phoebe was on the rebound and everyone knew rebound relationships were doomed to fail.

Besides, Ty didn't seem at all ready to commit to a relationship. Actually, neither did Phoebe.

Ruth needed to make some decisions soon, but not tonight with the clock ticking away and the morning and a full day at the bakery looming. *The bakery.* She turned over, fluffed her pillow, and tried to succumb to sleep.

It was still raining when she left the house early the next morning, a little gritty-eyed but determined . . . and still thinking about the bakery. In that first moment of wakefulness, she knew that she had come to a decision.

It wasn't just Ron's visit, his outrage, or even his pitiful demeanor that had pushed her there. She'd suspected it the minute she set foot in the bakery that first day. And now that she'd gotten those violets under her belt, she only needed Ron's stupid accusations about her relationship with Lars Harken to push her into action.

Ruth borrowed her mother's Wellies from the closet and stuffed her own rubber-soled shoes into the pockets of her raincoat. She grabbed the nearest umbrella from the stand and went out to face the day.

She hesitated only a minute under the porch eaves to look up at the sky. The clouds would break soon. It would be a sunny day. Her sunny day. Fingers crossed.

The sun was shining when Phoebe woke up. It always seemed brighter after a storm. But it wasn't the light streaming through the window that woke her up. It was Ty and his father arguing in the yard. She slipped out of bed and padded over to the window. Stuck her head out to see Ty perched precariously near the peak of the roof. Lars was on the ground, pointing and giving him instructions.

Ty looked down at the ridge of shingles.

"Not there," Lars called. "Over there."

Ty twisted to look behind him. His foot slipped.

Phoebe gasped as Ty slid two feet before he managed to catch himself, just before he reached the gutter and a long drop to the ground.

"Be careful," Mr. Harken ordered belatedly.

Ty seemed unconcerned and merely climbed back up to the ridge. Then he shook his head.

"You need a new roof," Ty said. "It's been patched too many times. I'll call Jerry Eames and see if he can fit us in."

"There's nothing wrong with that roof. It's not even fifteen years old and I got a twenty-five-year warranty on it."

"Well, if you want to sue whatever company installed it, go ahead. But there's bound to be a hurricane clause in the contract. You better hurry and do it or you'll be floating in your bed with the next big storm."

Mr. Harken grumbled something and went inside.

Ty climbed down the ladder to the ground.

"Did you get wet last night?" Phoebe called down to where Ty stood, looking up at the roof.

He swiveled to look up at her. "A leak from the overhang; fortunately, it was just the front bedroom. Not in use. But it started somewhere else and I can't find it. No telling what is under that last layer of roofing."

"Well, don't go back up there—it looks dangerous."

"Just because it was wet and worn and I was distracted."

You're always distracted, she thought. "Well, be careful."

"Right." He moved out of view. She heard him rummaging and clanking things in the yard.

He could take care of himself and she had work to do. After a quick shower and a dash of mascara as a nod to her job search, Phoebe grabbed her laptop and went downstairs. Granna and Vera had already had breakfast and were out in the garden. Phoebe poured herself a cup of coffee, made two pieces of toast, and took everything to the porch to work on her article about Charley and his vans.

And to be close to her laptop if any emails came in.

Ruth and Inez spent a busy morning not only baking and icing but also doing inventory and planning orders for the soon-to-be-burgeoning summer community.

Ruth had managed to go all morning without mentioning Ron's visit, but she couldn't keep it off her mind. She had to make a decision soon. Her girls were hanging on to their hope that their parents would mend their disagreements and get back to normal. Ron might or might not be duly chastised for the moment, but who was to say he wouldn't do the same thing again the next time he decided he needed to try something new? He should have taken up a hobby, not a new lover.

There was no one she could really discuss her feelings with. Her girls were too involved and dealing with their own reactions. And Alice, bless her, knew when to use her mother's advice and not interfere. The only thing she'd said was, "Every marriage is different. You have to decide how you want to live the rest of your life."

As if Ruth didn't have enough to think about.

So when the counter girl came in for her shift at two o'clock, Ruth asked Inez if she could stay for a few minutes longer. "There's something I want to discuss with you."

"Oh," Inez said, her face tightening with concern. "You've been awfully quiet today. Is something wrong?"

"I . . ." Ruth didn't know how exactly to begin. She wasn't completely sure what she was going to say. She just knew that Inez had been her best friend when they were girls and was close to becoming that friend again. If there was anyone to whom she could confess what a terrible muddle her life was in, it was Inez. "Let's go to that little coffee bar down the street."

"Sure," Inez said, glancing at the full coffeepot on the counter.

"We can check out the competition while we're there. They're bound to serve something besides coffee."

"Let's go see."

They left the counter girl, whose name was Sue, and walked the block to Beach Barista, which consisted of a dark wooden counter and a small display case of an assortment of croissants, biscotti, and pound cake. Ruth and Inez exchanged looks and ordered caffè lattes and biscotti.

They sat at one of the small square tables near the window, discussing the day's activities until their coffees arrived. It was almost as if they'd tacitly agreed not to start the conversation until then, because it was bound to upset the status quo.

But the coffees arrived.

"Hmm," Inez said. "Biscotti are not nearly as good as Sabatini's."

"No, they're not. You should send them a sample of yours."

Inez shrugged and said tentatively, "I couldn't do more by myself." She picked up her cup, looked at Ruth from behind it.

"It does look like it might be a bumper year for summer people," Ruth agreed.

"It isn't just the summer people," Inez blurted. "I couldn't have taken on the Garden Society luncheon if you hadn't been here. And the bakery is making more money. What if I—"

"Don't be ridiculous," Ruth said, feeling elated, then embarrassed. "I'm so glad I could help out."

"That sounds awfully past tense," Inez said, her face clouding over. "It's been remarkable. Between your skills and mine, we've really been able to up our productivity and selection. And the sheer quality of the presentation, people are taking notice. I couldn't have done it without you." Inez glanced down at her cup. Let her gaze linger there. "But I understand if you . . . I know it doesn't pay well, but business is picking up a lot and I might—"

"No," Ruth exclaimed, realizing that Inez thought she was going to ask for more money. "I've enjoyed every minute of it. I would have happily helped out just because we're friends. You're the one who insisted on a salary. But something just happened. It made me realize that I need to deal with my life choices. Ron made a surprise visit this past weekend. He said a lot of things. Some not-very-flattering things. He somehow made it all my fault. He's always made it my fault."

"Are you going back?"

"It depends."

"On what?"

"On whether you think you might still need me to work here after the summer crowd has gone home."

"Need you?" Inez's mouth dropped open. It was the same reaction she'd had when Tony Corrado had asked her to the senior prom, and when Ruth had told her that Ron asked her to marry him.

"I don't mean to sway you. I totally understand if it's not doable," Ruth said.

"Doable? It would be more than doable. I haven't been able to get anyone in the family interested. It's a long, unrelenting business with a low profit margin. Several places down island have shown interest in carrying our goods. It's hardly been worth doing lately, but if we could produce more and take on more clients, we could double our distribution."

"And do more catering," suggested Ruth.

"And expand into a little café," Inez said. "I've always dreamed of doing that. Not just those two little tables on the sidewalk. But more pastries, coffee, little sandwiches, maybe even serve afternoon tea." Inez clapped her hand over her mouth. "Listen to me carrying on. I can barely afford to pay you and a couple of kids to work afternoons."

"But *we* could." Ruth's own words filled the air. Words she hadn't planned on saying. At least not so soon. But after a second of sheer panic at hearing herself, she breathed again. She had her answer.

Inez seemed to have frozen mid-gesture.

And Ruth was afraid that she'd overstepped with her enthusiasm. The Sabatinis had owned and run the bakery for several generations. Maybe they wouldn't want her interference.

"Only if you think you would need an extra . . . I don't know . . . I thought maybe we could be . . . ." Ruth stalled to the next word.

"Partners?" Inez finished for her.

"Something like that. I have some money saved up. Married or not, I'm a Sutton and we always save for a rainy day. And I think I've hit that rainy day." And if Denny Welsh was correct, she would receive a more than decent settlement in the divorce. "But only if the family agrees. I don't want them to think I'm encroaching. I would never."

"They'd be delighted. Ecstatic. Tony and the kids have been trying to get me to sell for years. I know Mama and Papa will be very happy and relieved, and Nonna will bless you. She always said you would be the best decorator Sabatini's ever had. Besides, she made you an honorary Sabatini, remember?"

Inez frowned and stretched her hands across the table to clasp Ruth's in hers. "But are you sure? I've been poking along for so long just trying to stay afloat. Maybe this is just a dream I should keep tucked away in my heart."

Ruth squeezed back. "You propose it to your family and see what they really think. And we'll abide by that."

"Okay, I'll call them now." Inez reached into her purse for her cell.

"I didn't mean now," Ruth said.

"Are you chickening out already?"

Ruth could hear the phone ringing in the background. She shook her head. She had done her best raising her girls and being a supportive wife. It was time to do her best at what came next.

It was all settled within a matter of minutes. Inez's parents *were* ecstatic.

"Put her on speaker," they demanded, though Ruth could hear them loud and clear from across the table.

Inez tapped the speakerphone icon.

"We've been so worried about Inez," Mama Sabatini continued out loud. "She's working too hard, all the time. Nonna's here, she has something to say."

There was a commotion at the other end of the line, then a voice that had grown fragile but that Ruth still recognized said: "Welcome home, *la mia piccola* Sabatini."

"Whew," Ruth said, when Inez finally ended the call.

"Told you."

"What about your kids?"

"They won't care and if they do, Nonna will put them straight. How about yours?"

"That I don't know, but if I have trouble, I imagine Alice will put *them* straight."

"Then here's to us." Inez lifted her cup.

"But we'll keep the Sabatini name," Ruth said.

"Fine."

Ruth lifted *her* cup. They toasted and drank coffee that had become tepid while they'd been talking. It was the best caffe latte either of them had ever had.

Phoebe cut up chunks of watermelon, keeping one eye on the wall clock when she wasn't keeping it on the kitchen window and the lane outside. Lars and Ty had already arrived to start the grill and Ruth hadn't even called to say she was going to be late.

"Maybe she's having her nails done to go with her new hairdo," said Vera. "If something had happened to her, we would have heard by now."

Somehow that didn't make Phoebe feel any less anxious. Her mother always called if she was going to be late.

Phoebe glanced at the clock again. It wasn't really that late. It was just that Lars and Ty were showing up earlier lately.

"Why don't you go keep Ty company?" Vera suggested.

"What?"

"Go talk to Ty. He's out there with his laptop . . . all alone."

"I don't think he would appreciate the interruption." He was either happily fine-tuning his milk-jug project or conceptualizing a new one that he hadn't shared.

"I think he's a very attractive young man," Vera said.

"And smart," Phoebe added. "Why don't you go talk to him?"

"Ugh, hopeless, hopeless. I hope you're not swearing off fun because of your experience with the last one."

"No, of course not. It isn't something that's come up."

"Swearing off love forever," Vera moaned, warming to her subject.

"Aunt Vera, shush. Someone will hear you."

"Not daring to trust her heart . . ."

It was too much. Phoebe burst out laughing. "You don't need to worry about me. It's the twenty-first century and I'm extremely well-adjusted . . . except for being unemployed. Besides, having three family members monitoring my love life could have a dampening effect."

"True, but it would be fun for us. You'd better take that bowl of watermelon out to the table before you mutilate it any further."

Phoebe looked at the bowl. Big chunks, little chunks, and a bit of pulp. She should have been paying more attention to her knife than the clock. She carried it outside.

Ty was completely riveted to his laptop. Lars stood at the grill, so Phoebe sat down and checked her phone for emails, none offering her a job, and her messages. Nothing from her mother.

A few minutes later, Vera and Granna came outside. They were carrying a basket of French bread and a platter of the early tomatoes. Behind them, Ruth had stopped in the doorway.

"Attention, everyone," Vera announced. "Ruth has news."

Phoebe started to get up but a frown from Vera and she sat down again.

Her mother stepped off the porch step and came a little way into the yard to stand ramrod straight, weight deposited between both feet as if ready to do battle.

"You all know that my life has been going through some changes lately."

Phoebe braced herself for whatever the next statement would be because her mother showed no signs of slowing down.

"Well, I've made another big change today. Something I've wanted to do my whole life."

She had everyone's attention, even Ty's.

Ruth broke into a wide smile. "You are looking at the new partner of Sabatini's Bakery."

Chapter 19

Once the initial surprise subsided, everyone began asking questions and Ruth happily related how it had come about, the plans she and Inez were already making for enhancing the current bakery, and for doing some long-needed improvements and subsequent expansions. "But I'm starving," Ruth said. "Lars, man the grill, I'm just going to get changed and I'll tell you all about it over those rib eyes I saw on the kitchen table."

Lars saluted and trotted off. Vera and Alice went to see about the steaks, and Ruth went upstairs to change.

Ty looked up from his laptop. "Big news. I guess you'll be next?"

Phoebe nearly jumped out of her lawn chair. "Is that a question or a cattle prod?"

Ty shrugged. "Whatever you need."

Phoebe narrowed her eyes, but he wasn't joking or being smarmy. With Ty, what you got was what you got. His mind was in another place altogether.

"I have to be. Actually, this . . . this in-betweenness, it's making me crazy."

"But you're writing, aren't you? There are actually words in that laptop. Not blank documents with a title and page numbers and nothing else."

"No, thank God. I have plenty of material and the words are there. I just need to sell them. Or get on a staff somewhere that pays enough to live on."

"Not here?"

"Do you see a local paper anywhere?"

He closed his laptop.

"No, but you could freelance."

"I could. I'm pretending to do that at the moment. But it's nice to be a part of something bigger."

"Just not too much bigger," Ty added.

"Exactly. Gavin accused me of having no ambition. Or not enough ambition. Maybe he was right. But I don't think so. I just feel like my place is at the grass roots. That's where most things happen."

"And where most changes are made. You know how I feel about that."

"Yeah, and I think you're right. At least for your work. And that's the way I feel about news. I tell a story about Charley and his vans and that sets off another story, then that story sets off another. Maybe it makes a little change in the world. A lot of little steps can make big changes." Phoebe sighed. "Or maybe I'm just fooling myself."

"You don't strike me as the kind of person who makes a habit of fooling herself."

"Thanks."

The screen door banged open, and Ruth, who had changed into comfortable slacks and a T-shirt, emerged and held it open for Alice, who was carrying a platter piled high with thick steaks.

"About time," Lars said. "This charcoal is perfecto." He took the steaks from Alice and nodded to Ruth. A nod of encouragement? To show he liked her outfit?

All sorts of thoughts were running around in Phoebe's head.

The door opened again and Vera strutted out holding a champagne bottle high over her head.

"Where on earth did you conjure that from?" Alice asked.

"Bought it the day after Phoebe and Ruth showed up. Knew we'd have call to drink it sooner or later. Seems like tonight is the perfect time. Who wants to pop this baby? Ty?"

Ty looked around and reluctantly stood up. "Glasses?"

"Couldn't find the champagne flutes. It's the beach; those tumblers will do."

She lined them up and Ty expeditiously popped the cork and poured.

The glasses were passed, though Lars refused to leave the steaks. But he lifted his glass and called out, "To Ruth," through a cloud of hickory smoke.

"To Ruth," everyone chimed in.

Vera sidled over to where Phoebe and Ty were seated.

"Not to worry," she said. "I have another one waiting for you, Phoebe."

"For when I get a job?"

"That, too," said Vera and danced away.

Everyone seemed in excellent spirits and dinner passed in

lively animation. They all plied Ruth with questions and compli-
mented Lars on his steaks.

Phoebe listened and chimed in when she could. But mainly
she just smiled, while she panicked inside. She was happy for her
mother, even though it meant an end to their family as they knew
it. But that one sentence, *Something I've wanted to do my whole
life*, was like a clarion call to Phoebe. Time was wasting and she
didn't have a plan, not a concrete one, like new ovens and ex-
panding to include a café.

She reminded herself it had only been a few weeks, but it didn't
really help. She couldn't stay here much longer. The world was
passing her by, forgetting her existence.

Lars challenged Vera to a Parcheesi rematch and the older
adults left for the living room, carrying their drinks with them.

Phoebe and Ty cleared the table and took up their regular sta-
tions at the sink.

"Listen, they're already arguing about the game," Ty said.

"And enjoying every minute of it," Phoebe assured him.

"I know. It's weird. Your mom seems pretty happy."

"She does, doesn't she? I wonder if she feels like she wasted a
good part of her adult life."

"Nah, why would she? She had you guys, and this place,
and . . . Is that what you feel happened to you by staying at the
Sentinel for so long?"

"Only for the last few years. But I don't even regret those anymore. Gavin was never *Sentinel* material, which made him not my
material. Does that sound callous? I was simpatico with his father.
He had a vision of what a local newspaper should be. Strangely

enough, I learned something from both of them." She laughed, not a totally happy sound. "I was blindly busting my butt to save it, and all the while Gavin just wanted someone to take it off his hands. I'm smarter now."

"Well, screw him. You can't let other people's needs deter you from what you want to do. Or make you bitter."

Phoebe had been scrubbing the scalloped potato dish, but she stopped and looked directly at him. He'd been fighting that his whole life, from the taunts he got as a kid to his family's dismissive attitude now. And he was the least bitter person she knew. Well, she got it. If he wanted to help people while recycling trash, more power to him.

"Thanks, I needed to remember that."

"We can all use a reminder now and again."

"If you'll finish drying the silverware, I'll go see if they want anything more. And then we'll close the kitchen."

He just nodded. He was probably already off somewhere else, but Phoebe didn't mind. She knew it was somewhere that would make someone better off.

Ty watched Phoebe walk away, remembering how annoying she was as a kid. Questions, questions, questions. She'd been indefatigable. And she was indefatigable now. And strong.

He wanted to tell her just to forget everyone else and do it her own way. But he wasn't that irresponsible. He'd been lucky. One little part for some machine he didn't even remember had made him enough money to set him up in his life's work. And his successes kept enough coming in to pay a small staff while continuing to add projects throughout the world.

Would he still be doing this if he hadn't invented that part? Would he have given up and done something else? He didn't like to think so.

And he didn't think Phoebe would, either. But she was still young. It was a vicious, competitive world out there and he wanted her to succeed. She was a good journalist. He'd read her articles online. And they were spot-on.

She had a knack for identifying the things in the community that needed doing, found people who were making changes and wrote persuasively about them.

Hell, she had Charley yakking away like he wasn't a moody cantankerous recluse. Ty had to admit, she was kind of amazing.

The ringing of a cell phone put an end to that thought. Phoebe had left her phone on the table. He picked it up, glanced at the caller ID. Nobody he recognized, but it might be important. He was heading out of the kitchen to find her when he nearly ran into her coming through the door.

He handed her the phone.

"Thanks." She practically snatched it out of his hands and walked past him, through the door outside and into the driveway. A minute later he saw the top of her head pacing past the window and back again. He refrained from moving closer.

But he didn't move away; he just stood there. She was interesting. He never knew what she would be up to next. Enthusiastically mucking about with the garbage in the river sweeper, just because he said he needed a hand. Chatting away with Charley while they hammered and screwed and hauled and painted. Of course, it might just be a way of getting research for her intended article. But it seemed more than that.

Or maybe he just wanted it to be more than that. Because even though she was still Little Miss Magpie in adult form, asking hundreds of questions about his project and Charley's, they were intelligent questions and she seemed genuinely interested.

Put all that together with concern for others and a pretty nice face and body . . .

She was growing on him. At times she was pretty damn enticing. Or maybe it was just all the sly looks and innuendos from the older set that was moving his mind, and body, in that direction. But he was damned if he did and damned if he didn't.

If they did get together and things worked out, they would have a constant audience for the duration, and if it didn't, it would be embarrassing and awkward for the rest of the summer.

There was no way around it, acting on any attraction would be a disaster.

Phoebe read the caller ID. *O. Forrest*. The name sounded familiar, though she couldn't quite place it. It might be spam, but it could be the answer to her prayers.

She pressed Accept. "Hello?"

"Hi, Phoebe, it's Oliver Forrest with the *Boston Globe*. We met at the Press Association symposium a few years back. Simeon Cross and I served on a panel about feature articles. The three of us had dinner together."

Phoebe's brain had stuck at the words *Boston Globe* and she had to scramble to catch up. He worked for the *Globe*. She remembered him. Smart, energetic, a real newspaperman. She remembered dinner. He and Simeon had taken on the table next to them on the future of print news. She'd joined in without question.

". . . saw your article in the Kingston *Independent*. Glad you're still in writing. I sort of lost touch after Sim's death. A huge loss to the industry, and to his friends."

"Yes," she said, finally getting up to speed. "A big loss." How big of a loss came flooding back.

"I heard about the *Sentinel* shutting down. Too bad it couldn't be saved. It was a bright light in regional papers."

It could have been saved, she thought bitterly. *I could have saved it. Somehow.*

"Have you landed somewhere yet?"

Was he about to suggest someplace? "No, not yet," Phoebe said, clicking into pitch mode. "I'm taking a little time to work on several articles about individuals who are making a global difference." *A bit of a stretch at this point, but they all have great potential.*

"I'd be interested in talking to you if you can get down to Boston soon. We're looking for a features editor. Not sure if you're interested, but I'd love to touch base with you."

Features editor. A huge opportunity. And a highly competitive one. Though not the opportunity she would have chosen. She wanted to be in the field. She didn't mind the organizational stuff. God knew she'd spent the last three years doing just that. But she wasn't about to turn down the possibility of a job.

"I'd love to talk," Phoebe said.

"Great. The only thing is the job announcement goes public next Monday, so if there's any possibility you could get down this week?"

Phoebe willed herself to stay calm. "I can make that happen. I'm mostly self-scheduling at the moment."

Ollie laughed. "I hardly remember what that's like."

The words sent a thrill of reporter fever through her.

"Would the day after tomorrow be at all possible?" Oliver asked. "I'm swamped tomorrow. And I'm out of town on Friday."

Phoebe laughed. "That would be great."

"And bring your new articles if they're close to ready."

Not without a contract, she thought. "I'll email you some excerpts and bring some hard copies."

"Perfect." He gave her his work address. "Shall we say ten o'clock?"

"Ten o'clock. I'll see you then."

She ended the call. Stood where she was, since her knees seemed too shaky to hold her up. The *Globe* wanted her to come talk. An interview? It sure sounded like it. Day after tomorrow. She could be ready by then. She'd had plenty of time to spruce up her portfolio in the last couple of weeks. She huffed out a couple of breaths. The *Globe*. A big enterprise, not exactly local news, but they did cover local news. An editor's position.

Editors did get assigned articles . . . depending on the kind of editor. Occasionally. Sometimes . . . if they were lucky.

She had an interview. *Yes.*

She hurried back into the house and ran into Ty on his way out.

"I was beginning to worry," he said as they danced in the open doorway.

"I have an interview."

"That's great." He stepped aside, spitting her out into the kitchen. She did a little skip of excitement and ran to tell the others.

Four heads turned from the Parcheesi board.

Ruth jumped up and ran to give Phoebe a hug. "That's wonderful. Tell us all about it."

"Ollie Forrest from the *Globe*. They're looking for a features editor. It's a bit over my head," Phoebe cautioned, "but I'm going to talk to him day after tomorrow."

"Oh, sweetheart, I'm so happy."

"There's stiff competition. I'm not getting my hopes up."

"Well, I think they'd be crazy not to hire you."

"That's because you're my mother."

"Well," Vera said, "I guess it's time to break out that other bottle of champagne."

"Let's wait. It's a long shot," Phoebe said, then added, "I don't want to jinx it."

"Well, we're all very proud of you. Both of you," Alice said. "Ruth has a new business and Phoebe is up for a new position."

"So when is it?" Vera asked.

"Wednesday. Though I probably should go tomorrow and stay over somewhere. The meeting's at ten."

"Good idea," Lars said. "So you'll be rested for the interview. Ty can drive you. It's not like I need him around here when I have you lovely ladies to keep an eye on me, right, son?"

Ty frowned at his dad. "Are you feeling all right?"

"Sure. And while you're there, he can show you whatever it is he does for a living."

Phoebe winced. She couldn't believe the man was so dismissive of Ty's work.

"I do have some things I could do there." Ty shot her a look that on anyone else would have been pleading. Maybe he needed a break from his dad as much as his dad did from him. Maybe a break from each other would make them appreciate each other a little better.

"Yeah," Lars continued. "He's got a place up there, too. Don't know if it's nice enough for guests . . ." Lars cast a challenging look at his son.

"I couldn't impose," Phoebe said. "I'm sure there's a hotel near the paper."

"The rates'll be exorbitant in that part of the city. What do you say, son?"

"Sure," said Ty. "It's not a pigsty. And . . ." He paused to look at Ruth. "There are two bedrooms and separate baths."

Ruth smiled back at him, not reassured but amused.

"It's in Cambridge," Ty said. "But close to the T."

"Which she won't be taking," Lars added. "Since you'll drive her in."

Phoebe flushed. She'd been able to ignore the little jibes from Lars and the others so far. It was only natural, she supposed, that they would assume that since she and Ty were together for a summer, they might . . . whatever.

It was the last thing Phoebe needed. It would take all her energy and focus to reestablish her place in journalism again.

She sneaked a look at Ty to see how he was feeling about the whole thing. But he looked as blank as a face on a coin.

"Well, good, that's settled," said Lars.

"What?" Phoebe said. "I didn't—"

"Sure, that's fine," Ty interjected as if the suggestion had just reached his brain. "What time do you want to leave? I mean, if it's all right with you, Phoebe."

"If you're sure you don't mind," Phoebe said. Like it would make a difference if he did.

"Well, we better be going," Lars said. "Ty needs to get a good night's sleep if he's going to drive to Boston tomorrow."

The look Ty gave his father was indecipherable.

"Come on, Dad, it's been a long day. Good night. Thank you for dinner. And congratulations, Ruth. See you tomorrow, Phoebe."

Ruth just shook her head as they watched the two men walk away. "Ty has the patience of a saint."

"He does," Vera said with a satisfied smile. Even Alice looked awfully pleased with how things had worked out.

But Ruth came straight over to Phoebe. "You needn't give in to those three, if it makes you uncomfortable. I'll give you my credit card for a hotel."

"Mom, thanks, but I have credit cards and I can afford a hotel room. I just feel bad that Ty got lassoed into this. It was just another instance of his father trying to belittle him."

"No, not at all. You've just seen the worst of Lars. He's set in his ways, but he cares for Ty. And I'm afraid he's decided that you would be the perfect girl to make his son happy."

"Ty is already happy, so please disabuse him of that idea while we're gone. Neither of us is interested. Not Ty, and not me. Besides, I'm on the rebound and unemployed. I have issues."

Ruth laughed. "Oh, I'm sorry, I didn't mean to laugh."

Phoebe laughed, too. "Don't be. And don't worry, I'll be fine."

With Lars and Ty gone, they retired to the living room and switched to herbal tea. Phoebe could tell her mom was still riding a euphoric high. Phoebe was excited, too, but apprehensive about her own sudden possibilities.

She needed to send off her excerpts to Ollie Forrest, but not tonight. Tonight, she was just glad she was here with her mom, great-aunt, and grandmother in a comfortable place that felt like home.

Ruth took a sip of her tea and put her cup on the coffee table.

"I'm sorry, Phoebe, that I haven't had a chance to discuss things with you before this. It all happened so fast. And I don't want to put a damper on our wonderful day, but you need to know I've made up my mind. I'm calling Denny Welsh first thing tomorrow and telling him to start divorce proceedings. Inez and I always planned to run a bakery together. We made all sorts of plans when we were in high school. But then your dad and Tony came along . . . Now we have another chance to do that. I'm not going to turn down that opportunity again."

Phoebe opened her mouth, but nothing came out. How could a person feel glad and sad at the same time? She knew her mother was doing the right thing. Her father had broken trust with her, not to mention belittling her and embarrassing her in front of her family and friends. And as much as Phoebe wished things could go back to the way they were before, she didn't really. She'd never seen her mother so . . . inspired.

"Where will you live?" It was not the most important of the many questions that suddenly sprang to mind. But it seemed the most immediate.

Ruth glanced at Alice.

"You'll stay here, of course. If that works for you, Ruth. You can stay as long as you want. We can even set up a couple of rooms as a separate apartment."

"That would be excellent," Ruth said. "And you don't have to change anything for me, though I may want to move closer to the bakery at some point."

It was barely a ten-minute walk from the beach house, but Phoebe didn't point that out. Because it suddenly occurred to her. What was she going to do now that her mother was settled?

"I'm all right, Phoebe, really. You don't have to stay for me."

"But she has to stay for *us*," Vera broke in. "Besides, she doesn't have anywhere to go."

That was true.

"We have plenty of room," Alice said. "I love having family here again. We can make two apartments." She cut a sideways glance at Vera. "Three apartments."

And for the first time since they'd all returned to the beach house, Vera didn't argue.

Chapter 20

$\mathcal{T}$y was up early the next morning already questioning the advisability of leaving his father even for a couple of days, which was ridiculous. The man was perfectly capable of taking care of himself. If only he would.

He had work to do and he was grateful for Phoebe's meeting even if it meant putting up with his father playing Cupid. It made it possible for him to get back to the workshop where he might be able to get a good chunk of work done. Plus he really needed to make sure they were actively looking for a new publicist.

He'd already organized his papers, thrown some clothes into a duffel bag, and was now in the kitchen making a list of things to remind his father to do, headed by "Call the roofers." True, he might only be gone overnight, possibly two nights, if Phoebe needed to have a second meeting with the editor at the *Globe*. Or a third night, even. They might need to stay through the weekend. That would be nice. He could get a lot of work done in that time, but he couldn't take the chance. The leak was getting worse and he wanted to deal with it before the damage became structural, if it wasn't already.

He was checking the kitchen cabinets to see if he needed to do a quick grocery run when his father padded into the kitchen. He was wearing clean clothes—something that had been occurring with more frequency since they'd taken up with the women next door.

"What time you leaving?"

Ty sighed. His dad couldn't wait to get rid of him. Par for the course.

"After lunch. That way we'll avoid the morning rush and get there before the afternoon rush begins. It will also give Phoebe time to prepare for her interview."

"Take her out to dinner. Here." Lars reached into his hip pocket and pulled out his wallet. "Someplace elegant, not just a local dive." He took a few bills out and thrust them toward Ty.

"Dad, I can afford dinner. I don't need your money."

"You sure?"

"Have I asked for money since I left college?"

"Doesn't mean you didn't need it. And I would have gladly given it to you if you wanted to set up a business or buy a house. Something solid."

"I know, Dad." It had never been about the money. He knew they would never agree about what made a successful life. Ty was living exactly how he wanted and had the ability to do it without asking for a handout. And his dad would never be able to understand that, either.

"You know of a nice place?"

"Yes."

"And wear something nice."

"Okay, fine, but Dad, if you're expecting things to happen between me and Phoebe, stop it now. I'm leaving the country in another month or so. She's going to take a job somewhere and that will be the end of it."

"With that attitude you'll never get a wife."

Ty closed the cabinet door without even looking to see what was running low.

"Maybe I don't want a wife."

"Or a husband. I'm as open-minded as the next guy."

Ty doubted that, but he let it pass. "I don't want a husband, either. Anything you want at the store? I'll make a run now."

"Baloney. Better get extra since you're going."

Ty threw up his hands. "We had to toss the last batch out since we've been eating next door."

"Well, you never know."

"Fine. I'll be back in an hour. I need to stop by Charley's. I promised to pick up some stuff for him on our way back from Boston."

"Get your car washed while you're out."

"I was planning to."

Ty grabbed his keys and headed for the door before he lost his temper. It seemed like his dad was determined to make him angry.

"Ty."

Ty turned. "Yeah?"

"She's a nice girl."

"Look, I know what you're up to. It's not going to work. I'm happy to drive her. I'll take her to dinner. But don't start counting your grandchildren."

"I just don't get you."

"I know, Dad. You don't have to worry about me. I like Phoebe. She's very attractive. But you all need to back off."

"Your mother would be so disappointed."

Ty froze. That was a first. Turning his mother against him posthumously. It was a low blow. And not fair. Disappointed in what? The only thing she'd been disappointed in was that her husband couldn't understand or appreciate how successful Ty was. But she had, and that was enough for Ty. There were some problems that couldn't be fixed, like lack of imagination and resentment. As a scientist, he knew when to move on. They could accept him or not. He'd left that problem behind a long time ago.

He went out the door and let it slam behind him.

Phoebe spent the morning polishing her articles, then printing them out, just in case Ollie Forrest asked for a hard copy. It wasn't until Vera stuck her nose in Phoebe's bedroom and suggested that Phoebe should be choosing a power suit for her interview that she reluctantly closed her laptop. She could do some fine-tuning tonight if need be. Surely Ty had a printer at his place.

Vera took the laptop closing as an invitation to enter. She was followed by Granna, who immediately said, "Ruth just called to make sure you didn't need her."

"I'm fine. Journalists are not known for their sartorial elegance, sometimes even when they're in front of a camera."

"Still, you want to look professional," Granna said, then immediately edited herself. "Which you always do, but sometimes you just have to allow us a grandmother's and great-aunt's moment to do our thing."

"Yeah. What are you going to wear?" Vera asked and went to the hook on the closet door where Phoebe had hung her two choices for the interview: tan linen slacks, a royal-blue silk shirt, and an ecru boyfriend jacket, and a more casual work uniform of black slacks and white button-down blouse over a peach camisole.

"Do you two have any plans for tonight? Is he showing you the town? And what about dinner?" Vera began to rummage through the closet where Phoebe had stuffed all the extras she'd brought.

"I'm sure whatever I wear for the ride will be fine for anything we do. This is a work trip. I think that's what both of us will be doing tonight."

Vera stopped rummaging long enough to turn around and give Phoebe her best *You're kidding* look.

"Stop it. I like Ty. He's nice. And he's very kind to let himself be lassoed into taking me to Boston, but I'm pretty sure the reason he agreed is more about his own work and his relationship with his father than with me."

"It's not where you start, it's where you finish," Vera sang in a Broadway belt and added a hip thrust at the end.

Phoebe laughed.

Granna sighed. "Come along, sister dear, and stop trying to relive your life through the kids."

"Well, somebody needs to get the ball rolling." Vera shuffle-ball-changed toward the door.

"Remember, we'll all be sending you success energy," Granna said, and took a gracious-queen walk out.

Phoebe looked at her outfits—either would be fine. She took one last scan of the closet, thought *What the hell*, and pulled out her favorite going-out black sheath and an appliquéd silk hoodie that dressed it down just enough to let the world know she didn't need to try too hard.

She finished packing, checked everything several times, added extra chargers at the last minute, then stopped to survey her travel gear. It looked like she was staying a week.

Nerves, she told herself. About the interview, about spending two days with Ty without constant family input, sleeping in a strange place, and, well, if she were honest, a bit apprehensive about the chance of running into Gavin while she was there. Ridiculous—the *Globe* occupied two floors of a huge office complex and she doubted he mingled too often with the editorial staff. Plus, if he had heard she was coming, he would surely make himself scarce.

She carried laptop, portfolio, suitcase, and hanging bag downstairs twenty minutes before they'd agreed to meet. Ty's SUV wasn't even in his driveway. He'd probably gone to check on the river sweeper.

She just hoped he didn't resent having to put up with her for two days. She would make a point not to encroach on his time or his space.

He finally returned ten minutes before the agreed departure time in a sparkling-clean car—his father's doing, Phoebe had no doubt. He jumped out and ran into his house with a grocery bag. Phoebe ran to make a bathroom stop before they left. He was waiting in the kitchen when she returned.

"This all yours?" he asked, indicating her pile of luggage.

"Yes, I had help," she said drily, but not looking at her grandmother or great-aunt. She reached for her suitcase, but Ty was there before her. She grabbed her laptop, purse, and portfolio case and followed him out to the SUV, followed by Vera and Alice.

Lars came out of his house just as they got into the car. "Drive safe. Don't hurry home, stay the whole weekend. Show Phoebe the sights."

Ty just raised his hand through the open window and they drove away with the entourage waving goodbye.

"At least they didn't tie tin cans to the bumper," Ty said as they drove away.

Phoebe glanced at him. "Everything but."

"Don't feel uncomfortable."

"I don't. You either."

"Doesn't bother me."

And they didn't say another word for the first hour of the trip.

Ty seemed to be concentrating on the road, though knowing Ty, he was a thousand miles away standing thigh-deep in river muck or designing something no one had ever heard of but everyone needed.

It did cross her mind that it might not be the best state of mind for driving eighty miles an hour on a busy expressway. But so far, he'd been totally alert when the need arose.

So she relaxed and watched the scenery speed past, while she thought about her future and the interview to come. And she thought about the Charley article. How she planned to pitch it to

Ollie as an extended feature with a series of articles—if Charley and his friend up the coast were amenable.

The second article would follow the next steps, what happened to the finished vans, how the camp was set up, and the services and facilities provided, and a third article about the vets themselves, how they had become homeless, how they'd found Charley, and how it had impacted their lives.

"Let me know if you want to stop," Ty said into the silence. No music, hardly any ambient noise from the road. It was like they were in a cocoon of thought.

"I'm fine." Phoebe turned to look at his profile. Straight nose, firm jaw, no fuss, no muss, just like the man. "Listen. Go into work or do anything you need to do. I can take care of myself, so don't feel like you have to babysit me."

"I don't."

"Good." She looked back out the window.

"I'll go into the office tomorrow during your interview."

"It's all good, honest."

"But we could have dinner in my neighborhood tonight. There are some nice places." He seemed to add this as an afterthought.

"Okay." Somehow a perfectly normal relationship was beginning to sound very stilted. Maybe it had been inevitable, that awkward, what-are-we stage. Two single people thrown together, who get along, find each other interesting. Like each other. Their whole family obviously hoping for more, which was really uncomfortable, and so not a good idea.

How do you say "Let's just be friends" without it sounding like an insult? Sure, there was some spark between them. They were on the same wavelength more often than not. But they were both ignoring it, because this was so not the right time to embark on anything more than what they were right now.

Well, it was just overnight; maybe the situation wouldn't arise.

When the skyline of Boston came into view, Phoebe felt a surge of something that might be excitement, optimism, or sheer terror. The same feeling she realized she'd had six years before when she had decided against the *Globe* and for Simeon Cross and the *Daily* (at that time) *Sentinel*.

Phoebe hissed out a long, controlled breath.

And felt Ty's hand pat her knee. "Almost there and you can stop thinking for a while."

Her throat tightened inexplicably. For someone whose mind was so often off in some other world, he'd known exactly how she was feeling.

It was another twenty minutes before they entered Cambridge and another fifteen before Ty began driving through a warren of streets populated by a jumble of old and new buildings, brick warehouses, condos, typical triple-decker wooden houses, and midcentury constructions.

Phoebe caught an occasional sliver of what must be the Charles River.

She was beginning to think he was lost when he turned down a narrow street and into a small parking strip before a brick building, whose function wasn't at first identifiable. Not a warehouse, not an apartment complex. Something in between?

"Home," he said, and got out of the car. Phoebe got out,

grabbed her work stuff, and followed him as he strode down a brick sidewalk, her dress bag slung over his shoulder, and her suitcase and his duffel bag held in his free hand. He seemed to be in a hurry, so she hurried after him. She was surprised when he stopped suddenly at a double door that looked like it might have been a barn door in a former life.

"Stables," he said, before she could ask. "I'm this way." He led her to the left and down four steps and stopped at a single door, where he flashed a key fob and the door unlocked. "It's kind of minimalist." He held the door while she stepped inside. To darkness.

"Just a sec." She could hear him bringing in the luggage and depositing it on a hard floor.

Then she was standing in brilliant white light. And looking at a space light-years away from any imaginings she had had about the way Ty Harken lived.

"Wow," she said. *Minimalist* was too mild of an understatement. A wide rectangular room spread out before her. Couch, two club chairs, and tables at one end in front of a mantel-less fireplace.

At the other end, a sleek teak dining table with designer chairs was centered in front of a bank of windows that were completely dark, probably from what appeared to be internal light-blocking shades.

"Sorry." The light dimmed to a soft wash. "I haven't been here much in the last few months, so everything is in dormant mode. The guest room is this way." He passed her, carrying her suitcase and dress bag.

She followed him past the dining area and an opening to a spotless white kitchen and into a small hallway that led to a large bedroom, also with black-out shades, that looked so unused she doubted anyone had ever slept here.

And what did that say about his family? "Bath in there. Closet there." He opened the latter and hung up her dress bag. "The fridge will be empty except maybe some water, but we can pick up stuff for coffee and whatever later."

"Where are we?"

"A few blocks from Central Square. Is there anything else you need?" He stood, waiting.

"Are you expecting a tip?"

"Huh? Oh, no." He smiled and Phoebe realized she hadn't seen him do that very often.

"Then I'll just unpack so I won't be wrinkled tomorrow."

"I'll just be out there."

"Okay."

He gave her a funny look, then left without a backward look.

Phoebe came out twenty minutes later having changed into casual pants and a T-shirt and put on a bit of makeup. Ty was MIA, but he'd opened the blinds and light poured in from the outside.

And the view . . . Holy cow, the windows opened onto a panorama of a tree-filled park that sloped down to the Charles River. It was breathtaking in an urban way. The view alone must have cost a fortune, Phoebe thought, shocking herself and reminding that self that it was none of her business, even if she was a journalist.

She didn't usually think of things in monetary terms. Except in this case, his family had been carrying on about how Ty was irresponsible and couldn't hold a job. They patted themselves on the back for doing him a big favor by having him stay at the beach because he wasn't financially independent.

Unless Ty Harken had a sugar daddy or mommy, he was doing just fine for himself.

"Nice, huh?"

Phoebe started. She hadn't heard him come up beside her. He'd changed clothes and maybe shaved. And he seemed . . . different.

"It's beautiful."

"I haven't done much to the place," Ty said, glancing back over his shoulder. There was definitely a different feel to the man. *At home* came to mind.

"The apartment is very nice," Phoebe said. It was amazing.

"Were you afraid it was going to be some dive with dirty socks lying all over the place?"

"No, but I had no idea that reclaimable water was so lucrative."

"It isn't. I bought this place with what I earned from this invention I made when I was in college. I told you about it."

"Vera said you invented a—a doohickey."

"For lack of a more intelligible word, yeah."

"Do your dad and brothers know about this?"

He shrugged. "More or less. They know I tinker. And do stuff with water across the globe."

"But they don't know what exactly you do?"

"They just ask how I'm doing and I say fine and that's it."

"They've never been here?"

"Nope."

"You never invited them to visit?"

"No. They never invite me to theirs. And this is kind of a haven for me. Though my mother came a few times."

It sounded awfully lonely to Phoebe, but what did she know? He might have a fleet of best friends. They had never discussed their personal lives beyond her tell-all rant that night on the beach.

She sat down on the bare-bones couch. "You know, you can be weird sometimes."

"I know. I always have been. They're not comfortable around me, and vice versa."

"But they act like you're incompetent."

"Old habits. They work hard at the same thing every day, in the same place. To them, I just flit around from country to country, from one thing to the next, not keeping my shoulder to the grindstone. Not being responsible to whatever. It makes them uncomfortable. They won't change. And I won't, either."

"I don't know how you can be so complacent."

"Because it takes more energy than it's worth, a totally self-defeating paradigm."

And then she realized what this sudden change was. Ty Harken was home. He was a visitor at the beach, physically, mentally, and probably emotionally, even though he'd grown up there. Ty

Harken belonged here and Phoebe was beginning to think she was seeing her first extended view of the real Ty. And she liked him even more than the one she already knew.

"Are you hungry?" he asked.

"Starving. I was afraid you might be working and would forget to come out again. And I'd have to drag you back into the here and now by my rumbling stomach."

He smiled. "I set my alarm. I'm on strict orders from my father to take you somewhere nice and not to bore you to death."

Phoebe laughed. "You've never bored me yet. Have to stay on my toes, I never know what surprise you'll come up with next."

Ty shrugged. "Mechanical engineers are like onions."

"Hey. I saw that movie. The best."

"You like *Shrek*?"

"Yeah. A lovable character and the story hits every plot point that a good story needs."

"I just like ogres," Ty said.

He sounded so much like a twelve-year-old that she laughed again. And tried not to wonder how he could make her laugh when her future was so precarious, and why she had never laughed over stupid things with Gavin.

She quickly slammed down on that comparison and stood up. "Shall we go?"

"Sure," Ty said, turning around. "What shoes are you wearing?" He looked down at her feet and Phoebe had to resist the urge to do a Cinderella pose. She was feeling a little giddy. Probably from hunger.

"I thought we could have an early dinner, then walk around the square a bit. If those are comfortable."

"I'm good. I only wear my painful shoes for weddings and fundraisers."

"Me too," Ty said, and guided her out the door.

They paused just outside while Ty entered a series of security measures.

"I have a lot of equipment and computer stuff inside, hence the numbers and the black-out shades," he explained.

It was several blocks to the square, and while they walked, Ty listed a sample of the restaurants there.

She finally told him to choose one he liked best.

"You like Japanese?"

"Love it."

"I know just the place."

Phoebe would have walked right past Samie Sushi if Ty hadn't stopped her at a torii gate nearly completely covered with wisteria vines.

They ducked their heads and entered a courtyard lit by an array of paper lanterns, creating an atmosphere somewhere between exotic and kitsch.

Ty hesitated.

"What?"

"The food is really good here and the people, but I don't think this is what Dad had in mind. He said to take you somewhere nice."

"Too late now," Phoebe said.

A red painted door opened, and a diminutive Asian man

greeted them with a bow and a "Yo, Ty, my man" in a very thick Japanese accent.

"Hey, Samie."

"And lovely lady. Welcome." Samie bowed again, a purely theatrical move, then gestured them inside. Phoebe didn't miss Samie's nod of approval, and she suspected Samie had intended it that way.

"He's a bit of a character," Ty explained as soon as they were seated and Samie had shuffled away. "And laying it on particularly thick tonight, since I usually eat alone."

"Aw, how sad," Phoebe said.

Ty laughed. "Not at all."

Samie and his wife, whom he introduced as Margaret, began bringing food before they even ordered, and Phoebe and Ty finally let them just bring them the night's specials and a few other things Margaret thought they should eat.

When they finally left the restaurant, after a lengthy goodbye to Samie and Margaret, Phoebe was stuffed with food and a little dizzy from sake.

"I hope I can still get into my clothes tomorrow," she said as they strolled about the square. "That was delicious and I loved those two. Thank you."

"And you're already thinking about writing about them?"

"Too stuffed at the moment. But what a pair."

"Do you always have ideas for articles?"

"Almost always. I mean, people are fascinating, the things they do. Some of them, anyway. I'll leave the jackasses for other people to write about. I figured that out right away. Let other people chase breaking news; it's almost always tragic or smarmy. I think good stuff should have equal time. And don't say 'Pollyanna.' I know who she is."

"I wasn't," Ty said.

"I mean, look at Samie and Margaret—they took such care with the serving, they were a team. I bet they have amazing stories. And Charley. Who knew?" She hesitated. "And you."

He didn't react, so she kept going, even though she was semi-aware that maybe she'd drunk one too many sakes. "I mean. What an idea. One man's trash is another man's drinking water. It's brilliant."

"Remind me to give you a couple of aspirin before you go to bed tonight."

"No, seriously. Why shouldn't stories like that be news? I bet people—" She broke off. "Sorry, back on my high horse."

"It's a good place to be."

"Yeah," she said. "It is."

"Yeah," he said, and slipped her arm into his.

By the time they arrived back at Ty's apartment they were both feeling pretty chummy and Phoebe was beginning to think, *Why the hell not*, then she remembered she had a big interview tomorrow and way too much sake tonight.

"Well, thanks. I had a great time, but I'd better get to bed," she said as soon as they were inside.

"Yeah," Ty said.

She turned toward him, but he'd turned away and was reaching into the drawer of a sleek entry table. Pulled out a pad and pen, scribbled something down.

"Here's my Wi-Fi password. In case you need the internet. Don't steal any government secrets."

She frowned at him. "Was that a joke?"

"You have to ask?"

"Sorry," Phoebe said. "I can't always tell. You're not much one for joking."

He sighed. "No, I guess I'm not. Yeah, that was a joke, forget it."

"You can't blame me for wondering. You graduated from MIT, you still live in the area, so it wouldn't be a leap. And this apartment . . ." She looked around.

"Nothing so exciting."

"Aren't you taking the hide-your-light-under-a-bushel thing a bit too far?"

"Is that a biblical reference? I'm not tracking."

"You let your family think that you can't keep a steady job and are incapable of getting your shit together. Why don't you tell them what you do?"

"Are you back to that? They know what I do, but they'll never get it. I gave up trying long ago." He raised his eyebrows. "Okay?"

She pursed her lips and he capitulated.

"They come from the more-is-better school of thought. If you make money, you should use it to make more money. If you're successful, you should be more successful. Own a house? Buy a bigger one. Get ahead."

"Well, more money would allow you to do bigger projects, affecting more people."

"Jeez. You too? I'm going to bed."

"No, not me, too. I'm a journalist. It's my job to ask thought-provoking questions."

He turned on her. "Fair enough. Here's your thought-provoking answer. There are plenty of organizations with more money, doing big projects to aid lots of people. And that's great. But other people who are too remote or don't have the wherewithal to maintain those big projects need something that works for them. You give them a big machine and when it breaks down, they can't get Amazon to deliver parts. The system collapses and they end up using the parts for other things they weren't designed for. And they're back without potable water or arable land. We give them a working system that is renewable with things that are already in their environment."

"Like the milk jugs and fishing nets."

"Exactly. It's small, may look ridiculous to outsiders, but it works better than nothing. We're small enough to be flexible and can think on our feet. And what we build has a chance of longevity."

"You should speak from the heart more often."

"What?"

"Never mind. But if it's any consolation . . . I understand."

"I thought—was hoping—you might."

"But you still don't totally trust me?"

"Why are we having this conversation? Don't you need to get some sleep?"

"You're right—big day tomorrow. Good night . . . ogre." And with that she went down the hall to bed.

Chapter 21

"How do you think they're making out?" Lars asked as he studied the Scrabble board.

"I'm sure they're fine," Ruth said.

"I was hoping they might . . . you know, hit it off."

"They have," Ruth said, and rearranged her tiles in an attempt to make a word. Why was it that you were always plagued by either too many vowels or too many consonants?

"I don't know," Vera said. "Why do you think their generation is so . . . circumspect? In Alice's and my day, if we saw a good-looking man, it was a question of 'anything goes' until it wasn't and we parted amicably and went our separate ways."

"Speak for yourself, sis." Alice placed an *s* on the board followed by an *e* and an *n* to spell *sensate*.

"Damn, you have the best luck," Vera groused. "If I knew you'd manage to fill in that space, I would have used the corner."

"It's from having a pure heart," Alice said.

Vera snorted. "I could tell tales of our youth."

"But you won't."

Ruth loved it when the two of them teased each other like the sisters they were. It made Alice seem more accessible.

"What do you think, Ruth?" Lars asked, frowning at Alice's word.

"About?"

"About your daughter and my son?"

"Oh, Lars, I think they're both lovely people. And as much as it would please me to see them happy together, I don't think it's something we can direct. They'll figure it out with each other, or with someone else. Or they'll choose a different path altogether."

"That's what I'm afraid of. Ty oughta settle down."

"You may have to reconcile yourself to the fact that he may not. He seems very happy with his life."

"He'd be happier with a wife and children to take care of." Lars scowled and added an *r* to *taste* in the upper corner and got double word points for his trouble.

Ruth didn't reply. Though she did wonder how Phoebe and Ty were doing. If Phoebe was too nervous to have a good time. And hoped that they didn't embark on something that would bring both of them unhappiness.

Vera was all fine and good with her notions of free love. But nothing was really free, and Phoebe had just had a traumatic breakup, for all she appeared to take it in stride. Ruth didn't want her hurt again. And especially not because of Ty.

Ty lay in bed, thinking. Which wasn't unusual. He got some of his best ideas in that hypnogogic state just before sleep, but tonight he wasn't inventing. He was thinking about Phoebe sleeping on the other side of his apartment in the guest room.

There had been a couple of times that night when he'd considered asking her to sleep with him. But he was never really good at preplanning things like that. Besides, if they did, it might get really awkward if she stayed at the beach for the rest of the summer. And that would be uncomfortable for both of them.

And besides, he'd gotten an idea for an adjustment for the frame of the river sweeper, and figuring that out would be better in the long run—and not as embarrassing as Phoebe turning him down.

Phoebe was actually surprised to find herself sleeping by herself tonight. Not that she made a habit of sleeping with men who took her to dinner. It was just . . . Oh well, it was for the best. Rebound hookups never worked out, and she didn't want to jeopardize their friendship with an awkward morning-after. Besides, she should be concentrating on her interview tomorrow. Not fantasizing about sex with Ty.

Maybe he wasn't even interested. But there had been a couple of times on the walk back to the apartment that she'd been sure he was going to make some suggestion, move, something. But it never happened.

Thank God. This was no time to embark on any relationship with anyone, much less with someone who obviously had so many coping issues. Maybe he had been totally unaware of what she sensed he was feeling. Maybe he'd been thinking about milk jugs.

Had she flirted with him tonight? She didn't think so. Would he even have noticed if she had? He did have a tendency to lose focus during a conversation.

But she was pretty sure he'd been paying attention tonight.

Something she'd realized Gavin didn't do. Ever. Their conversations had mainly centered around the newspaper, or dinner menus, and sex. Sex was a big part of their relationship, which should have been a good thing. But they never discussed ideals. Or their hopes or dreams.

Phoebe sighed. For someone who had just told Ty she asked thought-provoking questions, she realized she'd never really asked them of Gavin. She'd merely buried herself in work, out of necessity to save the paper, she'd told herself. Now she wondered if it was to keep from having to acknowledge the truth.

Gavin hadn't been interested in keeping the *Sentinel* alive. He'd never come right out and told her he wasn't interested, but he had in many subtle ways.

But subtlety never had a chance when she was on a mission. And she'd been on a mission of loyalty to the *Sentinel* long before Gavin appeared on the scene. She had assumed, erroneously, that he would have the same mission.

It never occurred to her that he might have other dreams. Ones he should be free to follow, even if they led him to the *Boston Globe*.

And now here she was, knocking on the door of the *Globe* herself. She just hoped to hell she wouldn't run into him while she was there. Hopefully, she wouldn't have to see him tomorrow.

If she did run into him, she would be gracious. Maybe. Tell

him there were no hard feelings. At least on her part. And they could go their separate ways.

But she really, really hoped she wouldn't see him at all.

Phoebe was up early the next morning, feeling energetic, optimistic, and in need of coffee. What were the chances that Ty would actually have grounds in the freezer?

She found the remote that opened the blinds and was greeted by a sunny day, which she took as a good omen. Then she got into the shower and began to mentally prepare for her day.

It seemed it was easier to prepare her mind than decide what to wear. She'd ended up bringing three potential outfits, but after trying on all three, she decided to go for feel rather than look. Professional, but not too "done." Serious, but not worn to impress.

One last look, a straightening of the jacket collar, and she went out to face the day.

The first thing she noticed when she stepped out of her bedroom, computer case and portfolio in hand, was the smell of coffee. Thank heaven for that.

She put her things down on a dining chair and went into the kitchen.

Ty was there, taking cartons out of a reusable tote.

"I didn't think we'd have time to go out for breakfast so I went down to the deli and got some stuff."

It was quite a spread. Bagels, rolls, cream cheese in several flavors, butter, yogurt, bananas, apples.

She hated telling him that she had no appetite and wouldn't until her interview was over.

He poured her a mug of coffee from a Melior carafe. "There's milk in the fridge. I forgot to get sugar."

"Black is fine," she said, taking the mug and thinking this was almost as awkward as if they'd actually spent the night together.

"Bagel?"

"Thanks, but—"

"You can't concentrate on getting a job with your stomach growling every time there's an awkward pause."

She laughed. "You're right." She sliced a bagel and spread it with veggie cream cheese, then cut that in half. Offered half to Ty.

"I already ate. You want a plate?"

For some reason that made her laugh.

Which made him laugh. "I'm really much better at this . . . usually."

"But you have something on your mind."

"Yeah."

"Work, I hope."

"Always."

"Look, if you want to go to your office now, I can take the train or a Lyft or something."

"I'll take you. I wouldn't want you to get lost like Charlie."

"Charley got lost on the trains here?"

"Not our Charley. It's a song. About a guy named Charlie . . ." He looked at her for confirmation.

Phoebe shook her head.

"Kingston Trio?"

"Nope."

"I wonder if Granna Sutton still has the LP?"

"You heard it at Granna's?"

"Yeah, remember we lived there all year round. I spent a lot of time at her house. There's probably a YouTube video."

"Ty Harken, you are a wealth of arcana."

He shrugged. "That's a polite way of saying it."

"No, I love it."

"I want to drive you."

"Well, in that case," Phoebe said, startled by his insistence, "thank you."

She ate her bagel over the sink and took her coffee to the window. "You have so much light."

"Yeah, that's one of the reasons I got it. I have a drafting table set up in an alcove down the hall. It's nice."

They left early in order to compensate for any traffic.

"God forbid I make you late," Ty said as they stopped for a third light. "Not only my father but your mother, grandmother, and great-aunt would have my head."

"Well, if anything, we'll be early."

"Don't count on it."

He was right. After fighting traffic and navigating the one-way streets between the skyscrapers and office buildings of the financial district, Ty came to a stop in front of the office building that housed the *Globe* and forty-something floors of other businesses.

"Told ya," Ty said. "Fifteen minutes left to reach your final destination."

Phoebe laughed and stared up at the wide glass entrance.

"Daunting?" Ty asked.

"Nah," Phoebe said, forcing nonchalance—her heart was beginning to hammer. "They're on the second and third floors, probably in the old part." She pointed to the granite-and-limestone annex that had been transitioned from the old stock exchange building into the new skyscraper.

The words were barely out of her mouth before she said, "Oh shit," and slid down in her seat.

"What? You're wrinkling your jacket."

"It's Gavin. What the hell? What are the chances?"

"Probably pretty good if he's supposed to meet you."

"He has nothing to do with this."

"Then maybe he wants to make sure you won't badmouth him to whoever you're talking to."

"I would never."

"I know that, but does Gavin?"

It was a good question and it hit home. And she wasn't sure of the answer.

"Want me to go in with you?"

Phoebe cut a look at him. He seemed serious.

"Thanks, but I wouldn't want your car to get towed. I'll be okay."

"If you're sure. Just take your time and do whatever. Don't let him intimidate you."

"Not a chance."

"Or throw you off your game."

"Won't happen." She flashed him a smile that probably looked more like a grimace.

"You'll be fine. I'll be at the address I gave you until whenever. Plenty to do. If I'm out, Brandy will let you in."

"Thanks," Phoebe said, half listening. "Don't worry about me. I have your cell and vice versa."

She opened the car door.

"Wow 'em."

"From your lips." She got out and walked straight across the sidewalk and plaza and up the steps to where Gavin, seeing her, waited with a smile.

Chapter 22

I was hoping to catch you," Gavin said.

"Obviously," Phoebe said. "I'm sorry, but I don't have time to talk. Nice seeing you." Could she be more obvious?

Evidently she would have to be, because Gavin fell in step with her, which was a feat since she was striding at her late-for-a-meeting clip toward the revolving doors.

"You want me to show you around?"

"Thanks, but I think I can manage."

"You're angry."

"No, disappointed maybe, but better to have found out before we got any further." Phoebe jumped into the opening of the revolving doors, hoping to out-speed him.

But he stepped out right behind her. "Listen. I know things didn't end well. I totally accept responsibility."

Phoebe stopped. "It's history, Gavin. I'm over it. And I don't intend to discuss it when I'm going into a meeting." *Or ever.* "So let's let bygones be bygones and forget it. Goodbye."

Ahead of her, a wide beautiful staircase led to the second floor.

But the large blue *B* logo on the wall had her hurrying over to a wooden reception cubicle below.

He was right behind her. "I just hope our relationship doesn't color—"

She cast him a look over her shoulder "It won't come up. Relax. Now I have to go. I don't want to be late."

And finally he walked away.

She turned to smile at the receptionist. "I have an appointment with Oliver Forrest."

She was directed upstairs.

He was waiting for her when she stepped out of the elevator. Phoebe recognized him immediately, a stocky man with a white buzz cut and a slightly crooked nose.

"Mr. Forrest," she said, shaking his hand. "It's so nice to see you again."

"Call me Ollie. I thought I'd give you a quick tour and then go back to my office. We've made a lot of changes since you interned over at the old building."

"I'll say."

"We've leased two floors here. The space as well as the methods are much more fluid these days. A necessary reinvention to keep up with the changing world." He showed her into a large newsroom enclosed by windows on two sides. There were no walls or partitions. Several long rows of workspace ran lengthwise down the room, desk chairs and computer screens placed at regular intervals.

"We work on a revolving deadline these days; the old legacy

platforms don't mesh with today's news cycles. We're interfacing more in a hub paradigm. More efficient and more rapid." Ollie, however, seemed to be running out of steam.

"Impressive," Phoebe said, beginning to feel a little sick. Everything he said sounded good, but the "legacy" part was troubling. But he *had* said features editor.

"You probably are aware that our actual printing division has moved out to Taunton. And down here . . ." He led her to another workspace down the hall.

Phoebe had forgotten how big an operation it was. Busy and exciting, and she felt a rush of expectation. For a moment—then it dissipated. She wasn't sure why.

They walked past several doors, meeting rooms, and work pods partially concealed by frosted glass.

"Come into my office. It's one of the few things that is the same. We do have a few offices." He showed her into a room with a single window but finished in the same industrial carpet as the others.

"Have a seat." He walked around to the other side of a metal desk and turned to his computer. "I wanted to get you in here before we sent out the public notice. We'll be inundated and I didn't want you to get lost in the shuffle. I love what I'm reading from you. I knew from Simeon that you'd been practically running the *Sentinel* the last year before he died. And from what I've heard about the son, you still were. I'm sorry you couldn't save it."

"Not for lack of trying," Phoebe said, suddenly overwhelmed with sadness.

"It's happening all over," Ollie said. "It's getting more and more difficult to keep up with cable news, much less get it out to our readers. Fortunately, our electronic subscriptions are going quite well."

"The *Sentinel* was building an online presence, slowly but surely."

"I know you did everything you could to keep it going."

Phoebe nodded.

"When I heard it closed down, I thought immediately of you. We have an open position. I don't know if you would even be interested. It's an editorial position. Some of what you have been doing. But it wouldn't leave much time for your own writing."

And there it was, the thing that she had known all along. Editing, not writing. It was a great opportunity, but could she give up writing to give other writers a place in the news?

"You should think about the future, Phoebe. I'm selfish; I'll take every asset I can find to keep this paper dynamic. But in the end, you'll have to make a serious decision about your own career and future."

They talked some more. She told him about Charley and her vision for an expanded feature, a series of several articles. They reminisced a little and after another hour, she was walking out the front door, a little shell-shocked, a little excited, but mostly confused. She didn't stop to admire the building. She didn't want to risk another stealth attack by Gavin.

She crossed the street and walked down toward the wharf area. She didn't stop until she reached the Greenway and the fountain, where she sat down and realized she was shaking. It would be a big move. A bigger commitment. And the salary, while decent, wouldn't really be enough to live in Boston on her own.

That's why they have the MBTA, she reminded herself, which made her think of Ty and wonder what he was doing. She really wanted to talk to him. Just to reestablish her equilibrium. He almost always saw things with the clarity of a scientist, and she could use a little clarity about now. But it was obvious that Ty had lots of work he intended to do and she didn't want to be a bother.

She was angry at herself for not having handled the encounter with Gavin better. But he'd taken her off-guard when she should have been concentrating on the upcoming interview, and she resented him for it. But no harm done. And really, did they need to discuss anything about anything?

The answer was a big, resounding *Not in this lifetime.*

She should call her mom, but then she would just have to repeat it all again to the others. She texted that it had gone well, and she'd tell them the details when she got back.

Better just to have lunch and hang out for a while and then go to Ty's place of work. If he was still busy, she could leave her computer and portfolio with him and poke around Cambridge by herself.

Faneuil Hall was only a few blocks away. She deserved a quiet sit-down lunch where she could make notes from her interview. Maybe peruse the shops. Have some fun.

By three o'clock she'd had lunch, window-shopped to her heart's content, and was ready to call it a day. She tapped her carshare app and forty minutes later was pulling up outside a long brick derelict building that might have once been a factory, but now looked idle and forgotten.

"Cool," her driver said.

"Are you sure this is the address?" Phoebe asked.

"Oh, yeah. Big workspaces for local dot-orgs. And artists and greens and such. Good stuff."

It sounded like the right place. She gave him a cash tip and went through the heavy metal doors.

Phoebe couldn't help but make the comparison between this building and the one housing the *Globe*—both could be called minimalist, but whereas Exchange Place was state-of-the-art minimalist, this building was just down-to-the-studs minimalist.

There was a directory on the wall. She scanned down the names of the tenants: Artists Coalition, Daylight, Step Ahead, two architectural firms, an interior design studio—Phoebe rolled her eyes at that one—a few single names, and finally, WATER Reclamation Project.

She walked down the wide, stingily lit hallway, checking doors, some locked with heavy lockboxes and some ajar, through which she could see artists at work or people at desks.

WATER was directly ahead. There was no buzzer or intercom, so she tried the knob. The door opened and she stuck her head inside.

The first thing she noticed was the bright light and clean, crisp walls. Large silver-framed poster-size photos hung equidistant on the walls.

A beige couch and several black leather-and-metal chairs were arranged at the far side with a neat arrangement of high-end magazines displayed on a dark coffee table.

Phoebe stepped all the way inside and saw the top of a curly red head over the top of a computer screen.

From the other side of the screen a hand rose with one finger lifted.

Phoebe understood the universal signal for *Just a minute, I'm in the middle of something*. The hand disappeared followed by a grunt and the rapid repeat taps of a delete key.

The head appeared suddenly. The rest of the hair was as curly and red as the peak had promised. A pixie-like young woman grinned broadly. "Thank God you're here."

"I'm supposed to meet Ty Harken. Am I in the right place?"

"You sure are. You can sit right over there and fill this out while you wait." She pointed a plastic clipboard holding several sheets of paper toward the couch and then toward Phoebe. "Name, address, experience, the usual. But if you can put a sentence together and type, you're hired."

Phoebe stifled a laugh. "I'm afraid there's been a mistake. I'm not applying for anything."

The girl's face collapsed. "You're not from the university?"

Phoebe shook her head. "Sorry."

"You didn't come about the publicist job?"

"Nope. My name's Phoebe. I'm just a friend of Ty's. He does work here, right?"

"Work here? He's the boss. I'm Brandy."

"The boss?"

"Yeah. It's his foundation."

"Ty?" Had he ever mentioned he had a foundation? No, just that he was with a group who worked on projects. "I didn't realize."

"He didn't mention it, did he? He tends to compartmentalize life and work, most of it being work. Makes him seem a little socially awkward. But you probably know that already, being a friend. But when it comes to water, he's the best."

"I can see that," Phoebe said, wandering over to peruse the photos on the wall. Guatemala, Peru. "What's this big one? It looks like a dam."

"It is, but the dam isn't ours. See that grid in the lower-left quadrant?"

Phoebe leaned over and took a closer look. "Uh-huh."

"That's ours. It siphons off gallons of pre-polluted water and diverts it to the far side of the mountain. Affects maybe twenty villages that otherwise would have no water."

"I'm impressed."

"If you'll excuse me, I've got to try to fix this mess before he gets back." Brandy frowned at the computer screen. "Give me any problem with a fractal or a tort or even quality rating, but writing copy? I'm hopeless. Gina quit without notice. Her writing was pretty good, but her grades were crashing and burning because she was out partying when she should have been studying or working."

"What is it?" asked Phoebe. "Maybe I can help."

"A letter to a pack of prospective investors. It needs to be slick, hip, and persuasive. With bullet points—that part I get. But I'm not even the receptionist. We don't really have one unless we're expecting someone."

That sounded more like Ty. A shoestring operation. "What do you normally do?"

"I organize and file the necessary legal papers for each project.

I vet stuff before we send it to the lawyer or the government. Stuff like that. I'm studying environmental law at the U. This is my internship. And I gotta say, as far as internships go, good money and nice working conditions."

"You get paid?"

"Oh yeah, he's generous, but it is a nonprofit, so it's limited. But it also counts double for my intern hours, so that's okay."

"Well, I don't know much about fractals and nothing about torts, but I used to work for a newspaper."

"You're a reporter?"

"Sort of. Want me to take a look?"

"Would you mind? It has to sell these guys on investing in our new regional project. In Mexico. Can you believe there are actually people there who don't have drinkable water? They're right next door."

Brandy pointed at the large-scale map on the wall behind her. "That purple area. It's no-man's-land. Trapped between the states and the river. Totally dangerous, if you ask me. But they need water so . . . Anyway, these new possible investors are super rich, super hipsters. Most likely super woke. Can you help?"

"Let me give it a try." Phoebe shooed Brandy out of her chair and sat down. Brandy pulled up a second chair to sit next to her.

Phoebe read the paragraphs on the screen, then picked up a legal pad of handwritten notes. Two different scripts. She recognized Ty's scrawl in the margin notes; the other must have been the departed publicist's.

Phoebe quickly read through them, trying to get a sense of what Ty was after. It was pretty vague.

"Let's see. Rich hipsters." She hit Return a few times, then started a new intro. Moved some text around. Added a few sentences of her own. Got a few paragraphs down. Went back and changed out a couple of words. Read through it, while Brandy breathed over her shoulder.

"Brilliant. Keep going. It only has to be a page."

"Well, it's a start. But I'm not really sure what tone he wants. Do you have other releases?"

"Lots." She quickly left the room and came back with a folder filled with pitches and prospectuses. "These okay?"

Phoebe began to flip through the folders. "I see the data, but I think we need some appealing personal stories."

"Oh, yeah. We have a basic template we use for fundraising. But he wants this upscaled. Hang on." Brandy sorted through a stack of folders. Pulled one out. "I think we were planning on using some of these, but we ran out of time and a publicist." She plopped the fat manila folder on the desk. "There's more in the back, but Ty liked these the best."

Phoebe opened it to find photos of children, villages, and endorsements.

"Perfect. We can use these?"

"They've all been pre-cleared."

"Photos, too?"

Brandy nodded enthusiastically.

"Color?"

"Sure, we have all the equipment. We just needed . . . you."

Phoebe rifled through the material, found photos of a village. Matched it with a group of children, and a close-up of a kid named Luis, whose name she'd seen on one of the other pages. She looked back through until she found the citation. Snared a Post-it and wrote *Luis gets bottled water at school, when he can get to school.* And attached it to the photo.

The two of them hunkered down, choosing photos and quotations and interspersing them with bullet-point facts. Occasionally the door behind them would open and a young man or woman would ask a question or leave for the day.

"What's back there?" Phoebe finally asked.

Brandy looked at the closed door. "Workspace, specs, maps—it's a bit of a clutter."

"How many people work here?"

"Depends. The office is used mainly to have a storefront and a place for big design projects and problem-solving, and legal stuff. You know, office things. A lot of us are grad students. Three or four full-timers. It's fluid."

"It's impressive."

They whittled down the best photos, prioritized points, and Phoebe began to reshape her raw paragraphs into something that would move, educate, and excite. Another hour passed and they were well on their way to having a dynamic prospectus when Ty walked through the door.

"Am I late?"

Brandy and Phoebe burst out laughing.

Ty waited until they'd finished. "I see you two have met. Did the university send over an intern?"

"No," Brandy said. "But I found someone better." She grinned at Phoebe.

"Well, it's a work in progress," Phoebe said. "But it should give the intern something to work with once she or he gets here."

"Huh," Ty said. "How did your meeting go?"

"Good," Phoebe said. She stood, reached for her cell, and handed it to Brandy. "Put your cell number in and I'll send you my email if you want me to clean up the prospectus for you."

"Thanks," Brandy said on a whoosh of air. "Is it okay if I go? I've got class this evening."

"Go ahead," Ty said. "I'm not sure if I'll be in tomorrow. I'll text you one way or the other."

"Great. Thanks so much, Phoebe. Cheers." Brandy grabbed her purse from under the desk, slid her laptop into a case, and was out the door with a "Bye" and a "Great to meet you."

"She's a whirlwind," Phoebe said.

"She is," Ty agreed. "Did they offer you a job?"

"Early days yet. They have to do a public search. You didn't tell me that the place where you worked was *your* foundation."

"Didn't I? Well, it's really a group effort."

"Brandy says these photos on the walls are all your projects."

Ty looked around as if it was news to him. And maybe it was. Phoebe knew by now that when he was in the "zone" of water reclamation, he didn't pay much attention to his surroundings.

"Yeah. Thanks for helping Brandy out. She isn't really hired to do copy. Let me get my stuff and we'll go."

"Am I going to be allowed to see the inner sanctum?"

Ty, who had already started around the desk, hesitated. "Sure. Not much to see, just work stuff."

"I'm interested," Phoebe said, and joined him.

He opened the door and they stepped inside. It was a huge room, wall-to-wall windows and bright overhead lights.

"It used to be a cannery, I think," Ty said, looking around. "It's kind of chaotic."

"I think it's amazing," Phoebe countered, stepping past him into the space. Light poured in over drafting tables and shelves filled with rolls of what had to be plans.

Tables about the size of ping-pong tables held models of buildings and landscapes and miniature contraptions for every occasion. Not a cleared-off section in sight.

Two lone young men were bent over a spec sheet at the far end of the room, but the whole space thrummed with energy.

"This is where it all gets thought out?"

"A lot of it. But a lot changes on site. More than we'd like, actually."

"So it's not just you and a bunch of milk jugs?"

"What?"

"I was kidding. I had an idea that there was more to this story than you were letting on. This is a big operation, isn't it?"

"Pretty big."

"Why don't you . . . I don't know, brag more?"

His eyebrows furrowed. "To who?"

"Well, I'm proud of you," Phoebe blurted, then immediately felt stupid.

"Thanks."

She snorted out a laugh.

The two men at the end of the room looked up. And she

clamped her hand over her mouth. "I hope I didn't interrupt any great ideas."

"Nah, come down and meet Jonah and Frank."

They walked through a warren of papers, computers, and a giant printer to where the two men stood facing them, both grinning broadly.

As they got closer, one of them raised his eyebrows at Ty.

Ty introduced them.

"Hey."

"Hi."

And they stood there grinning.

Ignoring them, Ty explained what they were working on to Phoebe, then told them he and Phoebe were leaving.

"Sure."

"No problem."

"Have fun, man."

Ty turned Phoebe around but not before she saw Jonah give Ty a thumbs-up.

"They're sweet," Phoebe said, when the door closed behind them.

"They're scientists," Ty said.

"They like you."

"What a weird thing to say. Let's go."

Phoebe shook her head and retrieved her laptop and portfolio and watched as Ty went through an elaborate locking system and set an alarm.

"You're locking them in?"

"They can get out, then the system will automatically relock when they leave."

"Do you mind if I ask you a question?" Phoebe asked once they were in Ty's SUV and pulling out of the parking lot.

"Not as long as you don't mind if I don't answer it."

"Fair enough. Has your dad ever been here?"

"Are you kidding? One look at this and he'd have a coronary."

"I think you underestimate him. Besides, my Lyft driver said it was one of the cool places to be."

"It is . . . now. When WATER moved in, it was still pretty much an abandoned factory with a bunch of artists and start-up companies. I had the foresight to take a long lease."

"And you pay all those people?"

"I don't; the foundation does. It pays me, too."

"You're on salary like everyone else?"

"Of course, that's the point of the foundation—to use most of the money for the projects. I'm not destitute, regardless of what my family thinks. It's kind of early for dinner. Do you want to go back to the apartment and have a drink first?"

"Apartment," she said, recognizing a change of subject when she heard it, but not willing to let the subject go.

"Good, now tell me what happened at your interview."

Chapter 23

So basically," Ty said, his eyes fixed on the traffic ahead, "it boils down to do you want to be the facilitator or the freelancer."

Phoebe, who had worked herself into a state reliving her morning from that first meeting with Gavin—"He's such a worm"—and through the interview with Ollie Forrest—"You need to think about your career as a whole"—snapped her head toward him.

"You know, you have the most annoying habit of distilling everything down to the most simplistic terms."

"The simplest choices are usually the things that work. The more moving parts, the more things can break down or go wrong."

"In the mechanical world, maybe," Phoebe said. "A person's life is a little more complicated." She raised an eyebrow that he didn't see because he was looking forward. "Most people's lives."

"Because they don't keep it simple," he said, oblivious to innuendo.

"I don't know." Phoebe leaned back against the headrest and groaned. "Why is it that I always want to laugh when you're at your most irritating?"

"Why am I irritating? I merely identified the underlying argument. Either do your writing or organize someone else's to the best effect. They're both valid choices, as I see it. It depends on what you want to do."

"That's just it. I don't know. I knew until I had a choice and now I don't know."

Ty sighed. "Pros and cons," he said, and changed lanes.

"I don't know!"

"Of course you do. You just haven't taken the time to think about it in a rational way." He held up one hand, then returned it to the steering wheel. "It's all happened too fast for you to collate. If you want, we can order dinner in tonight and we'll make a list."

"You'd do that?"

"Of course. Why wouldn't I?"

Because you have your own work that you'd rather be working on. Because my decision doesn't change lives like yours does. Because I can decide for myself—should decide for myself—will decide for myself. But it would be nice to have his input. It would also be nice to have dinner, just the two of them with no family, no waiters, just them.

"Then, okay. Thanks. It sounds like a plan."

Ty looked over Phoebe's shoulder to the three sheets of paper she had spread out on the breakfast bar before her.

Sometimes it took killing a tree to form your ideas. Tactile learning. Tactile ideation. He did it himself.

He just didn't get what was bothering her so much about what to do. It seemed like an obvious choice to him. But it didn't matter what he thought. It mattered what she really wanted to do. It was pretty clear to him.

Or maybe he was wrong. It wouldn't be the first time. Just because you're really good at something doesn't mean you should have to do that thing for a lifetime. It had been a no-brainer for Ty when that time came for him. He wanted to do real things, not just brain things, sitting in front of a computer thinking of stuff.

Most of those things didn't impact the people who were just trying to get by and have their children survive childhood. His work was like the proverbial finger in the dike. He knew it. He didn't have any false illusions. But he knew it was what he was meant to do.

Why didn't Phoebe know?

Actually, if he thought about it, he was in a bit of a quandary himself. Usually he could see things without too much prejudice, but in this case . . . It had occurred to him somewhere during this trip to Boston that if she worked for the *Globe*, she'd be in the same town as him. They might get together sometimes. Except that he was often out of town. But if she freelanced . . . Stupid to go there.

He pulled his mind away, but it drifted right back into what-if territory.

She glanced up at him. "What?"

"Nothing."

"Okay, can I talk this through?"

"Sure."

She slid off the stool and began to pace, holding the papers like a hand of cards. "As an editor I'd be able to curate articles and organize them for best reading potential. I would have a desk, and a decent salary. But most likely no actual writing except for the occasional few inches to fill out copy or build out a theme. Staff writer: salary not as good, assigned articles, a chance to pitch a few ideas, not knowing if they would fly or not. Not sure they even have openings for staff writers in human interest. Not that I mind paying my dues. I mean, sometimes you find the most moving articles when you least expect it, like my food bank article when I was just out to do a PSA.

"Then there's always freelancing. No steady salary. Pay per article, mostly a feast-or-famine existence. And from what I've heard, mainly famine with an occasional feast thrown in. But I could also branch out to magazines. And I'd get to choose what I write about. But then I'd have to sell it."

Ty had been watching her pace, but now he stood up. "Fine, but what do you *want* to do?"

"I want to write, but it's not so easy for me. I didn't invent any doohickey to set me up or tide me over when things are slim."

"True," Ty admitted. "Doohickeys do come in handy sometimes."

She stopped in front of him and smiled.

And Ty did something he had no intention of doing—he kissed her.

She was too shocked to resist, he guessed, because she kissed him back. He was pretty shocked himself.

For a moment he lost himself; water reclamation, doohickeys, and hostile families receded into the dark. It was amazing.

Then his cell rang. He ignored it, tried to ignore it, would have ignored it, but Phoebe's cell rang next, and his euphoria was replaced by a sudden dread.

Ty jerked away, leaving Phoebe flustered and beyond. Then her cell rang again, and she made the obvious conclusion. Something was wrong at the beach.

Ty walked away, his cell to his ear, but she could hear the angry voice at the other end.

She grabbed her phone off the counter and walked in the opposite direction.

"Mom? What's happening?"

"Did Ty already get a call?"

"Yes. He's on the phone now." Phoebe cupped her hand over her mouth. "What's going on? Is it his dad?"

"Damn. I'd hoped to get to you guys before Dan did. Lars is fine. There is no reason for any drama. The dumbass climbed up the ladder to check on Ty's roof repair, and slipped. He was three rungs from the ground. Sprained his ankle and got a bump on the head. We took him to the hospital to get checked out. He's fine. No concussion and he has a soft cast, which he can walk on. There is no reason for you and Ty to hare back here. Unfortunately, Dan happened to call while we were at the hospital and learned what happened and now he and Scottie are on their way to the beach. Ugh, these men. There's absolutely no reason for everyone to be here.

"Your grandmother and Vera and I are staying with him until

the sons arrive. Not that he needs us, but I'll be damned if he's going to complain to them about Ty or let them badmouth him without anyone here to take Ty's side. So here we sit."

"I'm sure we'll come right back," Phoebe said, glancing at Ty. "I can hear his brother's accusations all the way from the other side of the room. I can tell Ty is getting pretty upset."

"Do you want me to talk to him?" Ruth said. "Maybe coming from a mother, he'll calm down. There's absolutely nothing to worry about."

"I'll tell him," Phoebe said. "Thanks. His call just ended. I'll call you back."

She knew before Ty reached her that they would be heading for the beach. "That was my brother Dan."

"I know," Phoebe said. "That was my mom. She said your dad is fine. He sprained his ankle but is mobile. But that your brothers are driving there."

"Dan didn't say he was fine. She's sure?"

"Yes, and said to call her and she'd give you all the details."

"Listen. Why don't you stay here in case the *Globe* wants to talk to you again. I'd better—"

"They can phone me. We'll both go. Then you won't be worried."

And your brothers won't blame you when you're not there to defend yourself. Not that Ty ever defended himself. But dammit, Phoebe would.

"Sorry."

"Don't be. Well, maybe about one little thing."

He frowned. Then his brow cleared for a second. "Yeah, I should have known it was too good to last."

Normally, that clumsy reaction would have set Phoebe off. But as she threw her things into the suitcase, checked for wayward chargers, and cleaned out the bathroom of toiletries, she concentrated on one part of that phrase: good.

It had been that and more. Damn Mr. Harken and his self-pity and his sons' willful misunderstanding of Ty's life.

They were packed and on the road within minutes. Ty spent the first half hour making calls canceling things he'd planned to do the next day. He'd definitely been planning to stay at least another day. How he had managed to make so many appointments in such a short amount of time was beyond Phoebe. Though it wasn't surprising; he was completely goal-oriented and efficient. But the most amazing thing was that he did it all without a sign of rancor, while Phoebe silently fumed for him from the passenger seat.

And not just angry for him, but for both of them and for the moment that might have become more, except for the selfishness of his family. She wondered what he felt—his eyes glued to the road, his posture upright, alert, but not tense, just . . . efficient.

And she couldn't help but wonder what might have been except for that phone call.

They made the trip in record time, though after Phoebe's first glance at the speedometer she decided it was better not to know, and didn't look again. Somehow they managed to make it without being stopped by the police, so it must not have been too bad.

Ty slowed as he turned down the lane to the beach. She could see a strange car in the Harkens' driveway and guessed Scottie and Daniel had arrived.

"I'll drop you off first," he said into the silence.

"Oh no, you won't. I'm not leaving you to face your dad and brothers by yourself. Anyway, I'm betting Mom, Alice, and Vera are there, too."

He cut a glance toward her.

"They weren't going to leave your dad alone to get into more mischief, and they won't leave you to face that onslaught alone."

"I'm an adult. I can handle it."

"No one doubts that for a second. But it's nice to have allies when you need them."

He reluctantly drove past the Sutton drive and pulled into his own, where he immediately got out and headed for the house. Phoebe hurried after him and they managed to walk into the living room together.

They were all there, both families. Scottie, who Phoebe recognized by his hair, had grown pudgy. Daniel wore a close-cropped beard that looked out of place at a beach house, not to mention on his face.

Ruth, Alice, and Vera flanked Lars, who was sitting in his armchair, foot on an ottoman with a soda and sandwich on the table at his elbow.

Ty stepped toward his dad, and the others all began talking at once. Phoebe's stomach growled; so much for a nice dinner out in Boston.

Daniel cut off Ty halfway across the room. He was a couple of inches taller than Ty, well over six feet, and his lean frame made him seem to tower over his brother.

"How could you leave him alone? The one thing we asked you to do, and then you go traipsing off to Boston. He could have been killed."

"Yeah," Scottie added. "Don't you even care what happens to him? We never ask you to do anything and the one time we do, look what happens."

"Yeah," Ty said. "And I feed him baloney, too."

Daniel's head snapped toward the sandwich. "You said you'd make sure he ate well. We trusted you."

"Hey," Vera broke in. "I made that sandwich and it's a damn good one if I do say so myself."

"Delicious," agreed Lars, who picked it up and took a large bite.

Phoebe glared at her great-aunt. She was just making things worse.

"We can't be running up here every time you screw up," Dan said.

Ty cocked his head as if he was considering the situation. Phoebe would have decked the guy, but she didn't see Ty being goaded into a display of force.

Then something amazing happened.

"You know, Dan. You're absolutely right. I'm terrible at playing nursemaid. I think it's best that I concede that point and just get out of your way."

Ty nodded slightly and then walked out of the room to dead silence.

"Where the hell do you think you're going?" demanded Scottie, springing to life as his face suffused with red. He looked just like he had years ago when throwing a tantrum—Phoebe had forgotten that about him.

"Upstairs to get my things," Ty said evenly and kept going.

"Well," Vera said. "Which one of you lovely young men is going to take over Ty's job? We'll set you a place at dinner."

"We can't stay here," Dan said. "We have responsibilities."

"Did it ever occur to you that maybe Ty has responsibilities, too?" Phoebe said.

"Well, sure. Some. But we thought it would be perfect for him. Give him a chance to get free room and board with very little work."

"You really don't have a clue, do you?"

"I don't know why you're getting so high and mighty," Scottie said. No doubt about it, the spoiled child had grown up to be the spoiled man. So much for "he'll grow out of it." "Just stay out of it. This is family business."

"Then be a family, Scottie. Jeez, you've always been a pompous little prick."

There was an audible gasp, probably from her family. Lars seemed to be enjoying the situation immensely.

Phoebe turned on him, but an urgent look from Ruth stopped her from saying what she really thought. She had to be content with glaring at Ty's father.

"We *are* a family," Scottie said. "But Dan and I also have responsibilities to our business, our families. Ty is the one who isn't tied down."

"Listen to yourselves," Phoebe said, not being able to contain herself. "Ty has responsibilities, too, serious ones, important ones, but you never bothered to find out what they are."

"Really, Phoebe. How dare you lecture us."

"Well, somebody needs to," Ruth said. "You're all behaving abominably. None of this is Ty's fault. Lars is the one who insisted that he drive Phoebe to Boston. Insisted. And how many times in the last few weeks has Ty climbed up on that roof because Lars refused to let the roofers come even after Ty offered to pay for a new roof."

"Ty offered to pay for a new roof?" Scottie asked incredulously.

"Clueless," Phoebe spat at him.

"And," Ruth continued, aiming her words at Lars, "even then you didn't trust him to do a good job. You had to go up and see for yourself, and got what you deserved. Now you've alienated your son, who only tried to help you. All three of you should be ashamed of yourselves."

They were all looking duly chastised when Ty came down the stairs carrying a backpack, a laptop, and a duffel.

Dan stepped in front of him. "Ty, don't be rash. You can't just leave Dad high and dry."

Ty looked straight at him, his face so bland that Phoebe wondered what it was costing him. And she ached for what his own family was putting him through.

"I'll send someone in a day or two to pick up the rest of my gear."

"He resents having to be here to take care of me," Lars announced to the others.

Ty stopped at that. And turned toward his father. "I don't resent being here, Dad. I resent *you* for not trying harder. You're not the only one who's grieving for Mom. We all are. It's not just about you." He jerked a cursory nod toward Alice and Ruth and Vera and strode out of the house.

Lars's mouth went slack. "You can't leave. Who's going to take care of me?" he cried, sounding suddenly feeble.

Ruth cast him a suspicious look. "One of your responsible sons can."

"Or not," added Vera. "Hell, maybe they'll decide to put you in a home. You'll get around-the-clock responsibility in a facility. That should make you happy."

"Vera," Alice warned.

"You forgot about the husband hunters," Ruth said. "I'm sure one of them would love to take Ty's place. Frankly, I preferred Ty, but to each his own. Let's see, there's that lovely blonde who brought the tuna casserole, or . . ."

"I hate tuna casserole," groused Lars, and tried to get out of the chair.

Dan and Scottie rushed to help him.

He batted them away. "I don't need help. I don't need a babysitter. I went up on the roof because I was feeling useless and lonely. It was stupid, but you can't babysit stupid away. I'm fine on my own. I want you all to go back to your lives, call me on weekends and come for holidays, but get your noses out of my daily life. I appreciate you, but you should be with your own families; they'll probably be worried with you on the highway this late."

Vera and Alice exchanged surreptitious glances.

"If you're sure," Dan said. "Jayne does get a little frantic dealing with the children by herself."

"Any self-respecting child would be in bed by now," Vera commented under her breath.

Alice nudged her with her toe.

"Do you need help getting to bed?" Dan asked.

"I'm not going to bed. But thank you for coming. Call me when you get home so I won't worry."

Left with that obvious dismissal, the two men took themselves off.

"Oh, great," Vera said when they were gone. "You've gotten rid of your other two sons. Now we'll be stuck with you."

Lars leaned back in his chair. He was looking tired. "What got into that boy? He usually just rolls with the punches. Makes me crazy. Now, when I thought he was finally showing some gumption, he up and leaves. Something must have happened when he was in Boston." He glared at Phoebe. "Did you have something to do with this?" His expression changed. "Just what did the two of you get up to while you were there?"

"We worked. Ty finally had a little time to do his own work instead of waiting on you all the time. That's all."

A glint shone in Lars's eyes. "I wonder. Maybe you're good for him."

Phoebe opened her mouth, but Vera beat her to it.

"You stupid man. You think playing your family against each other is a game? Two sons who couldn't wait to get back to their 'responsibilities,' while denigrating the key to their freedom to do it."

"Vera," Alice attempted.

Vera ignored her. "Ty didn't have to give up his life to come stay with you, but unlike Daniel and Scottie, he dropped everything to do it. Not because he needed a handout, but because he loves you. And you just keep throwing it back in his face. Well, it'll serve you right if you end up old and alone. Life is short. Much shorter than any of us expect. And you're wasting yours. Delores is gone. One day you'll wake up and Ty will be gone, too."

"Vera!"

"No, Alice, let me finish. I don't know why I should care what happens to you. Well, actually I don't. But I do care about Ty and he doesn't deserve this treatment from his family or anyone else."

Phoebe could only stare at her great-aunt as she steamrolled ahead. She'd never heard Vera talk like this. Had no idea she harbored such deep feelings. She'd always had a witty but slightly edgy view of the world. Except for that one night on the beach and her talk about the stars.

"I shouldn't have pushed so hard," Lars said quietly. "It's just gotten to be a habit. I didn't think he'd really leave."

Vera leaned over his chair and braced her hands on the armrests. "You should have thought of that before you pushed him out the door."

Then she straightened up and walked past the others and out of the house.

"Oh no. My stuff is still in Ty's car." Phoebe rushed out behind her.

Chapter 24

"Well," Ruth said. "You should be pleased with yourself, Lars. You've managed to clear the place in record time."

"I didn't tell them to come. That was Daniel's doing. Hell, taking Phoebe to Boston was the first time Ty has shown any interest in his personal life since he's been here. I wanted them to stay the whole weekend."

"If you're playing matchmaker with him and Phoebe, stop. Not that you'll need to now. You've fixed that."

"He didn't have to leave. He should have stayed and given them what for. Why won't he just stick up for himself?"

"Why? Why is that so important to you?"

"Because people will take advantage of him."

"I think he's quite capable of taking care of himself," Ruth said. "If I were you, I would call him and grovel. But not while he's driving. Or better still, go after him and talk to him man-to-man. And now Alice and I have to go look after our own brood."

"Good night," said Alice. "Enjoy your solitude," she added as Ruth steered them both out of the room and out the kitchen door.

"Ty's Jeep is still in the driveway," Ruth said in a whisper, and guided Alice away from the drive and toward the porch door.

"My goodness, don't tell me you're playing matchmaker after giving Lars a lecture on doing it."

"Of course not. But they seemed to have developed a rapport. And if they both end up here through the summer—though I suppose that won't happen after Lars made such an ass of himself. And he was making such progress; he was almost back to his former self."

"Maybe he scared himself," Alice suggested as she followed Ruth inside.

"You mean he doesn't want to admit he *can* live without Delores?"

"Well, think about it. A few weeks ago he just sat around moping and feeling sorry for himself. Lately, long stretches pass without him thinking about her. And most of the time when he does mention her, it's with fondness and happy memories, as it should be. Men are needy creatures. They try not to let go of one thing before grasping onto another."

Ruth stopped so suddenly that Alice had to hop out of the way not to run into her.

"Mother, sometimes you astound me."

"What a strange thing to say. Where are we going?"

"To the kitchen. I bet Vera is already there, nose planted to the window, and I have no intention of letting her or any of us spy on Phoebe and Ty. Let them deal with their own lives. Lord knows they've both got a lot on their plates right now."

Alice made a face. "I had no intention of spying, but maybe we should check. Vera will have the drinks made by now."

But Vera wasn't in the kitchen or the parlor or anywhere downstairs.

"Do you think she went to bed?" Ruth asked.

"At this time of night?" Alice said. "Hardly."

"You don't think she went back to Lars's for round two, do you?"

"That I don't know. Vera has always been straightforward; her humor is dry, her tongue can be sharp, but it's usually sharp with sarcasm. Tonight she was angry. Really angry." Alice cocked her head as if bemused. "I can't remember when I last saw her really angry."

Phoebe caught up to Ty just as he was taking her suitcase and portfolio out of the SUV.

"You were really going to leave without saying goodbye?"

"No . . . well, yeah. But then I remembered I had your life's work in the back, so I was going to drop it off at your house. Besides, I'm just going down to Charley's."

"And bunk out in one of the RVs instead of sleeping in your own bed?"

"Well, if I didn't, they would have been throwing around the guilt trip all night. I can think of more interesting ways to spend an evening."

So could Phoebe. She narrowed her eyes. "You're not upset?"

"Only because it cut our trip to Boston short. And that was my fault. Once I knew he was all right, I should have just hung up, but . . ."

"But you're a good son."

"Not especially."

"How can you be so fair?"

"How can a journalist ask that question?"

Phoebe rolled her eyes. "They were totally aggressive and nasty. And you just took it."

"Yeah, that drives my dad crazy. But it's pointless to get all riled up. They'll never change. Three peas in a pod, my mom used to call them. She was the only one who could keep them in check.

"It's just their way of coping with their frustration and their fear—go on the attack. Strongman tactics. It's the only way they know how to reach out. Which is weird; our mother was so compassionate. They're worried about our father; they're so afraid that if they don't do something, he'll have a heart attack and die. And they're petrified that I'm going to leave them to take care of him. The man's perfectly healthy—a few baloney sandwiches aren't going to do him in. But it's his choice. Not ours. Plus he's been more energetic since you and your mom came." Ty looked like he was fighting a smile. "I shouldn't tell you this, but he punched your father. It was kind of an accident. Neither one of them is in the best of shape."

"What? When did this happen?"

"I wasn't supposed to tell. Dad didn't want to embarrass your mom, but your father came over to accuse him of having an affair with her. He swung and missed and fell on my dad's fist. In retrospect it was pretty hilarious. Sorry, I shouldn't laugh."

Phoebe shook her head. The idea of two men fighting over her mother was . . . not ridiculous at all. She was a smart, caring person who deserved to be fought over.

"Actually, I think it's a compliment."

"Don't tell her or I will be in hot water."

"All right—for a while anyway. It's still too soon for either of us to see the humor in our situations."

"When my mother died, she left a hole. Ruth has been great trying to help, all of you have, but you can't fill that hole with trips to the lighthouse and lobster rolls. You have to learn to live with it. Only he can do that.

"It's been hell being in that house. Everything is just as it was before Mom died. Every vase, every picture. My mother is everywhere you look. Every time you turn you see something. Remember something. Occasionally it makes you smile for a second, but mostly it's just a kick in the gut. Everything is still there but her."

Phoebe reached out to touch his arm. He'd never opened up so much about his own grief.

"Frankly I'll be glad to leave. It's been exhausting trying to keep him from sliding back into depression. He'll have to figure it out on his own. I just wish we had come to some kind of peaceful coexistence before it ended."

"You had. He was coming around." She thought of her own father and how his absence hadn't even really affected her yet.

It probably wouldn't until the first holiday without him. But he had walked out on them, not died. They could always reconcile if they chose. But Delores would never be coming back.

"Don't worry. I'm not angry, I'm not hurt, I'm just done. I thought that with Mom gone, I should make a last effort to connect with him. A moment of febrile hubris on my part."

"You?" Phoebe asked incredulously. "I don't think I've ever seen you in feverish excitement."

He puffed out a rueful laugh. "If we hadn't been interrupted earlier tonight, you might have."

She smiled. "Sorry I missed it."

"Me too."

"That's not part of why you're leaving, is it?"

"No, but it's probably for the best, anyway. I'm not interested in a summer fling."

"Jeez, me neither."

"But I was really tempted."

"Yeah, me too."

"Maybe if you take the job at the *Globe*."

"Maybe. Which reminds me, your latest prospectus is sitting unfinished on my laptop. Brandy and I had a lunch date for tomorrow. I'll have to text her. But we can work remotely."

"I appreciate it, but you don't have to."

"I know, but I can do it. And I want to." She tried to read his expression. "So what's the plan? Are you really leaving? What about Charley? What about the river sweeper?"

"I'll stay on at Charley's for a couple of days to help him finish up some things we were working on. Charley managed on his own before I got here. He'll keep doing it when I'm gone. It will take me a few days to dismantle the sweeper . . ."

"But you're not leaving without saying goodbye to Mom, or Granna or Vera."

"Of course not."

"And make sure your dad's okay . . ."

He shrugged. "I'll have to come back to pack up the rest of my gear." He hesitated, then said, "It was great meeting you; I mean as an adult." A slight smile played across his face. "You were annoying as hell as a kid."

"I can be pretty annoying now," she said.

"Yeah, you can be, but in a good way. I hope you get the job."

"Thanks." She said the word, but it sounded hollow to her ears. "This is sounding awfully goodbye-ish."

He leaned over and kissed her cheek. "Maybe we'll see each other in Boston."

He handed her the laptop, then picked up the portfolio and suitcase and carried it across the driveway to her kitchen door.

Phoebe followed him, wondering what she wanted to say besides *Don't go yet*. He put her cases by the door.

"I won't go in. Tell everyone I'll see them before I leave."

"Okay. Call my cell when you're ready to dismantle the sweeper and I'll come help."

"Thanks, I will."

"I'll probably be dropping by Charley's tomorrow anyway. Ollie Forrest is interested in printing his story."

He nodded but didn't turn around.

"Ty!"

He turned, frowned.

"Why tonight? What happened that made you take a stand to-night?"

He shrugged. "You happened."

Phoebe's heart raced. Was he blaming her for taking him away from his family, or . . . ? "Is that a good thing?"

"Yeah. A very good thing."

"Oh. Good."

He got into his SUV. She stepped into the shadow of the house and watched him drive away. It was definitely a good thing. Weird, but good.

Ruth and Alice sat in the parlor sipping glasses of white wine and listening for Vera and Phoebe to return.

When at last they heard the kitchen door open, they both leaned forward to hear who it was.

"Ty and Phoebe," Ruth said in a low voice. She could hear them talking but she couldn't make out what they were saying. She told herself that it was probably private and she should not succumb to eavesdropping. But Phoebe was also her daughter and at a vulnerable time in her life.

"Well, at least Phoebe caught up to him before he left," Ruth said. "I think we should invite him to stay with us if he doesn't want to stay at Lars's. He'll still be close to Lars and it won't be as uncomfortable as camping out at the fish camp." She pushed herself out of the club chair. "I'll just go tell—"

The screen door slammed.

Ruth and Alice both jolted back into their seats and were innocently sipping wine when Phoebe walked into the room.

"He's really going?" Ruth asked.

Phoebe nodded.

Ruth stretched out a hand to grasp Phoebe's. "I'm sure it will all work out. Everyone was tired tonight; they'll all be thinking more clearly after a good night's sleep."

"I don't think so."

"It will be a first if they do," Alice said. "I was ready to give Lars a swift kick myself if Vera hadn't beaten me to it."

Ruth poured Phoebe out a glass and handed it to her, and Phoebe sat on the couch across from her.

"I'm sorry your trip to Boston was cut short, sweetheart. I wouldn't have even called if it hadn't been for Dan overreacting like he did."

"Yeah, me too," Phoebe said. "But it's a good thing you did. We would have come anyway and at least Ty didn't have to worry about his dad the whole way home. Dan didn't give him any details, just started yelling. I don't remember him and Scottie being such jerks."

"They aren't jerks," Alice said. "They're concerned about their father and going about it in the only way they know how."

"By attacking their brother? Like that's really going to help."

"Is Ty very upset?"

"He says no; he told me pretty much the same thing, but how could he not be? You wouldn't believe how successful he is. He runs a huge foundation, he does water reclamation projects all over the world, and all they do is put him down."

"I suspect it's a titch of envy," Alice volunteered.

Ruth and Phoebe both looked at her in astonishment.

"Their weird, geeky brother made it big," Alice continued. "He's good-looking, does good works, and is a successful businessman. A real catch if anyone was interested."

Phoebe's mouth dropped open. "How do you know all this?"

"I Googled him," Alice said. "I keep track of a lot of people that way."

"How many glasses of wine have you two socked away?" Phoebe asked.

"This is our first," Ruth said. "We were just waiting for you and Vera to get back so you can tell us how the interview went. But all this drama . . ."

"Did you see Vera when you were outside?" Alice asked.

"No. She isn't here?"

"No."

Phoebe sighed and took a sip of wine. "Did you look on the beach?"

"Vera?" Alice looked in the direction of the beach, as though she could see through the walls. "I suppose I could . . ."

"No, Mother. She probably just needs to regroup. She was rather spectacular."

"Are you worried?" Phoebe asked.

"No," Alice said determinedly. "Though she has been acting particularly odd lately. Haven't you noticed? No, of course you wouldn't. It's subtle and dates way back from when we were children. She was always doing things, but when she was really upset . . . she just did more. Until . . . Something is bothering her."

Vera had kept them all moving, Phoebe thought. More so in the last few weeks. But the phone calls, the talk about stars on the beach, her anger at Lars tonight. Was it all related? Should they be worried?

"She hasn't said anything to you?" Phoebe asked, putting down her wine. Ty and the *Globe* and Lars and the lateness of the hour—and now Vera missing—were all affecting her objectivity.

"No, and I didn't ask. I learned back in childhood that everyone has their own time for doing things. If you push them, they just get mad. At least Vera always did. Maybe I'm just being overly protective. It seems to be going around these days. I'm sure she'll tell us in her own good time."

Maybe she would, but maybe she wouldn't get the chance. She could be on the beach dying this very minute and here they sat not wanting to pry. Ruth and Alice hadn't heard that phone call. It would have piqued Phoebe's interest as a journalist even if it hadn't been her great-aunt on this end of the conversation. Should she tell them her fears? Was she blowing it out of proportion? Granna was worried. Better safe than sorry.

"I don't know if I should say anything, but I overheard her on a phone call a couple of weeks ago. I didn't mean to. It was dark and I was sitting outside, thinking. She got a call and brought the phone outside to talk. She didn't see me, and I didn't want to disturb her, so I just held still until she walked past. But I did hear her end of the conversation. She was upset; I could tell. Like it was bad news. She said something about how much time she had. I'm not sure what it was about. But it was enough so that I followed her down to the beach to make sure she was okay. She was sitting in the sand and she started talking about all sorts of things—the stars, the universe, and it sounded like . . . I don't know . . ." Phoebe looked desperately from Granna to her mother. "Maybe I'm mistaken, but . . ."

"It's okay, Phoebe," Alice said. "Just say it."

Phoebe looked at Granna and forced out the words she didn't want to say. "I think she's dying."

The air was sucked out of her lungs. Ruth and Alice just stared at her.

"At least that's what it sounded like. I asked if she was okay and she said yes. Maybe I'm wrong, I hope I am, but—"

Alice shook her head.

Footsteps sounded over their heads, then came down the stairs.

"She's been upstairs this whole time," Alice said.

A moment later, Vera appeared in the archway. She was carrying a suitcase.

Alice jumped up. "Vera! What are you doing?"

Vera's leaving. Phoebe knew it. And Alice did, too. Phoebe could see the disappointment in her eyes.

Ruth stood more slowly and went to stand by her mother.

Vera shrugged. "Phoebe, I wanted to hear about your interview, but with all the people leaving tonight, I think it's time for me to join the exodus."

"Why?" asked Phoebe. "You should stay here."

Vera took a step backward as if she hadn't expected an argument.

"Vera?" Alice asked.

"I have to go." Vera spun around and started for the door.

"Phoebe thinks you're dying."

Vera slowed, looked back over her shoulder. Then turned all the way to face them. "What? No, Alice. Not me. Someone else. Someone I love very much. I have to go now. I should never have come."

"When are you coming back?" Phoebe demanded.

"I don't know." Vera reached the door and then was gone. They heard the Jeep roar to life, then recede as she drove away.

First Ty, now Vera. Would Phoebe be next? Maybe it was time for her to go, too.

"Well," Alice said. "Now that that's settled, Phoebe, we want to hear all about your trip to Boston."

"But Granna," Phoebe said, the tears welling in her eyes.

Alice pulled her close. "Sweetheart, there are some things you can change and some you can't. Thanks to you, we at least know that Vera is not about to meet her end. She'll come back. Eventually. She always does."

Chapter 25

Phoebe slept late the next morning. When she stumbled down the stairs sometime after nine o'clock, the smell of frying bacon led her straight to the kitchen.

Alice was squeezing oranges into juice and Ruth was standing at the stove. Phoebe went to peer over her shoulder.

"Blueberry pancakes," Ruth said. "With organic bacon from the farm stand. They swore it would be the best we ever tasted."

"It smells that good," Phoebe said. "But why aren't you at work?"

"There are times when you need to be home. I called Inez and explained what had been going on, and she gave me the morning off. Now that we've hired another counter girl, life is a lot less hectic. Besides, we have a busy weekend coming up, so we'd already decided to take it easier the few days before, then it will be round-the-clock baking."

Alice handed Phoebe a glass.

"Thanks." Phoebe carried it to the table and sat down. "I haven't even asked how things were going at the bakery."

"You've had lots on your mind."

"Still do," Phoebe said, and took a sip of orange juice. "Why don't I have a juicer?" she said. "This is like heaven."

"You can have this one," Alice said. "I have two." She held up a shallow saucer with a glass reamer in the center.

"I was thinking something that plugged in," Phoebe said.

"But this is excellent for keeping your wrists in shape, something that someone who spends so much time on a keyboard should do."

"Hmmm," Phoebe said. "Why are we having such a large breakfast?"

"Because we all need pampering." Ruth put a plate stacked high with pancakes on the table. "Mother, sit down."

Alice carried two more glasses of juice over to the table and sat down.

When they were all seated and the pancakes, bacon, and maple syrup had been passed, Ruth said, "I just wanted you both to know that I've filed for divorce."

Phoebe's fork stopped inches from her mouth. She'd known this was coming. Still, it was hard to hear. Her mother had every right to do what she wanted. And after spending the last few weeks with her and seeing her transformation, Phoebe could hardly complain.

"This doesn't mean that you girls have to choose between your parents. This is between the two of us and . . ."

"It's okay, Mom. I know you both love us very much. We're all adults. We aren't mad and we don't blame ourselves or any of that other stuff."

"From your lips to your sisters' ears," Ruth said, and poured milk into her coffee. "Your grandmother and I have talked this over, and I'm going to stay here for a while until I get settled into the job and can look for an apartment."

"No hurry," said Alice, who seemed more interested in her bacon than the conversation. "And you're welcome to stay, too. So don't feel like you have to take the first job that comes along, though the *Globe* is a very reputable paper. But only you know what's best for you."

"It's not a done deal," Phoebe said. "There will be stiff competition. And frankly, I'm not sure I'm ready to give up reporting for editing just yet. I mean, it's a really important job, but I feel like I missed being out in the field because I was managing the *Sentinel*. Then again, opportunities like this don't come along ever."

"Eat," Alice said. "Life decisions can wait, pancakes don't."

Phoebe ate. Ruth and Alice tucked in and soon their plates were bare, the bacon platter was picked clean, and they all sat back, satisfied.

A phone rang. They all jumped and looked around for their cells.

"It's Inez," Ruth said. She talked for a couple of minutes, then ended the call.

"If we're all going to continue under the same roof, I think we should get different ringtones," Alice said.

"They *are* different," Ruth said.

"Only after you stop everything and listen for a few bars. It's wearing me out."

"I guess that means you haven't heard from Vera," Ruth said.

"She's only been gone since last night."

"I know. But we're all worried about her."

Alice sighed. "To think I was feeling lonely a few weeks ago."

"We don't have to—" Ruth began.

"And I wouldn't go back to that for the world. Having everyone here leaves PBS in the dust."

Ruth relaxed. "If you're sure."

"I'm sure."

Another phone rang.

"Mine," Phoebe said. "It's Oliver Forrest."

She slid her chair back and hurried into the hallway to answer it.

"Phoebe. I love the Charley article pitch. I'd like to talk more—are you still in Boston?"

"No, I came back to the beach last night."

"Too bad. But maybe we can do this over the phone."

When Phoebe returned to the kitchen, the dishes were done and Ruth and Alice were sitting at the table with their coffee cups.

"Well?"

"He wants to pitch a three-part series about Charley and his vans for vets."

"That's wonderful," Ruth said.

"Do you think you can persuade Charley to cooperate?" Alice asked.

"I don't know. He's been pretty accessible so far. And if I can convince him that it will help the same vets he's helping without making him a public figure, I think he might go for it. I'll go down and ask. The worst he can say is no."

"You go on," Ruth said. "I think I'll have another cup of coffee."

"If you're sure. I have to call Willa. I promised I'd call as soon as I got home from Boston. Thanks for breakfast. And don't worry about Celia and Daphne—I'll talk to them. Let me know as soon as Vera calls. I love you both bunches, but I better get cracking."

She was on her way up the stairs when her phone pinged. She glanced at the screen. Brandy.

Ty said you left. What's going on? Call me.

Phoebe stopped on the stairs, scrolled through to find Brandy's number, and pressed Call. She knew a hysterical text when she saw one.

"Phoebe, thank God. Ty called this morning to say you were already back at the beach and you weren't coming back. What happened? What am I supposed to do about the prospectus?"

"Family emergency that turned out not to be a real emergency."

"But what about the prospectus? He was cranky as all get-out and said he'd call back later. But who knows when that will be. He tends to lose track of time when he's working. I need to send out that prospectus pronto. I don't suppose you want to drive back? You can stay with me tonight or however long. It's not nearly as nice as Ty's place, but it's free."

"I can't get there right away," Phoebe said. "Lots of stuff going on here. I'll work up a layout and send it to you tonight or tomorrow morning at the latest. Then we can talk about it. I don't have great scanning facilities here, but if you like it, I'll email you everything and you can do the finish there."

"Whew! Thanks. I just about had a meltdown."

"Well, don't. I'm used to sliding into deadlines. It's a way of life. I won't let you down." Even if she had to drive all the way to Boston on her own. And she would be glad to do it. Two big writing projects in a matter of days. She hadn't felt this jazzed in ages.

She ended the call. And thought, *Mom, too. Good for her.* They were both having some kind of summer.

When she finally made it to her room, she changed into work clothes and called Willa. It went to voicemail. "Hey. I'm back at the beach. Interview went great. But I need feedback. Stuff is happening. Wish you were here. I'll call you tonight. Miss you, girlfriend."

She slid the phone into her pocket; put on her "muck" sneakers; stuffed her notebook, pens, and a sweatshirt into her backpack; and headed to the Point.

She chose the beach route rather than the lane. She'd hardly been on the beach since she'd been here, which seemed crazy, but there hadn't been a minute of downtime. And with a little luck, she wouldn't be having downtime for a long time.

It was low tide; the sand was dry and shifted under her feet. If she hadn't been in a hurry to talk to Charley—and maybe Ty—she would have taken off her shoes and walked barefoot in the warm sand, splashed her excitement in the surf, but there was no time for that today.

Her calves were aching by the time she stepped into the wooded area around the fish camp.

Charley looked up from where he squatted at the back of the truck he'd been working on. "Thought you might be showing up today."

"I told you I was willing to work for a story," Phoebe said, and squatted down beside him. "What are you doing?"

"Trying to figure out a way to make this one handicap accessible."

That was something that Phoebe had never even thought about. "Like a ramp?"

"Thinking more like a lift. Like delivery trucks have. Wish I had a big truck right now, but I don't, and some things can't wait."

Phoebe didn't say anything. She was bursting to tell him about her idea for Oliver Forrest, but she knew when to push and when to be patient. "Do you get requests from a lot of handicapped vets?"

"I don't know a vet who isn't handicapped in one way or another."

"You do good work, Charley." She swallowed a sudden tightness in her throat.

"Just do what I can do."

"But it's good work."

"Yeah, and I expect this is where you start pitching me some crazy-brain idea, ain't it?"

"You're too fast by half, Charley. Do you want to hear? Or shall we get back to the innards of this baby first? I can talk and work at the same time."

"Yeah, I figured that out pretty fast."

"Yeah? Well, I can listen, too."

"And I figured that out, too," Charley said. "Let me get my tools."

Phoebe climbed in the back of the truck. It had been gutted the last time she'd seen it. Now it had been insulated and covered in a white acrylic shell.

Outlets and wiring had been installed since the last time she'd been here. Charley had been busy. The specs for the interior—Ty's work—were spread out on the skeleton of a counter and held in place with empty beer bottles.

Charley dumped a box of tools on the floor and hoisted himself up.

"Thought you would have asked where Ty was by now."

She'd meant to, but got distracted by the lift idea. "Where is he?"

"Out at the inlet. Some group of no-accounts decided it would be funny to mess with the jugs. He's been working all morning to get it straightened out."

"Is he very upset?"

"Ty? Ty doesn't do upset. He just works it out. He's working hard today." He grinned at her.

She grinned back. "I guess it would be best just to let him work by himself."

"I think so, plus you're supposed to be working for me."

"You are a taskmaster, Charley."

"Gotta use help when it comes your way. Now tell me this exciting idea you're gonna try to sell me."

"Well, Oliver Forrest at the *Globe* loved the parts of the article I showed him. Oh, don't worry. He won't print anything without my—our—permission. But he's really interested in it. So interested that he wants me to do a three-part article. The one I've written that you've seen . . . And I thought maybe, if you and your friend Walter are on board, we could follow the van to the campsite. Introduce Walter and how you two came up with the idea and what part he plays in the journey. Then the last part would be with the vets, and how they're adapting to van life, then broadening the scope to what services are available and how that support system helps with all the things that I don't know about yet."

"I think that's gonna be a long article."

"Long and amazing," said Phoebe. "We'll make people aware of what can be done, and what they can do to help. I bet more people would be interested in supporting the effort if they knew the extent of the problem of housing. I mean, how often do people think about that, except for the occasional plea for donations in a television ad?"

"When they see them living on the street, then they get all freaked out about their property values."

It took Phoebe a second to process that one. "We can help change that, Charley. It's our duty to get people's attention."

"Damn, girl, you could sell sand to the Saudis. I'm not saying a definite yes, but we could use some cash and some cars and stuff. I'll talk to Walter."

"Great—now what are we working on today?"

They laid out a frame for a counter running lengthways along one side. It was sweltering in the truck and Phoebe was drenched with sweat by the time Charley announced a soda break. The soda was cold, the air cool beneath the pines, and the break all too short. And she'd still seen no sign of Ty.

"Break's over," Charley said. "I'll show you how to glue Formica."

They climbed back into the truck.

They cut and fit the countertop, and Charley had gone to find wide paintbrushes when someone called Charley's name. Not Ty. Phoebe stayed in the van. If it was the neighbors complaining about anything, she would come out and lend Charley her support.

"Well, if it isn't Lars Harken. Thought you'd become a hermit. Where you been keeping yourself?"

Phoebe shrank back. Lars was the last person she wanted to see. And he probably felt the same about her.

"Home, mostly; things have been not so good since Delores passed."

"Yeah. Sorry to hear about Delores."

"Thanks. It's been rough. I was looking for my son. Is he here?"

That was it; Phoebe had had enough. If he thought he could come here and bully Ty, too bad. Ty wasn't here. But she was. And she might do more harm than good if she interfered. She sat down on the floor to wait until he left.

"He's out by the inlet. Hear you kinda had a bit of a dustup."

"Yeah. We have a lot of those. What's he doing at the inlet?"

"Working on some contraption to get water to people who don't have all the modern inventions we have. Clever man, your son. Good with his hands."

"I don't know why he couldn't just be interested in cars. He could have a decent life as a mechanic. But he never was. Not even as a teenager."

"Oh, he was interested as far as it went. It just went past cars."

"He always turned down anything I could teach him."

"My man. Is that what you think? He's put what he learned from you into practice I bet a thousand times. We showed him what was under the hood of a car, but he just had bigger plans. But you and me and the others, we all helped him get there. He just had a different idea on what to do with that knowledge. You might say he's the next generation of the Saturday-afternoon Shady Oak Garage mechanics."

"I might say you're full of shit, Charley."

"You might, but you'd be wrong."

"Those were the days, weren't they? All of us together under that old tree."

"The new owners cut that oak tree down; had it pulled out by the roots."

"Yeah, I heard them at it one day," Lars said. "Damn shame."

"Said it was rotting. Afraid it might fall on their roof in a storm. Never did before."

A faint laugh from Lars. "We had some good times. All the guys together. Now they're all gone: dead or moved away."

"Well, I'm here. And you're here. And Ty's here, down by the inlet."

"I can't talk to him. I don't understand what he does and he doesn't think much of me. Can't say as I blame him."

"Hell, Lars, he's got a big heart, like his mother. Give him a chance. You want a beer? I got some cold ones in the garage."

"Wouldn't say no."

Phoebe nearly fell over, she was trying so hard to hear.

"So what are you working on?" Lars asked, his voice receding. They were headed toward the garage.

"I'm rebuilding a baby of a V-8 I salvaged off a 1995 Mustang Cobra. Car was totaled, but that engine . . . They don't build 'em like that anymore."

"Damn. I haven't seen one of those in years."

"I could use another pair of hands . . ."

The voices faded away.

When she was certain they were gone, Phoebe slipped out of the truck and made her way home.

Chapter 26

Ty yanked at a piece of slashed fishing net that was wound around a plastic shard of broken milk jug. Someone had done a number on his river sweeper, damn them. And from the number of beer cans he'd found in the water and on the shore, there must have been a few of them.

He never understood why some people got off on being destructive. And this had been purely gratuitous. No one was contesting his right to be there—no warring tribes or armies, not even a recalcitrant town council trying to sabotage the effort. Just a bunch of drunk locals with too much time on their hands and nothing in their brains but alcohol.

He didn't usually let stuff like this get to him. But today he was feeling pretty pissed, though if he was honest, which he usually was, he'd admit this had as much to do with his rift with his family. And the way he'd left things with Phoebe.

She'd offered to help him dismantle the sweeper. No need of that now. Someone had beaten her to it. If he'd known he might not see her alone again, he wouldn't have left her and her suitcases at the door without saying any of the things he thought he should say, wanted to say. Not that he actually knew what he wanted to say.

Face it; you bailed.

Now he was standing knee-deep in the water with a mutilated fishing net and a bunch of milk-jug pieces, feeling like he'd missed something important.

He shouldn't have let his brothers get to him last night. They were always the same. It never really bothered him before. At least not much. But last night, something in him just seemed to unreel and he'd reacted.

So now here he was, sleeping on a wooden platform in one of Charley's trucks, drinking Charley's god-awful coffee. Wondering how many pieces of the milk jugs he could salvage and recycle before they washed out to sea to kill fish who would mistake them as prey.

He waded over to the far bank, cut the tatters of net, and tore it from its support.

Splashed back into the water, dragging the net and plastic pieces behind him, and dumped the whole mess on the ground. He cut away the second side. Then stood looking at the rivulets of water draining from what had been his river sweeper.

As soon as it was dry enough, he'd put the whole mess in his SUV and drive it to the dump. There was nothing reusable here. And when that was done, he'd retrieve his stuff from the house and drive back to Cambridge.

Maybe he'd call Phoebe and ask her if she wanted to go out to dinner before he left. Somewhere away from both families. Just to make up for the dinner they'd missed to come racing back here for no reason at all.

There were some decent restaurants on the island. And really he owed it to her for dragging her away from Boston so quickly. What if they wanted to talk more about the editorship? She'd have to drive back—by herself next time.

Or maybe he should just drive away. He had plenty of work waiting for him.

They had a big project on the horizon, one that used more technology, covered a broader area, affecting more people living in a more varied terrain. He already had people working on it, but he should be there.

Tomorrow. Tomorrow he would pack it all up and go home.

He gathered up his gear and trudged, dripping and squishing, to the SUV, then drove through the woods to the fish camp.

He showered in the outdoor shower, changed into clean clothes, and went to find Charley. He heard voices coming from the garage and paused to listen, wondering if it was Phoebe.

But when he walked into the bay, he saw two men leaning over an old car engine Charley had decided to rebuild.

And a strange feeling spread though his chest. For a moment he considered quietly slipping back out the way he'd come.

What was his dad doing here? Leaning over an engine? Ty couldn't make sense of it. He had barely left the house in the last year, until Phoebe and her mom had come. He'd never once gone down to Charley's, that Ty knew of.

But here he was leaning over that engine like twenty years hadn't passed.

Before he could make himself move, Lars turned around to get something from the work tray; their eyes met.

Ty eased back toward the door. For a moment neither of them moved. While the tap-tap-tapping of Charley's wrench continued like a ticking clock—or a time bomb.

"Dad. What are you doing here?"

"Charley was just showing me this beauty. A five-speed V-8. For the '95 Cobra."

"Oh, didn't mean to interrupt," Ty said, and started to back out the door.

Charley kept tapping away.

"Don't go," said Lars. He looked back but Charley just kept tapping.

Lars put down the wrench and walked over to where Ty stood.

"I came down to ask you to come back home. Dan and Scottie were out of line. I shouldn't have let them harass you like that."

"No big deal," Ty muttered. What was he saying? It screwed up the whole reason he had for being here in the first place.

"Look, I know I've been hard to live with. I've let my own unhappiness taint everything."

"Dad, you don't have to say all this."

"Yeah I do. Vera said something last night."

Ty shook his head. "Don't let Vera bully you."

"It's not that; it's something she said about loss. And I realized." He stopped to take a breath. "When your mother died, a little bit of me died, too. But it was just a little bit. I've been acting like it was everything. But I still have you and Dan and Scottie. And even though the three of you couldn't be more different, you're my boys. And I—I love you guys and I want us to be a family."

Ty heard him, but it wasn't really sinking in. What did his dad really want?

"Come back to the house. You don't have to stay on my account, but you're welcome. I don't need taking care of. I need to take care of myself. You could come and go as you like.

"I'll get the roofers in to fix the roof. I didn't climb up there to see if you had done an adequate job; you always do. I did it to see if I still could. I'll call the Eames brothers first thing tomorrow and I'll pay for it. I have enough money. Your mother and I were always saving for a rainy day." He coughed out a laugh and his voice broke. "We were thinking about retirement and travel, not roofs, but whatever."

Ty's first reaction was to distrust this accepting father. He'd spent his whole life with his dad's attitude, his disregard, his lack of wanting to understand. This was not the way he and his dad interacted. And he wasn't comfortable with the new Lars. It left him wary and off-balance.

He wasn't sure he wanted to get to know him better. It was easier just accepting what it was.

"I've been pitiful and demanding, I know. I'll try to do better."

"Dad, don't."

"I lost Delores. I don't want to lose you, too. Come home, please."

Ty couldn't get his voice to work. He knew that things didn't change just because someone wanted them to. If he went back, they'd be arguing over baloney before dinner tonight. But there was one little sliver of hope that kept him from saying no. Last night he'd been ready to walk away from them all and not look back. A weary soldier who would never win the war.

But today . . .

"Just think about it." Lars walked to the bay door, clasping Ty's shoulder as he passed him.

Ty just stood there until Charley's tapping finally stopped and his head appeared from under the hood.

He took off his cap, smoothed back his long, sparse strands of hair, and pulled the cap back on. "Seems to me that's as good as you're gonna get. More than a lot of people get in a lifetime. May not have another opportunity."

Ty let that sink in, then ran to the door of the garage. "Dad!"

Lars stopped. Turned slowly back toward the fish camp.

"I have some work to finish here. I'll be late. If that's okay."

Lars nodded. "That's fine."

"Smart move," Charley said, coming up beside Ty. "Now what do you say we take a break and have a beer."

The first thing Phoebe did when she returned to the beach house was head for the kitchen and a tall glass of lemonade. Alice was sitting at the table with a cup of tea. Her cell phone was within reach on the table beside her.

Phoebe poured herself a glass and sat down with her. "Have you heard from Vera yet?"

Alice shook her head. "She'll call when she's ready."

Granna was always the coolheaded one of the family, but Phoebe could tell this was costing her some effort.

"Well, you can have a little quiet to yourself," Phoebe said awkwardly.

"Oh, I have plenty of quiet. It's been nice having you all back."

"It's been nice being here. Better than nice. Even though things are kind of messed up."

"Life tends to get that way, but think how boring it would be without the mess."

Phoebe huffed out a sigh. "I guess."

"Well, think about it. Have you seen your mother happier?"

Phoebe shook her head. "But will it last?"

"No guarantees, my dear. But if this doesn't, there will always be something else."

"I could do with a little less of not knowing what comes next."

"Well, that's not going to happen. You know what they say about plans."

Phoebe did. So far she was batting 0 for 0 in that department.

"Lars came down to the fish camp today," Phoebe told her.

"So that's where he was going. I was in the garden when I saw him come out his kitchen door and go around the back of the house. When he didn't come back I went to look, praying that he hadn't done some other stupid thing and was lying unconscious on the ground. But he wasn't there. Now my conscience can rest. What was he doing at Charley's?"

"I was working in the truck when he came and I just overheard part of the conversation, but I think he came to see Ty. But Ty wasn't there and Charley wanted to show him some engine, so when they went into the garage, I came back here. I felt kind of bad that I had inadvertently eavesdropped. I seem to be doing a lot of that lately."

"I expect it's an occupational hazard," Alice said. "Hmm. So Lars went down to Charley's. I remember Henry and Lars's father used to go down there. Then Lars would take his three boys and your dad would join them when he came down on the summer weekends. They'd meet some of the other local guys every Saturday to work on somebody's car. Shady Oak Garage, they called it, because there used to be a huge old oak tree on the Wilkinses' property. World problems got solved under that tree, more than a few fistfights; no telling what else they found to talk about all day. But it was a camaraderie that you don't find much these days. They'd come home dirty and smelly and reeking of beer, but they were easier to live with because they had each other. Did Lars see Ty while he was there?"

"I don't know. I left while they were in the garage."

"Hmm. I wonder if those two will show up for dinner?"

"I wouldn't count on it." Phoebe stood. "If you don't need me down here, I think I'll go take a shower."

"Go ahead, have a rest; you've haven't slowed down since you arrived."

Phoebe took her empty glass to the sink, then leaned over to give Alice a kiss on the cheek. She went upstairs, not to rest, but to shower and then finish up the prospectus for Brandy before dinner.

They didn't see Lars or Ty that evening. Alice and Ruth decided it was better to leave the men alone until they had sorted themselves out. The three of them ate on the porch with extra plates at the ready in case anyone changed their minds.

No one mentioned Vera, but she was on everyone's mind. And Phoebe noticed that Granna was keeping her cell closer than usual.

Things seemed more relaxed without Vera there, but also a little colorless. No one suggested a game or a walk or a trip anywhere. And when Ruth stifled her third yawn, they all decided to make it an early night.

Phoebe didn't go straight to bed but looked out her window, listening to the sound of the waves and wondering if she would miss them if she got the job in Boston. But what she was really doing was listening for the sound of an SUV in the Harkens' driveway.

But she knew it was futile. If Lars and Ty had talked that afternoon, it obviously had not helped heal the chasm between them.

She was just about to call Willa when she finally heard Ty's SUV pull into the Harkens' driveway and stop. Ty was home, but for how long? Had he come back to pick up his things, or was there a chance he would at least stay to say goodbye? She watched until the lights next door finally went out. Phoebe sighed in relief and crossed her fingers that the SUV would still be there in the morning.

I'm not finished with you, Ty Harken. Please stay.

She pressed Willa's number. Willa answered so quickly, Phoebe thought she must have been waiting for the call.

"Hey, are the kids asleep? Can you talk?"

"Absolutely. I've been waiting ages to hear how your interview went."

"I've been busy. First tell me about you. Did you go talk again to the food bank people?"

"I did and I took the job. The pay isn't great, but it's enough for now while I look for something with better benefits. In the meantime, it's doing something worthwhile for the neighborhood, which is gratifying and also looks good on a résumé. Me and the girls thank you."

"My pleasure and nothing you didn't deserve."

"So you'll never believe who's taking over the *Sentinel*."

"Someone bought it? I haven't heard a thing."

"Well, not in the sense that Gavin meant. But Nancy and Mitch. It will be small and entirely digital."

"Nancy and Mitch?"

"Yep. Sanje is helping them to get set up online. They're calling it the *News E-Sentinel*. It won't make them any money, but they'll still be in the newspaper business, and who knows, local news may make a comeback. Now tell me everything about your interview."

"Well, Ty from next door drove me up. He sort of got pushed into it by his father. I stayed overnight at his apartment."

"I'm listening."

"It's really nice. Did I tell you about him? I may have called him an airhead or something, but he runs this big foundation that reclaims water and his apartment is amazing."

"Okay, skip the real estate for a minute. What about staying at the guy's apartment."

"He has a guest room. I stayed there."

"That's disappointing, right?"

"A little. I really like and respect him, but I'm on the rebound, and he said he wasn't interested in a summer fling, but that was right after we saw Gavin."

"Hold on, girl, you're moving way too fast. Take it by the numbers. And start at one."

So Phoebe told her about staying at Ty's, and how Gavin was waiting for her at the entrance of the *Globe* building.

"He's got a lot of nerve," Willa said. "He was heading you off at the pass. He was probably afraid you'd say something true about him. What a . . . I can't even say the word with the girls asleep."

"Yeah, pretty much. I'm sort of embarrassed about how easily I got over him."

"A sign that you're one lucky lady."

"So I did the interview. Oliver Forrest knew Simeon. And we had a long talk, about the job and about writing. It was so good to be there."

"So did he offer you the job?"

"He can't yet. They have to do an open search. But it got me to thinking. About writing and where I see myself in the scheme of things. I showed him some of my articles and he was really interested in printing them. I don't know. I feel like I've lost a few years of writing trying to keep the *Sentinel* afloat. I'd kind of like to do more field work. But it's such a good opportunity. I'd be crazy to turn it down."

"You'll figure it out."

"I guess. I wish you were here. I miss you gobs."

"Me too. Maybe next month after camp is over and I've settled into the new job I can drive the girls out for a day."

"That would be fantastic."

"It would. Now tell me more about Ty."

Chapter 27

*T*he first thing Phoebe did when she woke up the next morning was to go to the window to see if Ty's SUV was still in the drive. And she let out a huge sigh of relief. Muddy and dented and filled with stuff . . . Filled with stuff?

He's leaving after all.

She pulled on the clothes she'd left on the chair the night before, passed a toothbrush over her teeth, and bounded down the stairs and out the door. She caught him as he carried a box piled high with papers out to the car.

"What are you doing? You aren't leaving?"

"Taking some stuff to Goodwill. It's about time we did a little cleaning out."

"Oh, whew."

He put the box in the back and turned to face her, frowned. "Is something wrong?"

"No," she said. "But . . ." She realized he wasn't paying attention but was looking at her hair.

She hadn't even thought about her hair. One hand shot to her head, attempting to push the wayward strands down where they belonged. That was the second she realized that she'd put her T-shirt on inside out.

"I was in a hurry. I wanted to catch you before you left."

"I have some errands to run, drop this off to Goodwill, go by recycling . . ."

"I mean, I thought you were going back to Boston."

"Not yet. We're going to give it another try."

She nodded, overwhelmed with relief. Which was a totally over-the-top emotion, but she didn't care.

"Good. Just checking." And she hurried back toward the house to do all the things she normally did before facing the world.

"Hey! Would you have missed me?"

"You know I would. Besides, there's something I want to discuss with you. But first I promised Brandy I'd get this prospectus back to her. See you later?"

"Sure, I'll be back in time for dinner."

Phoebe returned home feeling slightly embarrassed, but a whole lot happier. She stopped at the kitchen to snag a mug of coffee and went back upstairs to shower, change for real, and do a final proofread of the WATER prospectus before she sent it to Brandy.

After an hour of editing and fine-tuning, she sent it off. A few minutes later Brandy texted back. *This is fabulous. Thanks.*

Happy to help. Text if you need anything else.

A series of hearts and thumbs-up emojis followed. And another text read, *Ok if I call you?*

Sure.

Phoebe had just put down her cell when it rang. It was Brandy.

"Hey, what's up? Do I need to make any changes?"

"No, it's perfect. And gets me off the hot seat."

"Any news on a new publicist?"

"Not yet."

"Well, if you need help with anything else, let me know."

"That's what I wanted to talk to you about . . ."

That night Lars and Ty came for dinner, bringing the last of the husband-hunter casseroles. The local female interest in Lars had definitely taken a downward turn, and he and Ty seemed to have found a tenuous peace.

The next morning, the roofers came to give them an estimate. Lars argued that it was highway robbery, but it was mostly for show and the roofers enjoyed the game as much as he seemed to. They started the next week, with Lars footing the bill.

The two families fell back into their habit of having dinner together every night, though with Vera gone and Ruth spending more hours at the bakery, there was less motivation to take field trips farther than the beach or to the ice cream stand downtown.

The bakery was doing a bustling business and grew larger just from word of mouth every week. Each morning Ruth left earlier for the bakery and returned later each afternoon, more than happy to sip a preprandial cocktail while stretched out on a chaise in the waning sunlight.

Phoebe spent her mornings typing up her notes, researching

and writing her articles. Ty decided to set up a new and improved version of the milk-jug river sweeper.

Charley volunteered to sit up nights with his shotgun to scare away any would-be vandals. But Ty expressly forbid him to even consider interfering and threatened to "pull the whole damn thing out of the water if I so much as see a firearm."

Charley laughed, said he was joshing, and they had to be content with that.

A week passed and there was still no word from Vera.

Twice, Phoebe and Ty drove Charley up the coast to deliver vans, where Phoebe met Walter and convinced him to be interviewed. They met the current residents of the camp and interviewed those who were willing to talk.

Phoebe filled pages with personal stories and background on the camp from Walter. They visited the local support services and talked to someone from veterans affairs.

The *Globe* had opened the editor position to the public, but as long as she was working on Charley's article, she'd been able to shove the decision-making out of her mind. And when she wasn't writing, she was helping Ty collect trash or Charley gut the new arrivals. She'd loved every cantankerous, dirty, greasy, back-breaking moment of it. And she had another article series already in mind.

She'd talked to Oliver several times about editing in general and writing. He encouraged her to stretch some ideas and hone others. And she knew he was guiding her the same way Simeon always had, mentoring and giving her the freedom to grow at her own pace.

And she could see her writing jump to a whole new level.

She talked several times with Brandy about helping to publicize the foundation while the ongoing search for a publicist went unanswered.

"It's the summer," Phoebe said. "Everybody's at the beach. Wait until the next semester starts looming over their heads."

She hardly ever got to talk to Willa. Between juggling summer camp, childcare, and her new job, Willa barely had time for short texts.

Two weeks came and went and there was still no Vera.

Then one day when Phoebe, Ty, and Charley had made another trip up to Walter's to get his okay for publishing the final article, they returned in the late afternoon to find Vera's Jeep parked in the Sutton drive.

"She's back. Let me out here."

The SUV had barely slowed to a stop before Phoebe jumped out and ran inside and into Vera and her suitcase.

"Perfect timing," Vera said. "I just arrived."

She looked tired and pale, but much calmer than before she'd left. And when Alice volunteered to make tea, Vera acquiesced without comment. "I'll just take my things upstairs and freshen up a bit."

When she came down again, they were sitting in the parlor. Alice on the couch, Ruth in one chair, and Phoebe in the other. Vera had changed into the bright flowered muumuu she'd bought on their first outing to Kedding's Wharf, and her hair was pulled back from her face by two tortoiseshell combs.

She sat on the couch next to Alice, who handed her the china cup and saucer that only came out for special occasions. Alice had insisted on using it now.

They drank in silence for a moment, then Vera said, "I guess I should tell you where I've been."

It wasn't really a question, so no one said a thing, just waited for her to tell her tale. And what a tale it was.

"His name was Jon," Vera said. "We'd been traveling and doing things together for a number of years. He'd been ill for a while. When it was clear, to him at least, that he was going to die, he sent me away. At first I refused. Why would anyone want to die alone? I argued, I pled, I tried to convince him to get more opinions, more experimental therapies. But as he weakened, he grew more adamant that I should leave." She paused to roll her eyes to the ceiling and take a sip of tea. "But I was stubborn, I refused. He begged, said he didn't want me to see him drooling in his beard when he was too far gone to even recognize me. What a bunch of malarkey, I thought, and I held on.

"Finally, he was so distraught that I gave in and did as he asked. Though I convinced one of the nurses at the hospice to keep me informed. And I came here because it was close by and because, well, it's the closest thing I have to home."

Alice moved closer and squeezed her hand.

"I truly intended to respect his wishes. But as he lingered on, I began to question his motives for wanting me to leave, and mine for wanting to go back. But it wasn't until that night Ty left that I realized it wasn't fair—not to me, not to him. And I suddenly got it, why he asked me to let him die alone.

"He didn't really care about drooling. He was afraid I would try to keep him here, hell, refuse to let him leave when it was too painful for him to stay. And I would have. I would have made him try harder to live. It took Ty walking out for me to realize that sometimes you just have to let go.

"So I did what I always wanted to do—I went back. Not to try to keep him, but to send him on his way with my blessing. And suddenly I was so afraid that I had waited too long, that he wouldn't recognize me; not understand that I was there to let him go. And I panicked. That's why I left so suddenly. But when I walked up to his bed, he lifted his hand and I knew he recognized me and I knew I'd made the right decision."

Phoebe quietly wiped away a tear. Her great-aunt had been carrying this around all these weeks. Why hadn't she shared it with her family? Though she supposed there were some things you did just have to face alone.

She glanced at her mother sitting in the wicker club chair, her features composed, and Phoebe wondered what she was thinking.

No one spoke for a few minutes. Then Alice said, "He's gone?"

Vera took a deep breath. "Yes . . . well, for the most part."

"Vera?"

"Well, we always intended to spread his ashes over our favorite places we'd visited, but since I came straight here . . . he's in a box on the passenger seat of the Jeep. Would it be okay if I brought him inside?"

"Oh, Vera." Alice pursed her lips, then began to laugh.

"I didn't want to leave him alone." Vera started laughing, too, but the laughter quickly changed to tears. "I thought maybe we could spread his ashes here instead."

Alice wrapped her arm around Vera's shoulders. Ruth slipped out of her chair to sit on Vera's other side and they hugged and cried the way families did.

Then Vera smiled across at Phoebe. "Bunch of crazy old broads crying about death, but better than having to listen to us talking about sex."

Phoebe shook her head and slid to the floor to lay her head on Vera's knee and the Keyes-Sutton-Adams women cried and laughed until they were exhausted. Then they went out to Vera's Jeep to bring Jon inside.

Two days later Reverend Lester officiated at the goodbye ceremony. There were tears for the man none of them but Vera had ever known, some laughter, even some ad-lib singing. A joyful noise. They spread Jon's ashes in the sheltered lee where the bench looked over the sea.

That had been Lars's idea.

Life settled back into a summer island rhythm. And whenever they saw Lars out sitting on the bench, most likely they would find Vera there, too.

By the end of July, Phoebe was ready to submit the Charley series to Oliver Forrest. It took a lot of last-minute deliberation and waffling before she finally pressed Send.

She had no idea how long it would take before Oliver got back to her. Or if he would merely pass it on to the appropriate editor. He'd shown an interest in her work, for which she was grateful, but interest and a contract offer were too very disparate things.

There was still no word on the editor job. Which was normal and nerve-racking, while at the same time welcome, since she hadn't decided which career track she really wanted to commit to.

Ty was already working on the next WATER project, traveling back and forth to Cambridge when necessary. He sometimes tried to explain how it would work over dinner, which everyone listened intently to, even though most of it went over their heads. And Lars listened most attentively of all. He and Ty would never see the world through the same lens, but at least they were working on the things they did have in common.

On the morning they were to dismantle the sweeper, Oliver Forrest called.

"We haven't announced it yet, but the job's yours, if you want it."

They had a long talk about writing, her career options, her ideas for more articles. And after half an hour, she and Oliver both knew which was the best option for her.

She knew her family would support her decision either way. But it was with some trepidation that she made her way down to the inlet to tell Ty.

He was already at work taking down the last incarnation of milk jugs before the real one was installed in Peru. He looked up, a milk jug in each hand, and said, "What took you so long?"

"I—" She chickened out. "Just some stuff, sorry. What do you want me to do?"

They cut the milk jugs free, rinsed them, and let them dry in the sun, to be later returned to the recycling center. The fishing net was pretty mangled, and odiferous. But Ty insisted it could be repaired and reused.

And though it took several hours to dismantle and clean everything, they were finished sooner than Phoebe was ready for.

"Well, this is it," he said, as they stood looking over the open waterway.

"Not exactly."

He looked around. "What do you mean? Did we miss something?"

"I didn't mean this. I meant *it*. The life-goes-on kind of it."

"So your life is going on?"

"And . . ." she prodded.

"And . . . if you take the editor job, we could see each other—sometimes?"

"I'm not taking the editor job."

"Oh."

"But they did offer it to me."

"And you turned them down."

"Editors don't get to go out in the field or do their own reporting, at least not very much."

"And you want to write. I get it. You should write. You're good."

"Yeah, I should. Actually, I got a better offer. Two better offers."

His face went blank. "Better than the *Globe*? How far away is it?"

"Not too far." She chickened out again. "Oh, Brandy called. She told me to tell you she found a new publicist."

"Thank God for that. Why didn't she call me?"

"Guess you were busy."

"So what else did she say?"

"That this girl was really good and enthusiastic."

"Perfect. Tell her to hire her." He started gathering the milk jugs into the same plastic bags they'd arrived in weeks before. "Did she mention her creds? Who is she?" he said.

Phoebe licked suddenly dry lips. "You're looking at her."

"You? I don't get it."

"You know for a smart guy, you can be slow on the uptake. It was Brandy's idea."

"You mean you? You are the publicist?"

"If the boss says yes."

"I'm the boss."

"So what do you say?"

"But what about your writing?"

"Actually, there is a caveat. Ollie Forrest wants an article on your foundation and your projects for the *Globe*, starting with the river sweeper. So if you let me tag along and write my story, I'll do your publicity until Brandy finds a permanent hire. It's a win-win situation. I get to write, you get a publicist. And . . ." She hesitated. "We'll have a chance to get to know each other better."

Ty just stood there holding milk jugs for so long she wanted to kick-start him up again.

"Ollie Forrest has been wanting to do a monthly Sunday section. With longer in-depth articles on people who make a difference in the world, one van or milk jug at a time."

He didn't comment, so she kept going.

"I'd be a regional reporter, only with the regions changing and geared toward that area's readers. It'll be like glorified freelancing; the pay's iffy, but it's just what I want to do. Ollie agrees. I've lost several years of writing while I was managing the *Sentinel*, and I feel like I'm about to explode with ideas. I still have plenty of time to work my way up to editor. And when I do, I'll have the on-ground chops to be the best. What do you think?"

"You have to get shots."

"I love shots. Is it a deal?"

"It's a deal."

"Shake on it?"

"I can do better than that."

And they sealed the deal with a kiss.

That night at dinner they announced the new plan. Phoebe had decided to stick to writing.

She didn't miss the glint in Lars's eyes when she told them she would be doing an article on WATER for the *Globe*.

After everything that had happened in the last few months, it seemed incredible that she could be so happy, so optimistic. Her mother was off to a new start, Ty and Lars had made a start on a new relationship, and she was about to embark on a new and exciting writing career. She did feel a moment of nostalgia for the old *Sentinel*, and she was glad it would see a new life even in a smaller version, but this time she felt no need to go back and help.

She'd honed her chops at the *Sentinel* with Simeon Cross, but it took his son's losing it for her to find her way. She didn't even begrudge having to pay for the cake she never got to eat. Or the dress, or the reception hall.

Because she had a good feeling about where she was going and how she was getting there.

"Peru? It was on my bucket list," Vera said. "Now I can strike it off by proxy. Send me postcards."

"Are you still continuing with your bucket list?" Phoebe asked.

"One day, maybe," Vera said. "Right now I'm just trying to talk your grandmother into a trip to Boston." She shot Alice a cheeky grin.

Alice rolled her eyes.

Vera grinned. "And that, my dears, is just the beginning."

"A little trip might be in order," Alice conceded, as she looked over her family. "Now that everyone is settled . . ." *Until the next time.*

Acknowledgments

As always, many thanks to my agent, Kevan Lyon; my editor, Tessa Woodward; and the whole team at William Morrow. To the Weekend Away girls, who are always on board to climb every mountain and ford every stream (real or metaphorical, even if it isn't on the weekend) with me to discover a setting, a character, or a spur-of-the-moment what-if. And special thanks to Gail, Lois, and Pearl for their infinite patience and suggestions while I bumble about until I come up with the story I meant to write.

One day I stumbled across a news article about a veteran who wanted to find a way to help other veterans and began refurbishing vans for homeless vets. That man's service led me to Charley, and for that I am most grateful.

About the Author

Shelley Noble is the *New York Times* and *USA Today* bestselling author of *Whisper Beach* and *Beach Colors*. Other titles include *Stargazey Point*, *Breakwater Bay*, *Forever Beach*, *Lighthouse Beach*, and five spin-off novellas. A former professional dancer and choreographer, she lives on the Jersey Shore and loves to discover new beaches and indulge in her passion for lighthouses and vintage carousels. Shelley is a member of Sisters in Crime, Mystery Writers of America, and Women's Fiction Writers Association.

BOOKS BY
SHELLEY NOBLE

**BEACH
COLORS**

**STARGAZEY
POINT**

**BREAKWATER
BAY**

**WHISPER
BEACH**

**FOREVER
BEACH**

**THE BEACH AT
PAINTER'S COVE**

**LIGHTHOUSE
BEACH**

**A BEACH
WISH**

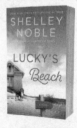

**LUCKY'S
BEACH**

**IMAGINE
SUMMER**

**SUMMER
ISLAND**

ALSO AVAILABLE · E-NOVELLAS BY SHELLEY NOBLE

Stargazey Nights
Holidays at Crescent Cove
Newport Dreams: A Breakwater Bay Novella
A Newport Christmas Wedding
Christmas at Whisper Beach